Kirdaars

...A Tale Of Character

Kirdaars

...A Tale Of Character

SATADAL LAHIRI
with contributions from
SONAM MALLIK

PARTRIDGE
A Penguin Random House Company

To order additional copies of this book, contact
Partridge India
000 800 10062 62
www.partridgepublishing.com/india
orders.india@partridgepublishing.com

TABLE OF CONTENTS

ACKNOWLEDGEMENTS

The space is probably not suffice to mention all who have contributed towards the formation of this novel. First of all accolades to my parents who have backed me throughout my journey . . . from infancy to adulthood; my sister, brother in law, my nephew . . . who always wanted me to do something new. My cousins and friends, who have been with me through thick and thin. My wife and my son Sounak . . . who I believe will definitely do a "Bailey" sometimes in the future . . . probably in a hope of desperation. I would also like to thank my inspirational teachers at school and college to be able to bring out . . . at times . . . the best in me. I would also like to thank the countless people I have come across during my professional career who have, at times, made me believe that the world, indeed is worth living. And definitely, would like to mention a ten year old child, Kithcu, fighting an acute case of renal failure, in an unforgiving world, trying to assert his right to live. And of course the person who stood beside me during the whole process of writing of this book . . . . my co-author, Sonam Mallik. Thanks to Partridge for giving shape of reality to the dream that had been just a dream even sometime back.

Thanks to all. This is just the beginning and I promise this will not end so soon . . . .

Needless to say, all the characters are fictitious. Any resemblance to characters living or dead is merely coincidental.

Let the journey begin . . .

We shall not cease from exploration, and the end of all our exploring will be to arrive where we started and know the place for the first time.

(T. S. Eliot)

CHAPTER 1

The Journey

He loves walking. Walking is, for him, not only a physical exercise but also a cerebral one. Walking allows him to think, and think he must because his thoughts and his ability to think have made him what he is today. Thoughts have never deserted him though, at times, they did appear to be illusions—a mirage, but it has always given shape to his being or as he called it—his *kirdaar*. He smiled to himself as he remembered the names he had once given to his study and bedroom—Khwabon ke Darbar (Kingdom of Dreams) and Kwahishon ke Mehfil (Congregation of Desires), places where his thoughts generally had taken shape and adorned features. Thoughts have always been his own, his inherent property, and they will remain with him till he is interred into the earth. So the walking will remain and also the thoughts—and the thought processes.

It was another of those surreptitious mornings in London, with rain, clouds, and sunlight playing hide-and-seek without any inhibition. Pedestrians were few and confused whether to hoist their umbrellas or wait for the weather to take a final call. He walked past the Bloomberg stall—hats and scarves of every shape, style, taste, and colour. Colours so blue that it can burn the back of your eyes, colours so red that you would like to run your lips over them. He passed the big display window of the

Chelsea Football Club counter—jerseys, caps, and all sort of accessories in bright colour reflecting the confidence the club exuded before the new EPL season began. Lines from a Bryan Adams's song 'We're Gonna Win' richly crafted across the doorway along with a wayward signature of John Terry.

He could see the studio now: BBC. The name itself is synonymous to an impeccable connection that every household has with the exterior world. This day was just another day of prominence to him. It was only an ordinary day when his literary exploits would receive some humble acclaim. A small interview with him had been scheduled in the morning hours about his newly published book—his first in the realms of fiction.

Salman Ilahi paused. His written doctrines have been published worldwide time and again. His interpretation of some of the exalted works of Urdu, Hebrew, and Arabic into English has found its place at the highest echelons of readership. But these are academic pursuits, not meant for the commoner in the streets, not meant for people who jostle back home in the crowded local trains of Mumbai and Kolkata, not meant for people who search for a semblance of their self in pages of text. This had been a thought that energized him to pen this portrayal of humans in different forms, shapes, colour as per the demand of circumstances like the hats at the Bloombergs. Men and women in their various avatars. Or as in Urdu—kirdaars.

As he briskly walked towards the main entrance of the studio, he could hear some people utter his name in hushed whispers, 'Salman Ilahi', 'Salman Ilahi.' He could feel eyes following him. People are excited to see him. He was overwhelmed. So many people know him. So many people waiting for him, braving the morning drizzle to have a glimpse of the author of *Kirdaar*. Or is it just a coincidence?

Is it just a gimmick by the publisher? He was pleasantly surprised to find himself waving at the small gathering and receiving a loud cheer from them in response. He could not help smiling at his new kirdaar of a celebrity.

Life usually comes to a standstill every Friday morning at Portland for a few minutes when Symphony music store play aloud some very nostalgic songs from around the world. People love to stand outside and listen to them. Just a few days back, an elderly gentleman had requested Symphony to keep playing the song 'Casablanca' by Bertie Higgins throughout the morning. Symphony had obliged, and it had become the talk of the town for a few weeks that followed.

Today Symphony was playing a Hindi tune from an old film that had appealed a lot to people like him. 'Dil Cheez Kya hai aap meri jaan lijiye . . . Bas ek baar mera kaha man lijiye.' (What's there in the heart, take my life . . . yet just once listen to what I have to say). The lyrics of the song were almost a personification of his late wife Ayesha who had always urged him to listen to her humble requests. He was shaken to reality when his host for the show Nafisa Ahmed ran out to escort him inside the studio. Nafisa, once upon a time, had been his student. A brilliant and determined girl, Nafisa always wanted to be in the limelight through her indulgences in drama, poetry, talk shows, documentary and look where she had ascended to. A few months back, she had proposed to write a biography on Salman Ilahi titled as 'The Life and Works of Salman Ilahi'. Though the project was yet to take off, Nafisa had not lost steam. She had collected a lot of writings of Ilahi for her project—some writings were so rare that Salman himself might not have kept track of them.

As Nafisa escorted him inside the studio, a loud cheer greeted them from inside. Members of Partridge Publication and the production staff, one by one, came up to him to shake his hand and congratulate him. Had they all read the book? Some said that it was fabulous. Some said it had made them cry. Some said it should be converted into a motion picture. Salman was rendered speechless. All his life there hadn't been a moment where he had lost words to utter. After all, he was the Labzon ka Sultaan (king of words). But today it was different. Today, he had been overwhelmed into silence.

One of the crew members quickly clipped a tiny microphone against his collar while another presented him with some tissues to wipe off the uncustomary droplets of sweat that had quietly congregated on his forehead. Others quickly got themselves seated in pre-arranged clusters. They were all ears to the deep baritone of the author and the impeccable choice of words, punctuated with meaningful lines in Urdu, which made listening to him a pleasurable experience.

'Camera, light, action,' screamed the bespectacled gentleman in the front row, and there was a deluge of illumination. Nafisa's soft voice elaborated, almost exaggerated the existence of Salman Ilahi in the most eloquent of verbose to the audience of the studio and beyond. The length of the introduction almost embarrassed Ilahi. He had a strong urge to interrupt Nafisa in the middle and say, 'I am only me, isn't that quite enough?'

'Sir, how do you feel?' Nafisa turned to Ilahi.

'Awkward!' came the pat reply. The audience was into splits at the spontaneity of the repartee.

'What inspired you to write a book on such an elusive subject, sir?' Nafisa continued to ask, unfazed.

'Life itself is an inspiration, my child. It makes everyone kneel. My rendezvous with the various so-called missionaries of fate gave me the strength to pen my thoughts. It is for everyone. It is everyone's life, each one's kirdaar.' Ilahi smiled at the audience. Their eyes glued to him, perhaps, anticipating some emotional discourse. After all, this was a book emotionally written.

'Tell us something about this book and about the fascinating characters,' Nafisa implored.

Salman Illahi looked around. There was too much silence that it stifled him. People waiting, almost with baited breath to hear him speak. Ilahi tried to run his eyes across the expectant faces seated with rapt attention. He was quickly reminded of his humanity classes in IIT, where he used to tell stories from the history of the world. But this is a larger audience, waiting to hear about the characters he had held close to his heart, waiting to hear about the roles they played, waiting to hear of their becoming from their unbecoming, waiting to laugh with them, cry with them, get angry and frustrated at the issues that cannot be tamed, to fall in love at a smile returned and out of love for a phone call not returned. And to relate their own lives with the characters because they are faces from the crowd like all of us here.

'The characters are real-life characters. They are not extraordinary ones but not ordinary ones too. They are people who have lived through rough and testing times to discover themselves. Their journey through pain, dilemma, controversies, helplessness, and all other impositions by life had been depicted here. What is more, their journey does not cease. The journey continues to the very end. We have to move with them, be with them, understand them, and perhaps . . . perhaps in the process, learn a bit about ourselves too.'

The applause hadn't ceased, even after Ilahi has made his exit from the studio after the two-hour session. Partridge Publications had provided him with a BMW for returning to his hotel. He looked around a bit. Symphony was still playing the same Hindi song the umpteenth time.

'Iss Anjuman mein appko . . . aana hai Baar baar . . . Deewaron, dar ko gaur se, pehchaan lijiye.'

(You have to come to this garden of flowers time and again, so try to familiarize yourself with the walls and the doors.)

Symbolic—perhaps this is a harbinger to another day . . . another story and this hallowed studio awaited him.

Salman got into the car. Let the day begin.

Dream tonight of peacock tails
Diamond fields and spouter whales
Ills are many, blessings few,
But dreams tonight will shelter you . . .

(Thomas Pynchon)

CHAPTER 2

The Ways of Kumar: Jamnagar, India

Jamnagar, a city quite unknown to the outside world, had suddenly made it to the front pages of all newspapers. The world's second largest grass root refinery was being built at an unimaginable speed and cost. The architect as well as the prime consultant for this project, Bechtel S. A., had made mammoth preparations for completing this project in record time. Reliance Industries Limited, the ultimate client, too, had taken all measures so that project comes off, as planned.

Jamnagar, a slumbering city in the Western coast of India, had suddenly shot into prominence. World's biggest construction giants were here; and it was aptly as Mr Dhirubhai Ambani, the chairman of Reliance Industries, had called it, 'A lifetime Opportunity Project'.

Moti Khavri was the war site. A huge tract of land expanding from Sikka Jetty to Vadinar demarcated the kingdom of Reliance Petroleum covering a sprawling area of sixty-four square kilometres. Engineers, technicians, architects, administrators were all at war with the perennial foe—time. It was time that was needed to be conquered. It was the unrealistic targets that were needed to be achieved. It was a modern-day replica though, at a much grander scale, the Hoover Dam Project.

'Welcome to the lifetime-opportunity project. I am your executive vice-president for this project, Abraham Verkey.'

Beamed the tall, dark and intimidating figure welcoming the fresh new engineering recruits.

'Let me also introduce my other team members,' continued A.V. looking sideways at the people standing beside him. 'Guys, please introduce yourselves. A.S., you start.'

'I am Ananth Shanker. I head the civil planning and execution departments. I have been with this company for the last thirty years.'

'All civil engineers, A.S. will be your task force leader.' A.V. adds. 'We think he is open enough to handle constructive criticism, knowledgeable and sensible enough to reject impractical criticism, and pleasant enough to ensure harmony. And if he is not, you tell me.'

The recruits were too nervous to laugh. This is the first time any of them has ever been invited to an executive VP's office. That too the VP of a company like Premiere Engineering and Construction Limited.

A.V. gestures to the other elderly gentleman to the right to speak up. 'I am Kaishash Choudhury. I am head, mechanical.'

The others followed one by one.

'I am Puneet Khandelwal. Chief of Logistics.'

'I am P. S. Hariharan, head plant and machinery.'

'I am Tejinder Pal Singh. I am in charge of Heavy Lifts.'

'I am Pushpak Raheja. Chief of engineering, civil and structural.'

'I am Swapnil Vasavada, head of finance and accounts.'

'I am Prithwiraj Shukla, in charge of Township and office administration.'

'I am Sanjay Saxena. Chief of the safety department.'

'I am Paulose Cherian. Head quality control.'

'I am R. K. Thakur. I am head of human resource department.'

As the last person nudged forward to introduce himself, the others quickly receded to the background to make way for him.

'I am Col. Rajiv Mehta. I am with the administration department as a consultant and have been deputed at this site to help A.V. execute this project,' announced the domineering character in a booming voice. 'Gentlemen', he continued after screening through the faces of the recruits. 'We expect a lot from our people. And you are no exception. This project, here, is meant to separate the men from the boys. The tarts from the engineers. Get into the mould as soon as possible and get your asses moving. We are here to create history.'

Colonel Mehta is amongst the most revered figures in the company. His fame is not only limited to his knowledge for project work but also for his ability to dominate any discussion or meeting in the most organized manner. His army background has ushered in a culture of discipline, dedication, and a sense of urgency into the company. He loved to dominate, almost bulldoze, people to meek submission. And he had been sent here by the management to use this very faculty of his to wring the maximum out of every individual attached to PECL, even in the most gruesome manner.

The gathering was dispersed. The recruits were escorted away to their residential quarters so that they can use the rest of the day to settle down in their new addresses. With the sunrise of the morrow, they were destined to breathe differently. Their lives were about to enter into new world, a cruel and gruesome world of project execution. The roles of the young enthusiasts of engineering was about to go through a process of metamorphosis. As they got ready to sleep off their fatigue and brush the night off their agenda, they were quick to realize something pretty quickly. This war is not going to be easy to conquer.

Colonel Mehta examined the expectant faces, all waiting for him to speak. Abraham Varkey quickly read through the posting letters before handing it to R. K. Thakur the head of HRD. It contained the postings of the twelve recruits, their tasks, responsibilities, and whom they would be reporting to.

'Shrikant Sharma and Vijay Dutt', R.K.T. read out aloud, 'you will be reporting to Mr Shyam Kamat of the Lower Aromatics. You will be responsible for the minor civil works of the Aromatic Xylene Project.'

'Aniket Shah, Vipul Jain, and T. S. Suresh', R.K.T. kept reading out from the list, 'you will be reporting to Mr Dileep Pranjal of HNUU.' He paused and looked around.

'Do you know what HNUU stands for?' Colonel Mehta interrupted. Though he expected no reply, he waited for a while before giving it out, 'Higher Naphtha Unification Unit. It is a very important system in the refinery.'

'Avik Agarwal, Sarvesh Gupta and Vikas Sathe, you all will report to Mr A. S. in planning.' R.K.T. turned to look at A.S., who seemed to be happy at the reinforcement.

'Kunal Sinha and Rushaad Gandhi, you are destined for FCCU. The heart of the plant. Fluidised catalytic Cracker Unit.' This time R.K.T. spelt out the contraction himself. 'You will report to K.P.R. Murthy.'

'Sunil Shekhar, you are in safety, reporting to Ajay Srivastava.' R.K.T looked around. 'Who's left?'

A hand spontaneously shot up. 'Kumar Sinha, sir.'

'Yes, Mr Kumar. Last but not the least. You will report to Mr V. Manivannan at Jetty, MTF site.' He smiled. He ran through his curriculum vitae and exclaimed, 'Wow, Kumar, you had been the goalkeeper of your college football team. You know, a goalkeeper is the first line of offense and the last line of defence. Our project at Jetty too is the gateway to the refinery. That is where the crude oil is supposed to enter our plant.'

'All the best to you, gentlemen. A great future awaits you.' A.V. summed it up as he came forward to shake hands with all of them individually.

The site visit was tiring. After all it was the biggest construction site in India. By the time they had returned to the CPO (Central Project Office), they were all very tired.

'Some coffee, folks?' enquired Vijay Dutt, a tall and lanky civil engineering graduate from Chandigarh. Some of them had already nodded in affirmation. They badly needed some energy. However, Kumar Sinha had other ideas. He was not keen on wasting time in the canteen. He would rather spend time studying the map of the refinery drawn so elaborately on the front wall of the CPO main entrance. It was overwhelming. So many units, each, linked to the other so immaculately. Each playing a role of its own in shaping the final products for the service of humanity. He kept reading—Jetty, MTF, CTF, OSBL, flare, CDU, VDU, HNUU, HTU, Merox, FCCU, LNUU, Aromatics Xylene, Aromatic Polypropylene, delayed Coking Unit, Tertiary Amyl Methyl Ether Unit, Sulphur recovery unit, Oxygen recovery unit, and so many other sub-units blinking in unison to demarcate a Gargantuan entity in the making.

The Jetty site was exquisite, a panorama in itself. The turbulent waves of the sea greeted Kumar as he stood on the barge trying to look beyond the horizon.

'This is a very pleasant site, sir,' Mahipal Singh, the know-all site supervisor, informed him. 'We all are like family members. We enjoy our work and the camaraderie.'

Mahipal Singh was a local construction worker with a lot of connections with the regional administration. Thus, the company thought it wise to induct him as a site supervisor to ensure harmony amongst the local populace. Mahipal Singh was not much educated, but he was a know-all at least to himself and his friends. Like other know-alls, he too always had a word of advice for all and sundry. He, however, had taken the pain and pleasure of taking Kumar around the site and introducing him to as many people as possible, whether they were relevant or not did not matter. Kumar didn't like to hang around with the other guys much. He was more interested in looking out at the vastness of the sea that lay in front of him. The sight enamoured him. Somehow there was a feeling of laze around the sight. The soothing breeze from the sea acted more like a lullaby rather than an energizer.

Kumar looked around. There was some kind of languidness in the way people here conducted themselves. Work seemed more of a secondary recourse; primary was rest and good food.

Kumar had grown up in a very secured atmosphere. Life in a small town like Jamshedpur was very tranquil and predictable. His parents never harboured sophisticated dreams and looked forward to Kumar graduating and settling down there with a job in any of the numerous Tata owned factories in the vicinity. But Kumar had other ideas. He wanted to scout around the world before settling down in a place of his choice. Selection at PECL happened not due to his good academic records but more because of his versatility. Unlike most of his compatriots, Kumar was more into sports, music, trekking, watching movies rather than being glued to course books. And Jetty, Jamnagar, appeared to be the idle place for him.

V. Manivannan was a short man. But his lists of achievement were by no means short. He was one of the youngest general managers in the company and rightly so since he had led a team of spirited engineers to complete a similar, albeit smaller in magnitude, project at Oman port before schedule. He had other feathers in his cap too. He had represented the company at the Energy Conservation Meet at Budapest and won laurels for the company through his innovative research work. Manivannan was different. He believed in people and their abilities more than their attitude. He believed in teamwork and collective contribution rather than authoritative control. He believed in technical efficiency and also in managerial finesse, blending the two into a winning combination.

'Good morning, Mr Sinha, rather good afternoon,' he chuckled, glancing his wristwatch. 'How did you find the site?'

'I have never seen something more grand, sir,' said Kumar, shaking Manivannan's hand.

'That's great. Welcome to the party. For the last four months, I too have been just admiring the scenic beauty of the site. Now, we need to start doing something,' said Manivannan, smiling. He gestured Kumar to sit while he himself got up and started pacing his small but well laid out office.

'We have a big task at hand, Kumar. Huge task. Our consultants have drawn very unsympathetic deadlines. I don't want to sound as a sadist, but probably you've come at a time when our honeymoon with the site is almost over.' Manivannan sighed.

'That's no issue, sir. I have come here to learn, work, contribute. I am not a poet to enjoy scenic beauties. I am an engineer,' Kumar replied in a voice of assurance.

'Engineers are humans too.' Manivannan smiled, and then coming forward, he said, 'We are always given the circumstances to bleed the greenhorns. But I believe that if someone takes up the cudgels in his hands, he or she can tame the circumstances, eventually. I would prefer you take some rest today. Tomorrow, we will assess the assessments.'

Kumar had developed an instant liking for Manivannan. His pleasing personality, poise, choice of words, confidence summed him up as a perfect human being and leader. Kumar thanked his stars for getting an amicable boss instead of a bully. He had come to know from his fellow recruits that there were quite a few bullies inside the plant.

It was a concerted team. Manivannan took Kumar around and introduced him to all the members of his team. Everyone looked friendly and helpful. Manivannan explained the tasks that they needed to complete by the month end, this being their imminent target. The plans and schedules were drawn and responsibility charts prepared and distributed. The bugles were sounded. The Team Jetty was ready to take the bull by the horn.

Jetty is always the whipping boy of any onshore-offshore project. Any delay within the plant is always attributed to the Jetty since it is the gateway of all consignments. Thus, all schedules of the Jetty are to be maintained, though with very stringent budgets and infrastructure. And what is more however efficient you might be, Jetty is always secluded from rest of the plant. Thus one has to learn to live in seclusion and also to live with blame.

The progress of the piping terminals was slow. Of course there were several hindrances to progress, one being neglect. The gross nonchalant attitude towards the requirement of Jetty by the management was hurting the company. Kumar was unable to understand the underlying reason behind this inappropriate thinking. Why was this not highlighted? Why do people bear such a feeling of jaundice towards Jetty and its people? Why is there a definite decline of purpose when it comes to discussions on Jetty?

'It's not jealousy, Kumar, it is policy. It hurts, but we have to live with it. It burns you within, but you have to bear the scars,' Manivannan explained after listening patiently to Kumar's concerns. 'Don't worry too much about it. Do not lose much sleep over it. This is not within our control boy. It is much beyond our grasp.' He paused, took a sip out of the water bottle in front of him, and concluded in a hushed voice. 'This is Kumar a part of Corporate Strategy . . . or if you can call it, Corporate Politics.'

'But why do politics, sir, when everything is there with the company? They are having no dearth of resources?' Kumar's intonation was more of surprise now.

'To survive, one needs to adopt some strategies. This is one such strategy,' Manivannan replied smiling.

'I don't understand, sir, but this has to change. By curtailing our resources, the company is not gaining anything. And we are working hard and getting nowhere.' Frustration was building up in Kumar's voice.

'Everyone knows that we are capable, and under the circumstances, we are doing our best. But someone needs to be blamed when it comes to targets. Jetty is always the punching sack which saves the larger interests inside the plants for the company.'

'Sir, then are we the scapegoats?'

Manivannan looked up. Took his time while lavishly taking another swig at the bottle. Then getting up, he came over to Kumar's chair and whispered. 'Yes, we are. But probably time has come to reverse this age-old policy. And I feel someone will surely take it up.'

'Why someone . . . why not you, sir?' Kumar thought. 'After all, you are the most respected figure when it comes to Jetty work.'

Manivannan walked out of the room, leaving Kumar with a very disturbing thought, almost a dilemma. Here in front of him was a dream project where, if proper resource be provided, the most superlative Jetty and Marine Tank Farm can be established in record time. At the same time, there was this irrational strategy of the management to choke the resources of the Jetty for building excuses for the delays in the main plant.

Some process should be devised such that it ends up in a win-win proposition. May the process be a detour from the previous methods? May it be that it doesn't follow any set rule? May it be that it happens through Kumar's ways!

All people dream, but not equally.

Those who dream by night in the dusty recesses of their mind, wake in the morning to find that it was vanity. But the dreamers of the day are dangerous people, for they dream their dreams with open eyes, and make them come true.

(D. H. Lawrence)

CHAPTER 3

Tina's World

This was the awards night. The annual fashion show award is a very high-profile affair. Countless celebrities, bureaucrats, and famous entities grace the occasion. This is a gateway to fame—unadulterated fame. And this night was no exception. The world was to witness new talented faces emerge in the world of fashion. Good Eveninggggggg . . . Mumbai.

The backstage was full of characters, some pragmatically trying to organize the sequence of the programme while some engaged in animated discussions on endless concerns. Smell of perfume, sweat, and more perfume filled the atmosphere. There were colours all around and countless flashes from cameras that punctuated the atmosphere with periodic brilliance of silver. The esteemed dignitaries awaited as did the dazzling diadem of glory, honour, prestige, and glamour awaited the victor.

Amongst humongous applause, the master of ceremony ushered in the ramp walkers. Quite a few celebrities and who's who of the world of glamour too walked the ramp. The actresses of yesteryears had a special entry, which drew and appropriately too, a standing ovation. Can you take your eyes off the beautiful models, walking the ramp in glamorous clothes and dazzling jewellery? The evening was ascending to an unprecedented level. The rock band, IgKnight, played some of their most famous numbers and did some very popular covers from the past.

They ended with the famous 'No Matter What' of Boyzone:

> I don't deny what I believe,
> I know what I'm not . . .
> I know my love's forever,
> That I know . . . no matter what.

Probably the last lines had more bearing to Tina's life.

Tina Rodericks. And now Tina Ray. This was the special evening she had always been dreaming of. Excited is too mild a word to describe her state of mind this evening. It was something much, much, beyond. She was almost in a trance. Her hard work, sacrifice, dedication, and capability were about to achieve the due recognition. She has been working very hard ever since she graduated from IIFT. Fashion designing was always the profession she wanted to be in. There had been opposition from her family due to their ignorance of the same.

Mr Jacob Rodericks was a resolute and formidable gentleman. He had almost singlehandedly established the bakery business that is so famous in this part of Mumbai. People swear by the rum balls of Gaylord Bakeries. From Dadar to Matunga to Sion to King's Circle and up to Antop Hill, Gaylord is a household name. Jacob always managed to come up with new flavours every Christmas, and this innovative instinct of his had been very generously passed on to his children. Tina, the eldest amongst the siblings, was the biggest beneficiary. From her very school days, she had developed a penchant of helping her father in the bakery. Her designer cakes and cookies were instant hit with orders coming in from places afar like Pune, Kolhapur, Nasik, and even some cities of Gujarat.

This is the kind of innovation that Tina had brought about in the world of fashion technology. New ideas, concepts, colours, and combinations had created a revolution in the fashion world. Her enigmatic Theme Collection was voted the most innovative collection of the year. Tina had never imagined that it will be so big. She was almost stirred to tears when the anchor announced her name. The applauses took an eternity to stop, and when it did, Tina didn't know where to start from. Tears rolled down her cheeks as she held the gold plated close to her heart.

'I owe this evening to my family, friends, and my dear teachers, who have always inspired me. My special thanks also to St. Xaviers, Mumbai, and St Marys for shaping me into what I am today. This is my first Fashion Era Award, so pardon me for being so choked with emotion, but I do promise that this will not be the last one. Love you all, and thank you for making me feel so special.' She managed a smile amongst the sniffles and also managed a glimpse of the blurred image of her brother George Rodericks clapping away in the most frantic manner. George was the only member from her family present at this evening.

Tina was quickly crowded by photographers and admirers as she descended from the podium. It wasn't that she was not savouring the adulation but was more interested to break free and run and embrace George. By the time Tina got free from the crowd, George was gone. Tina kept on trying George's number without any success.

George had always been by her side since childhood. Though he was five years junior to her, she had always found in George, a close friend and confidante. They always discussed matters most important to them for hours. But those were times that were not anymore now. Life is different for George now. After dropping out of college, George had started a construction business in partnership with some of his friends, all of whom, like him were college dropouts. There was huge resistance from Mr and Mrs Rodericks, who wanted George to complete his studies and take over the family business. George never listened to his parents and went ahead with his own future plans. The business never developed rather it drained them financially. Almost every day debtors made rounds of their house in King's Circle, demanding money and threatening of dire consequences.

George got himself into regular feuds with his so-called business partners, and things took a very ugly turn when George eloped with Rochelle, sister of one of his dubious business associates, Michael. A frantic search was launched for them by the police and Michael's family only to be informed months later that George and Rochelle were leading a married life in another part of the city, with an inclusion to their family, a baby boy.

Thereafter, George has been in touch with only Tina though their telephonic conversations had diminished considerably. Tina had met George once in these four years of tumult, and this was another occasion where she could have met her dear brother. But George probably did not want to spoil Tina's evening, and also he was wary about his parents being there and creating a scene.

Once out of the humdrum, Tina called home. Jennifer, her mother, picked up. She had been very sick in recent times and had been advised bed rest.

'Mom, I have won the award.' Tina's voice choked with emotion.

'I know, my child, I am so happy for you.' Her mother's faint voice was hardly audible.

'Where is Dad, Mamma, is he keeping well?' Tina enquired.

'You know your dad, he cannot stay at home. He is very busy with some party orders.' There was a feeling of pain in Jennifer's voice.

'Mamma, it would have been so wonderful had you been there tonight. You should have seen the packed auditorium and even the celebrated designers and models applauding me right through the programme. Mamma, you and Dad would have been proud parents.' Tina almost sobbed.

'I know, my child. I was myself dying to be there. But my knees do not support me these days, darling, and your dad wouldn't miss even an evening at the bakery. Were all your friends there, my child? What about Amit, was he there?'

Before she could reply, the line got disconnected. Tina kept staring at the instrument in her hand wondering whether to call back or wait to see whether her mother calls her back. It has been ages since they had talked at length. All conversations seem to come to a common termination. Amit. Dr Amit Ray, Tina's high-profile husband.

Amit is a merited heart specialist. Merited is the word. Patients swear by his name. His observations, diagnosis, treatment, medication have been spot-on over the years. He has always been a hot property with whichever hospital he joined. Now, he was associated with the Escorts Heart Foundation and numerous other hospitals and medical colleges spread all across the globe.

Amit had been extraordinarily merited since childhood. Being born to parents in the teaching profession, the atmosphere at home was always that of academics. Right from early days in school, Amit had a penchant of becoming a doctor. His focus and dedication got him to realize his dream years later. Today he is not only a famous doctor worldwide but also a well-known figure in society. People look up to him and love to hear his no-nonsense comments on issues ranging from politics, academics, economics, and culture. Needless to say, he was well-read and well associated with some of the finest brains in academia.

Tina and Amit had been married for three years now. Tina had always admired Amit for his wit, intellect, and seriousness. She liked his silent nature—a sharp contrast to the loud and vociferous boys all around their neighbourhood. Tina cherished the quiet evenings they used to spend either at Five Gardens at Matunga or Shivaji Park at Dadar.

For Amit, Tina was a constant source of inspiration. She was always there whenever he needed her; even in rainy and slushy days, they managed to spend some time together. The whole world seemed to slow down when he was with Tina. He could see the insides of him within her eyes—her eyes. Those large dark eyes, so expressive yet so soothing, so concerned yet so passionate, so serene, tranquil, and yet so full of life, so hypnotic; and the innocence of natural beauty glorified the image that this girl carried. Tina was so full of life that her mere presence would get an otherwise docile Amit animated.

Amit had never thought that he could muster enough courage to propose Tina. He had rehearsed several times in front of his bedroom mirror the lines he wanted to utter in proposition of his love towards her. But every time, he ended up talking about books, studies, and music. Tina knew, as a woman always does, that Amit had a special feeling towards her. She had been waiting to hear from him the eulogy of his feelings for her.

A conference in Bangalore came about, and Amit had to leave Mumbai for a week. It was painful—a very disturbing break to the routine that had become so much part of their living. Amit had realized that this separation, though a temporary detachment, was too cumbersome to bear. On his return to Mumbai, he rushed straight to Gaylords at King's Circle. Tina was overjoyed to see him after a week. A week's separation—only a week's separation had brought about a sense of desperation in both. Amit did not make any fuss about it and very politely announced to Mr Rodericks that he was in love with Tina and wanted to marry her. Though stunned at this proposal, Mr Rodericks could not help but nod in approval. This issue had been discussed at home several times, and Tina had been able to convince her parents that Amit was the person she would be the happiest with. And they knew that it was true.

Memories also took her back to the trip to Shillong, which they had embarked upon, soon after marriage. Their romance had flourished amongst the enveloping mists and the whispering trees, sticking together in the abode of the clouds. They had spent some priceless moments of joy in the cosy cottage of Hotel Pinewood Ashok, sitting beside the smouldering fireplace, losing themselves in each other's eyes. Hours had tumbled without notice as they lived every moment in the mirth of togetherness. On their last night as they sat out in the garden watching with silent appreciation at the place they had fallen in love with, they had discovered themselves again, in a more meaningful manner. As in most hill stations, night comes on suddenly and with great stealth in Shillong. Gazing down the hills, they had witnessed the mesmerizing sight of millions of fireflies lighting up the mountains. They, like other visitors, had brought back those images of a charmingly, refreshing place where the orange blossoms vie with the forget-me-nots and tiny children in their blazers walk up the lovely streets. Shillong had ignited amongst them an eternal bond of love, trust, and belief.

Tina was jolted into her senses when some of the members of the organizing committee asked her permission to allow crews from the media to interview her. Before Tina could accord her consent to the request, the media was upon her. Questions and counter questions from all the reputed news channels continued for the next half an hour before she could escape on the pretext of taking a break to freshen up. Her phone had been continuously on the buzz either they were calls from her friends and colleagues or text messages from her work associates, clients, and vendors. However, she stopped to read out a text message scripted in Hindi, and a smile ran across her face. A message from Salman Ilahi, her teacher, and now one of Amit's patients.

'Manzil yeh nahi . . . Ab to sirf ek lamba safar ka iraada kiya hai . . . Door talak jaana hai hume . . . Ye kisise nahi . . . Khud se waada kiya hai.'

(This is not the destination yet, this is just the will to go on a long voyage. I have to go a long distance, and this promise I have made to myself and no one else.)

It was quite late at night by the time Tina reached home. She could see the lights upstairs from quite some distance. Probably Amit was awake, or maybe he had forgotten to put them off. Tina glanced at her watch, 1:30 AM. As the vehicle pulled up at the portico, she could feel the silence within the house. There was something sinister about this silence. It has been a part of her life for some time now. The silence somehow managed to make mockery of her achievements. She had always fought against this silence, this nothingness that has descended on her life. She couldn't remember when last she and Amit had dinner together. Suddenly, their relationship seemed to be the remains of a compromise.

Tina looked around. Everything was perfect. The best of furniture, tapestry, decorative—there was perfection all around. Their dream house, at the most enviable of locations at Juhu seaface, could not graduate into a home. It remained a house for two celebrated professionals racing against each other to establish their superiority. Tina was never in the race before. She loved to design, innovate, create fusions of colour, texture, and fabric. She had been always passionate to discover new meanings with the inanimate. She never wanted to compete on a subject that is bereft of competition. However, Amit's demeanour towards her profession had been disturbing, almost derogatory. According to him, fashion was nothing but seduction. It was a way of titillating the audience with ravish show of flesh. And all the followers of fashion and apparel design were victims of lecherous and nefarious tendencies.

The insult was too much to tolerate. No one is entitled to belittle the hard work, dedication, and creativity of an individual—no one. Creativity is like worship. It is one of those faculties that separates us humans from other insensitive primates. Tina had wept for several days in protest of such heartless hypotheses about her dream profession. But Tina was a very strong lady. She had quickly dried up her tears and added fuel to her ambition to yearn for the pinnacle. She had never topped in academics neither in school nor in college, but this was a different world. A world full of unsporting, insensitive people. She looked at the gold-plated statuette. Perhaps this was the beginning. And yes, as Ilahi sir had rightly said, this was a promise to herself that she needed to keep. The world outside, for now, is rendered secondary.

The celebration at INIFD was huge. Her old colleagues, mentors, professors, and students of INIFD had organized a colourful evening in commemoration of the grand success of Tina. All the staff of her boutique 'The Magenta' were also present. It was a proud feeling to be felicitated by the institute that had taught her the basics of fashion design.

INIFD is the first educational institute in the world to completely digitize education to change the learning landscape for thousands of students across all INIFD centres!

INIFD has revolutionized the entire field of Design education in country, keeping in sync with today's rapidly changing dynamics of the fashion World. World class education facilities, indigenous curriculums blending theory with practical experience, industry interface, and showcase, has helped INIFD to stay leagues ahead in fashion and design education. INIFD prepares students for professional excellence in design, fashion, and business by providing the premier educational experience that fosters creativity, career focus, and a global perspective. The biggest example of excellence for this institute was Tina, who had emerged in the world of fashion design as an enigma. Truly this was a proud moment for everyone associated with the institute.

Thronged by photographers and admirers, Tina had to struggle to reach out for Rosy, who had been trying to catch her attention. Rosy worked in her boutique and was one of the most trusted compatriots of Tina. She handed her an envelope, where the emblem of Vizion Creations was deeply embossed. With trembling fingers, Tina tore open the tip of the envelope to reveal a congratulatory letter with an offer at the bottom.

We would like to offer you the task for the costume designing of our upcoming home production, "The Legend of Alexander." Please let us know if you are interested.

—Raj Mathur (Producer, Director, Cinematographer)

Tina stood there, speechless. Were things happening a little too fast, or are these too small compared to what the future beholds?

Tina met Salman Ilahi at the doorway. The very sight of the graceful old man was soothing enough to calm down racing nerves. Ilahi smiled at Tina and bent to plant a kiss on her forehead.

'You have made me very proud, Tina,' he said in unadulterated mirth.

Just as Tina was about to say anything in response, Amit made an aggressive appearance at the doorway.

'You know that I have to leave for Amsterdam today. Where the hell are my suits?' he shouted. 'You are only bothered about those bullshit fashion shows. Bloody lecherous business. Get me my suits immediately instead of bragging around about your unchaste escapades.' He stormed inside. Tina quietly followed him.

Salman stood there awhile. He was shocked at this outburst from Amit Ray, whom he had always known as a soft-spoken, caring, benign, and compassionate person. Why are the ways of the world so cruel, he thought to himself. Another human being, steadfastly degrading into self-decline.

Salman sighed as he muttered the once famous lines of his motivator, Mirza Ghalib.

'Woh Firaq aur who Vishaal Kahan . . . Who sub-e-rozo-maho-saal-kahan . . .'

You've gotta dance like there's nobody watching,
Love like you'll never be hurt,
Sing like there's nobody listening,
And live like it's heaven on earth.

(<u>William W. Purkey</u>)

CHAPTER 4

The Rathods

The train finally ended its meandering course through meadows of shrubs of stunted growth and rocky terrains, as it jogged to a halt at the platform of Jaisalmer Station.

Rajasthan—the name itself—symbolises a rich heritage of culture and ethnicity. A historic land of valour carrying on its shoulders centuries of glorious ethos. This is the land where civilization took shape before even history dawned upon the Western World. This is a land where the caresses of nature are in abundance and the hospitality of the people lure many a tourist to its domain. The charismatic monuments so ubiquitously spread across this land that everything looks to have a bearing with the facades of history. Apart from the history and the vastness of the tradition and culture, what distinguishes Rajasthan more is the music.

The music and dance of Rajasthan is the most lilting tribute to the spectacular beauty, the undulating sinuousness and the brutal harshness of the landscapes and to the hardiness and heroism of the people who live in this land of the kings and queens. Vibrant, vigorous, graceful, sinuous, plaintive, and martial—the dance and music of Rajasthan in India evoke the desert in all moods. Music and dance in Rajasthan is deeply ingrained in the life of Rajasthan.

The vibrancy of Rajasthan is never completely discovered until you engulf yourself in the music and dance of

Rajasthan. A tour to Rajasthan would be incomplete without experiencing the folk music and dances of Rajasthan. The music and dances of Rajasthan are so appealing and soothing that it matches so well with this strange and wondrous land of culture. The cool stillness of the desert after the searing heat of the day and the upsurge of life in the short-lived rainy season or spring are filled with soulful, full-throated music and rhythmic dance of Rajasthan. The state of Rajasthan has a very vibrant, highly evolved tradition of performing arts, carefully nurtured and sustained over the centuries.

Being a land of royalty, the rulers of Rajasthan, have all along been great patrons of music and dance. Patronized by erstwhile royalty, the music and dance of Rajasthan follows a legacy that dates back to several centuries. The rich folklore and culture has added some more sparkles to its glory making Rajasthani dance and music a treasured jewel in Indian culture. The tradition of court dances and music performance of Rajasthan still can be seen today in the cultural nights making the grandeur of bygone Rajput era alive in front of you. Needless to say, the music and dances of Rajasthan draw inspiration from its legends that abound in valour and courage as also romance.

The striking feature of Rajasthan's music and dance scene is that there is great variety. In fact, nothing much has changed since the time of their inception, probably a thousand years back. The music and dance of Rajasthan are rooted in tradition. Although music and dance of Rajasthan are an integral part of the daily life of Rajasthan, it is more pronounced during festivals. Songs of ancient poets like Kabir, Malookdas, and Meera have become an integral part of the Rajasthani folklore. Apart from festivals, music and dance of Rajasthan are also performed during special occasions like marriage and childbirth. Enjoy a dance performance, and we can say for sure that you can't help yourself from shaking your body in the hypnotizing melody and beat.

The music of Rajasthan is very vibrant and the manner in which Rajasthani music has evolved by absorbing the unique features of its adjoining states like Gujarat, Haryana, and Punjab has meant that Rajasthani music is bold and evocative. Rajasthan has already carved a niche for itself not only in India but has also been very popular overseas, courtesy of the Festival of India shows that are conducted in a select few western countries. The State Government of Rajasthan has provided patronage and opportunities for self-employment for folk artists by organizing festivals and cultural programs. Rajasthan has also aroused and directed the interest of the local people towards our rich cultural heritage.

All the regions of Rajasthan have their distinct folk entertainment. The dance styles differ and so do the songs. Interestingly, even the musical instruments are different in Rajasthan.

The hilly tracts of central and southern Rajasthan are rich in community entertainments because of the lifestyle of tribes like the Bhils, Meena, Banjaras, Saharias, and Garasias.

The Jogis in Rajasthan were well-known for their recitation of the great ballad Nihalde Sultan, Shivji-ka-byawala, and songs about Gopi Chand and Bhartrihari. Most of these musical communities of Rajasthan live a rural base and function as wandering minstrels travelling from village to village around Rajasthan. There are many other artists in different art forms that use music as an accompaniment in Rajasthan.

Eastern Rajasthan is fertile and affluent, with plenty of patrons to sustain professional entertainers like the *bhats*, *kamads*, *bhopas*, *kacchi ghodi* dancers, and *kathputli* (puppeteer).

There is a great tradition of popular poetry, which is written under the rival banners of Turru and Kalangi. This is sung in groups in Jikri, Kanhaiyya or Geet (of the Meenas), Hele-ke-Khyal, and Bam Rasiya of Eastern Rajasthan. Group singing of classical bandishes called the Dangal or taalbandi is also unique to this region. Bhopas are singing priests of various deities or warrior saints. The Bhopas of Mataji wear costumes and play the *mashak*.

People in the harsh scantily populated desert areas of Western Rajasthan have very little leisure for merrymaking. Therefore, in this region, entertainment is provided by professional performers like the Bhats, Dholis, Mirasis, Nats, Sargadas, and Bhands who have been performing the age-old musical soirees in Rajasthan.

Folk traditions and classical forms found royal patronage in Rajasthan. A major school of the sophisticated classical *kathak* dance form originated in Jaipur as did Dhrupad singing. The rulers of Jaisalmer extended patronage to the Manganiyar community in Rajasthan.

State and royal patronage elevated some of these musicians into Kalawants in the royal courts of Rajasthan. The music of Rajasthan had acquired a sophistication that was absent from the rustic tones of the others. The famous Maand of Rajasthan, which is a unique style of singing and a core melody, is their creation. True to its desert environment, the Maand speaks of love, separation, chivalry, and revelry. Ballads are an integral part of the professional repertoire; and Dhola Maru, Moomal-Mahendra, Doongji-Jawarji, Galaleng, Jala-Boobna, Nagji-Nagwatnti are the most popular ones. The Mahabharat and the Ramayan are popular themes for ballads, and the Mirasis and Jogis of Mewat have a delightful folk version of the former while Hadoti has the Ramayan of Dhai kadi.

The brightness of its life, the legends of its heroism and romance, is captured in the vibrant and evocative music of this desert land. There is a richness and diversity in Rajasthani music which comes from a tradition that is old and undisturbed and from a culture that has imbibed the best from its neighbouring states of Sindh, Gujurat, Malwa, Mewar, Haryana, and Punjab.

Music which rich evocative heroic plaintive and joyful governs all aspects of Rajasthani lives. The voices both male and female are strong and powerful. The numerous songs sung by the women reflect the various feminine moods and strong family ties that govern their lives. Peepli and Nihalde are songs imploring the beloved not to leave her or to return to her as soon as he can.

There are songs about the family comparing every member to the numerous ornaments worn by women. The festivals of gangaur and teej celebrating marital bliss and the brief but splendid monsoon of Rajasthan call for special songs without which no celebration is complete.

Men and women of Rajasthan sing devotional as well as festive songs. Songs by the saint-poets like Kabir, Meera and Malookdas are part of the folk repertoire. They are sung all night during the *raatjagas* (all-night soirees spent singing devotional songs) which are held as thanksgiving to a particular deity. The resonant singing of the Rajasthani folk is accompanied by music from simple instruments like the Baara and Algoza that usually give a beat or a drone to offset the poetry.

Fairs and festivals bring an even greater riot of colour and music into lives of these desert people. Holi, the festival of colours, brings forth the joyous, lively rhythms of the change and *dhamal* songs, marriage, childbirth, the visit of the son-in-law, all call for song and music. Even children have their own special songs called the *saanjhi* and the *ghulda*. Favourites that are sung at all times are the Panihari Eendoni, the famous Kurjan Digipuri-ka-raja, and the Rasiya songs of the Braj region.

The hard life of the desert dwellers made them seek means of making life more pleasant by developing their artistic talents. There are many traditional communities who are professional performers, and their skills are handed down from generation to generation. The Bhat and Charans are bards, who could inspire the Rajput warriors with accounts of heroic deeds by whipping up patriotic flavour or even ridiculing the royal families with their satire.

The wandering balladeers, like the Bhopas, who sing about the Marwar folk hero-Pabuji, travel from village with their *phad* painting and rawan hahha entertaining people with their ballad. There are many singing communities in Rajasthan known as the Dholis, also known by other names like Mirasis, Dhadhis, Langas, Manganiyars, Kalbelias, Jogis, Sargaras, Kamads, Nayaks or Thotis, and the Bawaris.

Today their musicians can be heard all over the state and is popular even on the national and international circuits. The best flavour of this rich artistic talent can be savoured during various fairs and festivals of the state, especially during the Desert Festivals (Jan-Feb), the Pushkar Fair (Oct-Nov), the Marwar Festival (Sept-Oct), and the Camel Festival (Jan-Feb).

Ilahi had been to Rajasthan several times before. He had a special liking for this place, especially Jaisalmer, where he and his mother—along with his sister and brother—had once lived and where he had spent quite a few years of his childhood. As he disembarked from the train compartment, he could feel the rhapsody of the morning breeze gushing in to embrace him. Suddenly, there seemed to be more colour in the skies, more voice in the warble of the birds, more life added to the otherwise mundane atmosphere. Jaisalmer had recognised him, even after a space of two years.

Jaisalmer is a former principality in Rajasthan state, NW India. Its terrain is largely a sandy or stony waste and constitutes a section of the Thar Desert. Jaisalmer was brought under the Mughal Empire by Akbar in 1570. It became a British protectorate in 1818. In 1949 the region was incorporated into Rajasthan state. It is now a rail terminus and strategic military post close to the Pakistan border.

This desert fortress close to Rajasthan's border with Pakistan was founded in the twelfth century as a staging post for camel trains travelling between India and Central Asia. Jaisalmer is a golden sandstone city with crenellated city walls, a magnificent fortress and a number of exquisitely carved stone and wooden havelis. Seen at sunset from afar, it glows with the luminescence of a mirage. Jaisalmer's impressive fort crowns an 80m (260ft) high hill and about a quarter of the city's 40,000 inhabitants reside within its walls. Little has changed here for centuries, and if ever a record-breaking effort were made to pack as many houses, temples, and palaces into a confined space, this would be the result. The fort is honeycombed with winding lanes and has formidable gateways, a maharaja's palace, a ceremonial courtyard, and beautifully carved Jain temples. The most beautiful of the havelis built by Jaisalmer's wealthy merchants are Patwon ki Haveli, Salim Singh ki Haveli, and Nathmal ki Haveli.

Despite its incredible picturesqueness, you don't have to look very hard to realise that Jaisalmer is crumbling at an alarming rate. Its disintegration has finally brought local, governmental, tourist, and archaeological interest groups together and a 'Jaisalmer in Jeopardy' campaign has been launched in the UK.

As he stood at the platform slowly, coming into terms with his old home, a slight commotion brought him back to the present. There was a group of people who had quickly surrounded him, some with garlands, some with rose petals, and one of them with a placard with the name Prof Salman Ilahi carefully crafted on it. These people were from the Rajwada Karm Sanstha (Rajawada Working Committee) and had come to receive Ilahi. After all, he was the chief guest of the annual *mushaira*. The chief organizers for this event were the Rathods and the Sisodias. ArjunSingh Rathod, the indomitable leader of the Rathode clan, was one of the founder members of this cultural committee. A very respectable businessman, ArjunSingh, was known far and wide for his for his almost astonishing ability to organize functions of a grand scale within a very short time. Not only was he influential, he was also very well respected by people from every strata of the society. And needless to say, he was well connected too. His business of timber and furniture has also made him to travel a lot and in the process had given him lots of opportunities to know people . . . understand people.

ArjunSingh and his family had been very fond of Ilahi. He was like a family philosopher for them, apart from being a good friend of ArjunSingh and a good guide for his two sons. Ilahi also treated them as an extended part of his own family, especially Ramsingh, the younger son of ArjunSingh, who was quite like his own son. From playing chess to discussing politics and business, they have done it all together like any father and son should do.

Ramsingh Rathod maintained a particularly royal life. Endowed with the best of amenities of luxury at his disposal, he did not mind brandishing an affluent lifestyle. However, unlike other rich kids of his ilk, he was well read and well educated. He had completed his civil engineering from a reputed college and had developed a technical bent of mind. Thus, the family business of timber did not interest him much. He related himself with activities laced with sophistication rather than being layered with rusticity.

Ramsingh lived in a world of his own. His tastes did not match with that of his kith and kin. He chose Western Music over the local folklores to soothe himself. His attire was outlandish too. Instead of the traditional *dhoti*, *kurta*, and *paggar*, we were more into T-shirts, jeans, and designer caps. The Rathod clan, however, has always been steeped in tradition and were firm believers in a value system that had descended through centuries, into an era where some of the principles they followed were termed irrational, illogical, irrelevant, and bizarre. There has been always a murmur of discontent at the unconventional, almost outrageous, propensities of the younger Rathod. But he remained unperturbed. He was a man of his own making. He followed the jurisdiction of his interims and his bohemian instincts. He was a king of his own making, independent of the canonical and conservative thought processes of the society.

Salman Ilahi looked around the huge haveli. It was nothing less than an alcazar—an acropolis—with beautiful rose gardens, orchards, architectural fountains, and picturesque dispositions. The atmosphere was filled with fragrances from the fresh smelling flowers all around. The green grasses—a rare sight in Rajasthan—appeared greener, bathed in sunshine, and reflected the meticulous nurturing, tendered to them to guarantee their sustenance. The sight itself was having a charm, so refreshing, so rejuvenating that it almost escalated to the degree of intoxication.

'Welcome home, Bhaisa,' exclaimed ArjunSingh as he rushed out to greet him.

'ArjunSa was dying to see you,' Ilahi said, giving him a tight embrace.

Arjun Singh had made elaborate arrangements for Ilahi as was evident from the large table laid across the covered-garden veranda decorated with flower pots and exquisite seating arrangements. Peacocks and parrots took turns to scout for some commission against the brilliance they projected to the environ.

'I hope the journey was not tiring,' said Arjun Singh gesturing for Ilahi to take a seat.

'Not at all. Not this time of the year,' replied Ilahi.

'You are looking quite pale, Bhaisa. Is Mumbai giving you a very hard time?' Arjun Singh looked genuinely concerned.

'No, Arjun. This is old age. Can't you see how much I have greyed?' smiled Ilahi.

'Bhaisa, I know how disciplined you are. Your habits are so exquisite and your demeanour so cool. I have never ever seen you in anger. You are so very close to God. Then why do you appear so mellow, Bhaisa? What is bothering you?' Arjun Singh plodded on stubbornly.

'Kirdaar . . . Arjun Singh, kirdaar,' said Ilahi smilingly. 'Kirdaar has changed.'

'Means?' Arjun asked unblinking.

'Wohi Kaarwaan, Wohi Raastey, Wohi Zindagi, Wohi Marhaley, Magar Apne Apne, Muqaam Per, Kabhi Tum Nahi . . . Kabhi Hum Nahi!'

'Still not understood?' Ilahi laughed.

'Kirdar badal gaye, ab badli si yeh kahani hai, Zindagi mein mithaas thi ab zeher ke paani hai,

Mere zakhmon par marham na lagaao, Mere paas bas yehi ek us ki yadon ki nishani hai.' This time he recited aloud before getting up. It was time now for namaz.

Arjun Singh accompanied him to the guest house, still wearing an expression of bewilderment. Perhaps, he rued at the fact that his skills in comprehending the linguistic skills of his friend was so limited, that he could neither decipher nor appreciate the feel within the envelope of the eloquence—the mellifluousness of decorative words. He was just another novice in the realm of grandeur of languages.

The evening was at its glamorous best. Mewari, the gorgeous auditorium of the city centre, had been garnished with illumination and decor. There was music in the air. People had congregated in scores to witness an extravaganza of cultural curricula in the most colourful of outfits rendering a feel of ecstasy to the proceedings. An instrumental duet in violin and sarod set the gathering with the perfect mood. And the flute presentation provided the setting for the entry of the chief guest for the evening, the MP (member of parliament) from Jaisalmer, Mr Vikrant Parmar. Tipped to be the next minister of finance, for the state of Rajasthan, Parmar was a very influential person. Known for his penchant for art and culture, Parmar was a very close ally of the Rathods and the Sisodias. Every election, he is heavily funded by these two sections to ensure a landslide victory for him.

As Parmar descended to his recliner, Arjun Singh took the opportunity in introducing Ilahi to him.

'I have heard lots about you,' Parmar said, shaking hands with him. 'Today, I have got the opportunity to hear you.'

Ilahi smiled at him. 'Today, artists will play your kirdaar, sir. They will sing, recite, dance . . . and you will be a spectator. And rest of the year, so will talk, sing, and we . . . will play the kirdaar of listeners,' he replied.

Parmar chose to divert the topic to some relatively benign attributes. He knew that there can never be a decisive conclusion on arguments regarding the gap between promises and performance of a leader.

After a series of folk dances and desert songs, it was time for some other forms of music. The announcer called on stage Ms Megha Joshi, a budding singer from Mumbai.

Megha was a nightingale of a singer. Her sweet and soulful voice made inroads to the heart very easily and effectively. Whenever she sang tuneful numbers from touchy tunes, the hapless audience was moved to tears. One particular song that was in tribute to her mother was exemplary, peerless, divine. Even, Ilahi developed goose bumps on the impact of the powerful yet delicate rendition by this girl. There was a minute of silence as she finished the song—silence of awe—.the audience was numbed to speechlessness, spellbound. Then there was the applause that reverberated around the auditorium in a thunderous alacrity. Even Vikrant Parmar couldn't help but give her a standing ovation.

Ilahi was the last performer of the evening. He looked around the packed audience and smiled. 'After such fantastic renditions, how can I spoil this evening with my ordinary harangue?'

'My life orbits around my kirdaars,' he continued. 'I am like you, who play contrasting yet distinct roles to mark my existence. I don't rule the circumstances . . . But the circumstances dictate me. I fall, rise, fall again, and rise and become resolute or bow down under the burden of responsibility. I am you, who revolt against any injustice yet lose voice when strength deserts me. I am like you.' He paused, looked around. All eyes were fixed at him in unconditional attention. 'I fear to venture in the dark. I am afraid of apparitions against my windowpanes on stormy nights. I feel jealous of the myriads who ride their luck while others fall back into the beaten tracks, even after going through all the necessary ordeal. I feel apprehensive about my children when they stay away from me for long. I am one amongst you. I am also at times irritated with my country and my countrymen . . . angry with the government, frustrated with the law and order situation, and aggrieved by the impoverished condition of the majority of our population. But yes, I still hope . . . like you do, at the light at the end of the tunnel will again be visible . . . So I wait and play through all the kirdaars life has to offer me.'

aaj phir din ke ujaale se dar gaya koi . . .
Jaise sooraj par hi ilzaam dhar gaya koi
aaj kal shehar mein ayinon pe paabandi hai . . .
aks apnay se, sunaa hai, ke dar gaya koi

Ramsingh was awake unusually early. Ilahi was pleasantly surprised to see him walking up to him as he sat on the garden chair cherishing the beauty of the morn. Sun, the harbinger of life, had just made its auspicious appearance at the horizon spreading its silken golden streaks across the vastness of the sky.

Ramsingh stooped to touch his feet. Ilahi was pleasantly taken aback. Ramsingh was not the kind to touch feet. Somehow, this attribute had been missing from his otherwise charming constitution. Ilahi signalled him to sit beside him. He liked his company. His methods of searching for methods in the madness of the world sometimes amazed Ilahi. Why does he engage himself so vehemently to unravel the unravelled?

'So, Ram, when do I get the invitation of your marriage?' Ilahi Joked.

Astonishingly, Ramsingh took much longer to reply than he usually does. 'I don't know,' he replied wryly.

Ilahi could gauge his distraction. He was not the one to reply without looking in the eye.

'What's wrong, Ram?' he inquired. 'I see some change in your demeanour.'

'It's love, Professor.' That's what Ramsingh had always called Ilahi.

'Love is everywhere. Especially in Rajasthan.' Ilahi smiled.

'I am in love, Professor. And I know I cannot live without it,' Ramsingh said.

'So what's so wrong in it, my son? Go ahead and confess your love. And Allah is great, you will soon be able to convert this lover of yours into your life partner,' Ilahi Beamed.

'What if she is not a Rajput?' enquired Ramsingh.

'Well then, it will require some convincing,' replied Ilahi almost in a casual tone.

'Professor, you have always paid heed to all the tantrums that I have thrown in the past. At times you have been like my mother though I have never seen her, my brother, friend, and my guide.' Ilahi could see tears brimming at the rims of his eyes. 'Professor, help me with my life. You can best convince babasa.'

Ilahi was perplexed. He knew with what vigour the Rathods maintained their caste culture. His intervention in this issue ruined his relationship with ArjunSingh forever. However, if he did not listen to his heart, which prompted him to think in favour of this child, who may have discovered true love the only time, he could never look at himself in the mirror.

Ilahi pressed at the folded arms of Ramsingh and was almost moved to tears at the unadulterated smile that he got in response.

Listen to the mustn'ts, child. Listen to the don'ts. Listen to the shouldn'ts, the impossibles, the won'ts. Listen to the never haves, then listen close to me . . . Anything can happen, child. Anything can be.

(Shel Silverstein)

CHAPTER 5

The Sport Star

'What kind of name is this?' Murmurs developed from several sections of the classroom. The vice principal had just introduced the new student to join Standard XI Bio section—Arman Bailey. What a name—a kind of hybridization between the Orient and the West. 'Children, please welcome a new member to our family.' Father George Fernandez, the vice principal, rumbled on in his lifeless monotone. 'It's a matter of pride for us that Mr Bailey, the president of Habbit Bobbins Corporation, has chosen our school for his son to study in.' Father Gearge looked around the class, perhaps in anticipation of a round of applause. When there was none, he continued again, 'Arman hails from Australia. He has spent his life till now in Australia, and this is the first time he has come to a different country. Please make him feel at home. And, Arman, this is your new home, and all your friends here will help you out with everything that you need.' Arman nodded in gratitude to the vice principal before taking his seat at the far corner of the classroom. He could perceive that all eyes were glued to him.

Arman was tall, had a good built, and had a very serious face. Though he hailed from Australia, he strangely had immaculate Indian looks. He was not as fair as Australians should be and uniquely enough had black hair and brown eyes. Actually, Arman had inherited his looks and nature from his mother, Alia, an Indian by origin, born and brought up in the city of Mumbai. Arman's only inheritance from his father, Jonathon, was his accent.

Jonathon was a very jovial and amicable person. Hard work, dedication, and an indomitable spirit have catapulted him to the helm of an organization that has found a huge market in India and neighbouring countries. He had been to India before—once before—when he had spent three marvellous, eventful, memorable years in Mumbai as an enterprising young engineer. His quest to learn Hindi and Urdu had given him the opportunity to meet Alia Ilahi, the daughter of an extraordinary, iconic scholar, who was not only a pundit of languages but also possessed extensive knowledge of science, arts, and literature. Jonathon had amassed treasures of knowledge and the wealth of love in those three historic years. His marriage to Alia had been a quiet and low-profile affair prior to their departure to Australia. The birth of Arman added more meaning to their lives, and together they formed the most adorable family in the neighbourhood. Jonathon was back to India again, eighteen years later. And this time, he was not merely a soldier in the ranks. He was the general.

Arman had been a very silent and secluded child since his early days. He never mixed with his peers much. He loved to play alone with unconventional toys and uncanny props, which he modulated to suit his kind of play. Since very childhood, his suppleness and agility was immense. He was a fast runner and very fit and quick in his movements. Words had come to him late since he was not particularly inclined to enhance his vocabulary. Everyone suspected that Arman was a child with autism, a neurodevelopmental condition which mainly affects areas of social interaction and communication.

Alia and Jonathon were both worried with this little kid. They took him to scores of child psychologists and ABA centres, all around Tasmania, in an effort to bring about some semblance of normalcy in him. But Arman remained unconventional, unmoved by all the therapies tried and tested on him. Arman was bereft of emotions and preferred to stay within himself.

Desperate, Alia finally sought the help of her father. Though not a doctor, psychologist, or psychiatrist, Alia knew that her father, Salman Ilahi, somehow, would be able to achieve what professionals in psychology could not. Ilahi obliged by coming down to Australia to stay with his daughter and work out some method for young Arman.

Arman was entrusted to Ilahi, who stayed with him through night and day, slowly establishing himself at first as an acquaintance then as a friend and finally a buddy whom Arman could trust and understand. Arman was happy with Ilahi. In fact, he was overjoyed. Ilahi slowly started teaching him how to read, talk, and play conventionally.

Arman was eight years old when Ilahi took him to a cricket coaching camp in South Hobart, where young children were being taught to play and understand the wonderful game of cricket. Slowly, Arman started taking interest in the game. Initially, he only used to watch the bigger boys go through their motions. Slowly but steadily he started getting himself acquainted with the nuances of the game. There is a peculiarity about these autistic children, some of them at least, that they do not forget things easily and also certain things which they learn, good or not so good, become their part of life. They learn things the hard way through a tedious process of activity recognition. But they learn, albeit in a very slow, sluggish manner. They do not feel the way others do. They don't see things with the same percept that of their peers. The concept of Autism had shot to prominence after Dustin Hoffman's enactment of an autistic character. Several other films too had been projecting this behavioural disorder to project the uniqueness of this irregularity of the psyche. Autism has no cure. Only through therapy can one reduce the effects. Arman was destined to live in this world of orderliness with this malaise of mental disorder—though a mild one.

Arman took fancy for all aspects of the game, fielding, batting, bowling, and also wicket keeping. His only misgiving was that he was not expressive and cricket is a vociferous game. The Australians play it hard. In Australia, the game had graduated from the benign gentleman's endeavour to a highly competitive and professional sport. It is performance and not popularity that dictates your destiny as a cricketer.

❧

Not only students of eleventh bio but also students from rest of the sections and classes of Loyola School, Jamshedpur were bewildered by this new inclusion in their ranks. Not that Arman had become popular, but people were generally mystified by his peculiar nature. He liked to be alone, all by himself, not quite keen to talk or be friendly with people. Most of the time he appeared lost and adrift. He hardly involved himself in class activities, and his interactions with people around him were bare minimum. His solitude had a bearing of strangeness. He struggled with studies and other curricula and was soon designated to the anonymity of the back benches.

Not that he was totally friendless; there were a few amongst his classmates who were genuinely concerned about him.

It is pertinent to mention here that Loyola School was primarily a boys' school. The inclusion of girls happened only in standard eleven and twelve. Thus, girls were few, and everyone knew them. Sacred Heart Convent School was the able counterpart of Loyola since it was an all-girls school. Some of these girls, who used to grow up hating Loyola, would ultimately join the school in plus two and become diehard fanatics for the system. Loyola School was legendary. It was held in high esteem in the academic circles of India. The specialty of Loyola was and still is that it creates all-rounders. It laid equal stress to the physical, intellectual, spiritual, moral, and extracurricular development of each student. These students grow up to become trendsetters in different parts of the world, in different paths of life.

Anil Sinha was the class councillor. He was one who could mix with one and all very freely. He was an absolute lovable character bestowed with a witty disposition. He spread good cheer and best of humour in the class and wherever he went. Then there was Rajat Gupta, hugely popular for his handsome looks and stylish nature. He had an aura of sophistication that came from his being part of the lineage of the famed Gupta clan. Guptas were rich business owners of Jamshedpur. Kaushik Dhar was another character. He was absolutely brilliant in studies, being head, neck, shoulders above the competition. He had an air of superiority about him and rightly so because people knew that his academic records were hard to beat. Navin Chaddha was a self-proclaimed casanova. His character was an effort towards impersonation of the legendary Don Juan with comical effects. Roopam Gandhi—creative, passionate, a fantastic public speaker as well as a good sportsperson.

Let's talk about the girls too. Rishita Pradhan. A beautiful lady in the making. You call her a showstopper, a head-turner. She was surely the cynosure in the campus. Boys longed to talk to her, and girls were jealous of the attention she received.

Shruti Khanna. Another ravishing damsel. However, this girl was more down to earth, was more affable and cordial. She was good in her studies and thus was popular amongst the teaching staff too.

Nandini Arora. This girl was of the silent type. Very particular with her sense of duty and responsibilities. She always indulged in sensible discussions and was rarely found to hang around uselessly with gangs of boys or girls, inside or outside the campus.

Priyanka Singh. A very bubbly and effervescent girl. Loved to laugh around, joke around, and be active throughout the day. She had a good sense of humour and was one of those characters who enjoy school and college life to the fullest.

Vinita Garg. She was the executive, with a stern and serious personality. Though a bit of a tomboy by nature, she commanded respect amongst her compatriots due to her connections and contacts. After all, she was the daughter of the chairman of Crescent Corporation, a big corporate house in the Indian Subcontinent.

Payel Sardesai. This girl was a born analyst and critic. Her analysis of films, programmes, even characters were always spot-on. Her comments were always taken into account when any new initiative was to be taken up by students. Her opinion did matter since they were very honest, rational, to the point, and unbiased.

Loyola Plus two was a hep and happening crowd, and there was huge competition amongst the sections. In every department of schooling, there was competition—be it studies, debates, quizzes, be it organizing skits and musicals or sports.

One annual event everybody used to look up to was the intersection cricket tournament. This was organized by the plus two, for the plus two, with the whole school as spectator. Generally, this was fierce competition, and the junior boys, who looked up to the seniors as their heroes, enjoyed the on-field spectacle and the off-field tussle with utmost intent. This was also a great stage for showcasing one's talent, glamour, and capability.

The class was almost in a huddle as Arman entered the classroom. Anil Sinha was vigorously scribbling names on a full scrape white paper while the others were talking about batting orders, fielding positions, etc. Cricket always drew Arman's interest. So he tried to get into the huddle to understand what exactly was going on.

'What's going on?' Arman asked innocently to the boys in general.

'We are working out our class team for the tournament,' replied one of them wryly.

'Is it?' Arman got interested. 'I too play cricket. Can I be included?'

Some of the boys turned around to face him. 'Dude, this is not a charity cricket match. We have to win this tournament. At least we need to beat XI Maths,' they almost said in unison.

Anil was more sympathetic. Looking up from his scribbled paper piece, he said in a consoling voice, 'The team is selected, but don't worry, you can help us out in the nets.'

Arman was taken aback. Why are these boys not giving him a fair chance? They probably are not aware of his capabilities, so they should have tested his skills. They should have told him to have a practice session with them.

'Can you please accommodate me for some of the matches?' Arman pleaded.

'Sorry, champ, the best team has been selected,' announced Roopam.

Best team? How can it be the best team when other people have not been given a fair chance to compete? Arman was visibly very disappointed. He sat in his corner seat the whole day without even going out during lunchtime and waited for the day to end. His non-inclusion to the class cricket team kept on playing in his mind making him feel more and more agonized, angry, and heartbroken.

While on the dinner table, he spelt out this disappointment to his parents, and needless to say, they were both concerned. As it is that poor Arman is not expressive enough and now this incident may not augur well for his already-disturbed psyche. Alia and Jonathon both tried their own methods of pacification for they knew that they could not afford for Arman to have a psychological breakdown, given his fragile and impressionable mental condition. They started spending quality time with him in an effort to distract him from his present state of dejection.

The jubilee park, at the heart of the city, was one of the greatest attractions. A spread of green in the midst of a city built around a mammoth steel plant is arguably a rarity. The jubilee park has it all, from musical fountains, rose garden, zoological park, children's park, landscaped walks, a beautiful artificial lake, a musical fountain display, and much, much more. Jamshedpureans draw their oxygen for sustenance from this precious zone so precariously maintained by the enigmatic subsidiary of Tata Steel, JUSCO. Arman loved jubilee park, especially at late evenings when the fountains were at full flow. The statue of Jamshedji Nessarwanji Tata, the founder of the steel plant and the city, in the middle of the park, always enamoured Arman.

'Dad, did J. N. Tata ever play cricket?' he had once asked Jonathon.

'I don't know, but I have heard that he had great interest in the game,' Jonathon had replied.

After a brief interval of silent pondering, Arman had further enquired, 'Don't you think, Dad, he would have made a wonderful cricket captain?'

Amused, Jonathon could not prevent himself from asking, 'Why so?'

'He was a good strategist, Dad,' Arman had replied. 'And to be a good leader, one has to have a strategic mind.'

'Who told you all this?' Jonathon had been pleasantly surprised at this recourse on leadership from his son.

'Well, Dada did. He told me about leadership. And he has also told me that one day I will the captain of a cricket team.' Arman gleamed. Incidentally, Dada, his grandfather, Salman Ilahi, had been in constant touch with Arman over the telephone. They have been in serious discussion over Arman's omission from the class cricket team for some time. And it was also certain that this mentor of his would be soon making a welcome arrival to Jamshedpur for providing Arman with some more lessons on leadership . . . or patience maybe. He also knew that Arman was waiting for that impatiently.

There were seven teams in fray: XI Commerce, XI Maths, XI Bio, XII Commerce, XII Maths, XII Bio, and a combined Arts section. The first match was between XII Commerce, one of the favourites and XII Maths.

In an almost one-sided affair, XII Commerce thrashed XII Maths by seven wickets. The curtain-raiser ended up to be a damp squib. But there were more exciting contests in store because the next day XI Maths was to play XI Commerce.

Both teams were strong and full of characters that were hugely popular. A huge crowd had gathered to witness the thirty over aside contest that promised to be a humdinger. Raj Bhatia won the toss, and a huge roar emanated from the XI Math's camp. Maths were to bat first. They had some very good batsmen in their squad, and they had planned to put up a sizeable score before exploiting the crumbling pitch with their array of swing and spin.

Commerce, though, had other ideas. Their loss in the toss did not matter much for them. Their bowlers had been instructed strongly not to provide the opponent batsmen with any room to play cuts or pulls. They bowled wicket to wicket with decent pace and a clever field setting. Maths batsmen were unable to get them away. Under pressure, the famed batting line-up began to crumble. Chinks in the formidable armoury was exposed.

The XIth Commerce won the match by chasing down the ordinary target that Maths had set for them. But Maths did not go down so easily. They did put up some fight in the end to make the contest a bit interesting.

It was XIth Bio's turn now. Their first match was a tough one, against the formidable XIIth Commerce. Arman and all his classmates cheered noisily as Anil won the toss. The toss is always important. It somewhat dictates the proceedings. The one who wins the toss gets a chance to caste his opinion over the cricketing transactions. Bio opted to bat first. Arman somehow thought that they would have done well had they bowled first. It was a disastrous start by Bio. Their batting order disintegrated in no time against some very disciplined and controlled bowling performance by the Commerce team. Bio could put up a very modest total which was overtaken by Commerce without much labour.

Meanwhile in another match, XIth Maths won a very tight match against XII Bio. So it was a day when both the bio sections were beaten.

Arman was very disappointed at the performance of his class team. He trudged back home with a very heavy heart. A loss is a loss, so what if it's against a stronger team. We play a match to win, and even if we may not come out victors, we should be happy that we gave the winners a tough fight—that they had to earn their victory. But here their team had almost gifted the match to Commerce without even a semblance of fight. As he neared home, a familiar perfume revived his senses. He could not hold himself back from rushing inside. The dejection that was weighing him down had suddenly evaporated.

There on the dining table was the bearer of the sweet perfume—his dearest friend, guide, and philosopher, his grandfather, his dada.

The next few days were humiliating for XI BIO. They had lost their next two matches too. XII Maths had trounced them, and so had Arts. This arts team was the weakest team in the tournament. It was preassumed that all the teams would have a cake walk against them. But XIth Bio was such a disorganized team that even the minnows of the event gave them a nightmarish outing.

Arman and his dada spent a lot of time together. Their discussions moved around the school, the subjects, the town, and over and above everything was the Cricket tournament. Dada was a very good listener, one of the finest listeners one can ever come across.

Dada also had that never-ending stock of tales from history. Tales that were entertaining and also imparted a lot of inspiration. Arman could sit for hours on end and listen to those enchanting narratives. The bond between the two kept strengthening with every such tale of subjects that mainly revolved around acts of valour, courage, benevolence, and leadership. Dada had come to Jamshedpur with a purpose to bring forth a *kirdaar* which he had been nurturing with so much care and warmth.

The class was in total bedlam. Students were irate at the shameful defeat of their class in all the three matches and especially against the Arts, the most fragile side.

Payel Sardesai was very vocal since morning. 'The team has been an embarrassment,' she announced. 'We need a change. We are playing XIth Maths next, and a defeat against them would be very, very shameful.' Her face was red with resentment.

The XIth Maths was their arch rival. They were adversaries in everything: studies, sports, extracurricular, popularity—everything was up in contest. At the moment, Maths were sky-high in confidence after having defeated XII BIO in their last outing, and XI Bio were low in morale after their three consecutive defeats. The turnaround looked a very distant possibility.

All morning Anil Sinha had been at the receiving end. He had been, like never before, in a loss of words to explain the debacle in his team's performance. He was trying to put together some desperate measures to resurrect the wilting spirits of his team. Amongst the jeers and the angry criticisms, Anil took courage to announce his measures for rectification.

'The match against maths is four days later. We will have a trial match between us before that amongst ourselves. The class will select the team according to the merit of players and their performance in the practice match. Does everyone agree?' He waited for a consensus.

The class unanimously roared in agreement.

Jonathon was amazed at the quick transformation in his son's mood. Just a few days ago, the child had been melancholy and morose, and now there was a spring in each of his steps. He looked happy, attentive, and focused. His son appeared animated, expressive, vibrant, energized, and above all happy. This was in sharp contrast to what they had been accustomed to in connection to Arman's moods. He was truly perplexed. That night after having dinner, Jonathon could not prevent him from telling Alia about his curious observation. 'Alia, your father is a magician. He has performed a miracle with our son.'

Alia could only nod silently in confirmation. She had always known that her father was truly a genius.

They called it BIO A and BIO B. Arman was in the B side. Sriram Bhagat, their captain, a member of the existing team, had opted to bowl first. Determined to prove their mettle, the A team batters played with caution and responsibility. The A team looked to be controlling the proceeding with ease. Something drastic was needed to be done by the B team players to make a match out of it. After a lot of pondering, Sriram chucked the ball to Arman, who gleefully accepted, what appeared to be a faint flicker of an opportunity for him to make a claim for a place in the side.

An overenthusiastic Arman started with two consecutive wide deliveries and followed it up with a full toss which was put away easily by the set batsman. Someone from the crowd howled out some expletives. Others just shook their head in disappointment. As Arman Bailey walked back to his run up, Sriram ran up to him for some words of admonition and encouragement.

The batsman, Hemant Sharma, could not read the pace of the ball this time. The ball deviated just a shade after pitching, beat the half-forward lunge of the bat, and uprooted the off stump. Wicket. Arman had struck.

Next delivery was even better. The new batsman, Sameer Sen, could only see the ball zip through his bat and pad to crash onto middle stump. Timber. Another wicket. The next delivery was another peach of a delivery. The ball swung ominously from outside off-taking the edge of the bat to the wicket keeper. From 63/0, the A team was reduced to 63/3 in the space of three balls. The class was dumbfounded. They were witnessing some extraordinary specimen of swing bowling.

Sohail Akhtar was yorked. Karthik Dhar was caught at second slip. Bivash Dutta was bamboozled by the pace and could only see his stumps get shattered.

The A team slipped to 95/8 in no time, and soon the full team was dismissed at a paltry 113 runs. Arman ended with an emphatic figure of 21/7. He had taken seven A team wickets at the expense of only twenty-one runs in only five overs. Arman Bailey had announced his arrival. Needless to say, the B team did not have to break much sweat to canter home.

XI Maths were to bat first. Anil, the captain of BIO, had resisted a huge urge to let Arman bowl the first over. He wanted to use Arman as a surprise element against their arch rivals and rightly so because the maths players looked a bit complacent right from the beginning. They played aggressive cricket batting with utter disdain against the mediocre bowlers of Bio. Unable to restrict the flow of runs, Anil turned to his ace. Arman's first over was not very effective.

He bowled slow and straight and let the batsmen play freely against him. The Bio players looked dejected in anticipation of some kind of success from their newly discovered hero.

Arman did not disappoint them in his second over. Anshu Jain, the celebrated opener, was caught plumb by a magnificent inswinger. Amit shah had no clue of the delivery that followed. In a fraction of a second, the ball clipped his right pad to crash onto the stumps. Wickets started tumbling, and suddenly Goliath had started taking a lot of pounding from David. Bio did well to restrict maths to a modest total of 128 runs. It was a big morale booster. Bio was a transformed lot now. Arman's bowling had brought back in the camp the belief that was lost. And what a dramatic transformation had come about Arman. He was no longer the lost, absent-minded, shaky teenager. He was now the epitome of determination, passion, and attitude. There was a distinct intent in his confident steps. His thoughts were more organized, and there was a sense of belief in whatever he did. His focus, his passion, and intent mixed with a hint of aggression was evident by the way he conducted himself in the field. This was metamorphosis—a complete evolution of the psyche, and Loyola School, Jamshedpur, stood evidence to another rising star, ready to get his name etched in the annals of history.

The XIth Bio survived some tense moments to beat Maths convincingly and trigger off frenzied celebrations. And rightly so, XIth Bio was back in the reckoning. If they managed to win the other two matches with comprehensive results, they might qualify for the finals. And looking at their present forms, it was appeared to be a distinct possibility.

XIth BIO won the next match against XIth commerce without much ado and inched towards the final with only one hurl in front of them XII Bio.

Arman had taken his dada along for the parents-teacher meeting. All the teachers, including the ever grumbling Chemistry teacher Father Bonneli, lauded his remarkable turnaround. He had improved substantially in his studies too. His marks definitely reflected a sudden change in his attitude and approach. Ilahi was proud at this remarkable change that had come upon his grandson. He could not ask for anything more. It was a rewarding feeling. It was a poetic justice.

> Muddat se apne kabiliyat pe fakr kiya tha,
> Muddat se chirago se parchaai ka zikr kiya tha,
> Ab ye jalwa-e-raunak ka jasn suhana hai . . .
> Sochta hoon khamakha hi humne itna fikr kiya tha.

The XIIth Bio posted a mammoth total for XIth Bio to chase. It was a formidable total, 188 runs. Though Arman had bowled brilliantly, the other bowlers had leaked far too many runs. The onus was now up to the batsmen. XIIth Bio had very good bowlers in their team, and the crumbling track suited them. Soon, XIth Bio was staring down the barrel having lost half of their side before putting even fifty runs on the board. It was now the turn of Arman to do some magic with the bat. The battle between bat and the ball intensified. With each hit to the fence, XIth Bio sent shivers into the spines of their seniors. Arman stuck on, fighting a lone battle. However, XIth Bio finally succumbed to the disciplined bowling of XIIth Bio and were sent crashing out of the tournament. The fight back was epic. They had lost the match by a whisker, only seven runs. They had almost done the improbable. Arman Bailey remained not out on eighty-one. It was a emphatic display of stroke making, leaving even the opponents with a lasting impression.

The XIIth Bio and XIIth Commerce locked horns in the grand finale, and Commerce emerged the deserved champions. A lot of fanfare and celebrations were followed by the awards ceremony. Father Gregory Thomas, the rector of the school, announced the winners of all the category of awards. Everyone clapped out loud as one by one the awards were read out and the winners summoned to the podium. Finally, it was the turn of the most coveted award—that of the player of the tournament. 'The player of the tournament is unanimously chosen by all faculty members, Armaaaaan Baileeey,' the otherwise stoic Father Thomas announced with a flourish. Arman could do nothing to hold back his tears. As he came up to the podium, Father Rector gave him a big hug. The applause reverberated around the school corridors out in the open, along the avenue streets of Jamshedpur, and rang out to each house, gathering, hamlet. Here . . . Here is a performer who overcame the challenges of destiny, to take a baby step in conquering destiny.

'Say a few words, Bailey,' implored Father Thomas.

Armaan looked around the huge gathering. All eyes were glued at him. Many of them probably did not know even a fortnight ago that Armaan Bailey existed.

'I can only say something, Loyoleans. If you have a dream, better start believing in it,' he said in a semi-choked voice.

A loud cheer emanated from the assembly and reached out to the sky in a crescendo.

We're all seeking that special person who is right for us. But if you've been through enough relationships, you begin to suspect there's no right person, just different flavours of wrong. Why is this? Because you yourself are wrong in some way, and you seek out partners who are wrong in some complementary way. But it takes a lot of living to grow fully into your own wrongness. And it isn't until you finally run up against your deepest demons, your unsolvable problems—the ones that make you truly who you are—that we're ready to find a lifelong mate. Only then do you finally know what you're looking for. You're looking for the wrong person. But not just any wrong person: the right wrong person—someone you lovingly gaze upon and think, "This is the problem I want to have."

I will find that special person who is wrong for me in just the right way. Let our scars fall in love.

(Galway Kinnell)

CHAPTER 6

From the Hallowed Corridors

On a particularly cold evening, one of the prominent residents at the Lala Lajpat Rai Hall of Residence of IIT Kharagpur was going through a mental tumult. Life, as it looked to him or as he looked at it, seemed to jeer at his whole existence. He had been going through the trauma of losing his edge over his competitors, which he had been trying hard to maintain all these years. They are not only catching up, they are surpassing him. Even the revered professors who did swear by his abilities till recently had started doubting his capability of keeping up with the lofty standard of the institution. His steady decline in merit had also prevented him from calling home and lying to his people about his artificial prosperity. The Laplace theorem and the Fourier series returned to haunt him every night robbing him off even the last iota of slumber that remained in his eyelids. He was tired of a life that seems to endlessly drag on without any substantial tangibility. His credibility, for which he had drained a significant measure of his livelihood, had nosedived to a downward trajectory . . . to the abyss of no return.

He straightened up to adjust the noose he so carefully had crafted with the ambidexterity of a garrotter. Life appeared to be now just a momentary impulse. Just then, out of nowhere, one of his favourite numbers of Eric Clapton wafted through the air. He was lulled to the doorway as if in hypnotic animation. The song was being played by his unsuspecting next-door neighbour. Swapnil glanced at his watch. Two-thirty AM. He was pleasantly surprised at the fact that his early-sleeping neighbour was up till so late, playing the choicest melodies he can go miles to listen. He thought of bidding his friend a final adieu before giving life a final go. Death can be procrastinated by five minutes.

Minutes turned into hours, and the night yielded to a golden morn. The noose was carefully tucked away and the other accessories of self-decapitation were put out of sight. With the morning light a fresh lease of life had returned to the abode of enlightenment. There was a fresh spring of life in every step of Swapnil Chowdhury, a new chapter in his life had begun.

Welcome to IIT Kharagpur, where even a trivial film song can transform gloom of death to the glimmer of prosperity. Where hope and desperation play hide and seek amongst the hallowed corridors of technical excellence. Where dreams, desires, ambition, apprehension culminate into a single pursuit. The reach for the pinnacle . . . of unfathomed glory.

BB was up from his bed early because he was required to meet the members of the organizing committee of the Annual Spring Fest, to connive upon a novel and innovative event for the forthcoming fiesta. Spring Fest was knocking at the door. It happens to be the one of the prestigious Festivals in this part of the country and has already attained lofty standards over the years in the community of academia. The expectation of everybody within and outside campus has always been on an ascent. The challenge was to create an ingenious concept wrapped up in the mould of entertainment delivering some message of pertinence across every classification of society.

BB had been outstanding with such events and acts of entertainment giving them his own distinctive flavour that was highly appreciated by all and sundry. Coupled with this talent of his was his extraordinary knack of excelling in his department of Computer Science.

Algorithm Laboratory, Software Engineering, Theory of Computation were areas where he had already stamped his supremacy over his contemporaries. But the subject close to his heart was AI—Artificial Intelligence, which is the skeleton of the most enigmatic of all subjects . . . robotics. Ironically, however, these academic successes did little to gladden BB. His realm stretched far beyond the confinement of academics, much beyond the boundaries of class rooms and libraries into the territories of the unknown, unconquered, unsurpassed regions of human behaviour. He always wanted to Grow up into someone different, someone offbeat.

Last year the erstwhile organizing group had introduced the event where collages were synchronized with distinctive songs played in the background, and one of the naughty groups had played the mercurial number 'Choli ke piche kya hai' (what's beneath the bikini) bringing about an uproar amongst the audience. This year it was the turn of BB and his team to come up something more significant and subtle. Parameters had been set too. Pramila Roy the head mistress-like third year student of architecture had already issued the dictate to eliminate vulgarity and innuendoes and to take special care in maintaining 'the dignity of ladies'.

The Algorithm Laboratory was due in fifteen minutes—a time enough for the organizing group to hurriedly exchange some opinions over a few puffs of a circulated shaft of nicotine.

Abir, one of the masterminds in the team, suggested that the event must be rocking with lot of rock and roll with splashes of light and laser.

Sipping the hot tea from an earthen tumbler, Sunil, a self-styled unheralded dramatist proposed that Indian culture and heritage must be portrayed in a solemn and dignified manner. Shyam took a counter from Robin and drew a vociferous puff from it and suggested that it must reflect the 'technical instinct' of an IIT student.

'All bloody run-of-the-mill thoughts', reckoned BB, visually frustrated at the mediocre levels of imagination of his peers. Tossing away the cigarette butt, he stood up abruptly and headed towards the lab.

At the doorway, he almost bumped into Dr A. K. Shom, a stalwart in the faculty and also a member of the cultural committee.

Dr Shom stopped to smile at him. His smile has always been contagious. Whatever one's state of mind be, one usually ends up smiling back at him.

'Don't be too worried, Bibhuti,' he said in a low voice. 'I know you will come up with some extraordinary idea this time. The whole college is looking up to you.'

'And', he added after a pause, 'everyone knows that you can do absolutely anything. Anything.'

BB kept watching until the silhouette of the professor waded out of sight. Whether what he said was in challenge or in appreciation did not matter, for Bibhuti Bhushan, alias BB, too believed that he only *can* . . . and he will.

Bibhuti Bhushan was born to a humble parentage at Dooars in the peripheries of North Bengal and brought up in the enchanting and tranquil ambience of tea gardens. His father, Subhash, a manager with one of the tea estates at Vannabari—though had been detached from academics for quite some time—had been paranoid of getting his only son educated in the best of Institutes. Subhash had a penchant for Literature and nature, thus prompting him to name his only son after the eminent Bangla, litterateur Bibhuti Bhushan Bandopadhyay, whose phenomenal endeavours with 'Pather Panchali' (the tale of the road) and 'Chader Pahar'(the mountain of moon) had been phenomenal work in the world of Bengali Literature. Subhash had repeatedly read out excerpts from Chaderpahar to a very young BB in an effort to give BB's impressionable mind a literary texture. This had Bourne results. BB had grown up with a distinctive though process. His methods, though innocent, reflected the creativity in his character.

Usually BB's day started at seven in the morning with his journey to school; the only available school in the locality of Vannabari Tea Estate, walking through the pebble-aid makeshift road between two plantation sections of the gardens . . . hopping, running, dancing. The waist-high fresh green plants as if joining him in his merriment. The twenty-minute walk from the bungalow to Vannabari tea estate secondary school was always a pleasure for BB. The astringent aroma of tea leaves worked as energizer for his indomitable spirit. BB can see Itwari aunty plucking the leaves from the bush. Itwari aunty helps his mom in household acts beyond her works in the garden. She waves at BB and cautions him to keep safe. Yes, he had to keep himself safe. He had bigger things to do.

Tea plantation is no less than an art. Precaution is required to be taken at every stage of growth and development of the plants. The plantations are taken special care of by the vigilant supervisors. Strict discipline and decorum is maintained for the processes of cultivation, collection, and maintenance. Team effort, timeliness, and discipline are the major attributes that provide the morning cuppa with the kind of flavour that gets mankind on the move.

BB had always admired the orchestrated acts of weeding, spraying, and plucking of two leaves and a bud and tossing the same to the basket at the back. The dedication and the skill of these ladies often made BB wonder whether machines can ever replace this traditional work process. Can any machine match the exactitude and the devotion that these women involve in their work? Perhaps one day economy will force machines into these plantations, and perhaps from that day, tea will have a different texture—an artificial texture like that of the world at large.

Kalamandir was the only school in the locality with wooden wall and roof made of asbestos. The number of class rooms are limited, and there is scarcity of teachers too. Boys from neighbouring tea estates also come to this school.

Students belong to two broad categories. The elite class or the children of the managers and executives of the tea gardens enjoyed certain privileges that the other category of students, the children of the estate workers, could never even dream of.

However, very few children of the workers could afford this particular school. Like Budhua, BB's best pal and Itwary auntie's son, many drop out midway, unable to sustain the monetary demands on a regular basis. Understandably so, because it was the women folk who earned while the menfolk were more engrossed with their indulgence with alcohol and opium.

Amongst all subjects, BB had developed an inherent liking for history. History amazed him, amused him, inspired him, made him sit up in admiration of the makers and propagators of history through acts of courage, thought, schemes, strategy, benevolence, kindness, dedication, and . . . and deceit.

One particular lecture of Kalipada Sir, the inspirational but cantankerous history teacher, had made a permanent impression to his mind . . . and perhaps to his aspirations too.

'Abraham Lincon was the sixteenth president of the United States. Lincoln led the United States through its greatest constitutional, military, and moral crisis—the American Civil War—preserving the Union, abolishing slavery, strengthening the national government, and modernizing the economy. Reared in a poor family on the western frontier, Lincoln was self-educated and became a country lawyer, a Whig Party leader and a source of inspiration for generations to come.'

Kalipada Sir had gone on to describe some landmark achievements of Lincoln and had paused several times while describing his assassination outside an opera.

Lincoln had lived and died for a cause: equality. Equality that is so sadly missing in every department of livelihood. We are born to be slaves of systems and other human beings. Man is a slave of his brother man. We are slaves of unexplained dogmas and rituals that sometimes defy logic and also of laws and rules that are always generic and never individualistic. Equality, even in the smallest measure, can bring about so many smiles . . . So much happiness, so much peace.

It was 10:10 PM when Lincoln was shot at. Since then all watchmakers around the globe have given a permanent time to their watches when on display, 10:10. The coincidental smiley has immortalized the last minute of this phenomenal human being on earth.

The bell knelling the end of class acted always as an interruption to BB's thoughts. It was time to go home . . . Along the sundrenched rows of shiny leaves, along the small santra orchard, full of rotund balls of sweetness, along playfields surrounded by small outgrowths and shrubs acting as boundaries, and along the meandering pebbled path that led to his house, among several houses, reflecting their tales of neglect and dilapidation.

BB had been a topper all through, and hence, there were no superlatives left in the dictionary of his teachers to attribute. This time, however, the principal had something else to say. He had especially invited Subhash to meet him in his office. It was a special occasion. The principal was not always keen in meeting people in person. This gesture, thus, was a special one.

On entering his decorated and spacious cabin, Subhash was greeted warmly by the principal. Gesturing him to take a chair, the principal ordered for some tea and snacks.

A moment of silence followed, filling the room with an air of silence.

'Your boy, Subhash,' at last the principal spoke, reclining himself to his chair, 'is extraordinary. Do a favour to him. Take him somewhere else.'

Another moment of solemn silence descended. Subhash could not figure out why the principal was speaking in such a pessimistic tone.

The cloud lifted somewhat as the bearer entered with the bone china cups of steaming tea along with some sandwiches. The aroma of the fresh garden tea hung loose in the zephyr as a source of rejuvenation.

'Sir, this is our land, our mother. Where will I take Bibhuti? He is so small,' Subhash mumbled on helplessly.

'Bibhuti is our star in this ensuing darkness, Subhash,' said the principal, this time facing Subhash.

'This land needs a Messiah. Subhash, I can see the traces in Bibhuti. He can bring about the change, and mark my words, he will.' The principal's eyes lit up as he completed the sentence.

The Spring Fest ended with a bang as it had begun.

Now it was the time for campus interview. Jobs from Major MNCs and domestic companies were up for grabs. The campus was teeming with HR representatives of various companies lurking in hunters' demeanour, scouting for most appropriate candidates for their organizations. Every student also had made up their mind to opt for the employer of their liking.

Simultaneous campus selections were happening in various pockets of the institution with students scurrying to and forth from one camp to other, unable to decide what pay packet and which location suited them the best.

BB, however, was rather calm amongst the pandemonium. There was a reason to this tranquillity. The special program in the Spring Fest called the Psyanide had been a standout feature. The juxtaposition of various state of psychology mixed with pleasant and pungent feeling of the soul was not only unique in presentation but also a thought-provoking affair. After all, life is an oxymoron full of paradoxes . . . To some, however, life is just froth and bubble.

One of the prospective employers, a globally renowned consultancy firm, was enamoured by the thought process underlined in Psyanide. They had specially taken some time from BB to have a light discussion over a cup of coffee. They had developed an instant liking for this extraordinary character and the light discussion culminated into the most lucrative and honourable job offer to have ever hit the IIT campus. BB had become a celebrity instantaneously.

⸻

With a heavy heart and bits and pieces of memorable moments spread over four years of melodramatic existence in the hallowed campus remained coming to him as the rickshaw tugged him along to the majestic railway station of Kharagpur. He was leaving behind a past that probably would have lost forever into the alcoves of memory. Abruptly, life appeared lonely in the crowded platform of Kharagpur. As he jostled into the a local train bound for Howrah, he realized that this is but a baby step towards his ultimate goal—to evolve, to become, to revolutionize . . . and to create for himself a world of his own.

The vastness of Howrah station, teeming with people, sent a striking message to his psyche that Bibhuti Bhushan was just another face in the crowd. The flight was delayed by one-and-a-half hour and reached the Bangalore Airport at 4:30 PM. BB took some time to figure out the conveyor to collect his luggage as it was his first ever air travel.

The company had sent a vehicle to the airport. BB found that the chauffer clad in white uniform

holding high a placard with his name printed on it— Bibhuti Bhushan, CBD, OASIS.

The sedan started running, leaving behind high risers, malls, flyovers, offices of huge repertoire, and finally took BB to transit house in BTM layout. The girder erection activity of the new flyover drew BB's attention. Yes, construction of such magnitude was required at his home town too.

One of the two-storey buildings behind central silk board was the new address for BB along with six others colleagues.

The next morning, a huge Volvo bus carried them to the office—a momentous journey of one hour.

Whitefield. India's supreme effort of creating its own silicon valley. A spectacle of its own enraptured in the beauty of architecture. This was the new India, an emerging India, a rising India.

BB stood spellbound. Here was he, looking in amazement at the glory of a nation subdued by its own maladies. India glittered, shone, radiated its splendour of grandeur and supremacy. BB stood there for a while looking around the glint of stupendous growth. Suddenly, his nation, his poor nation, looked different, looked majestic.

The entry to office was not very easy as it took around one hour to complete all the access control formalities and issue of smart card-based access.

Five new entrants had joined, and the HR partner, Urvashi, took them to a small conference room and handed over the joining documents. It took almost an hour to fill up all the stuff that had to be filled. After filling up approximately thirty documents repetitive in nature, BB finally got to sip some coffee dispensed from the vending machine. Needless to mention that there was a huge difference in taste in the coffee served in IIT canteen that oft Oasis Consultancy Services.

Urvashi informed that Mr Murthy, the location head, will be starting the induction program shortly. Sharp at eleven-thirty, Murthy the dark chubby figure in gold-rimmed spectacles entered the conference room. With a brief introduction, he presented a small AV, depicting the formation, background, context, success story, and road map of the organization. Vinay and Baibhab were assigned to be part of the Application Development team, and BB was assigned the role of a service delivery leader handling a key banking account. Murthy also did not forget to mention that OASIS had received a high-level escalation from the GM of a client bank just the previous day.

In this unit of OASIS in white field, there was a dedicated sales team, a small group pre-sales team, which assisted the Sales Team technically. There was also a technical support wing with a division of domestic and offshore operation. Some distinct account management teams are there taking care of some of the *big* accounts with special focus.

The domestic technical support team was always facing issues as the majority of solution offered by the sales team remained incomplete. The sales team always got rewards for earning revenue for the company and meeting targets while the support teams was always reprimanded and were left to clean the garbage.

In two months' time, BB gradually leant all the delivery parameters in scope. OASIS was engaged in managing hardware infrastructure, database, core banking application, and user training modalities. There was a perennial problem with the compatibility of the application with the DB versions. BB took extra effort to engage the experts from the Lab of the Database OEM and managed to get the patch specially developed for the application. The trial balance had become error free, the SOD (Start of Business) and EOD (End of Day) operations had never been so easy and accurate. It was appraised by both the GM of the client bank as well as the VP of Oasis. In a span of three months, BB had stamped his mark as a distinct enabler and problem solver. Oasis received repeat orders for the integration of the ATMs with core banking applications across the country. All these were possible because of the hard work of the three testing months. BB's awesome communication skill also impressed many. Mr Rakesh Verma, country manager sales, saw the potential of BB as a sales leader and had already started his discussion with one of the directors to pull him out of delivery and put him in sales team to focus on business development in the Middle East.

However, there were certain aspects to the job that BB never liked. There was too much of blame game and leg pulling that kept happening all around. The service and the sales departments were perennially locked into confrontation over deliverables, with each blaming the other over issues that looked petty and unnecessary. Intradepartmental strife was one of the prime items of every agenda, and sometimes these wrangles came in the way of harmonious coexistence. To be able to survive this unabated onslaught was a virtue in itself. Survival required guile and adaptability.

One very alarming feature in this way of life had struck BB. In this fast-paced corporate livelihood, success came at a cost. One had to be part of some lobby to be able to move ahead. People who are meek, too dedicated, and unaware of the mindset of the contemporaries are easily waylaid and sidelined. He realized that in this kind of world, if one has to ascend the staircase to success, one has to pull down people from the rungs above. Here, success happens through a process of elimination. BB knew he had to wait for his chance. BB knew he had to make use of the opportunities that arise out of others weaknesses. BB knew he had to exploit the weaknesses of his colleagues and bosses. BB knew that sometimes he also might have to appease the mighty, stooping to the lows of flattery and sycophancy. BB knew that if he did not eliminate people, Caesar might die. And BB, alias Bibhuti Bhushan, was no Julius Caesar.

The director, Mr Joseph, invited BB on a Saturday evening and collected his feedback on the Service Delivery Management. He was quick to offer him the role of Country Sales Leader, which involved frequent foreign trips and a lot of strategy making. BB did not want to disappoint Mr Joseph. After all, he was a stalwart in the company. At the same time, he also did not want to leave his task halfway through. His immediate boss Arun Kashyap had been relying on him heavily. Kashyap was a good man, at times too helpful than was necessary. He was slowly moving up the popularity chart. His popularity had won him accolades from clients as well as his management. Kashyap had become a threat to people in power because Kashyap was steadily gaining power.

The most unbecoming factor of Kashyap, however, was his overdependence on his down line. Of course, Kashyap never did anything himself but passed on every job to his subordinates and made sure that the job gets done effectively and before time. He also made sure that the credit for every job done is received by him first before it gets to his team. Yet Kashyap was good because he never attempted to know how these jobs were being done.

But he had to take a call. Mr Joseph was waiting for his reply. BB finally nodded his acceptance to Joseph's offer.

That evening, while sitting in his semi-darkened room, Bibhuti Bhushan, alias BB, realized that he had taken another baby step towards greatness. He was slowly learning the art of betrayal. He knew his decision will put poor Arun Kashyap into a different orbit. He also knew that this decision of his would please M. M. Joseph immensely. But what he knew most was that he would return to take the vacant space of Kashyap and restart the job that he had left incomplete.

Brutus had been born again.

Bibhuti Bhushan had passionately adopted a very common dictum into his life.

'Flow with the times . . . otherwise be influential enough to change the times.'

So be sure when you step, Step with care and great tact. And remember that life's a Great Balancing Act. And will you succeed? Yes! You will, indeed! (98 and ¾ per cent guaranteed) Kid, you'll move mountains.

(<u>Dr Seuss</u>, <u>*Oh, the Places You'll Go!*</u>))

CHAPTER 7

Change of Track

The project war room at Mumbai House was buzzing with activity. The representatives of all the project verticals of PECL had congregated in this hall of eminence where some historic decisions have been made over the years. Two full days had been devoted to Jamnagar Project, and rightly so, since it was the biggest project being executed by the company. Top executives, including the president, project control, Mr R. K. Sood, a person of immense stature, had been specially invited to review the progress of each department of Jamnagar project.

Kumar was awestruck by the sheer magnitude of the room which resembled nothing less than an amphitheatre. Project managers can be seen rushing around with files and half-scribbled papers while others violently typed away some last-minute alterations in their PowerPoint presentations. Manivannan appeared pretty relaxed even under the stressful circumstances. He smiled reassuringly to Kumar and handed him a bar of chocolate. Manivannan knew that Kumar was fond of chocolates. These ten months together had got them to know each other as well as their likes and dislikes pretty well. And these small gestures of Manivannan at testing times made him all the more special, as a person, as a guide, as a leader.

The meeting opened in a grim note as the chief of finance, HQ, Mr R. N. Joshi, spelt out the sombre numbers regarding the billing and collection. The invoicing for the finished goods were definitely lagging by some distance. The collection had also been ominous. Some of the billing were more than 120 days old. Revenue collection was definitely an area of concern for a company of PECL's stature. And off course, the goal for any company should be to make money and ensure growth in a sustainable basis. R. N. Joshi finished his discourse on money matters with a gentle reminder.

'Remember, turnover is vanity, profit is sanity, and cash is reality,' he reminded. And it was a fact that the company was fast garnering a hefty top-line, but the bottom line definitely required strengthening.

The baton was now passed on to the engineering and planning departments. The slowness of drawing submission and approval was brought under heavy hammer. Engineering has always been the Achilles Bone for the company. The dearth of skilled and trained manpower in the market has triggered a sense of worry in many corporate houses. Many a youngster has, over the years, migrated to foreign MNCs, after having gained substantial experience with companies like PECL. Thus, engineering has always been starved of quality manpower. Mr R. M. Bansal, the vice president, Engineering and Design, went through the slides presented by the engineering team. There were too many areas of weakness that needed to be urgently addressed. Outsourcing was not the only remedy. They also needed the advanced softwares that were available in the market to be able to stand by the deadlines issued by the consultant. A training program in Staad Pro, Solid Edge, and Tekla softwares was announced for the design engineers with immediate effect. These high-end softwares would enable design and estimation in civil and structure to be foolproof and fast, that's what the predominant belief was. There were some further debates regarding civil quantity verification. There were some arguments over the quantity of earthwork, which surpassed the actual quantities by quite a margin. Tedious calculations and verifications were resorted to resulting in a lot of cross talk and pandemonium. Abraham Varkey restored some orderliness by announcing a tea break. It was a welcome break for all. People immediately rushed out of the gloominess of the war room, either to relieve themselves or take the luxury of a few puffs of cigarettes.

'Welcome back,' announced Sumant Dayal, the convener of the programme as people started taking their respective seats. The grind was about to begin one again and this promised to be grilling session.

The focus had now shifted to execution. Already a pensive mood had set in. The projector beamed on the giant screen a bar chart showing the comparative progress of the different sites. The chart also defined some notable milestones that had either been reached or missed.

The first site to be pulled up was CDU, the Crude Distillation Unit. The discussion on CDU also invariably got connected to VDU, the Vacuum Distillation Unit and HTU, Hydro Treating Unit. All these three are so interlinked that the sites looked similar in progress, collection, and in the context and content of the replies made by their representatives to questions posed by the authorities.

HNUU (Higher Naphtha Unification Unit) and LNUU (Lower Naphtha Unification Unit) were another two parallel sites which had shown significant progress in the last few months. And why not, after all, they had at their disposal some of the most sophisticated and modern machinery to boast. Three towering Manitowoc Cranes along with the finest collection of Demag and American 9490 Cranes. The construction work has been steady and in tune with the set targets. Mr K. R. Singh, the overall boss of the Naphtha recovery unit, bore a confident look. A feel-good factor descended on the coterie, Naphtha had given them a rare moment of cheer.

Aromatics had been struggling with dewatering. The open trenched for U. G. Piping usually got filled up with water creating havoc with constructive progress. The area being at a lower terrain got filled up with water even during days of slight showers. Discussions rambled on in the topic of dewatering without any appreciable solution at sight. The problem was referred to Mr Shammugam, an expert in drainage planning to take up the matter with utmost seriousness and rid the site of this menace of water logging.

Before they broke for lunch, one of the assessors threw a note of caution in the air. 'Jetty and FCCU, be ready for a not very pleasant afternoon.'

The lunch was a huge spread up buffet in another of the mammoth halls of Mumbai house. Mouth-watering delicacies selected from the best Indian, Continental, Chinese, Thai, and Italian cuisines were up for the taking. A mixed extravaganza of aroma filled the room, and people hustled around with plates, in an effort to stomach the enticing culinary delights with fiendish appetites. It was difficult to choose between Chicken Cacciatore, Chichen Tuscan, Chicken Piccata with Linguin, Chicken Korma, Chicken Sesame, Chicken Regaata, Lamb in Oyster Sauce, Mutton Rezaala, Asparagus Mutton Stir Fry, Chichen Tandoori, and an endless list of choicest non-vegetarian food. There were lots for the vegetarian folks as well. A rich choice of Paneer recipes, vegetable lasagne, mixed vegetables with coriander garnish, Herb Risotto, Mushroom Chilly were some of the mouth-watering stuff. The most alluring was, however, the collection of desserts. From Raspberry puddings, Tapioca Pavlova, Fruit Salad, Creamy Caramel Custard to Shrikhand, Amrakhand, Rasmalai, Rasgulla, Gulab Jamun, Ice Cream, and much, much more.

Post lunch the ordeal started with the utility departments. The CLD (Civil Lay Down) and the CPP (Captive Power Plant) came under heavy scanner. The power distribution network and the load calculation of each unit was sought, and explanations were demanded. Sanjeev Ranjan, the head of the utility department, had a tough time explaining the assumptions taken while calculating the load requirement. Though these issues had already been discussed in various forums, the authorities chose to seek more explanations and elaborations on the same subject at this forum too. The services department was also not spared. Part of the delay in the execution was also attributed to the inadequacy of logistic support. The expectation from the logistic department was mammoth, and Ranjan and his team were well aware that all of it cannot be fulfilled.

Mr Sood was getting restive now. He was most intent now to review the progress of the two most important areas of the project: the Jetty and the FCCU. He cleared his throat and summoned for the hard copies of the respective presentations of the two constructional entities. He leafed through the pages repeatedly, at times referring to A.V. about the authenticity of some of the figures that appeared in those miniature booklets. It was clear from the expression of the president that he was not at all happy with the progress of these two paramount projects.

'I am absolutely dejected to see such depressing figures.' Sood almost exploded. The room was rendered speechless at this sudden display of emotion. 'We had deputed our best engineers to these two sites of prime importance,' he continued. 'But instead of taking the lead, both these sites have become our bottleneck. Month after month, quarter after quarter, these two sites have shown only snails progress. We have provided you with all possible amenities, yet you refuse to improve. Please tell me, what is so wrong?'

There was a momentary silence. It hung around the hall like a pall of gloom. First, it was the turn of the towering figure of R.B.R., the boss of FCCU. He gave a series of explanations. How FCCU, being the most sensitive zone, had to undergo several quality checks before installation activities and how due to the involvement of several agencies the number of protocols to be followed increased from time to time. The delay was also attributed to the delay in shipment of critical equipment from Jetty even after providing Jetty with the schedules well in advance. Questioning looks greeted Manivannan and team as if they were standing in trial of some heinous crime.

After putting up a plethora of excuses in defence to the allegations of the management, R.B.R. took his seat. He wiped away the sweat from his brow as he took his seat. An aura of contentment had already come upon his otherwise troubled countenance.

'Who will explain the status, programme, and progress for Jetty?' A.V. enquired in a muffled intonation. 'Manivannan, will you?'

Kumar had already stood up even before Manivannan had a chance to reply.

'Introduce yourself,'. A.V. said in a demanding voice.

'I am Kumar Sinha. I have been working in this company at Jetty and MTF sites for the last eleven months,' replied Kumar in a loud resounding voice.

'Isn't there anyone more senior who can do the explaining part?' asked A.V.

'Sir, I think I will be able to handle all your queries. I am well prepared,' replied Kumar in a mild display of his inherent rigid pertinence.

'That's what you think. But we seem to think otherwise,' said A.V. gravely.

'No problem, Verkey, let this lad continue.' Sood was more relenting.

Manivannan's reassuring smile provided the much-needed encouragement for Kumar to continue.

'Sir, I would like to draw your attention to the construction versus resources graph that we have defined in the first slide of our presentation.' He paused for everybody to take a long hard look at the pictorial. 'The notable point is that with the blatant reduction of resources, the output of Jetty and MTF have suffered.' He paused again, perhaps in anticipation to some repercussion. On the contrary, there was silence all around.

'In every system there is a constraint. The identification of the constraint, you will appreciate, is one of the most crucial step towards achieving the set targets or goals of the organization. It is the constraint that dictates the speed at which throughput is achieved. Also, the constraints, once identified, should always be exploited, and all other operations should be subordinated and synchronized in tune with the constraint, and finally strategies are needed to be devised to elevate the performance of the constraint.'

'So have you figured out the constraint of Jetty?' Colonel Rajiv Mehta interrupted.

'Sir, I am more intent to present before you the constraint of the project as a whole,' replied Kumar.

'That's off course, Jetty,' the colonel exclaimed in dismay. Like the colonel, to everyone else, it looked quite obvious.

'Sir, if you look up at the steps that characterize a constraint, you will discover that Jetty is not the constraint anymore,' Kumar said, politely refuting the charge of the colonel.

'If you allow proper resource in machinery, manpower, and funds, Jetty can achieve the set targets with relative ease,' Kumar continued to explain. 'However, FCCU, the project on whom a major chunk of the revenue is dependent upon, has been provided with all amenities to show good progress.'

'So you mean to say, FCCU is the bottleneck for the project?' protested K.P.R. Murthy, the diminutive project leader of FCCU.

'There's nothing wrong in being a constraint, Murthy Sir,' Manivannan said with a chuckle.

'In order to help FCCU shed their tag of a constraint, we must first rid it of its inherent constraints,' added Kumar.

'Inherent constraints? What's that?' Mr Sood looked puzzled and a bit confused.

'As Mr R.B.R. had explained a little while ago, there are many issues that are affecting the progress of the site,' explained Kumar. 'Those are the inherent constraints.'

'One of them is deliverables of Jetty,' quipped R.B.R.

'Yes, sir. The inability to deliver as per your schedule is our constraint,' replied Kumar.

'Then how do we get to eliminate these bloody constraints so that the project is put back into the track?' Sood enquired with a hint of impatience.

'In my opinion, sir, we need to reaccess our resources and reallocate them,' replied Kumar.

'Can you kindly elaborate?' snapped Colonel Mehta.

'Sir, we are not reusing our resources as per the demand of the constraint. We need some additional equipment and manpower so that we can open up a late evening shift to offset the delay caused by the slowness of drawing approvals. Also, there are a few high calibre equipment idling at HNUU, Cocker Complex, and the CPP, which can be re-allocated to jetty so that their capability gets a fillip.'

'You mean to say, that for the time being all attention needs to be shifted to these two sites?' asked A.V.

'The necessary attention,' the colonel was quick to correct him.

'Can we be more specific about the kind of attention to be given?' A.V. was determined to dig for the details.

'Sir, all the sites should synchronize their activities as per the demand of FCCU. And FCCU should in turn re-modulate their activities to synchronize with the progress of Jetty,' explained Kumar.

'Another area which is needed to be analysed is the cause-and-effect syndrome. What we generally see are the UDEs or the Undesired Effects that fan out of various activities. We chase these effects instead of finding solutions for the causes that give birth to these UDEs.' Kumar paused once again, letting the thought to sink in.

'For example. A lot of accidents had stalled the progress of our site in the past months. The reason for these accidents were gross negligence to safety and haste. We have taken measures to step up safety measures and a general consciousness of safe working. However, if we investigate deeper, we realize that the root cause is the demeanour of our sub-contractors. If they are paid in man-hours for jobs at height and risky locations, instead of item rates, the hasty methods of working can be substantially reduced, if not eliminated,' Kumar explained.

There were murmurs all around. The course of the meeting had been successfully navigated by this fresh new chap to a different but definite direction. The arbiters were also made to sit up and take note of this alternate discourse.

It was now time for some decision making. The top bosses, seated on the podium, had a long meaningful discussion amongst themselves before making public their twenty-point agenda.

Jetty was given extra machinery, enough to sustain their workload in a uniform manner. Utility department was given specific requirements for different sections so that they may focus on the areas of importance. Aromatics received new sets of submersible pumps for draining out the accumulated water so that their schedule of U.G. Piping is not delayed. And FCCU got some additional manpower and someone special to take control of their construction planning—Kumar Sinha.

Winter nights in Mumbai are always special. The weather is most pleasant at this time of the year. The honking traffic, glaring lights, the jostling crowd does not seem that irritating after all. One can spend hours at the Juhu Beach, looking at the sea and getting lost in the merriment around. Gas balloons wafting in the air being chased by colourful children. People thronging the brightly lit Pav Bhaji stalls, lengthening the queue as time rolled on. Couples sitting cosily at the edge of the rocks whispering sweet nothings to each other, under the perennial threat of encountering someone who might recognise them. But the periodic roar of the waves drowned all. Even thoughts that crowded the apprehensive mind.

'Here, with Jetty with love.' Manivannan laughed loudly as he handed Kumar a bar of chocolate. The seemingly innocent statement almost startled Kumar. His next consignment appeared to be more than just intimidating. It was an imposing task to plan for the construction schedule of the biggest site in the history of the company. Cumbersome is an understatement.

'It is an opportunity, not easy to come by,' said Manivannan, still smiling. He had perhaps been reading Kumar's thoughts. He, off course, was very good at it. 'I know there will be opposition. Old people will never accept the new thought process too quickly,' he added. 'No one surrenders his dominion too quickly. But remember, men are not good or bad . . . it is the circumstance that decide their kirdaar.'

'Kirdaar? What's that?' Kumar had come across this word for the first time.

'It means roles, acts, characters,' Manivannan replied. 'Pity, a Tamilian knows more of Urdu than a North Indian.' Manivannan laughed.

'Not North Indian, sir,' Kumar answered gravely.

'Oh, sorry, East Indian,' Manivannan corrected himself.

'Only Indian Sir. Only Indian.' Now it was Kumar's turn to laugh. For once, he had stumped V. Manivannan.

I missed you, Angel. Not one day went by that I didn't feel you missing from my life. You haunted me to the point that I began to believe Hank had gone back on his oath and killed you. I couldn't escape you and I didn't want to. You tortured me, but it was better than losing you.

(Becca Fitzpatrick, *Silence*)

CHAPTER 8

The Doctored Life

The silence of the shadows greeted him. There were shadows all around and so was the silence. For the past three years, he has always returned to the reception of silence. The din outside, the smell of formaldehyde, the crowd at OPD faded away at the driveway to the Ray mansion. It is seclusion like a faraway resort, distancing itself from the humdrum of the city. It is seclusion, by choice. Seclusion by destiny. By design.

There was a steady breeze outside, lending voice to the enveloping silence. The clamour of loneliness had always bruised him. But again it was loneliness by choice.

Like any other doctor, Amit detested death and disease. They were the two adversaries that people in his profession had been fighting against since time immemorial. But here at home, the fight was against loneliness, solitude.

Amit, Dr Amit Ray, readied himself for another sleepless night after having served himself with an incomplete dinner which perhaps symbolized his own incompleteness.

Tina had not yet returned. Not that he was too concerned about the timing of her return, but he had been sceptical about the profession she had chosen. Fashion. It looked so very artificial, like some fabricated truth. Perhaps, both of them chose to stay busy to keep themselves removed from each other. Life had changed appreciably over the years.

Time had hurt, time had healed, but the remains . . . the scars were still evident. Life was now more of a compromise, bereft of reasons or aspirations.

Amit's stature in the medical world was phenomenal, incredible, remarkable. His popularity was not only reflected by the unending queue outside the OPD but also through various magazines and journals that published his opinions regarding various issues of the medical world. The number of O.T.s he attended were a feat in itself since no other doctor came even close to those numbers. Dr Amit Ray was a name to reckon with in the medical world. His stature was unparalleled; his opinions were unchallenged, his processes were immaculate, and his success . . . enviable. All that glory aside, his personal life bore a lore of bitterness. The love which once had been the essence of living for both of them appeared forlorn and extinct. The professional success meant nothing as he sat silently in the shadows of desolation.

Amit had never supported Tina in her endeavour to become a designer. He had always thought of this profession to be vulgar and meaningless. He had always insisted that Tina stay at home and be more of a wife than just a companion. His Bengali upbringing had prompted him to believe that a wife always stayed at home looking after the domesticities and catering to the children. The concept of a working wife, that too in the glamorous domain of fashion design was alien to him. He had frantically opposed this pursuit. But Tina too had been adamant. She yearned to steer away from the shadows of Amit's profession into a world of her own. She wanted the world to know her differently. She wanted the world to respect her for being her and for not being the wife of another successful professional.

It was well past midnight Tina came in. She looked ruffled and visibly exhausted. They only shared a glance and did not find the importance to exchange any word. The silence still ruled between two individuals who had been madly in love with each other just a few years back. There had been times, not very long ago when, they used to draft out excuses to be with each other. They had been entwined, integrated, interwoven into a fabric of a single entity. Amongst hectic schedules, torrential rain, life paralytic strikes and numerous such obstructions, Amit had taken out time for Tina.

And Tina . . . she had always been a paragon of devotion. She took care of even the tiniest aspect of Amit's existence. She even attended special cookery classes to learn Bengali dishes to treat Amit every now and then with some of his choicest Bengali food. Those were the days when Amit yearned to get back home. He knew Tina would be waiting for him with good food and a world of affection. And on reaching home, he would spend hours describing his day to Tina, who in turn would listen to everything with admiration and intent.

Amit got up from his rocking chair and walked out into the balcony. A blanket of repose had draped the neighbourhood. He felt jealous of the peacefulness that symbolically defined each home. He stood there awhile as if standing in defiance to the mandate that the night held. Sleep for him was not easy.

Tina was fast asleep when Amit entered the bedroom. Some scattered books, magazines, and diaries lay scattered all around the room. The magazines were all pertaining to fashion, which hardly evoked any interest in Amit. He picked up a diary instead, leafing through the scribbled pages of notes, schedules, and reminders. As he ran through the pages of insignificant comprehension and inconsequential derivations, he stumbled upon a small poem, scripted in carefully organized letters at one corner. He read it through, once, twice, several times.

Little Angel

I look at your sleeping face,
And I cannot help, but sigh . . . .
Throughout the day you have made me
Laugh, sing, dance and cry . . .
Your little body and your gurgling glee . . .
Had kept me busy like a bumble bee . . .
Peaceful, beneath the blanket blue . . .
My little Angel . . . . cannot take my eyes off you!!!

Amit was dumbfounded. He kept reading those innocent lines over and over again. He could see Ayan in those lines. His tiny outstretched hands trying to reach for Amit's head. His tiny feet scrambling in an attempt to climb on his back. Ayan was the little bundle of joy that had lit up the Ray household ever since he had arrived. As soon as he had learnt to walk, he toddled his way to almost all the neighbouring households making himself an instant favourite amongst all nearby residents.

He was an affectionate child. Always busy as a bumble bee making a plaything with whatever he could lay his hands on. Tina had been very particular with his food and habits so that little Ayan never fell unnecessarily sick.

Ayan was an active child. Always fond of running around, jumping, playing. His gurgling laughter echoed around the locality throughout the day and sometimes till the deep recesses of night, when he kept himself awake, waiting for his father.

Ayan was a lovely boy. His lively nature produced a world of animation wherever he went. Tina and Amit would love to keep watching little Ayan go about his innocent set of activities throughout the day. Whenever, Tina went visiting her parents at King's Circle, Mr Rodericks would treat Ayan with the most majestic of cakes and pastries he had on offer. Ayan loved cakes and would carry back home a booty of such savouries, carefully packed and labelled by Mr Rodericks.

Ayan was also the cynosure at his school. His teachers would love to play with him and listen to his various incomprehensible dictions. Ayan was growing up fast and with him grew his almost insatiable curiosity. He was curious about everything, from cars to table fans. From screw drivers to papa's stethoscope.

Tina, in particular, was always kept on tenterhooks. Balancing herself between her job and Ayan was becoming a very demanding task. Amit had been adamant not to leave Ayan under the care of a governess. He wanted Tina to relinquish her job to give full-time attention to Ayan. Tina had argued that her job timing was flexible. She only attended her boutique when Ayan was at school.

It was Tina who used to take Ayan to school and pick him up on return. She always managed to be on time before and after school hours. It was a routine she never missed out.

It was strike day. One of the political outfits had declared a shutdown in protest of the arrest of one of their leaders. Shops were shut. Public transport was paralyzed, and even schools and colleges were ordered to declare a holiday all of a sudden. Poor Tina was left stranded. She had been frantically looking out for a public transport to be able to reach Ayan's school to pick him up. She could not reach Amit's number too. His hospital informed that he was busy with one of his heart surgeries. Tina had dropped a message on Amit's cell phone, hoping that he gets the message, post operation.

The epicentre for all the mayhem was near Little Angel School. Heavy street fights and stone pelting had broken loose in this part of Mumbai. The school authorities frantically dialled on to the numbers of parents so that the little angels are taken to safety.

The explosion happened all at once. No one had an inkling of what was coming. A powerful explosive planted in the vicinity went off without even signalling any signs of alarm. The powerful explosion ripped through a part of Little Angels School. Disaster had struck. Inhuman motives produced some ghastly casualties.

Ayan had been covered with a white sheet of cloth in the casualty ward when Amit entered. Sobs, sniffles and wails filled the atmosphere. Amit, Dr Amit, who had been steady at sights of death, stood perplexed. Ayan had departed without a word, without a smile. Ayan had left them without even warning them of his departure.

Somehow, Amit could not believe it. There can be something . . . something that can be done. Some bloody medical miracle. How can he live without Ayan? Amit could see one of those tiny hands sticking out of the sheet. Come, Ayan . . . reach for me . . . come, Ayan . . . Papa's home early today.

Amit, kept the diary aside. Tears had filled up his eyes. He went over to the basin, washed his face, and waited for another day to begin.

To love. To be loved. To never forget your own insignificance. To never get used to the unspeakable violence and the vulgar disparity of life around you. To seek joy in the saddest places. To pursue beauty to its lair. To never simplify what is complicated or complicate what is simple.

(Arundhati Roy, *The Cost of Living*)

CHAPTER 9

NAZM—a Tragic Poetic Life

Zindagi yuun hui basar tanhaa, Quafilaa Sath aur safar tanhaa.

Apne saaye se chowk jaate hain, Umr Guzaari hai is Quadar tanhaa.

Raat bhar bulaate hain sannate, Raat kaate koi kidhar tanhaa . . .

Din Guzarta nahi logon mein, Raat hoti nahi basar tanhaa . . .

Mehfilo mein raunak hum se hi hai, Phir bhi na jane kaise reh gaye tanha.

Life has been spent alone; travellers are there, but still the voyage is lonely. I shudder at my own shadow. I have spent my life, thus, lonely. The silence of the nights beckons me. How do people spend nights lonely? It's difficult to spend the day amongst people but cannot spend the nights lonely. I have been the life of gatherings, yet I don't know how I have remained lonely.

The momentous scripture greeted all onlookers passing the famous Petunia Road of Matunga, Mumbai. This has been the famed abode of the Ilahi's from time immemorial. At a glance, the mansion reflects a feel of neglect and desolation. The once ornate walls courageously bore the ravages of time. The replica of an illustrious past could be sensed from the flair of architecture that spoke in volume of the times that were. The relics of reputability still commanded respect amongst people who know and revere history.

Like many other such mementos of the past, this mansion has also witnessed some remarkable phases of history. It had pained to withstand the trauma of partition and also celebrated the emergence of a new India. It had witnessed the boom of a capital market and also watched in dismay the debacle of money machinery at the hands of a maverick called Harshad Mehta.

This is a heritage, that's what the old residents believed. This is a seat of learning where even the walls reverberate with exquisite eloquence of superlative oratory. The magic of words was afloat in the sereneness of the air. The very environ was woven with a fabric of Urdu, Hindi, Arabic, Hebrew, English, German, Italian, Spanish, and whatnot. The collection of treatises was such rare in nature that they would put any decent private library to shame. There seemed to be a little bit of rhetoric, dipped in a flavour of mysticism, in every aspect of the mansion. Life appeared in the drapery of verse, ornamented in prose, and wrapped in hues of tears and laughter. The world began and ended at this doorstep for Salman Ilahi. A distinguished world. A world of graciousness and solitude.

It has been some time now that Salman Ilahi had been living alone in this huge house. It has been a queer life for Ilahi. There was a time when this very mansion used to be full of people. The sound of voices and laughter used to echo around till late at night. There was a time when during the holy month of Ramadan, the lawn, which is now an Elysium of weeds, used to be illuminated majestically in welcome of eminent guests for Iftaars. Iftaars do not happen here now.

Neither do eminent guests come. Only memories lurk in every darkened corner of silence and solitude.

Salman Ilahi was in all consciousness when the partition of the nation occurred. It still is and will forever be the defining moment for the two nations, India and Pakistan. Those who have witnessed, read, or even heard of those nightmarish turn of events will recall that mayhem left the most indelible mark on children. Partition had infused an invariable vehemence of hatred in the minds of the progeny that subsequently kept being taken forward in form of some legacy.

Part of the problem with the semi-amnesia regarding Partition in the Indian subcontinent is the fact that the underlying motives are still inseparable from current political realities.

The very motive for partition is the raison d'etre for Pakistan and, indirectly, Bangladesh. On the Indian side, there often seems to be a knee-jerk reaction towards blaming the British entirely for initiating partition.

In sum, none of the communal parties involved finds it in their interest to study, recall, and assuage the wounds of Partition. This sounds cynical, I know, but it was a very successful bloodbath for all sides as it handily satisfied their political need for victimization and segregation in lieu of social integration.

In this world of hatred, only a few could keep their head and their faith in humanity and humaneness. For Abid Ilahi, it was a test of his resoluteness. The idea of leaving his birthplace in favour of some foreign land. He along with his wife Zoya and three children Salman, Salim, and Zaara had taken a firm accord to stay put in a land they knew and revered as their own—India.

The tempest of partition raged through the nation inflicting more psychological wounds than physical. The nation was suddenly thrown into a mode of delirium with its citizens converted into lunatics. One such lunatic was Kehav Rathod, a fanatical Rajput, who had been elevated into a rabid rabble rouser, had been creating havoc in the streets of Mumbai in the name of instilling justice. But justice is always for the sane . . . for the insane it is only vengeance.

Keshav had always fostered a feeling of aversion against all Muslim inhabitants of Mumbai. His proclamation of ridding Mumbai of its Muslim populace had been giving him a lot of political mileage. His political ambition coupled with a sense of ruthlessness had turned him into a savage. He had attained some dubious distinction too. He had led a mob into Victoria Terminus Railway station and lynched several poor passengers trying to flee the burning city. He had also burnt down two madrasas where small children used to study. He had broken into some of the fruit shops at Mahim and had gutted some restaurants run by Muslim owners. Backed up by the frenzied groups of irrationals, Keshav continued his vandalism unabated.

According to Keshav, he was concerned for a Hindu future. And his argument was as that of Pastor Martin Neimoller, who had warned regarding his incarceration by the Nazis:

They came for the Communists, and I didn't object— For I wasn't a Communist;

They came for the Socialists, and I didn't object— For I wasn't a Socialist;

They came for the labour leaders, and I didn't object—For I wasn't a labour leader;

They came for the Jews, and I didn't object—For I wasn't a Jew;

Then they came for me—And there was no one left to object.

There was one person but in the whole of Bombay to confront this frenzy. Abid Ilahi. A teacher by profession, Ilahi took to the streets in protest of this organized decimation of Muslims. It was not in retaliation, it was more in a mode of negotiation. Negotiation for peace. For harmony, both communal and social. Negotiation to coexist.

Talks succumbed to swords, and words failed to calm the fury generated through a deep-rooted hatred that had engulfed both the sides. There was no room for reason.

Abid Ilahi along with seven of his friends were mercilessly stabbed in broad daylight at Matunga station. The lifeless bodies lay there in a pool of blood for several hours. A huge price for peace . . . for democracy . . . for reconciliation of faith. No arrests were made; in fact, no police complaints were entertained at all. A pall of gloom had descended on the Ilahi Mansion. Life appeared paralyzed for Zoya and her children. People in the neighbourhood for whom Abid had several times gone out of the way to help looked alien. The otherwise serene air of Bombay appeared rancid at the stench of blood.

Help came from an unexpected quarter though. One fine morning, Keshav Rathod and a few other party leaders came to visit the grief stricken family. Keshav's brother Jaisingh had also come along. Jaisingh was not amongst the fanatic lot. He was a business of repute and was known for his altruism and generosity. God fiery by nature, Jaisingh never fostered any ill will for believers of different faith. He was amicable to all, kind towards all.

During his visit to Ilahi mansion, he was touched by the good manners of the children. The rich culture the practiced in etiquette. He was moved. He realized that the lives of these children would be affected greatly if they were to stay on in Bombay. Zoya's brother, Asif, was a resident of Jaisalmer. He had come down to stay with the kids and his widowed sister at Bombay after Abid's death. He was quick to recognise Jaisingh Rathod. After all, Jaisingh was a reputed figure of Jaisalmer and Arif Mirza had been working in one of his numerous timber estates for several years. Arif appreciated Jaisingh's concern for the family and also his suggestion of shifting the family to the more peaceful domains of Jaisalmer. Jaisingh also proposed to induct Zoya into one of his childcare clinics, which he ran for free for underprivileged children. Arif did well to convince Zoya since she had been reluctant to leave the place for which her husband had sacrificed his life. But Arif's reasons were too logical to defy and mainly for the sake of the children finally Zoya accorded her consent.

Salman, Salim, and Zaara were all good at studies. It wasn't much difficult for them to adjust to new curricula at a new place. They were immensely popular too for their wit and witticism. Especially Salman, who from very childhood, had the gift of amazing oratory. He was also a tremendous story teller. Children used to sit for hours at their home listening to various anecdotes Salman used to pick up from history and transform those commonplace events into captivating anecdotes through his tremendous skill of oration. Salim was a gifted singer. His rendition of sufiana as well as Rajasthan local folklore had everyone captivated. Functions in the school or the locality were incomplete without any presentation from Arif and Salman.

Zaara was different. She liked helping her mother with household work after coming from school. She would help her mother with cooking, washing of dishes, cleaning the house, knitting. Yet Zaara was an outstanding painter. Her various sketches of whatever her mind had recorded in Bombay looked lively on canvas and reminded men of the ghastly sin they had committed against their brothers in a fit of frenzy. Her depiction of peace through the colours of flowers and birds and the heavenly green pastures she had once encountered in Kashmir won her accolades from far and wide. Her painting hung in the corridors of her school at the child clinics where her mother worked, at the majestic Haveli of the Rathods and also at various locations of their makeshift house here at Jaisalmer.

Arjunsingh Rathod, son of Jaiaingh Rathod, was an avid admirer of Salman. Arjun never paid much attention to studies. From a very young age, he had started helping his father in business, and by Jaisingh's own admission, Arjun was very good at negotiations. But Arjun also liked poetry, music, and would travel far and wide to attend cultural programs. His admiration for Salman grew immensely as he slowly came to grasp some words in Urdu. Their friendship grew strong with each passing day and with the creating of each new Nazm by Salman.

No sooner had he passed, he stepped into high school, then his father got Arjun married to Roopmati, the daughter of Virendra Rai Ahlawat, the erstwhile zamindaar of Rewi. Roopmati was only ten at that time, and Arjun was sixteen. Custom had it that the Rathods shall either get married to the Ahlawats or the Ranawats to keep intact their place of pride in the echelons of the Rajputs. This was a very rigid tradition. There have been umpteen numbers of mishaps in the history of Rajasthan when daughters or sons have been sacrificed for refusing to abide by this ritual. These episodes of honour killings are blotched in red in all treatises of history, in black-and-white. But for Arjun and Roopmati, there was no such fear. They had been obedient children to their parents, and elders and had shown total faith to all the customs that were prevalent in their lives. It was a grand affair, lasting for not less than seven days. The house of the Rathods, the adjoining lawns, even the road that led to the place, had been deluged with illumination. There were fireworks everywhere. Huge arrangement for food, and music were organized with special provision for the hospitality of the outstation guests.

Rajputana culture was on full display. Guests arrived in traditional attire of expensive coats and salwars carrying swords within exquisitely embroidered scabbards. Some of them also carried guns, and they fired in the air to express their happiness over such event. The festivities continued till late at night, and Jaisalmer remained awake in celebration of Arjunsingh's entry into the threshold of a new life.

Salim was not a particularly healthy child. Though blessed with a strong voice, he was not bestowed with good health. He regularly fell ill. He started losing appetite and also appeared to grow pale and weak. Local doctors advised rest and a diet of fruit and vegetable as the recipe for recovery. Salim was subjected to bed rest, in anticipation that the rich diet and special care would get him better. But the situation worsened soon, and Salim had to be admitted to the hospital. He was diagnosed with jaundice and acute anaemia. Salim could not survive the joint attack and left for his heavenly abode peacefully in sleep. People who knew Salim and his melodious voice mourned deeply the loss of a prodigy, and the Ilahi household wept at the loss of a son.

Zoya had been considerably weakened by this unexpected bereavement. The shock was too hard for her to handle. Though Zaara took intense care of her, Zoya showed little signs of recovery from her state of trauma. It was hard on Salman too. Though he had graduated into an earning member of the house, yet there were other responsibilities too. Zoya was racing through her teens, and Salman needed to start for a search for a match for her. His uncle, Arif too had been rather concerned about getting Zaara married. Zaara, on the other hand, was more concerned about her mother. Her health, both physical and psychological, had been steadily deteriorating. Someone constantly needed to be by her side to cater to her various needs. She had become too frail to move around or even voice an opinion in this debate regarding the nuptial obligations of her daughter. After a lot of coaxing and convincing, Zaara finally agreed to spell out Kabool Hai in a low-profile ceremony, where she got tied into holy matrimony with Saiful Akhtar, a building contractor from the suburbs of Mumbai. Saiful was the selection of Arif Mirza since he had been knowing him and his family for a long time. Saiful was a thorough gentleman. He was well read and widely travelled, and for Zaara, he was the perfect match that Salman had been looking for. Saiful and Zaara left for Mumbai soon after their marriage, leaving Salman to cater to his ailing Ammi with the help of his uncle Arif and friend Arjun.

Zoya repeatedly failed to respond to medication, and one fine morning, when the world woke up to a new dawn, Zoya remained in her state of eternal slumber. Zoya's demise was like a bolt from the blue. Salman was left alone in this world full of characters. Salman Ilahi's search for kirdaars had started with the discovery of his own.

Salman returned to Mumbai, leaving the good and bad memories of Jaisalmer behind, in search of a new life. He continued his studies as well as part-time teaching, which got him enough to cater for himself. He was heartily welcomed by the remnants of his neighbourhood, after fifteen long years. The Ilahi Mansion again came alive with its lone resident.

Salman, however, never relinquished his literary pursuits. In fact, he became more focused and dedicated. His discourses on history and literature began getting published. Salman also started translating renowned works in Hindi and Sanskrit into Urdu. The number of readership began to swell, and soon Salman Ilahi had created a niche for himself in the literary world.

Salman met Shenaaz in a function where a mushaira was organized, and high-profile poets from various parts of Mumbai had come to deliberate their verses. It was an august gathering. Shehnaaz had come with her father Rafiq Ali, a renowned poet and scholar, who was also supposed to brandish his skills of oration.

Shehnaaz was seated apposite to Salman. And poor Salman could not take his eyes off her. Her grace, beauty, elegance had overwhelmed Salman. Shehnaaz looked visibly perturbed at this unwanted attention. As she rose to change her seating position, Salman managed to whisper an audible note, 'If you ever go near Taj Mahal, do take a box of make-up with you. Taj Mahal may need it.'

Shehnaz blushed at this unprecedented and eloquent piece of adulation. She receded to a corner but kept looking at Salman from her hideout. Soon it was time for all to leave. As they departed, Salman and Shehnaaz exchanged a few glances and smiles. Salman once again took the opportunity to whisper, 'Tum woh Kaynaat ho, woh satrangi Nazaara, jise dekhne ke liye ek jhrokha nahi . . . aasmaan chahiye.'

(You are that rainbow . . . you need a whole sky to see, not a window.)

Shehnaaz was flattered. She could not hide her pleasure at the generous shower of praise. As Shehnaaz's father came near, Salman hurriedly wished her Khuda Hafeez and was about to leave. Shehnaaz whispered smiling, 'Darte ho [are you afraid]?.'

Picking up a piece of paper from his Sherwaani pocket, Salman quickly scribbled a few words before handing to a startled Shehnaaz. It was their first love letter.

Rone se darta hoon.

Juda hone se darta hoon . . .

Meri aankhen bayan karti hai . . .

Main sone se darta hoon.

Jo haste ho to kyon

Palko ke Goshen bheeng jaate hain . . .

Main iss tarha hasne se darta hoon . . .

Jab se khwab me dekha hai tumhe . . .

Main sone se darta hoon . . .

Hastein hain lekin har baat pe hum . . .

Kyoki main rone se darta hoon.

Salman kept meeting Shehnaaz sometimes at college, sometimes in the library, sometimes on the way to college. The frequency of their meeting slowly began to increase. A mutual sense of admiration was fast bringing them closer to each other. Shehnaaz was a very sensitive girl. She could gauge Salman's mental condition by simply looking into his eyes. She was caring too. Almost always she carried some foodstuff hidden in her dupatta for Salman. She knew he took very little care of himself. The love and care was becoming an addiction—a necessary feature of living. Shehnaaz also had become addicted to Salman's charm and his intoxicating verses. His words touched the soul, and his magical voice made the heart beat faster. A unique chemistry had developed between them. They could feel each other's presence amidst a crowd. They could feel each other's absence within intervals of their meetings. Their lives had become so intertwined with each other that living separately had become an anathema. They longed to unite—to become one.

Arif Mirza was a frequent visitor to Ilahi Mansion. He was very fond of Salman in particular and was more of a friend than an uncle. He had noticed Salman's change in demeanour in the last few visits and had been worried about it. Salman looked to be introverted, lost in thoughts, not eager to participate in discussions that Arif tried to indulge him in. But Arif was no novice. He was quick to find out the reason for Salman's strange behaviour. One evening, when Arif and Salman were sitting across the fireplace ambling away time, Arif found the moment opportune to break the silence.

'Barkhurdaar, ishq chupta nahi chupane se.' (Son, love cannot be kept hidden, no matter how much you try). He said all of a sudden.

Salman was taken aback by the statement. Embarrassed, he lowered his head and tried to look away. Arif burst into an instant laughter. He kept on peppering Salman with questions which he tried his best to evade. But true love doesn't stay hidden for long. It appears writ on the face. It emerges with every sigh and gets underlined with every expression. Love cannot be hidden. Love cannot be kept away from the tangible world. Salman was but another mortal, which, finally, made him confess to Arif about his love for Shehnaaz. Arif was overjoyed. In fact, he used to worry quite a lot about Salman and his lonely way of living. Many a times he had tried to convince Salman to find for himself a companion. But Salman never heeded. He was perhaps in love with his solitude. Now he craved for companionship, he craved for compassion, he craved for love.

Salman had carefully crafted a poem of Mewlana Jalaluddin Rumi on the wall:

A true lover is proved such by his pain of heart;
No sickness is there like sickness of heart.
The lover's ailment is different from all ailments;
Love is the astrolabe of God's mysteries . . .

Arif's gaze fell on it, and he was quick to understand that he needed to pursue the matter with Rafiq Ali. He wanted to see his nephew happy at any cost.

Arif's proposal was greeted with cheer by the Ali household. Rafiq himself was a great admirer of Salman. He had always followed Salman's literary exploits with great interest. Arif Mirza's proposal was something he secretly had been fostering in his mind. Even Arif was overjoyed. He never expected that the proposal would be accepted so meekly by a person of such a high social bearing. But what mattered most is that it brought happiness to all.

At the request of Salman, the *nikaah* was kept a low key affair. Only relatives and close friends were invited to bestow blessings and good wishes upon the new couple. The rest of the rituals were completed at the Holy Shrine of Baba Haji Ali. But Jaisingh Rathod was not ready to leave things at this. He had organized a gala reception in honour of the new couple at his palatial house in Jaisalmer, and at his behest, the new couple along with Zaara, Saif, her two-year-old son

Shoaib, Arif, and Rafiq and family once again landed up at the majestic locales of Jaisalmer. The festivities that followed had a combined fervour of Idd and Diwali. The atmosphere was replete with orchestrated happiness. A new had emerged with a promise . . . happiness.

⌘

Riaz and Alia, though twins by birth, were very dissimilar in character. Riaz was hot-headed, volatile, whereas Alia was silent and understanding. From a very young age, Riaz had been very ambitious. His yearning for money and expensive clothing frequently got him to cross swords with his father. Salman always wanted his son to become pious, benign, honest, and humble. He almost always prevented Riaz from indulging into unnecessary expenses over items of fancy and fashion. He wanted Riaz to study. However, Riaz was more inclined towards the glitter and glamour of the artificial world of fashion. Riaz got himself into wrong company too. His friends were ones who indulged into gambling and drinking and were established rowdies of the marketplace. They often got themselves into trouble over drunken brawls and had earned quite a lot of disrepute in the locality.

Alia on the other hand was a very obedient and studious girl. Another feature of significance was her striking good looks. Alia was not a particularly talkative girl and took more interest in reading and sketching rather than indulging in useless gossips with other girls of her college. She was very kind hearted too. She always took care that the stray dogs which at times chanced to enter the college premises, never went unfed. This virtue, of course, had been inherited from her mother, who herself had been very kind to animals and in particularly with dogs and cats who had no identity or religion, unlike humans. Alia was also a very sensitive and emotional girl. Even small admonishments such as punishments rendered out to her classmates by irate teachers used to upset her. She believed in a world of peace, happiness, and fair dealings. Her concept of an ideal world at times made her the subject to jokes from her classmates. Yes, she was different and too soft for the world to accept.

Shehnaaz had always been worried about her two children. Time and again, she had pleaded with Salman to do two very important things. One was to get Riaz to rectify his ways, and two was to get Alia a match with someone as sensitive and kind-hearted as her. Salman had always laughed at her propositions, not that he was not worried, but because he had a couple of other most important task in front of him. One was to take Shehnaaz to Haj, and the other was to get her treated for the persistent pain in her forehead she had been suffering from since the last three years. She always downgraded it, saying that it was a symptom of her weakness. But Salman feared of something more sinister.

Salman was equally concerned about Riaz's future. They had regular sessions of discussion regarding Riaz's goal in life. And almost every time, the discussion had to be cut off midway due to Riaz's disinterest of taking such discussion to any kind of conclusion. He continued with his disruptive way of life, and Salman always was left wondering what would be the best forms of reform for this unruly child of his. The father-son relation had, however, been strained beyond repair. Riaz and Salman no longer took interest in talking to each other. The silence between them had escalated into an unbearable pitch . . . unbearable. They were like two strangers living under the same roof.

Riaz did not prolong the misery further, and one fine morning, he left the house for good. For quite some time, there was no news of Riaz. Even his delinquent associates were unable to provide proper information regarding to Salman. Salman, however, remained calm. He always consoled his wife that Riaz would definitely return as soon as he exhausts his pocket money. But Shehnaz never ceased to worry, and a mother's worry is always of a different proportion. She would always wait for Riaz till late at night with his dinner in anticipation that he would suddenly make his appearance at the doorway looking tired and hungry. Days accumulated into months, and the wait for Riaz persisted. And one day, Salman received news from one of Riaz's dubious associates that Riaz had been spotted in Delhi working for some political outfit. He had been involved with several skirmishes with the police and was on the run to escape arrest. Salman was both scared and rattled at the news. He took special care that none of the information got home and especially to Shehnaaz; otherwise there might be ominous ramifications.

But Salman was unable to hide the sordid information that had quickly spread in the neighbourhood like wildfire. A news that was devastating, contrite, disconsolate. Riaz Ilahi along with his three colleagues had been shot dead while trying to illegally cross over to a neighbouring country. Riaz's concocted face printed in the newspapers appeared to bear the sinister intent that he harboured in his mind. But the story of gore and gruesomeness that described the story of the encounter was too difficult to go through. Shehnaaz was shattered, maddened by grief. Her grief had drained her of all physical and psychological vigour and vitality. She had been thoroughly wrecked at the death of her son. It was a macabre death. Unthinkable. Unbearable.

The police did not hand over Riaz's body even after repeated requests from Salman. The lawmakers required documents to establish Riaz as the son of Salman, and no document was adequate. Riaz was, thus, interred as an unclaimed, unidentified entity under the jurisdiction of police forces.

Salman returned empty-handed from Delhi, heartbroken and thoroughly shaken. He was also terrified at the thought of facing questions from Shehnaaz about Riaz. However, he held on to his nonchalant composure. He did not want his brother-in-law Saif to know how devastated and empty he felt. As they approached home, they were greeted with some commotion from the Ilahi mansion. As they rushed inside, they were further greeted by another scene of utter devastation. Pushing aside a weeping Zaara and a wailing Alia, Salman met his wife. She had been laid on the floor on a full-size mattress strewn with flowers. Incense sticks threw around the errands of vespers. Salman silently took the hand of his bereaved wife, and everything appeared standstill. Shehnaaz had slept off her worry, her grief, her anxiety, her pain. Her quiet mutiny with the times that had befallen had been a solo effort. She had chosen to depart the scene of crisis in the most peaceful way. She had slept to the journey of her heavenly abode.

Salman was rendered silent. He and Alia chose the lay Shehnaaz to rest under a beautifully carved tombstone that wore a hue of blue and white and had some precious words inscribed on it.

'I stand alone gulping the lazy sun, slouching in sky, avoiding everyone

A chaotic day, finally descending, darkness sprouts in a happy ending.'

The night starlit sky hung in silence from above, as if offering words of consolation to the inconsolable Alia. Salman kissed her forehead and led her on the way home. Numerous people had gathered to express their consolation to the father-daughter duo. Salman turned around as a hand silently touched his shoulders.

'Jonathon,' he exclaimed in surprise.

'Sir, I am back,' replied the tall Australian. 'Now don't think yourself to be alone.'

If you want to find the real competition, just look in the mirror. After awhile you'll see your rivals scrambling for second place.

(Criss Jami)

CHAPTER 10

The Tournament

Sports is a great leveller. For a game like cricket, especially, where there is more than the mere dynamics on the field. The cricket field is a didactic arena which defines the art of leadership, team building, strategizing, and temperament to subtle limits. Yes, cricket is about talent, about hand-eye coordination, about fitness, temperament, and leadership. But cricket is also about strategies, leg pulling, sledging, politics, and cheating.

Times have allowed cricket to graduate from the gentleman's game to a most competitive and aggressive sport. And cricket has, over the years, developed more as a mind game. More often than not, a cricket match is won or lost in the mind before the act is enacted on the field.

Human mind neither sleeps nor hibernates. The visual cortex at the back of our head is bombarded with electrical signals as we open our eyes. It receives, processes, and stores enormous amount of data. Even when we sleep, the brain cells remain active for their own survival. Our mindset dances to the tunes of our continuous thought processes. Cricketers are no exceptions. Aggression, anger, fear, success, failure are certain keywords which preoccupy the cricketer's mindset. This relates to their professional and personal life. But the impact which it creates affects their cricketing abilities even if it originates from their off-the-field personal life. Every day can be a different day for all cricketers. We cannot expect Ricky Ponting to go and score a century every innings he plays. His level of concentration ought to be at different levels on his various innings.

The world had taken a full circle. The fever of cricket had once again returned to grip the campus of Loyola. The spirit of competitiveness could be felt all around. Once again, all the classes were busy selecting the best possible team composition in an attempt to establish supremacy in this event of prestige.

This time around the event was being organized in an even grander scale. The field and the pitch, the seating areas, the players' zone, had all been given a necessary facelift. The fight had already reached the classrooms and was reflected in the notice board of the portico, where each team announced their composition with slogans and labels of encouragement. But XII BIO was running in a bit of crisis. There was a huge amount of dissent over the leadership of the team, which everyone felt was the reason for their debacle last year. The debate went on endlessly, and finally, Mr Philip Cordero, the class teacher had to intervene. Under his behest, a consensus was drawn to select the captain and the vice captain of the team. Siddhath Singh was a unanimous selection for the post of vice captain, and there was definitely a gasp of surprise that released from the classroom at the announcement of the captain of XII BIO . . . Armaan Bailey.

Armaan and Siddharth got together pretty well. Though Armaan generally remained a quiet listener, Siddharth preferred to be animated, expressive, and vocal. Siddharth was the one most overjoyed at Armaan's supple elevation to this hot seat. And Armaan . . . he was left astounded. As if the world had come within his grasp, a world that all of a sudden appeared much, much more liveable.

At home too, there was an atmosphere of celebration. The otherwise silent, diffident, reserved, reticent Armaan had discovered a new voice in the world of words. Jonathon, in particular, was overjoyed at this transformation of Armaan. He had never seen him to be so happy. This recent development had ushered in a tide of euphoria in the Bailey household.

But amongst all this hoopla, however, Armaan engaged himself in readying himself for the job. Under the watchful guardianship of his guide, his grandfather, he had come to terms with the various aspects of the game. He had learnt about strategizing through various discourses from his dada . . . of how Douglas Jardine had employed the Bodyline, the fast-leg theory bowling to curb the prodigious run scoring ability of Sir Donald Bradman. He had also learnt of how Greg Chappel had induced his brother Trevor to bowl underarm to prevent the batsmen from playing a lofted shot. He had also learnt how the duo of Bob Woolmer and Hansie Cronje had employed various measures against world-renowned batsmen to make them look ordinary. And above all, what captivated him most was the life of Mike Brearley. Everyone knows that Mike was a captain of the English cricket team, but only a few know that Mike had never contemplated to be a cricketer . . . least a captain. Though his ability with the bat and ball was limited, his thought process as a cricketer has immense. His ability to turn things around against the run of play can be attributed to his god-gifted instinct to think out of the box. Armaan wanted to be like Brearley. He wanted to beat his adversaries by the turn of strategies and not mere skills of cricket. So there began a rigorous training process of transverse thinking, working out various permutation combination with the select batting and bowling line up. A lot of brainstorming, conjecturing, questionings, and debate happened over the telephone relentlessly.

'This time our STD bill is going to eat away half of my salary,' said Jonathon while having breakfast one morning.

'But isn't it worth it?' Alia smiled, visibly pleased at the tremendous transformation that had taken place in Armaan over this short period.

Jonathon could only nod in affirmation, for he was not to forget the stress and pain they had gone through to induce Armaan with the behavioural patterns of a normal kid. He was not to forget the struggle they had to go through to conjure up money, to be able to pay for the visits to psychologists, behavioural experts, and emotion therapists. He was not to forget the nagging thought that drove them to the point of craziness, about the future of their son, the unslept nights that they had to endure consoling each other and chasing away thoughts of despair and depression. Jonathon knew that the almighty had been kind to him, to Alia, to Armaan, and to everyone, even remotely connected to them because they were happy, and happiness grows as it spreads. He believed that the future had in store greater surprises.

The tournament began with a bang. The opening match ended in a tie. The XI Maths and XI Bio ended even sevens in a highly exciting, nail-biting encounter.

The XIth Commerce was, by far, the best team on pen and paper. Even before the start of the tournament, they had been branded with the tag of the Favourites. And they did justice to the tag, when they mauled a hapless XII Maths in a high Octane combat. All attention was now on the new look. XII Bio team who were to start their campaign against XII Commerce. The Commerce team had always been unpredictable. They were a side that enjoyed a world of support. And what is more, they had fielded an unchanged team. All their last-year players had been retained in the squad. Bio was aware that they were up against a perfectly knit, unified team.

Bailey lost the toss, and Bio was sent to bat first. It was not a very encouraging of starts for Bio. They quickly got themselves into trouble by losing a few quick wickets to some disciplined bowling. Bailey came to bat at the fall of the third over to steady the boat. Bio survived some anxious moments to post a respectable total on the board. Bailey scored an unbeaten 65 runs—a responsible innings that befits a captain. Though the target was not very stiff, only 166 runs, Bio had a good bowling attack and a very innovative captain.

Commerce started steadily, working cautiously towards the target. A bit too cautious, probably. Bailey's field setting had been spot on from the very beginning. Though commerce had not lost any wicket in the first 16 overs, they could only muster a mere 60 runs. It was this time that Bailey chose to bring himself on. The guy who had turned things around last year with his swing bowling, however, chose to bowl spin. Everyone, including the Bio teammates were surprised, unaware that they were about the relentless hours that Armaan had put at the nets under the watchful eyes of Hari Singh, who was his father's colleague and a spinner in the state cricket team. People were also little aware that the barren pitch of last year, which assisted swing and bounce, had maligned into a deft turner. Also, little did they know that during their last visit to Australia, Jonathon had arranged a meeting with the legendary Shane Warne. And there had been a prolonged session of discussion and training. Shane Warne had been benevolent enough to share with Armaan the creativity and the mysticism of spin bowling. Armaan Bailey had carefully stocked his arsenal with lethal weapons capable of mass destruction of batting line ups. And here was he to unravel his new Avatar in front of the partisan crowd, who had been vociferous in support of Commerce.

Armaan's first delivery was a googly that hurried on to the bemused batsman who could only plod at it half-heartedly. Armaan followed it up with an off break. The batsman, aware of the fact that the Required Run Rate was rapidly climbing up, went for a big hit. The ball did enough to dribble past the edge of the bat to dislodge the off stump. The sound of timber sparked off an instant celebration in the Bio camp. The floodgates had opened. One after the other, the commerce batsmen fell to the guile of Armaan Bailey, who accounted for seven such batsmen. The rest was completed by the fast bowlers Siddharth, Narayan, Karan, and Dubey. The XII Bio had flagged off their campaign in the most emphatic manner.

The XII BIO went on to triumph over their next set of opponents in the same authoritative tune. The XIth Maths and XIth BIO were effectively dumped aside. What was important here was that the other players were peaking too. Each player looked focused and motivated and played their part in putting up inspired performances. The body language had changed because victory always brings about changes. On one hand, victory brings in confidence, belief, and; joy but on the other, it also brings about a sense of complacency, vanity, and pride . . . and the attitude that one attains at the end of the day after being bathed by success defines character. And it is not always only skill that makes one a true champion. It often is the character.

It was a Sunday and Derbytime. Arch rivals XII Maths and XII Bio were to lock horns in a high-voltage encounter. A lot of things are at stake whenever these two teams collide.

Pride, being the foremost. Maths, was full of talented and handsome individuals. But again, they were individuals in a team and not a team of individuals. However, this time, they were determined to exorcise the ghost of last year's defeat and avenge the humiliation they had been carrying for one long year. They had been specifically working out strategies to counter Bailey, with bat and ball. But there was one other aspect they had badly missed out during such sessions of brainstorming—his captaincy. The most lethal, potent weapon that Bio carried with them. Like Mike Brearly had one famously said, 'You need to think yourself to win, the rest will always follow', Bailey believed that teams can be beaten by the process of thinking. Performances are mere reflections of thought processes.

Bio was soon all over Maths, and it was not only Bailey who was performing. The total team had worked itself into a fantastic rhythm. Wickets tumbled, and Maths looked completely helpless in front of a continuous onslaught of pace, swing, spin supported by athletic fielding and intelligent field settings. It was then that controversy erupted. Mohit Raj edged a delivery to the keeper. An appeal went up in unison from the Bio team. The umpire Mr Lalit Prasad looked blank for the faint snick had lost its decibels in the roar of the crowd. The leg umpire too had heard nothing. It was up to the batsman now to own up to his own undoing. Mohit Raj shook his head and stood the ground. The whole Bio team was stunned in disbelief. This blatant form of cheating was beyond their comprehension. It was a sharp violation to the lofty principles the school had proudly propagated over the years. Cheating was a word quite alien to the lexicon of the school.

But we are built to cheat. Our DNA demands that we take the opportunities that increase our chance of survival.

In Stanley Kubrick's adaptation of *Arthur C Clarke's 2001: A Space Odyssey*, it is the bone-wielding apes who viciously club the unarmed apes. No lingering guilt about what is fair inhibits their bloody victory. But these are primates fighting over territory in a tooth-and-claw scrabble without values to impinge their survival instincts, distant cousins of refined cricketers imbued with a sense of moral duty to a sport that has long been elevated above other recreation as a bastion of fair play.

However, it is the codified rules, empirical rather than moral, that ultimately define a sport. In football you cannot touch the ball with your hands, in rugby football, you can. Bereft of guidelines a sporting contest debases back to the savannah. Medieval unruly versions of the beautiful game involved neighbouring villages fighting to move a ball from one field to another. These riotous matches with surging mobs hacking, wrestling, and lurching back and forth across muddied fields—much like a Five Nations clash from the 1980s—were banned in 1314 by an Edward II Royal Decree that declared 'hustling over large balls' as an act 'from which many evils may arrive'.

Cricket, conversely, has often been taught in an effort to instil morality and sportsmanship. The phrase 'it's just not cricket' has been popularised to describe underhand behaviour in wider society. The MCC, the owner of the Laws of Cricket since the eighteenth century, included a preamble on this 'Spirit of Cricket' in its updated 2000 code: 'Cricket is a game that owes much of its unique appeal to the fact that it should be played not only within its Laws but also within the Spirit of the Game. Any action which is seen to abuse this Spirit causes injury to the game itself.'

Occasionally players do contravene this near-mystical ethic of cricketing spirit. In 1981, six runs were needed from the last ball of the third World Series Cup final between Australia and New Zealand, and Australian captain Greg Chappell instructed his brother Trevor to bowl underarm. New Zealand's no. 10 Brian McKechnie blocked the grubber and then hurled his bat away in disgust. Outrage followed, and the Australian Cricket Board acknowledged that Chappell's action 'was within the laws of the game', but as the MCC would formally state, 'that it was totally contrary to the spirit in which cricket has been, and should be, played'.

The unwritten code of fair play had been broken, and a week later, the law was changed to ban underarm bowling. Like religion, the Spirit of Cricket is a concept universally understood but not universally practised.

In this boiling encounter of equals, Mohit Raj stood his ground when he knew full well he was out. Sensing that he might escape justice, his face was that of a boy wiping away the crumbs of a stolen cookie. Never has he looked more like the nefarious Malfoy from Harry Potter than when he realised his stay of execution.

It is the same player, whether on the village green or the school tournament arena, stuttering, 'I really wasn't sure if I'd hit it' who demonstrates an ancient skill not only to others but also to oneself.

'In a competition for mates, a well-developed capacity for self-deception is an advantage,' writes philosopher John Gray in *Straw Dogs*. 'The same is true in politics, and many other contexts.'

Including, one would argue, when at the crease.

'If they believe the lie', says Victor Gombos, a psychologist at California State University, 'it's easier to be convincing.' That golden duck turned into a century is sweeter still if the guilty man can free himself of the crime.

The walk-or-not-to-walk conundrum is a direct test of moral fortitude against genetics—a measure of character extended to home umpires in club games when they, as well as the appealing fielders, are well aware that the ball held aloft in the keeper's glove did indeed feather their teammate's bat and a prime example of how lying, whether to oneself or to others, is a preprogrammed ability.

'Almost all children lie,' notes the director of the Institute of Child Study at Toronto University, Dr Kang Lee. After studying 1,200 children, Lee claimed that lying 'is a sign they have reached a new developmental milestone' and evidence of a fast-developing brain. He was quick to negate the link between juvenile deception and graduation into adult fraudsters and, we presume, dishonest cricketers.

Whether Mohit not walking constitutes a lie is debatable. No one asked him if he had hit the ball. And as many great batsmen have done before him, he is entitled to wait on the umpire's decision. But a cheat? If so, he is certainly not the first or the last.

In a survey conducted for the MCC and the Cricket Foundation, one in twenty children questioned admitted they were proud to have achieved victory dishonestly. With twenty-two players involved in a cricket match, that correlates to at least one dedicated cheater per game. This will to sporting power, to win at all costs, was highlighted in Dr Robert Goldman's 1984 survey that claimed over 50 per cent of athletes would take an undetectable drug that assured them five years of glory.

Darwinism teaches that a quest for truth is often contrary to our survival. The truth is that Mohit edged the ball to the keeper and the deception prolonged his life. Here, the 'victory' gene, as I shall briefly rename Dawkins 'selfish' original, is in conflict with what is considered fair play.

Morality is built on the shifting sands of time, place, and culture; and in natural selection, the human mind pursues evolutionary success, not values.

Therefore as we evolve, the rules and how they are applied, must adapt too. Sporting laws that fail to keep players in check will die off like dodos. Cricket changes because we are inventive mammals with the capacity for creativity—cheating.

The decisions will improve. Leg and third umpires will see and hear with Orwellian focus. The ministry of truth will reign over every high-definition microsecond of every televised game, and on-field umpires such as Lalit Prasad will only try to improve upon the art of decision making by peeking through idiosyncrasies of deceit.

And cheating will advance too. Each mutation of advantage will result in a tweak of governance. While the coming youth play warped forms of our beloved game and we casually forget this is a sport born on grassy meadows with curving bats and gates of sticks instead of stumps—an evolving game—our fading generation will hark back to a time when cricket was cricket and a batsman could stand his ground whether he had hit the ball or not.

Mohit remained the top scorer of the Maths innings. And Maths was relieved to have posted a reasonably challenging target of 140 runs in front of Bio.

Bailey could understand that the controversial reprieve of Mohit was playing in the minds of his team. A feeling of injustice always harms good intentions. The need of the hour was to stay focused amidst the counterproductive opinions that echoed around the playfield. Before the batters went out into the middle, Bailey got all the players into a huddle. This was the first time, probably, they were into a team huddle. Under the given circumstances, it was indeed a necessity. All the players eagerly waited for their captain to speak. Taking brief turns to look at each member of the team, Bailey spoke slowly. 'We know what has happened in the past. It cannot be undone. What we have to do now is to be ourselves out in the middle. We should not get swayed by what people think about us or what people think that we should think about us. Our patriotic duty towards our believers, supporters, parents, loved ones, school, society, and nation is to win and prove to all that one who resorts to nefarious means cannot end up in the podium. We have to once again bring forth the dictum that people who forget history are condemned to repeat it.' Smilingly he added, 'Remember Ben Johnson.' A huge roar of laughter went up from the Bio boys and a loud round of applause as Sumit and Siddhath walked into the middle to initiate the run chase. Though Maths had a strong bowling attack, they found the going difficult against the resolute opening pair of Bio. The match that held promises of a humdinger turned out into a damp squib. The XIIth BIO went on to win by a whopping eight wickets.

Suddenly everyone had started taking note of Bailey, the captain—his calculated methods and his wise bowling changes. His alteration of the batting line-up and his shrewd field placements were all topics of animated discussion. As the tournament progressed, more people got attracted to the enigmatic style of cricket of Armaan Bailey. His leadership had brought about a complete transformation in the ability and attitude of the Bio team. And the whole school was a witness to this change. They were all a witness to the positive results that good leaderships bring about. A good leader often inspires the ordinary to attempt for the extraordinary.

The match against the combined Arts team was a cake walk. Arts chose to surrender most meekly to the marauding Bio boys without putting up any sort of resistance against them. But the final league match was the toughest of the agenda—a dress rehearsal for the finals. XI Commerce, who had won all their league matches without much sweat, stood between XII Bio and invincibility. Armaan did well to rest most of his performing players to avoid unnecessary injuries before the finals. However, commerce played with their best team.

As the match progressed, the imbalance of attitude could be seen most transparently. Whereas, commerce was putting their all out effort to win the match, BIO was merely content in giving the substitutes more chances to bowl and bat. It was as if BIO was more into a practice session rather than being in a match against an equal adversary. On the other hand, Commerce was playing the match in utter seriousness. They believed that by winning this match, they would automatically enhance their chances of winning in the finals. Commerce did win, albeit by the smallest of margins. But victory is always sweet. The inconsequential victory was only a morale booster for XI Commerce. The finals were a couple of days away, enough time for Bio to regroup and decide upon the decisive strategy that will slay the invincible commerce side.

There are three things worth noting here. One, as already mentioned before, cricket is a game of uncertainties. And this thirty odd over a side-shortened version was a more unpredictable affair. Even the most favoured side might bite the dust to a seemingly weaker opponent by twists of fate. Two already mentioned before too that success always brings forth two major emotions: confidence and complacency. Champions are those who let confidence eclipse complacency. And third, there is a ruling in the world of successes. It is called the law of average. It is a rare occasion in life where you can remain unbeaten through a series of encounters. There will be instances where you will, no matter how strong you might be, falter. Though, this law of averages is generally a psychological phenomenon. It does exist. And it can catch up with you at most crucial times, robbing away your title of invincibility.

The final match, by no means, was an ordinary affair. Elaborate arrangements had been made to make the occasion look special. The decorations, the sound system, the players dug out area, the seating arrangements for the spectators—everything was given special attention to. The junior classes were called off along with the senior classes, to allow all to witness an encounter of equals. The teachers and nonteaching staff were also very eager to be part of this electric atmosphere.

The occasion was graced by Dr Amir Ali, the only representative of the state to the BCCI (Board of Cricket Control, India). His enthusiasm for the game was such that he arrived early enough to be able to follow the match from the toss of the coin. After being introduced to the members of either side, Dr Ali tossed the coin, which fell in the favour of Commerce. They decided to bat. Before the Bio boys walked out to take the field, they went into the famous huddle. Words of inspiration strengthened their will to win, the slogan that ranged out from the Bio section of the crowd reflected that will. 'Commerce has won the toss, BIO will win the match.'

The crowd was treated with some exemplary bowling and fielding stunts by Bio. The lush green outfield allowed the fielders to throw themselves around providing the much required 'Spectators Delight'. Commerce too showed glimpses of mastery through authentic stroke making and crisp running between the wickets. The match had started in the correct note, and the initial stages already had enough in it to get the audience glued to their seats in excitement. Commerce was scoring in a brisk rate. Their aim was to post a total close to two hundred runs which will of course be an imposing total for any team to chase against their famed bowling attack. But the Bio captain had some other ideas. Commerce had already galloped to sixty runs within the first eight overs when Bailey came out with another of his novel strategies. The Diamond System. Six bowlers of different acumen, bowling in tandem. If the first bowler is primarily an outswing bowler, the next would be one who makes the bowl come into the batsmen. The next over would be bowled by someone with less speed but more accuracy. Spinners would bowl the middle overs. A very immaculately thought process that keeps the batsmen guessing and makes it utterly tough for them to get into some kind of rhythm. It casts a spell of suspicion on even seasoned campaigners when they encounter such strategies. For here all the elements are tested—sight, adaptability, instinct, and above all temperament. It is a test of all senses.

Commerce was taken aback by this strategy. Before trying to fathom what had hit them, they had already lost half of their side. Till now commerce had been only playing against teams in terms of cricketing skill, but here they were up against a thought process, which required more than mere cricketing skills to overcome. The field was immaculately set too. Each over had a different set of field. Sometimes, the field was reset between consecutive balls. The batsmen were flabbergasted. There was uniqueness in every stratagem, something Commerce had never ever could have thought about. In their utter astonishment, they soon witnessed their innings getting folded even before they could reach the three-figure mark.

The supporters of commerce were stunned into silence. They could just watch on in utter dismay as BIO stroked themselves to a comfortable victory. The XIIth Bio was crowned the new champions. Celebrations were let loose and all the Bio students ran amok, smearing each other with colours and setting off a barrage of fireworks. Dr Amir Ali heavily praised Armaan while handing him the winner's trophy and the trophy for the player of the tournament. Dr Ali was visibly pleased to know that Armaan was the grandson of Salman Ilahi, who had once been his teacher. He announced his willingness to host a party in honour of the winning team and also invited Reverend Father Principal to join XII Bio at his residence, not very far away from the school. He also whispered to Armaan that he should not forget to get his parents along.

Dr Ali's house itself was an avid indication of his great passion for cricket. He had named his house the Pavilion. The lawn had been carefully crafted into a mini cricket field with two adjoining practice pitches. Dr Ali's both sons were in the state cricket team and had been selected for the Ranji Trophy squad. The entrance itself had some resemblance to any pavilion. The flavour of cricket was scattered all around. Dr Ali welcomed his guests with open arms and led them into a huge open courtyard where already some eminent people of the town were present. Dr Ali introduced his guests to everyone. He, of course, had a special mention for Armaan, calling him the emerging prodigy of Indian Cricket. Jonathon and Alia had accompanied Armaan. And Dr Ali thanked them immensely for keeping his request.

'What have you thought of, Armaan?' Dr Ali's question almost startled Jonathon.

Before he could find an appropriate answer, Dr Ali chose to reply the question himself. 'Jonathon', he said, 'your son is a genius. Do you know that?'

Jonathon was taken aback by this sudden admission by this eminent gentleman. 'He can think way ahead of people in his age group,' said Dr Ali looking into the eyes of the Senior Bailey.

'But, sir, he struggles with his marks,' stammered Jonathon.

'No, son.' Dr Ali was adamant. 'Don't gauge him by his marks. Marks do not portray the thinking capacities of a human being. He is not destined for these nine-to-five jobs. He is meant for things beyond. And mark my words, if you allow him to have his way, he can become a legend.'

Jonathon almost laughed in disbelief. Though it was good to hear these words of praise for his son, but reality depicted something else. Armaan was still an autistic child. His behavioural patterns were much different than children of his age. His interaction levels were low; his capability to grasp even commonplace instructions was considerably weak. He barely got pass marks in his subjects though he was being tutored by the best teachers in town. Jonathon could not help wonder what extraordinary spark did Dr Ali see in his child to come out with such lofty statements.

'Sir, if you can guide him, he will surely do much better,' said Jonathon in a tone of subtle diplomacy.

'Of course I will,' replied Dr Ali in the most emphatic manner, almost startling some of the guests seated at the corner table.

Dr Ali lowered his voice almost to a whisper as he moved closer to Jonathon. 'Boy, your son can read minds. He can see through intentions. He can discover your instincts even before you yourself can discover them.' Taking a pause to sip some of the mango juice he had been holding on to, Dr Ali once again looked deeply into the eyes of Jonathon. 'Your boy is no ordinary child. He is a great prodigy.'

Probably for the first time, Jonathon turned around to give an investigating look at Armaan, who in turn was busy observing the fishes in the large aquarium. Though the innocent appearance of Armaan gave nothing away, Jonathon could sense a strong feeling building up within his beloved son. Probably the hints of genius he had been showing had been misconstrued by the world as unconventional . . . or autistic.

The thoughts that kept playing in the minds of Jonathon was probably also orchestrated by the lyrics of the Elton John number being played in the background: "The Circle of Life."

From the day we arrive on the planet
And blinking step into the sun
There's more to be seen than can ever be seen
More to do than can ever be done . . .

He's not perfect. You aren't either, and the two of you will never be perfect. But if he can make you laugh at least once, causes you to think twice, and if he admits to being human and making mistakes, hold onto him and give him the most you can.

(Bob Marley)

CHAPTER 11

Ways of the Heart . . .

'**D**o you remember me?'

'Why are you asking that?'

'People generally tend to forget . . . or pretend to.'

'I am surely not amongst them. By the way, where are you now?'

'At home in Jaisalmer doing nothing.'

'Why? You were such a brilliant engineer.'

'Dad is forcing me to take over some of his business, and I don't like to do non-technical stuff. Mute trading and negotiations are not my cup of tea. I want to do something different, something more challenging.'

There was a brief pause. As brief as a sip off the coffee cup . . . but for someone in wait, it appears like eternity.

'Are you there?' The impatience could be felt even in the typed words.

'Ah . . . yes,' came the almost reluctant reply.

These modes of communication is, however, ruled by one invariable discipline—the Internet speed. Though, by mere coincidence, but too often to be of comfort, the internet speed opts to lower itself decisively, to put an end to meaningful conversation.

This time too, poor Ramsingh was rendered helpless by the intolerable no-speed of the Internet as he stomped out of the Internet café in frustration, mumbling a mixture of some of his choicest expletives in Hindi and English.

This had become a routine exercise. Ramsingh had been rendered busy by the lure of the Internet café more than the profitability of business. This was an uncontrollable obsession. The fire that had been simmering since the days of college had been rekindled. The embers had been reignited into a bonfire. And when cupid strikes, it does not heed to any choice . . . whether it is place, time, society, or logic. There has never been logic to love and there cannot be . . . Love remains and will continue to remain an enigma. Unexplained.

'Where are you now?'

'I am in Mumbai. Working in a boutique.'

'But what about the degree in architecture?'

'Well, I did something extra too. I did a course in apparel design as well. I like to follow my heart. And life is too short. We need to do things pretty quickly, isn't it?'

This time the silence was from Ramsingh's end. He did not want the conversation to meander on meaninglessly. At the same time, he did not want to type something that would upset the other party. However, mustering up enough courage, Ramsingh typed in almost slow motion.

'Did you not miss me all these years. I mean after leaving college?'

'Sometimes. And you?' the reply came faster than expected.

'Yes, I did. And I still miss you.'

Once again the conversation was punctuated by a confused silence.

There was a further interruption. Ramnik Chedha, the owner of the esteemed café, was getting impatient to go home.

'Sir, it is almost midnight. Can we close now?' he enquired hesitantly.

'Go on. But let me have the keys. Collect it from me tomorrow, here itself,' replied Ramsingh without even looking at his bemused face.

Poor Ramnik had no choice but to relent to the whims of the imminent heir to the clan of the Rathods. And he had started getting used to this regular ordeal.

'Why didn't you get married?' came the question, which was least anticipated.

'I can ask you the same question.'

'I had been through tough times, Ram. My father passed away as soon as I graduated. I had to support my family— my mother and my little brother. So I joined a boutique in Bombay as a design assistant.'

'Sorry to hear that, but why didn't you remember me then?'

'Could not remember anybody. The people who really took care of us that time, Dr Amit Ray and Mrs Tina Ray. God bless them.'

'Can't we start from where we had left off in college?'

'No, Ram. It's not possible. This is not college life. This is reality.'

'So what if this is reality? Why can't we face reality?'

'We can't. Because we have social obligations. Look, Ram, you know your society. I know mine. They don't converge at any point.'

'Are we to live our lives as per the dictations of society? Is this what education has imparted upon us?'

'This is reality, Ramsingh. Just reality.'

Jamnadas College of Engineering and Architecture. An institute that has garnered good faith and repute over the years by imparting quality education in this Northern regions of India. The college, has over the years, produced some excellent engineers in the discipline of civil engineering and architecture. The institute also had an enviable faculty especially in civil engineering. Various concepts in concreting and soil engineering had been developed by the eminent professors and the research scholars here. MOST (Ministry of Surface Transport) was the biggest benefactor. Every modification to their specification was brought about by JCEA. The latest development in slip form paving had also been developed to some extent by JCEA.

Another feature of JCEA was the strict decorum that it maintained throughout its premises. There was always an air of cordiality in the atmosphere and time, and again the college organized various entertainment programs to ease the students off the curricular pressures. The college administration cared for the wholesome development of individuals, and therefore everyone was cajoled into participation in every event that the college organized.

This time around, a trip was for all second year students in civil and architecture had been organized to Jodhpur. This was the time of the fall. Winter had slowly started to recede into oblivion, making way for the pleasant autumn climate of soothing breeze and colourful landscape. Nature suddenly appeared to have been wrapped in a smear of colour. There was colour everywhere because round the corner was HOLI—the auspicious festival of colour and fervour, of love and mirth. HOLI is a celebration of togetherness, of unconditional unity. And it was unity in totality as all students assembled in the lawn of Hotel Ghoomar to participate in the auspicious Holika Burning. It's a bonfire of sorts, which precedes the actual celebration of HOLI. It is a custom where all woes and troubles are subjected to fire, to rid humanity of all kinds of maladies and misfortune. It is a process of welcoming happiness, prosperity, and love in a world full of strife and altercation. It is a process of ushering in hope into the gloominess of competitive lifestyle.

Hotel Ghoomar was decorated in the traditional fervour of Holi. A huge gathering, besides the college students, had congregated in the majestically decorated lawn, where a bonfire was about to be lit up amidst songs and chants in praise of Lord Krishna. As the Holika got lit up by Prahlad Kakkar, a famous industrialist of Jodhpur, a huge chorus of 'Jai Sree Krishna' filled up the air.

Thandai, a fermented drink, considered auspicious during Holi was being served to people who were willing to indulge in a bit of revelry. Ramsingh Rathod along with his band of hooligans, whom the college had rendered the pseudonym of 'The B Boys' were the first to pounce on the intoxicating delicacy.

Ramsingh was merrily pouring his third glassful, when one of the architecture students, who was also the co-leader of the trip, approached him with a tone of dissent.

'What is this going on? Can't you guys restrain yourself from having such filthy stuff?' she scolded.

'Restrain?' Ramsingh laughed disdainfully. 'But why? Isn't life already full of restraints?'

'Only the savage lead irresponsible life,' rebuked the petite lady.

'And I have not risen above that level yet,' Ramsingh replied with a smile. 'The truth, actually, lies only in savagery. All else is pretence or delusion.'

'Then there is no such thing as civilization?' questioned the lady in utter amazement.

'There is, but that's only a dark veil over reality, just a decor.' Ramsingh laughed as he took a big gulp of thandai and walked away into the crowd of revellers, leaving the co-leader stupefied with his crisp and pointed replies.

By the time the bonfire had subsided, thandai had taken its toll. A vast majority of the crowd, which had by now appreciably thinned down, were high on spirits. Most of the girls in the group had retired for the night, and most of the boys too. Only a few, who were awake, were busy playing pranks with each other and having fun in the process. Streaks of laughter went up from time to time, and nobody complained.

Ramsingh was engrossed with the dying remains of the once vivacious Holika, trying to rejuvenate it with twigs and dry leaves that were strewn around.

'We didn't complete our argument,' the voice startled Ramsingh. Looking up, he saw the co-leader, standing right in front of him. She looked pretty in her red lehanga-choli. Very pretty in fact. Her whole persona had a certain glitter that mesmerized any onlooker. Ramsingh was enchanted. Quickly recovering his senses, he retorted, looking at her straight into the eye. 'What argument?'

'Well, about civilization and all that.' She smiled at him, lowering herself slowly to sit beside him.

She listened silently as Ramsingh went on to elocute his reverie about the narrow-minded approach of the middle-class girls who must argue about the good and the bad in every little thing when nothing in itself is either good or bad. It is one's approach to it that makes it so. How about the naked body of a woman? Is that, in itself, good or bad? The great artists of Ajhanta and Ellora have depicted women almost naked. The statues of Khajuraho are not only nude but are also locked in erotic embrace. Liquor can be condemned because it causes physical ailments and economic defluxion. But at the same time, its potential as a medium for relieving man of stress, even though temporarily, cannot be denied. It helps him transcend time and space while it makes him capable of impersonal thinking at the same time. Wine is not, of course, the only source of intoxication. It is there in meditation or in the eyes of someone you love. But our bourgeoisie are all idolaters. They make idols of hackneyed, worn-out ideals, to put them on a pedestal of hypocrisy and worship them.

'You seem to be quite a rebel yourself. By the way, I am Neha.' She smiled as she extended her hand of friendship. Needless to say, the hand was gleefully accepted.

After the daylong tomfoolery, smearing of colours on each other, splashing water, throwing balloons stuffed with coloured water, and dancing to the beats of the *dholki*, the group had once again gathered that evening at the lawn of Ghoomar. A musical evening had been organized to culminate the whole program melodiously. Singers from all around Jodhpur had assembled here to render their part of melody to the function. But the highlight of the program was the opening song 'Bande Mataram' from the film *Anandmath*. A glorious tribute to the motherland scripted by the prodigal Bankim Chandra Chattopadhyay in his 1882 novel, *Anandmath*.

Mother, I salute thee!
Rich with thy hurrying streams,
bright with orchard gleams,
Cool with thy winds of delight,
Dark fields waving Mother of might,
Mother free.

Glory of moonlight dreams,
Over thy branches and lordly streams,

Clad in thy blossoming trees,
Mother, giver of ease
Laughing low and sweet!
Mother I kiss thy feet,
Speaker sweet and low!
Mother, to thee I salute.

Who hath said thou art weak in thy lands
When the swords flash out in seventy million hands
And seventy million voices roar
Thy dreadful name from shore to shore?
With many strengths who art mighty and stored,
To thee I call Mother and Lord!
Though who savest, arise and save!
To her I cry who ever her foeman drove
Back from plain and Sea
And shook herself free.

Thou art wisdom, thou art law,
Thou art heart, our soul, our breath
Though art love divine, the awe
In our hearts that conquers death.
Thine the strength that nerves the arm,
Thine the beauty, thine the charm.
Every image made divine
In our temples is but thine.

Thou art Durga, Lady and Queen,
With her hands that strike and her
swords of sheen,
Thou art Lakshmi lotus-throned,
And the Muse a hundred-toned,
Pure and perfect without peer,

Mother lend thine ear,
Rich with thy hurrying streams,
Bright with thy orchard gleems,
Dark of hue O candid-fair

In thy soul, with bejeweled hair
And thy glorious smile divine,
Loveliest of all earthly lands,
Showering wealth from well-stored hands!
Mother, mother mine!
Mother sweet, I salute thee,
Mother great and free!

The song had everyone mesmerized. The hypnotic tune and the feel of patriotism descended on each and every person present in the function. This is a song of Indianness; and it soars above all petty differences, whether it is religion, caste, creed, and culture. The selection of the song and the beautiful rendering of the same had brought about a transformation in the atmosphere. An envelope of solemnity descended. Every member present was made conscious about their being an Indian in the most sublime manner.

This is what Neha Joshi can do. She can weave magic with her voice. She can cast a spell on the audience through her hypnotic renditions.

After two hours of music in the form of song and dance sequences, the program came to an end amidst heavy applause. However, the standards set by the opening song could not be matched by the rest of the programs, and everybody went home with the lingering tones of Bande Mataram still ringing in their ears.

Ramsingh was mesmerized too. He stood amidst the dispersing crowd almost in a trance. The song had also etched a lasting impression with him. Standing in the back row, his eyes met Neha's as she followed the others to the exit of the auditorium. She stopped to allow him to catch up with her.

'You sing too well. Your voice touches the soul,' gasped Ramsingh, trying to recover from the trance that he had been transformed into.

'Thanks, at least you liked something in a middle class girl.' Neha smiled.

'No, Neha, you are different. You stand apart in a crowd,' said Ramsingh almost in utter spontaneity.

'One song. And I become different?' Neha could not suppress her laughter.

'The song has given a glimpse to the purity of your soul. The song has brought forward the hidden innocent human being inside you,' said Ramsingh, not heeding to her laughter.

As they bid each other goodbye for the night, Ramsingh realized that he had met someone, his heart had yearned for. He had met someone who had come straight out of his dreams. He had met someone who had a heart as pure as the silvery moonlight that filtered through the leaves of the banyan tree that stood in front of the hotel, in all its grandeur. As he inched back to his hotel room, Ramsingh realized that suddenly his heart had been throbbing a bit faster. He realized that his wait for the next morning would stretch to eternity, because sleep had somehow decided to desert him.

JCEA campus was never a very appropriate location for lovers to meet. Always a hub of activity, JCEA campus remained crowded till late evenings. However, Ramsingh and Neha managed to sneak into ignorant corners, to spend some quality time together. Their closeness grew with every meeting, and more than their respective courses, it was the lure of being together that drew them to the college even during days of vacation.

'Neha, do you still sing in functions?' The words flashed in the computer screen in depiction of Ramsingh's typical ways of innocent questioning.

'Yes, I do. It's my passion.'

'Why don't you come to Jaisalmer then? We have the annual function where people far and wide come to participate.'

'I will try but cannot promise.'

'It's my request. I cannot wait to hear your mesmerizing voice.'

'Oh.' Neha could manage only manage an expression as she blushed at the shower of praise.

Neha had kept the request of Ramsingh and also had fulfilled his expectation by captivating the audience through her soulful singing. Ramsingh could not hide his mirth as he introduced Neha as his special friend to his friends, relatives, and accomplices. Neha had become nothing less than a celebrity amongst the residents of Jaisalmer. Her performance had brought in a lot of offers from different organizers in Jaisalmer requesting her participation. But Neha was more intent in spending the little time she had in Jaisalmer with Ramsingh. Though most of the time, they were unable to meet each other in person, they managed to stay in tough through the chatting window of Yahoo. Sometimes they chatted through the night with Ramsingh hooked onto one of the computers in Ramnik Chedha's cyber café and Neha glued to the screen of the internet outlet of the hotel. These long hours of endless discussion had started taking some meaningful shape in their minds too. But it is a common phenomenon for people in love that it is most often that during the time of detachment do the lovers actually confess about their true feeling to each other. These two youngsters were no exception. The time had come for Neha to return to Mumbai. That night as they sat across their respective computer screens, suddenly words eluded them. Neither of them knew how to start or where to start from. After the exchange of the customary pleasantries of how are you, how the day has been, etc., both sat in utter silence unable to progress with the conversation.

'Neha, these three days were probably the best in my life,' Ramsingh finally mustered the courage to break the silence.

'That's great to hear, Ram,' replied Neha.

'Neha, I don't know how you will take it, but let me be honest with my feelings . . . I want to spend the rest of my life with you. Tell me, Neha, have you never, even in your wildest dreams, seen us as a real couple?'

There was a long silence which got Ramsingh extremely restless. Each passing second wrecked havoc with his emotions. He was unable to wait any longer. His reckless fingers kept on typing repeatedly in almost a mad resolute. 'Are you there?'

Finally, when the wait had almost turned Ramsingh insane, the computer at the other side started to respond.

'Ram, I would also like to spend my life with you. You are a wonderful person, undoubtedly. I have also dreamt of us being together, as a married couple. But, Ram, we do not get whatever we dream of, do we?'

'But where is the problem, Neha?'

'You know the problems, Ram. Our castes do not match. You only told me once, how aggressively orthodox your people are when it comes to inter caste marriage. Also, Ram, you are dependent on your family business. If you go against the will of your family, your source of sustenance maybe snatched. I never would like such a thing to happen.'

'Neha, I know that a lot of convincing has to be done. But we will do it, Neha. And as far as family business is concerned, I told you before that I am not interested in it. I want to go to Mumbai and look for a job. I am a qualified civil engineer, Neha, and I believe that I have the capability to get selected in top-notch EPC companies in India and abroad.'

'Look, Ram, this will give you a lot of pain. It is not easy to live happily after having upset everyone.'

'Neha, it is my life. And if my happiness upsets everyone because it goes against some irrational tradition, then why should I keep bothering of everyone's happiness? Look, Neha, we cannot make everyone in this world happy. But at least we can make ourselves happy. Let's try that.'

'Ram, you will suffer being away from your family and loved ones. They might not accept you for life.'

'Neha, I know that it will be difficult convincing my family. It might take long, maybe a lifetime. It might not happen too. But, Neha, I cannot sacrifice my happiness on the altar of some false set of reasoning. I am ready to share the rest of my life, in happiness, in woe with you and only you. Neha, are you there with me?'

'Ram, I fear the repercussions . . . but your words give me strength. I do not want to lose you. I am with you, now and forever.'

The interview room was almost like a medium-sized banquet hall. The size probably appeared larger due to being sparsely populated, with only four people occupying a capacity room of more than 200 people. Ramsingh glanced through the faces of the three other occupants. The one sitting right beside him was an aged gentleman in his late fifties who introduced himself as Sunil Nigam, a heavy-lift crane operator who had come to collect his transfer papers of his new destination. He had also told Ramsingh about the nagging worry that he had at the back of his mind. His daughter's wedding was near, and he had to make himself available for making the total arrangements and getting transferred at such a time would mean less holidays and lesser time for the family.

The one seated right behind looked to be a grim character. He looked busy with a sheaf of paper, which he kept on leafing through time to time. The third character was seated on the extreme left. Somehow, the guy looked a bit like a foreigner. He had an athletic physique, with hazel eyes and fair complexion. Before Ramsingh could interact with the other two, he was summoned to the room where the jury was seated to have the final round of questionings.

Ramsingh took his seat after sharing greetings with all seven members of the jury.

'Mr Rathod, we find in your curriculum vitae that you had been jobless after passing out from your college. May we ask why?' asked one of the senior members in the panel, unblinkingly.

'Sir, first of all I was never jobless.' Ramsingh was confidence personified. 'I had been supporting my father with our family business.'

'But your family business is not civil engineering, Mr Rathod.' The questioner was adamant.

'But it is good money, sir. Our turnover is approximately sixty crore rupees,' came Ramsingh's straight-face reply.

'You are talking about sixty crores turnover to a company whose turnover is 6000 crores, my son.' The gentleman sneeringly smiled.

'But I am also talking of a 65 per cent bottom line, sir,' Ramsingh's reply somehow stunned the members into silence.

'You mean you have worked in a 65 per cent margin?' questioned another member who looked more like a character from a comic book.

'Yes, sir. We know how to create value addition.' Ramsingh smiled.

'Then why are you willing to leave the family business and venture into something difficult?' questioned the only lady in the panel.

'Because', Ramsingh paused to move his eyes across the face of each member of the panel, 'I want to create history in civil engineering.'

'What kind of history, Mr Rathod. Can you elaborate?' This time it was J. Nandi, vice president (Roads).

'PQC, Sir, PQC,' replied Ramsingh, straight-faced.

'What do you know of PQC, Mr Rathod?' asked another relatively younger member.

'Everything, sir. From GSB laying to WMM, to DLC, to the survey of the final layer and the quality of slump, the temperature of concrete. The speed of paver. The cutting techniques and the final texturing of the road. Should I spell out the IRC codes or the MOST guidelines?' Ramsingh ended as the panel once again fell silent.

'Mr Rathod, you have mentioned that your favourite past time is sleeping.' One of the members smiled. 'But I am afraid in this company sleep will be a sparse commodity.'

'Sir, if you read correctly, sleep is my past-time activity, not my prime time activity,' replied Ramsingh, triggering off an orchestrated laughter from the panel.

'Lastly, Mr Rathod, can you briefly summate the system of PQC?' Mr Nandi enquired.

'PQC succeeds DLC, which generally is a levelling course. PQC is generally done with the help of a slip form paver. The batching plant provides concrete to the tippers with very less slump. The slump is kept less to avoid segregation. When the concrete is dumped in front of the paver, the temperature of the concrete should be less than fifteen degree calcium, and that's why the batching pant should be supplicated with a chilling plant. The auger of the paver ensures uniform feed to the paver screed, and the vibrating box ensures proper vibration of the concrete to the particular level. The mason platform allows the mason to provide the particular surface finish to the concrete, and the texturing and curing machine which follows the paver gives the final touches to the texturing of the final surface of the road. Then cutting of the green concrete is done after approximately four hours to ensure smooth cut and smooth insertion of the filler material,' Ramsingh ended in a flourish.

The room fell silent once again. They had realized long ago that they had found the appropriate person to help them complete their first super expressway project in time.

'Thank you Mr Rathod,' was all Mr Nandi could manage as he extended his hand as did the rest of the members.

As Ramsingh was leaving the room, the grim-faced guy made his way inside. Ramsingh returned to the mini banquet hall to find only the foreigner sitting in one corner. Ramsingh approached the curious character cautiously.

'Hi, I am Ramsingh Rathod,' Ramsingh extended his hand to the stranger.

'I am Armaan Bailey,' replied the stranger standing up. 'Nice to meet you, sir.'

Before they could exchange further pleasantries, the grim-faced guy re-entered the room. Both of them turned to him in unison.

Gingerly, the character in white shirt and bark trousers approached them. 'Hi I am Kumar Sinha. Welcome to PECL. Both of you stand selected.'

On the way to the company guest house, the trio got to know each other a little bit more. Ramsingh was in fact extremely livid. His first objective in life had been accomplished. This small success had partly taken away the rancid thoughts that were playing around in his minds. For the time being he chose to forget how his father had vehemently reacted to his proposition of getting married to Neha. How his father and his other paternal relatives had issued threats of inflicting serious injuries to the girl and her family. He also chose to forget how his father had proclaimed publicly that he did not mind snapping all ties with Ramsingh if he chooses to go against the tradition of the Rathods. As they drove through the historic causeway of the marine drive, he realized that he had taken the first baby step towards independence. To the dismay of the driver and his other two co-passengers, he pulled down the window glass to be able to deeply inhale the air of liberty.

Armaan had been selected to be a part of the corporate cricket team of PECL and would be representing the side in all upcoming cricket tournaments. Kumar Sinha looked quite impressed with Bailey. He showed a lot of interest in the titbits of cricket that Bailey shared with them. Ramsingh also took keen interest in the discussion and butted in sometimes with comical questions regarding the game.

'Why do we have three stumps for wicket?' Ramsingh asked suddenly.

'Well, err . . . That is the rule,' replied a bemused Bailey.

'Maybe, for better assessment of LBW,' Kumar chirped in.

'Then in ladies cricket there should be only two stumps,' replied Ramsingh sending the other two into splits.

'Well, Mr Ram, you seem to have a good sense of humour. Do you know any good joke, without cricket of course?' Bailey smiled.

'Ah well, plenty. But let me ask you a question first,' said Ramsingh smiling mischievously.

'What?' Bailey was almost taken off guard.

'How would you tell your girlfriend that you want to go to the toilet on first date?' asked Ram.

'Will be back soon,' replied Bailey and Kumar after looking at each other.

'A better way would be, Dear, I've to go to shake hands with my close friend with whom I'm going to introduce you later,' said Ramsingh, and all the three laughed out loud.

'One of my friends once told me', continued Ramsingh, 'that his eight-year-old son was so naughty that he had got their maid servant pregnant.'

'How's that possible?' exclaimed Kumar.

'Well, he had punctured all the condoms kept in my friend's cupboard,' replied Ramsingh throwing them both into another bout of laughter.

By this time they had reached the elegant company guest house. They were heartily welcome by Mr Mathur, the caretaker of the majestic bungalow. After freshening up in their allotted rooms, they again met in the hall, where the table was laid out with some light snacks and refreshments. Bailey took the opportunity to call home and inform his parents about the proceedings of the day. After that he made another call. This time to his grandfather, his dada, who seemed to be equally excited about Armaan's new assignment and promised him to meet him at his guesthouse the next day. Armaan always loved his dada's company, so needless to say that the youngster was overjoyed.

'Hey are you the son of Alia Behen?' Ramsingh had made his assumptions from the teletalk that Armaan had been having.

'Yes, sir,' replied Bailey.

'Hey, you are my little nephew. I am your Ram uncle dear. Remember, Jaisalmer?' Ramsingh exulted.

A tight embrace followed. A typical Rajput embrace, hard and strong.

The good news of Ramsingh getting selected had made Neha ecstatic. Her co-workers at Magenta took turns in congratulating her since everyone knew about her courtship. Tina was also very happy for Neha. She had always treated her like her younger sister, and why not, it was Neha who had been by her side during her tough times. Tina was quick to organize a dinner program at her place to commemorate this milestone in the life of her sister and friend, Neha. So Ramsingh, his nephew Armaan, and newly acquired friend Kumar Sinha were invited for dinner at the grand mansion of Dr Amit Ray to celebrate the occasion. And at the special request of Ramsingh and Armaan, Salman Ilahi also accorded his consent to join the celebration.

It was a very pleasant evening. Neha and Tina had decorated the place with limited resources to dazzling immaculacy. The professional touches, layered with the icing of a lot of emotion, could be perceived at the selection of colour, food, illumination, and music. Dr Amit Ray was himself present to welcome his guests. His easy and amicable nature was enough to make them feel at home. Dr Ray had heard quite a bit about both Armaan and Ramsingh, so it was not difficult for them to instantly find out topics for discussion.

Soon Tina and Neha too joined in the discussion, and light laughter and a sense of enjoyment filled the atmosphere. Dr Amit announced that since he had to catch a late-night flight, he would be taking their permission to leave early.

Dr Amit glanced at his watch, fully aware that the most distinguished guest of the evening would not disappoint him by turning up late. At that very moment, Salman Ilahi appeared at the doorway, a sight of a man clad in spotless white—a sight that fills the heart with reassurance.

Salman Ilahi too glanced at his watch while exchanging smiles with Dr Amit, for both the watches showed to the minute correctness, the time to be 8:00 PM to perfection. Salman Ilahi's punctuality remained unquestioned, unchallenged.

Agar Yakeen Nahi Aata To Aajmaye Mujhe,
Voh Tasavvur Hai To Fir, Aaina Dikhaye Mujhe,
Nacheez hoon par hawa ke rukh ka parwah rakhta hoon,
Kyuki muhabbat ne banaya hai karazdaar mujhe

(If you don't believe me, do test me; if you have any image of mine, do show me the mirror; I am not capable but I do keep track of the weather, since love and affection has made me indebted).

Everyone broke into a spontaneous applause as Armaan rushed to give his dada a tight embrace. He was followed by Ramsingh and Dr Amit. The only person who needed to be introduced to Salman Ilahi was Kumar Sinha. Neha had also had an earlier interaction with Ilahi when Tina had introduced Neha to him.

Salman Ilahi somehow came to like Kumar instantly though Kumar's perpetual grim expression was not a particularly likeable feature with everybody. At this outing, he felt himself as the odd man out. Here everyone somehow knew one another. Only he was a stranger to all.

Salman Ilahi could feel the uneasiness that Kumar possessed. A master of communication, Ilahi immediately indulged into some general discussion with Kumar. And what was more, due to Ilahi's presence, no one took part in the drinks session. Feeling the discomfiture of Kumar, Dr Amit decided to give him company for a peg or two. Ilahi had noticed the spark in Kumar, which makes him so different from the others. He doesn't speak much of himself, but in his concealment, there was enough revelation of his character and belief.

Dr Amit was the first to leave. As everyone escorted him to the driveway, where his driver waited for him in the new Peugeot, they took turns in asking him about various issues related to his profession, taking turns to shake hands with him before he disappeared inside the car behind the confines of the tinted glasses. The car soon throttled itself out of sight. They should watching the trail of the vanishing car for a while before returning to the table, elaborately arranged with the best of delicacies one can only think of. Salman Ilahi was overjoyed to find his favourite sweet dish, rice pudding, amongst the delicacies. Tina had taken special care to prepare it up to the liking of Ilahi. This has been one item that Ilahi had been having at their place whenever he had been invited.

The prime topic of discussion as they all indulged into filling and refilling their plates was obviously about Ramsingh and Neha. Ramsingh had promised Neha in full publicity that he would try to find a residence for both of them in Lonavala as early as he possibly could and then decide upon the time best when they could tie the knot. Everyone including Salman Ilahi stood in full support of the course of action decided upon by Ramsingh.

Before taking leave, Salman Ilahi announced that he had been invited by the institute for Fundamental Research to deliver a motivational lecture the next evening.

'If you all find the time, please come. It will make me feel good,' said Ilahi before taking leave.

Tina, Kumar, and Bailey decided to take a stroll outside leaving Ramsingh and Neha alone for some moments of privacy.

'Are you married, Kumar?' Tina asked all of a sudden.

'No, ma'am,' replied Kumar, almost wryly.

'Any girlfriend?' teased Tina.

Kumar smiled. He turned around to face Tina. 'When I was in college, I had some. But here, in PECL, it's difficult to find a girl, leave aside girlfriend,' he said sarcastically.

'Then why don't you change the job?' asked Tina.

'It's not only "a job", madam,' replied Kumar.

'Then what else is it?' questioned Tina.

'It's life.' The emphasis on the word proved that Kumar meant it.

'You mean . . . you never think beyond your job?' Tina enquired further.

'Yes, I do. I watch films, visit pubs, watch cricket on TV. I do it all. But somehow everything comes back to ground zero. The thought of getting projects completed within the stipulated period within the budgeted cost is a never ending passion. One who gets into it gets into a perpetual spiral.'

'Don't you ever feel that there is life beyond your profession and job responsibilities?' argued Tina.

'There surely is, and it should be. But, madam, in the pursuit of excellence, somehow, the outer world doesn't look of much interest anymore.' Kumar sighed.

This time it was Tina's turn to give Kumar a meaningful look. It was very difficult for Kumar to decipher what that look meant. Was it a sympathetic look? Was it a look of bewilderment? Whatever it was, it surely meant one thing. Young chap, you have only one life (without counting the reincarnation thing). Enjoy your life . . . don't watch it waft away in front of your eyes. Live it now . . . here.

In the guest house, Kumar kept tossing in his bed. Time and again, the words of Tina Ray came back to haunt him. Was he really wasting his existence? Was he really in pursuit of something incredible, unique? Or was he compromising his rights against his responsibilities?

When they reached the auditorium, it was almost filled to capacity. This was the final session underway. The first two sessions had been conducted by some corporate speakers, which did not attract much response. But this was the final session, where the most prolific speaker of the meet, Salman Ilahi, was assigned the task to draw the crowd. And even before he had spoken a single word, even the last seat had been taken.

'The pope asked Michelangelo: "Tell me the secret of your genius. How have you created the statue of David, the masterpiece of all masterpieces?" Michelangelo's answer: "it's simple. I removed everything that is not David."'

He cleared his throat, looked around at the expectant faces, and continued in a more authoritative voice.

'Let's be honest. We don't know for sure what makes us successful. We can't pinpoint exactly what makes us happy. But we know with certainty what destroys success or happiness. This realization, as simple as it is, is fundamental:

negative knowledge, what not to do, is much potent than positive knowledge, what to do.

'Thinking more clearly and acting more shrewdly means adopting Michelangelo's method: Don't focus on David. Instead, focus on everything that is not David and chisel it away. In our case: eliminate all errors and better thinking will follow.

'Ladies and gentlemen, all that I say tonight finds significant application in professional life as well as personal life. It only depends on the individual how he chooses to apply these principles.

'The Greeks, Romans, and medieval thinkers had a term for this approach: *via negative*. Literally the negative path, the path of renunciation, of exclusion, of reduction. Theologians were the first to tread the *via negative*: We cannot say what God is; we can only say what God is not. Applied to the present day: we cannot say what brings us success. We can pin down only what obstructs or obliterates success. Eliminate the downside, the thinking errors, and the upside will take care of itself. This is all we need to know.'

'Some of it is already going above my head,' Ramsingh whispered.

'Mine too,' agreed Bailey.

But Kumar was still, listening and registering all the words that left the podium.

'As a professor and writer. I have fallen into a variety of traps,' continued Ilahi. 'Fortunately, I always managed to wriggle out from them. Nowadays when I lecture at seminars in front of doctors, CFOs, CEOs, investors, politicians, bureaucrats, or government officials, I sense a kinship. I feel that we are sitting in the same boat . . . After all, we are all trying to row through life without getting swallowed up by the maelstroms. Still, many people are uneasy with the *Via*

Negativa. It is counterintuitive. It is even countercultural, flying in the face of contemporary wisdom. But look around, and you'll find plenty of examples of *Via Negativa* at work. This is what the legendary investor Warren Buffet writes about himself and his partner Charlie Munger: "Charlie and I have not learned how to solve difficult business problems. What we have learned is to avoid them." Welcome to *Via Negativa*.'

'God, this is some sort of alternative thinking that Dada once told me about,' Bailey whispered to Ramsingh.

'But this is something I'm hearing the first time,' replied Ramsingh.

'Don't worry most of the people out here are hearing it the first time too,' said Kumar.

'Let me ask you some simple questions which I believe very few have asked themselves.' Ilahi smiled.

'What are thinking errors? What is irrationality? Why do we fall into these traps?' asked Ilahi almost breathlessly.

'Two theories of irrationality exist: a hot and a cold. The hot theory is as old as the Aravalli mountains. Here is Plato's analogy: A rider steers wildly galloping horses, the rider signifies reason and the galloping horses embody emotions. Reason tames feelings. If this fails, irrationality runs free. Another example: Feelings are like bubbling lava. Usually, reason can keep a lid on them, but every now and then, the lava of irrationality erupts. Hence, the name, hot irrationality. There is reason to fret about logic: It is error free. It's just that, sometimes, emotions overpower it.

This hot theory of irrationality boiled and bubbled for centuries. For John Calvin, the founder of a strict form of Protestantism in the 1500s, such feelings represented evil, and only on focusing on God could you repel them. People who underwent volcanic eruptions of emotion were of the devil. They were tortured and killed. According to Austrian psychoanalyst Sigmund Freud's theory, the rationalist ego and the moralistic superego control the impulsive id. But that theory holds less water in the real world. Forget about obligation and discipline. To believe that we can completely control our emotions through thinking is illusory . . . as illusory as trying to make your hair grow by willing it to.'

Someone in the crowd laughed. 'Must be a bald man,' chuckled Ilahi, bringing out laughter from many more.

'On the other hand, the cold theory of irrationality is still young,' he continued. 'After the second world war, many searched for explanations about the irrationality of the Nazis. Emotional outbursts were rare in Hitler's leadership ranks. Even his fiery speeches were nothing more than masterful performances. It was not molten eruptions but stone-cold calculation that resulted in the Nazi madness. The same can be said about Stalin or the Khmer Rouge.

In the 1960s, psychologists began to do away with Freud's claims and to examine our thinking, decisions, and actions scientifically. The result was a cold theory of irrationality that states: thinking is in itself not pure but prone to error. This affects everyone. Even highly intelligent people fall into the same cognitive traps. Likewise, errors are not randomly distributed. We systematically err in the same direction. That makes our mistakes predictable and thus fixable to a degree . . . but only to a degree, never completely. For a few decades, the origins of these errors remained in the dark. Everything else in our body is relatively reliable—heart, muscles, lungs, immune system. Why should our brains of all things experience lapse after lapse?

Thinking is a biological phenomenon. Evolution has shaped it just as it has the forms of animals or the colours of flowers. Suppose we could go back fifty thousand years, grab hold of an ancestor, and bring him back with us into the present. We send him to the hairdresser and put him in a Hugo Boss suit. Would he stand out on the street? *No.* Of course, he would have to learn some Hindi and English, how to drive and how to operate a cell phone, but we had to learn those things too. Biology has dispelled all doubts: physically, and that includes cognitively, we are hunters—gatherers in Hugo Boss or H&M or any other modern outfit.

What has changed markedly since ancient times is the environment in which we live. Back then, things were simple and stable. We lived in small groups of about fifty people. There was no significant technological or social progress. Only in the last 10,000 years did the world begin to transform dramatically, with the development of crops, livestock, villages, cities, global trade, and financial markets. Since industrialization, little is left of the environment for which our brain is optimized. If you spend fifteen minutes in a shopping complex, you will pass more people than our ancestors saw during their entire lifetimes. Whoever claims to know how the world will look in ten years is made into a laughing stock less than a year after such a pronouncement. In the past 10,000 years, we have created a world that we no longer understand. Everything is more sophisticated but also more complex and interdependent. The result is overwhelming material prosperity but also lifestyle diseases such as type 2 in diabetes, lung cancer, and depression to name a few and errors in thinking. If the complexity continues to rise, and it will, that much is certain, these errors will only increase and intensify.'

There was a hushed silence all around. Everyone wondered where the discussion was taking them to. But whatever was being said was indeed something to think about. Ilahi paced the podium, took a sip of water from the glass tumbler on the table before continuing.

'In our hunter-gatherer past, activity paid off more often than reflection did. Lightning fast reactions were vital and long ruminations were ruinous. If your hunter-gatherer buddies suddenly bolted, it made sense to follow suit regardless of whether a sabretooth tiger or a boar had startled them. If you failed to run away, and it turned out to be a tiger, the price of a first-degree error was death. On the other hand, if you had just fled from a boar, this lesser mistake would have only cost you a few calories. It paid to be wrong about the same things. Whoever was wired differently exited the gene pool after the first or second incidence.

'We are the descendants of those *Homines sapientes* who tend to scarper when the crowd does. But in the modern world, this intuitive behaviour is disadvantageous. Today's world rewards single-minded contemplation and independent action. Anyone who has fallen victim to stock market hype has witnessed that.

'Evolutionary psychology is still mostly a theory but a very convincing one. It explains the majority of flaws, though not all of them. Consider the following statement: "Every Hershey bar comes in brown wrapper. Thus, every candy bar in a brown wrapper must be a Hershey bar."

'Even intelligent people are susceptible to this flawed conclusion—so are native tribes that, for most part, remain untouched by civilization. Our ancestors were certainly not impervious to faulty logic. Some bugs in our thinking are hardwired and have nothing to do with 'mutation' of our environment.

'Why is that? Evolution does not optimize us completely. As long as we as we advance beyond our competitors, we can get away with error-laced behaviour. Consider the cuckoo.

For thousands of years, they have laid eggs in the nests of other birds, which then incubate and even feed the cuckoo chicks. This represents a behavioural error that evolution has not erased from the smaller birds; it is not deemed to be serious enough.

'Any questions?' Ilahi paused.

Someone from the rear had raised his hand.

'Yes, please.' Ilahi invited the questioner.

Before the questioner could start with his question, Ilahi requested him to introduce himself.

'I am Bibhuti Bhushan Das,' announced the candidate.

'Well, BBD,' exclaimed Ilahi.

'Only BB, sir, that's what people call me.' The gentleman smiled, clad in dark blue suit and a red tie.

'OK, Mr BB, what's your question?' asked Ilahi.

'Don't you think that today, we think more in short-term favour, which, sir, is hurting our future? Don't you think that our thoughts should be more based upon the future, which is becoming more uncertain, by the way we think of it?' asked BB.

'Mr Bhushan or BB, you are right. We have thought processes that are more or less based on our present circumstances. But how have these circumstances come about in the first place, has anyone questioned that?' said Ilahi in agreement to the argument.

'I have a small explanation to the same.' BB was not finished yet.

'In that case Mr BB, can you please share the stage with me?' invited Ilahi.

The spotlights were not focused on the new speaker. Dressed immaculately for the occasion, this gentleman carried with him an aura of sophistication. On reaching the stage, BB and Ilahi engaged themselves in a brief embrace before Ilahi passed on the microphone to him.

'A second parallel explanation of why our mistakes are so persistent took shape in the mid 1990s,' BB announced. 'Our brains are designed to reproduce rather than search for the truth. In other words, we use our thoughts primarily to persuade. Whoever convinces others secures power and thus access to resources. Such assets represent a major advantage for mating and for rearing offspring. That truth is, at best, a secondary focus is reflected in the book market too.' Looking at Salman Ilahi, BB made a comment that made Ilahi laugh out loud. 'As sir would vouchsafe, Novels sell much better than nonfiction titles, in spite of the latter's superior candour.'

BB thanked Ilahi before passing on the microphone to him. A shake of hand and another brief embrace followed before BB strolled gracefully across the audience to take his seat at the rear of the auditorium. A section of the audience who had understood the subject clapped in appreciation.

After thanking BB, for his brief and meaningful participation, Ilahi continued with his further explanation on though processes.

'Finally, a third explanation exists. Intuitive decisions, even if they lack logic, are better under certain circumstances. So-called heuristic research deals with this topic. For many decisions, we lack the necessary information, so we are forced to use mental shortcuts and rules of thumb.

'If you are drawn to different potential romantic partners, you must evaluate whom to marry. This is not a rational decision. If you rely solely on logic, you will remain single forever.' The statement drew guffaws of laughter from a section of the crowd.

'In short, we often decide intuitively and justify our choices later. Many decisions pertaining to career, life partner, investments take place subconsciously. A fraction of a second later, we construct a reason so that we feel we made a conscious choice. Alas, we do not behave like scientists, who are purely interested in objective facts. Instead, we think like lawyers, crafting the best possible justification for a predetermined conclusion.

'So forget about the "left and right brain" that semi-intelligent self-help books describe. Much more important is the difference between intuitive and rational thinking. Both have legitimate applications. The intuitive mind is swift, spontaneous, and energy saving. Rational thinking is slow, demanding, and energy-guzzling in form of blood sugar. Nobody has described this better than the great Daniel Kahneman in *Thinking, Fast and Slow*.'

A hand shot up immediately from the audience. 'Yes, gentleman,' Ilahi relented.

'Sir, I am Kumar Sinha. Do you, after knowing all these human disillusions, lead an error-free life?'

Ilahi smiled at the questioner. 'Since I started to collect cognitive errors, people often ask me how I manage to live an error-free life. The answer is I don't. In fact, I don't even try. Just like everybody else, I make snap decisions by consulting not my thoughts but my feelings. For the most part, I substitute the question, 'What do I think about this'? with 'How do I feel about this'? Quite frankly, anticipating and avoiding fallacies is a costly undertaking.

'To make things simple, I have set myself the following rules: in situations where the possible consequences are large, I try to be as reasonable and rational when choosing. I take out my list of errors and check them off one by one, just like a pilot does. I've created a handy checklist decision tree, and

I use it to examine important decisions with a fine-tooth comb. In situations where the consequences are small, I forget about rational optimization and let my intuition take over. Thinking is tiring. Therefore, if the potential harm is small, don't rack your brains; such errors won't do lasting damage. You'll live better like this. Nature doesn't seem to mind if our decisions are perfect or not as long as we can manoeuvre ourselves through life . . . and as long as we are ready to be rational when it comes to the crunch. And there's one other area where I let my intuition take the lead: when I am in my circle of competence. If you practice instruments, you learn the notes and tell your fingers how to play them. Over time, you know the keys or the strings inside out. You see a musical score, and your hands play the notes almost automatically. Warren Buffet reads balance sheets like professional musicians read scores. This is the circle of competence, the field he intuitively understands and masters. So find out where your circle of competence is. Get a clear grasp of it. Hint: it's smaller than you think. If you face a consequential decision outside that circle, apply the hard, slow, rational thinking. For everything else, give your intuition free rein.'

Ilahi looked around for the response. People were too engrossed to even applaud to this momentous lecture. To this revolutionary explanation of human thought processes.

Ilahi ended in his customary manner with one of his choicest verses of Mirza Ghalib:

Na tha kuchh to khudaa tha, kuchh naa hota to khudaa hota,

Dubayaa mujhko honay ne, na hota main toh kya hota?

Hua jab ghamm say yoon behiss to ghamm kya sarr kay katnay ka,

Na hota gar juda tann say to zanoo par dharaa hota,

Huye muddat key ghalib marr gaya par yaad aata hai,

Har ek baat par kahnaa key yun hota to kya hota . . .'

Life is a series of natural and spontaneous changes. Don't resist them; that only creates sorrow. Let reality be reality. Let things flow naturally forward in whatever way they like.

(Lao Tzu)

CHAPTER 12

The Realization

Rajni Sawant was being wheeled into the emergency room when she asked the doctors to ease the needles so that she could call her office. Dr Pradhan was extremely annoyed and said things could wait, but Rajni pleaded, 'Just a quick one, please, as there are clients who will come all the way. They need to be informed. Please, I am sorry . . .'

Rajni was the divisional manager, Client Relationships, at Oasis Consultancy Services. In her fifth month of pregnancy, Rajni was in no position to risk her baby, conceived with extraordinary difficulty using IVF technique. What was more, she was in the eighth year of her marriage and had been through several miscarriages, including a messed up IUI three years ago at the hands of another doctor. Rajni had a lot at stake. The conception itself was very tricky, and she had been warned by her doctor to be on bed rest for the first few weeks, as far as possible. But various reasons compounded, and she returned to work. Today, Rajni had stood up to put a file out into the transfer box when Mitali Sen, her colleague, noticed the blood stains and . . . Anyway, here she was at Mercy Hospital. 'Unexplained spotting during IVF pregnancies are cause for concern,' Dr Pradhan was telling her more firmly than was his usual tone.

Between yelling ward boys and rushing nurses, Rajni spoke to Senior VP Mallika Prasad, her boss, about the seriousness of the situation. Mallika almost shouted from the other side, 'You are crazy ! I was in similar situation during my pregnancy, and I didn't even report it to the doctor. You overreact and make your situation sound so big and serious all the time!' adding, 'Make sure you enter your medical leave on the system immediately.' Rajni said she was being hospitalized and would do it as soon as she was discharged. But by evening, she had received two reminded SMSs, followed by two emails as well. Mallika was both concerned and anxious for the organization.

Rajni's condition was known to the company. When she had conceived five months ago, she had discussed it with the HR and her boss. Thus, the company was fully briefed and aware of the IVF procedure she had been through—what it entailed, what precautions she needed to take, and how she could be supportive. Of course, it did not require any special care to be taken in most cases. But in Rajni's case, it was different. The company was aware of her miscarriages and the fact that her child was conceived through IVF. Nothing was hidden from the company. They also knew what a fine worker she was. Her ratings, promotions, and performance all reflected her ability and skill.

As for Rajni, she knew what the risks were, what the stresses were, what the expectations hinged on her, her own dreams and wish for a baby. But there was also a clear area of her brain, unadulterated by emotion or illogic, that she was not going to allow work to be compromised if she could avoid it. If anything, work was only going to make her happier and the baby, happiest, creating a great environment for her pregnancy to thrive.

Rajni's family, maternal and in-laws, were like the Oompa Loompas of Willy Wonka's chocolate factory. They stood by to do anything she or her baby needed, camping as they all did under one large roof. For they knew that their daughter was a DM at Oasis and her dreams were as much theirs. There was no undue social pressure on her.

Rajni was no mean worker. In the seven-odd years, she had been at Oasis, she had raised its business with private banks, sourcing most of its relationships and taking the profile of Oasis to an altogether new page. It was all this hard work that had earned her very high ratings and the DM ship.

When she conceived, Rajni was clear that she would take the work-out-of-home option from her fifth month, i.e., September, and when medically permissible, she would try and come into work as well. She had discussed her leave management with her boss and HR. The company went into discussion and returned saying that they were unable to give her the work-out-of-home option and instead suggested that she take medical leave. Rajni did not sweat too much over this. If something suited the company, she was always partnering that even if it came to her with a cost attached. And technically, everyone had agreed upon this, HR, her boss, and others connected. All approvals came in, and Rajni went on leave from 1 June as the doctor suggested that she stay rested in her third and fourth months. The baby was due in January; after which, she would commence her official maternity leave of six months. Most Oasis women availed of five months.

During the medical leave, in the third and fourth months, Rajni was working from home through webcam and conference calls and was in touch with her clients, continuously delivering on all her portfolios. So she was advising clients, selling software products, training online, taking care of all service-related requirements of clients and coordinating with the office to ensure timely delivery . . . everything just short of her physical presence at work. What was more, the clients dealt with her with the same ease as before. Rajni herself had realized how easy it was to continue to work if technology was integrated into one's work.

Two days later, when her own gynaecologist, Dr Kamini Goel, had seen her, Rajni was moved out of emergency. But Dr Goel said she was worried about the unexplained spotting and was unwilling to withdraw the 'bed rest' order. In short, after the prescribed bed rest of two months, the emergency caused in the fifth month made her doctor risk-averse.

Mallika did not take kindly to this and said stiffly over the phone, 'You need to have your options clear and take a call between your professional and personal priorities.'

In the interest of space, no mention is being made of what various near and dear ones said to her. But Rajni's mother, a lady of undue sweetness, would not even hear of it. Her jaw dropped as she said, 'Travel 26 km every day in this condition? Impossible.'

Mallika, however, asked Rajni to resume work. Now, Rajni was truly taken aback. Here was her whole family on tenterhooks, and there was Mallika behaving like this was the common cold. Why was Mallika being difficult? Rajni wrote to the business head, Bibhuti Bhushan, and sought his intervention. HR and Mallika had asked her to submit her hospital discharge summary so they could have it verified by their company doctors. This had hurt Rajni a lot.

This was a new age company with widely known women-friendly policies. And she had been a DM with eight years employment. 'This is embarrassing,' she told BB. 'If this is my state, what about the lesser girls in the company? Your secretaries, clerical teams, the doers who hold the grassroots together? Don't assume they are not watching all this. Are you sending out the right image of the company?'

BB had enough to deal with. He understood Rajni's argument and did not understand why Mallika was agitated. But he had no time for the next three weeks to even call anyone, let alone meet. BB barely went home on some days. That was how much work lay on his plate. But Rajni's words did bother him. 'Leave this to me,' he told Rajni. And he conveyed his concurrence and support to her medical leave to HR and Mallika.

In September quarter, Rajni topped the zonal performance in her region, despite having been on medical leave. If this should have spoken volumes, it did not, sadly. For when the quarter-end appraisals were out, she was admonished for 'not delivering on new business'! New business during medical leave? Something was fundamentally wrong.

But Mallika was tough. 'You have to be meeting new prospects, building business. You have not travelled at all. What do you want me to say?'

Rajni realized something was not right. This was an insane comment, but she continued to advise clients and clock revenues. As someone would say later, 'When you bend backwards and put your all at risk for work, it is not valued. You worked during leave and queered your pitch. You must remember this is a dog-eat-dog world!'

Rajni went into labour prematurely in December. Of course, she had come to work in October and November, putting her whole family into a grip of anxiety. A C-section had to be performed as the baby went into trauma. Her brother came in time to warn everyone at home to not to tell her 'I told you so'. 'Don't blame her, don't scold her, she is getting enough of that at work.'

Yet within two weeks of this, the company informed her that her yearend rating had been downgraded to BA, below average, and she was repeatedly questioned by junior officers in HR and Mallika's department if she was planning to continue working, was she quitting, would she join back exactly when her maternity leave finished . . .

Rajni was very depressed with the company, with their bedside manners, and with their insensitivity after all the poster talk of being a gender sensitive organization. So much for their MNC status, their MBAs and their superficial sophistication. How can it be that a senior management made up of educated men and women think that once the baby is 'out', the woman is back to normal? Or did they not know that a body that carries a baby and delivers it undergoes trauma, blood loss, tears and ruptures, and needs to heal first? Can they really be so ill-informed, or are they maniacally performance conscious?

Her brother Vivek's viewpoint was that Indians are good with textbook knowledge but not general knowledge. 'Which is why the average male asks, where are my socks?' he said.

Rajni knew he was attempting humour, but she was not amused.

Then, something unusual happened. The company kept sending her messages and e-mails asking her if she was planning to return, and Rajni confirmed each time, 'Yes, I will be at my desk on eighteenth of May.'

Mallika confirmed to her that her portfolio of clients would be handed back to her once she returned, and that in the interim, it would be managed by the investment team, and no relationship manager would be deployed from elsewhere.

Rajni was more confounded now. On a day-to-day basis, she had never seen this side of the company. But now, in a crisis, she saw their total lack of elegance. Surprisingly, within a week of this, three clients informed her that they had been introduced to a new Client Relationship Manager (CRM). When the clients expressed their preference to stay with Rajni as they were even now on conference, Mallika had told them this: 'I am not sure if Rajni is coming back. And even if she does, she is not likely to be in a position to deliver her duties as she does not have any family support.'

Arvind Ramalingam, one of her clients, a CFO with a large pharmaceutical house, called Rajni and shared this. Rajni was more confused now. Where was the need to make personal talk with clients? Why did Mallika talk like this? This only deepened her doubts about intelligence and elegance. Do we hire intelligent people or clever people? The bad taste had turned bitter.

BB returned from his trip to US of A to find the office in a total disarray. After a quick briefing from his secretary, he realized that something had rationally gone wrong with the functioning since people, especially the lady employees, looked demotivated and demoralized. He needed to repair the damage quickly.

The whole episode of gross mismanagement of the criticality of Rajni's condition had escalated into a mass feeling of disregard and disgruntlement. A pensive feeling had replaced the otherwise energetic atmosphere.

BB was quick with his thinking and priorities. Leaving all other work for a later date, he immediately dropped at Rajni's place, with gifts, fruit, and some pleasantries for the newborn.

The silence and the forced formalities were proof enough of the disappointment and the dejection that the recent turn of events had filled her mind with.

'Okay, Rajni, listen', said BB, breaking the uncanny silence, 'I am a vice president too. I rub shoulders with many men, at work, at the club, at seminars, my clients . . . Let me gauge what is going on here. No male management has ever sat down and thought about all this. They do not do that, not in India. Yes, smaller organizations in the services sector in the service sector, like ad agencies or consultancies, think and cogitate a lot about these things, and they do, in fact, have a clear understanding of all this. It does find its way into their policies.' He paused to see if she was listening. Satisfied, he continued, 'But large organizations, especially MNCs, depend entirely on the parent company to give them a process, which they will adopt. They will very rarely evolve a system by themselves. Now, cultural differences have to find their way into policy, and this is where we come a cropper because of our white skin fixation.' He paused again as Rajni's mother brought in some sweets and coffee.

'As for men, if they have not watched their sisters' deal with crisis, they do not know what crisis is,' he continued. 'Whatever words they speak are from MDP programmes.'

After taking a deep sip to the coffee, he said, 'The women, hear me carefully, are breaking free from an old system . . . All you women. So deal with the ill-treatment, the abuse, the attacks, the assaults, everything . . . without feeling bad. Fight it, of course, you must, but be a soldier. Don't weep. Don't feel sorry for yourself. This is a battle you fight, a price you will pay, so that your progeny live a better world. For what is going on . . . is change, and change always agitates!' Then looking at the bundle in the crib, BB said, 'Welcome, ole chap, to the world, where you will have to learn good manners without seeing any!'

Next morning a huge report went up to the management. The board was forced to sit together to take stock of the effects that had arisen from the unforeseen turn of events that had occurred in the recent past. Rectification was required, that too urgently.

BB's report was hard-hitting. It demanded at paradigm shift in the management's mode of conduct. It read as follows:

Would you trust people who are dishonest, unfair, or are conspirers? Would you do business with an organization that nurtures values of ad-hocism and has feudal decision making processes that are not based on evidence but on lies to endorse its actions which are then covered up? Of course not. How dare I even suggest that you would condone such behaviour?

So if you would not, then you are unlikely to work for or engage with the Oasis Consultancy Services. It is likely that you would not approve of Oasis's conduct or that of Mallika and the HRD. Unfortunately, it is equally or more likely that you too will just look the other way if somebody like Rajni was discriminated in your organization. My worry is not about Oasis but most organizations in our country. If you look away, then you may use four rationalizations to decrease your guilt.

a) It's not my problem; HR must handle this.
b) If women want to be treated as equals, they have to learn that an organization's goals come before an individual's well-being.
c) This is a gender issue. We should hold workshops to sensitise the organization.
d) It does not happen in my company.

Let me confront these, beginning with the last one. Let us not kid ourselves. Organizations are not an oasis of equality (pun intended), they are a microcosm of the society. We live in a discriminating and excluding society. More women die to ensure that men have more power. More women remain out of schools, face malnourishment, have no access to healthcare without husbands' permission, get raped and abused by the men who are supposed to protect them, stay at home to ensure that men work. More women lose their right to property to ensure that men own property. Women MPs wait for decades for a reservation bill to become a law. So organizations normalize such discrimination. Rajni getting discriminated is an effect, not the cause.

Now to the third point. This is not a gender issue alone; it is an integrity issue. Each time someone like Rajni is discriminated against or forced to give in to the organizational might, it is dishonesty. Look at the number of lies the organization would have to overlook to get away like Oasis did. It would have to lie at every step of the process of discriminating against her.

The second point: It is not that there are some kind of women who fight for their equality or who want to be treated equal to men, and to qualify for it, they have to prove to men that they are worthy of such equality. All women and men have to be treated equally—in letter and spirit, by all organizations and society. If they do not, it would challenge the very basis on which society is formed . . . on the principle of interdependence and respect for each other's rights. Even if a single person's rights are violated, and in the case of gender inequality, the rights of half the human race is violated. The society loses its 'humanness' and pushes itself towards the realm of being uncivil and animalistic. The equality between men and women has to be substantive and tokenistic. A maternity leave that lowers your performance rating does not create for substantive equality. It is a step towards being animalistic. Oasis Consultancy Services has lost the right to be seen as humane.

The first rationalization is of denial. It is your problem too because if your organization conspires against your colleagues, it will soon conspire against you. I am not asking you to be paranoid, but do be intolerant when others are deprived or exploited. Be so because tomorrow it could be you.

Rajni, perhaps you kept quiet for seven years in the face of many such normalized conspiracies. The reason organizations get away with such behaviours is because the Rajnis and others remain silent and the Mallika's get co-opted.

Look out! Be intolerant! Speak up!

The management was shaken. Rajni was instantly inducted with a promotion, to take up the place of Mallika, who in turn was saved from being fired by a benevolent BB and was asked to report to him instead.

BB had instantly become a hero for the Oasis staff management, to Rajni and also Mallika. The staff was happy with the instant justice that was meted out, and the management was happy that the incident did not boil out of proportion and the order of the house was restored.

That evening BB got a call from Siddharth Gowda, an independent director to Oasis and leader of the opposition party in the Bidhana Soudha (State Parliament).

'Mr Bibhuti', the voice from the other and side was cleft and clear, 'I must congratulate you for handling such a sensitive case so adeptly.'

'Thank you,' BB responded smilingly.

'You know what', said the voice on the other side, 'you are suited more to be in a minister's role.'

'Really.' BB was not amused. These politicians think everyone to be amongst their tribe.

'Think about it seriously, Mr Bhushan, I can change your future,' Said the voice before disconnecting.

The situation at Oasis was changing fast. As the company kept growing with growing opportunities, the pressure to perform surpassed every other priority. It was merely a world of zombies; Pavlov would have been proud though. The money, respect, power, admiration, and adulation were, however, not pleasing BB enough. Somehow he felt that he had to get bigger and had to go beyond so that his profound ideas get utterance.

After days of self-conjecture and brainstorming, one late evening, as he sat in his office lost in his thoughts, the phone rang. He could recognise the voice in the other end. Siddharth Gowda. After exchanging some formal pleasantries, Gowda came directly to the point. 'Mr Bhushan, what have you thought?'

'Mr Gowda, I need to understand things. Can I meet you at your office tomorrow?' enquired BB.

'Welcome aboard, Mr Bhushan. Tomorrow at 10:00 AM,' the voice was ecstatic.

No human face is exactly the same in its lines on each side, no leaf perfect in its lobes, no branch in its symmetry. All admit irregularity as they imply change; and to banish imperfection is to destroy expression, to check exertion, to paralyze vitality. All things are literally better, lovelier, and more beloved for the imperfections which have been divinely appointed, that the law of human life may be Effort, and the law of human judgment, Mercy.

(John Ruskin)

CHAPTER 13

The Road to Eternity

'**R**oads are built by everybody,' said the task force leader in a humourless monotone. 'Even monkeys make roads. Even dogs do. A road is a prime necessity for movement. It is the very first requirement of society. Better infrastructure means better economy. But making a good road is nothing less than an art.' He paused to scout the faces of the people present in the room before continuing. 'We have been entrusted with a very significant patch of the super express highway, one of the first in India, by the Indian Government. The future of roads in India depends on the success of this project.' Once again he paused to look at the faces of the spectators before continuing with the overtly repetitive statement that every project manager or TFL invariably puts forward. 'We are working with very stringent budget and strained resources. For the success of the project we need maximum utilization of resource and effort.'

There was a long silence as the TFL read through the names and the origin of the candidates who stood in front of him. At long last, he raised his head from the printed sheaf and addressed the small congregation once more. 'I am B. K. Thakur, you can call me BKT. I am the TFL for this project. By the way, who is Mr Kumar Sinha?' he asked looking up.

Kumar raised his hand in mute obedience. 'Well, Mr Kumar, you have come with very strong recommendations from the VP. Hope you can live up to his expectations,' said the TFL, looking straight into his eyes.

'Surely, sir,' replied Kumar in a grim voice.

'Your records in Jamnagar were exemplary. Especially the turnaround you brought at FCCU. Some bloody theory you started implementing. What was it?'

'TOC, sir. Theory of constraints,' replied Kumar.

'Yes yes, here no such theory will work. Everything here is a bloody constraint,' said BKT in a dismissive manner.

'Vinod Kanojia, Ramesh Chadha, Kamal Dixit, Avinash Banoshe, Sharath Joshi, K. P. Rao, P. Solomon—all stalwarts of road projects,' exclaimed BKT. 'Rajeev Kumar, you have a very good team.' He turned to the project manager.

Rajiv Kumar, the stout gentleman in his midforties, smiled in utter contentment.

'And of course, Mr Ramsingh Rathod. You seem to know a lot about PQC.' BKT turned to Ramsingh.

'Yes, sir, I do.' Ramsingh was once again confidence personified.

'Good, from tomorrow, your training starts with the team from Wirtgen. You have thirty days to get trained, after that you are all by yourself. And I want results.' BKT's last words were more like a hidden warning.

'Neha, the schedule is very hectic these days. And there is only one Internet connection in the whole hostel.' Ramsingh typed the words as fast as he could.

'I am worried about you, Ram. Please take some rest from time to time,' pleaded Neha.

'Neha, after the training gets over, I will take a few days off and bring you here in Lonavala. It is wonderful place, Neha.'

'Ram, please take me with you after you have settled down . . . and after we are married. Take me with you forever.'

'Yes, Neha. I want to bring you here with me forever.'

'Hey, Rathod, can we switch off the light?' called out an irritated Solomon, who had had a particularly tiring day at the paver.

Poor Ramsingh had no option but to log off from the conversation unceremoniously and retreat to the warm terrains of the blanket of his bed.

'This paver is a very sophisticated one,' announced Josef Sneider, the team leader of the Wirtgen training squad. 'As you have seen in the last few days that there are a lot many things to be taken care of, before, during, and after paving. It is a synchronized effort of all the departments engaged in concrete production, survey, quality control and assurance, RMHS, intercarting, paving, curing, etc. And let me tell you, guys, this particular terrain is pretty tough to pave. All the best.'

The month long rigorous training program with the slip form paver had given the group the confidence to take up the challenge.

Lonavala-Khandala, the twin cities between Mumbai and Pune, are spectacularly located. Situated at an altitude that makes it considerably cooler in comparison to Mumbai or Pune, it has been attracting tourists from all over the world for ages. Lonavla, in particular, comes to life during the monsoon season as the countryside turns lush green with waterfalls and ponds. With so many waterfalls all around and the picturesque setting with the lush green valleys and the misty sky and the woody viaducts, Lonavala gets transformed into a tourist's paradise during the monsoons.

Both Pune and Mumbai are cities of prime economic significance to India. An expressway, where speed limits and go up to 160 km/hr, will same considerable amount of time for transportation either way. Though there was an existing highway between the two cities, but was ill planned, ill constructed, and thus unproductive. The express highway was not only a challenge for the companies and consultants engaged in construction but for the administration as well. The ministry at the centre as well as the state were looking at it as a tangible gimmick for the upcoming elections. The governing bodies for road construction viz. NHAI (National Highway Authority of India) and MSRDC (Maharashtra State Road Development Corporation) were also determined to prove a point that they too can get world-class roads laid in India, on difficult terrains.

PQC (Pavement Quality Concrete) itself is a cumbersome process. After a process of meticulous laying, spreading, grading, compacting of the subgrade with the finest quality earth, consecutive layers of GSB (Granular Sub-base) and WMM (Wet Mix Macadam) are laid and compacted as per the IRC guidelines. On top of the final layer of WMM, DLC (Dry Lean Concrete) is laid. DLC is a levelling course and the precursor to PQC.

PQC is laid by the monstrous slip form paver. This equipment has a lot of attachments and controls to be maintained to perfection to ensure the quality of the surface required for heavy traffic to ply unperturbed for the next fifty years.

The earthwork along with the retaining walls and the toe walls, the overpasses, underpasses, culverts, and the minor bridges had been progressing as per schedule. The management had not been losing much sleep over the progress of the concrete structures and the other auxiliary work. Even the tunnelling work by blasting the rocky mountainous outgrowths was progressing as per plans. The loose stones left behind after blasting had to be bound together by shotcreting. Even this perilous activity had been progressing to schedule. In short, all activities from earthwork to launching the girders for the elevated corridors were not the cause of worry for PECL and the ones connected with the expressway. It was PQC laying that had been the concern.

PQC was an activity of the night. Since the temperature and the air velocity generally are under control and within the limits, PQC or paving is carried out at night. So for the PQC team, it was night shift till the last stretch has not been paved.

The paving started from Rajmachi Chowk, a high point over the valley of Khandala. The arrangements had started from ten in the morning of shifting the paver, the TCM (Texturing and the Curing Machine), the dowel bars, the concrete cutting machine, the light masts, the excavators, the curing tankers, and all other associated items. The otherwise silent and secluded Rajmachi Chowk had become a hub of activities that afternoon.

There was another set of preparations going on at the batching plant site, where three automated batching plants, newly imported from Italy, called ORU (Officine Reunite Udine spa) were being set up along with the fleet of Tatra tippers, newly imported from Czechkoslovakia. The bugle was sounded for a war of a different kind—a war of man against himself in an effort to prove his ability to triumph over his humanness.

Kumar, Ramsingh, Suraj, Vinod, Solomon, Ramesh, Dixit, and Rao made a formidable team indeed. The Wirtgen team had done enough to build a strong understanding between them. Each one contributed to the best of their ability with proper cooperation and understanding from the other team members. Kumar Sinha planned immaculately. Guided with his concepts of Theory of Constraint and

CCPM, he managed to keep good control on his resources and ensure decent output in terms of paved area. Ramsingh's and Dixit's knowledge of concrete and the various aspects of the mix design kept the quality under control; and Suraj, Vinod, Solomon ensured that the paver and all allied machinery work properly without any breakdown.

Ramsingh took time out from the robust schedule to hunt for a decent house in the vicinity. There were only a few houses that suited the budget of Ramsingh, and the suitable ones were located in remote localities. Ramsingh for looking for the dream house to house his dream. Meanwhile, the pressure for achieving more was increasing with each successful stretch of PQC. Rajeev Kumar and BKT were already being heralded as the heroes of the expressway in the legions of PECL. Rajmachi was completed in record time and the paver was now weaving its way across the serpentine terrains of Khandala. The paver moved on, keeping all the pundits and critics agog.

Ganesh Chaturthy had come upon Maharashtra. This a festival, eagerly awaited in this part of the country. The arrival of Ganesh Chaturthy also marks the end of monsoon in this part. A fortnight of festivities engulfed the whole of the state, bringing about an essence of undisrupted joy to every household.

Ramsingh had taken this opportunity to shift to his new home in Valvan, a picturesque locality in the heart of Lonavala. Flanked on each side by Valvan Dam and the famous Matarani temple. He took special care to articulate the interiors with choicest pieces of furniture and the best of available decors in and around the locality. He had planned for an elaborate house-warming ceremony for which he had specially printed decorated invitation cards to be distributed amongst friends and special guests.

Having made all the arrangements to limits of satisfaction, Ramsingh headed for Mumbai to reveal the news to his beloved that he had crossed the second major milestone in his life. On his insistence, Kumar Sinha finally agreed to accompany him to Mumbai.

Ramsingh had always garnered a special feeling for Kumar Sinha. He respected his assured presence, his professionalism, his dedication for work, and his never-say-die attitude. He admired Kumar's guts to accept challenges, his ability to convince even diehard cynics of the theories he professed and also his capability to lead men and horses in the field of war. Ramsingh also had a special affection for Kumar. He knew that Kumar was a few years younger to him and thus had a brotherly sort of affiliation towards him. On the other hand, Kumar had no such weaknesses. Kumar had never had any weakness for anyone special. Ramsingh Rathod was only a team member for him. Kumar only believed in a single pursuit—to win. For him, everything in life was a race to the victory podium. This professionalism was, however, never part of his personality in his younger days. In fact, he had grown up in a very boisterous atmosphere. Having street fights, playing football in the rain on grounds that had more puddles than grass, flying kites all afternoon on the terrace, going to trek on the unsafe terrains of Dalma Hills were some of the routine activities of Kumar and friends. But below the happy-go-lucky surfaces of Kumar Sinha resided the stubborn character who dreamt of becoming big someday. Money and power were not the attributes he goaded for . . . but greatness. Kumar believed that one day the world will remember him as a master of his trade, a connoisseur of his discipline.

They were in time to catch Dr Amit Ray at his residence, just about to leave for the hospital. He appreciated Ramsingh's choice after seeing the photograph of the house. At Rathod's insistence and several requests, he finally agreed to grace the occasion of house warming with his presence. Tina was obviously happy that things were turning in the right direction. And Neha—she was already transported to the seventh heaven of happiness.

Ramsingh took time to visit Neha's mother and brother, who had welcomed him with full cordiality. Her mother, particularly, was very happy for her daughter. But at the same time, she was equally pained to know that Ramsingh had renounced his family ties to strengthen this association. She requested Ramsingh to establish contact with his family and take their blessings before starting his family life. But Ramsingh knew that it all would come to no avail. His family would never accept his getting married outside the clan and would come up with all kinds of hindrances to stop him from doing so. Neha's mother, however, was an old woman. And she attached a lot of value to family attachments. But Ramsingh was not ready to relent. His apprehension about his family was also a stark reality. He was aware how hostile his tribe of Rajputs were. He was aware that his return to Rajasthan will surely result in an eruption of the state of fury his whole tribe has been harbouring. He didn't want to lose the little world of love, peace, and satisfaction he had created of his own by getting into loggerheads with his fellow Rajputs by getting into the communication mode with them. He was happy amongst friends, who were more receptive to him being him, rather than where he came from.

Marriage was the topic of the discussion as they all sat in Tina's drawing room. Neha, Ramsingh, and Tina were the more vocal participants whereas Kumar and Armaan were keener to being mute spectators. According to Ramsingh, marriage should not be stipulated by religion, caste, or any kind of discrepancy. Humans should come together as humans. Whereas Tina stressed on the fact that everybody should have a fundamental right to choose his or her life partner.

'Why don't you say something on this Kumar?' Suddenly Tina turned on to him.

Kumar looked flabbergasted. He had never encountered such topics after having left college. He could just shrug his shoulders as a gesture of ignorance towards the subject.

'Have you ever been in love before?' asked Tina teasingly.

'Not exactly,' Kumar stammered.

It was not common to see Kumar Sinha hesitate. He had never faltered before even the most challenging sessions of questionings from the top brass of any company. He had never been found in search of words while taking part in any discussion. But here, he had been pitted against people who are from different plains. Who asked questions that attacked the heart more than the mind? Here no theories work. No CCPM, TOC, Six Sigma, or Lean. Here, only the heart listens—only the heart answers.

'What do you mean by that? Can you elaborate a little?' Tina was persistent.

'I . . . err . . . once had a crush on someone in college. Just talked a few times that's all.' Kumar looked embarrassed.

'Well what did you talk about? What is the constraint in your being my friend, or should we become friends, Murphy might strike?' Ramsingh laughed.

'Well, she might be married by now,' Armaan said.

'Yes yes, why will she wait for a dolt, who will never propose to her?' joked Ramsingh.

'Where's she now? Are you in touch?' asked Neha almost sympathetically.

'Were you really in love with her?' It was Tina again.

'Well, she's dead,' answered Kumar in a dry voice, bringing the discussions to a screeching halt. The buzzing room suddenly appeared to have worn an attire of silent alarm.

Kumar stood still, looking out of the window, with his back towards the rest of the occupants of the room. Everybody looked at each other, unable to select a proper sentence to utter. Neha was almost into tears. She slowly walked up to him and, in an almost an inaudible voice, whispered, '*Bhaiyya*, sorry to have racked up old wounds. We didn't mean to hurt you.'

Kumar could hold himself no longer and burst into instantaneous laughter.

'I'm sorry, but I had to say something otherwise you people were killing me with your fusillade of questions.' Kumar laughed.

'It was a very cruel way to do that, Kumar,' said Tina in a very dejected voice.

'Please do not say such things, Bhaiyya. Death is something too sinister, and to lose someone whom you love is like death itself,' said Neha.

'I'm sorry. Didn't ever thought that it would have such enormous repercussions,' admitted Kumar apologetically. 'But I know that such things will never happen to good people.'

The housewarming ceremony was a grand affair. Ramsingh had specifically taken care of the individual tastes and expectations of the invitees, as is the ritual of the Rajputana style of hospitality.

The celebration and singing continued till late in the night. The house with its fabulous interiors, choice of colours, and the majestic setting had been appreciated by almost everyone. The house stood as a symbol of affection that bound the two souls together. It stood as an able replica of the happiness that honest hard work and unconditional love had brought about.

Like all good things, the days of celebration had also come to an end. The days of revelry had now given way to serious work at the project site. The management had tightened the schedules further so as to make up for the losses incurred during the rains and the Ganesh Chathurthy celebrations. Work had started in a war footing once more.

The Khandala elevated corridor was being merged with the Kune Viaduct. This was a major activity since the whole of the traffic of the national highway had to be diverted along another makeshift road. Safety was a major concern at this stage. With heavy girders being lifted overhead and mass concreting of the deck slabs being done by Boom Placers, it was extremely important to provide the traffic below safe passage, without getting hurt or humbled. The local population too cooperated with the workforce to ensure there were least hold ups and the work progressed properly towards completion. They had never seen a road being built in this colossal measure. Everyone waited for this road to be built—from politicians to architects, from motorists to tourists, from transporters to real estate owners, from policy makers to the owners of the thatched roof tea stall owners.

This was not merely seen as a road that would link the cities of Mumbai and Pune. It was looked upon as the road to eternity.

The paver moved on, throttled by the robust Duetz engine that relentlessly pumped energy to the monster to leave behind a concrete pavement, that for the next fifty years would allow motorists to zoom across at speeds that they had only been imagining of. The paver moved on, chugging with it the vibrator box, the Dowel bar inserter, the surface finisher, the TCM, spraying and texturing the surface to completion. The paver moved on, following the sensor string on either side of the machine that provided the machine with the level and direction. The paver moved on as the Tatras relentlessly kept pouring the low slump concrete on the polypropylene parchment to be spread in front of the augur by the bucket of an excavator. The paver moved on night after night, sleeplessly, creating new records in progress and quality.

Ramsingh was getting fidgety as the days passed. Now that he was living alone, he was being confronted with a world of difficulties. The dearth of time had rendered some of the essential chores like cleaning the house, washing clothes, cooking food, a much demanding ordeal. Time and again poor Ramsingh had to take refuge in the company guest house along with other bachelor inmates like Solomon and Kumar.

After hearing about the sorry state of affairs of Ramsingh, Neha was pained. Now that Ramsingh had found an able house and was also doing fine professionally, it was felt by all that a quick marriage, allowing the pair to live together can alleviate the misery of Ramsingh. Tina was quick to take up the discussion with Neha's family. Her pleasing nature and power of conviction was enough to sway Neha's mother to accord her consent. And Neha . . . well, she was waiting for this day. Her happiness knew no bounds. She was all too excited and impatient to graduate to Mrs Rathod.

Tina Ray's nature as a human being always surpassed her professional character. She knew that she would lose Neha as an employee at Magenta as soon as she got married. But she laid emphasis on the well-being of Ramsingh and Neha above all her professional aspirations. She was the one who had catalyzed this relationship into a bond of perpetual oneness.

So they assembled once again at the court at Bandra, for entering the signatures of the bride and groom in the marriage register to authorize themselves as husband and wife. Dr Amit Ray, Tina Ray, and the whole Magenta faculty stood witness from the side of the bride, whereas, Kumar Sinha, Solomon, Suraj, Vinod, as well as the whole paving team along with Bailey, Salman Ilahi stood witness for the groom. After the formalities got over, a small party was hurriedly organized in a nearby restaurant, so that the paving team may be released for their nocturnal escapades.

Before leaving for Mumbai, Kumar Sinha handed over the marriage gift to the newlyweds on behalf of the paving team. The reservation slip of one of the finest resorts in Goa, the most happening tourist destination in India. He also handed over the keys of his own car to Ramsingh. He knew that Ramsingh preferred to drive down to Goa rather than take any kind of public transport.

As the team from PECL led by the very able Kumar Sinha took leave from the couple and other well wishers around them to pave their way to glory, Ramsingh Rathod stood beaming at his newest and greatest acquisition, his beloved, into the folds of his checkered life.

Neha could not hide the feeling of pride that he had acquired for having fashioned a life of her own in association of Ramsingh, who had forsaken his tribe, his hometown, his family to win her love.

Armaan Bailey was thrilled to pieces. For him, it was like a hard fought victory against a home side, garnered through a complete team effort. This victory was for him a motivation to bring about an inspirational performance in the upcoming Corporate Cricket Challenge.

While Tina and Dr Amit Ray standing side by side reminisced the time when they had stood at this very office of registration. Though time had snatched away some gloss from the promise of togetherness, their hearts somehow believed that wounds, even severe, do heal with time.

And Salman Ilahi—he was happy too. Happiness and togetherness had always made him happy. But this happiness was special. The victory of love over senseless rituals had brought upon him a sense of triumph too. He looked up as if to search for Shehnaaz amongst the congregation of stars. Probably on a day when love had stamped an authority in the world of wrongs, he missed her more than ever before. The mood of the moment made him mumble a few lines of Ghalib, which depicted the aptness of his feelings.

Tere Waade par jeeye hum, to yeh jaan jhoot jaana,
Ke khushi se mar na jaate, agar eitbaar hota.
Ye na thi humaari quismat, ke wishaal-e-yaar hota,
Agar aur jeete rehte, yehi intezaar hota.

Mr and Mrs Rathod, on the other hand, readied themselves for the short and sweet sojourn to the shores of Goa—the beginning of the bigger voyage of life together.

Last night I wept. I wept because the process by which I have become woman was painful. I wept because I was no longer a child with a child's blind faith. I wept because my eyes were opened to reality . . . I wept because I could not believe anymore and I love to believe.

(Anaïs Nin, *Henry and June: From 'A Journal of Love'— the Unexpurgated Diary of Anaïs Nin*)

CHAPTER 14

Fashions of Life

In that far-off land of kaleidoscope imagery, there were candy-coated flora and fauna, appliquéd Ferris wheels and carousels, techno-indulged Indian street art, sequined animae. As you delve deeper into this whimsical wonderland, things get more and more curious. 'Oh my god, this embellishment is done with gold latex!' 'The detailing is not from fabric, it is acrylic!' This is a pilgrimage to the world where nothing would be what it is because everything would be what it isn't. And contrary wise, what is, it wouldn't be. And what it wouldn't be, it would.

Welcome to the exuberantly imaginative world of Magenta, where dreams are given colour and fabric. Where passion is writ large on the caricatured figures in the large drawing boards. One is drawn in like Alice in Wonderland, awestruck, childlike in curiosity and euphoric in each discovery.

The finest of Indian Luxury dressings are born out of the imagination of the specialists here. The ascetics in the organized precision of the craftsmanship and the understated sophistication of the fabric evoke a Zen-like serenity and calm.

The contrasting natures of the designers' self-expression connect with the dichotomy of human nature. And there lie the two sides of emotion in design: self expression of a designer and connection with an audience. In the modern culture of self-actualization, everyone from professional coaches to spiritual gurus and pop psychologists insistently pose one question, 'Who are you?' and almost always answer, 'Who you are in mix of beliefs, philosophies, ideas, and experiences that shape the way you perceive the world.'

What are you passionate about? What moves you? What does beauty mean to you? What incidents have shaped you? Your story—how only you see and feel the world—is your unique identity. How you express it is your message.

This idea is not limited to the scope of the design industry as is evinced by Chiara Ferronato, a globally recognised leader in talent strategy and a pioneer in building the business case for brand humanization. Chiara's contribution in helping Tina build up Magenta has been formidable. Her assured presence by the side of Tina, when in need, had provided her the necessary confidence to move in the right direction in a difficult industry.

Tina too had shaped the business in an alternate mode. Her approach to design had been more individualistic in nature. In a contribution to the Vogue magazine, she had once declared, 'I want to know you for the real you. I want to celebrate your personality . . . every nook and cranny. Real success has always been about knowing ourselves and staying true to that core. No one is perfect, and no one is expected to be perfect. Authentic people are exciting, original, and refreshing. The essential element of an exciting, vibrant workplace culture that leads to knockout performance.' Perhaps that explains why the iPhone is a culture, Apple, a religion.

According to Tina, there are three levels at play in design and how people process it—visceral, behavioural, and reflective. The first refers to the look of the product, the aesthetics; the second to functionality and use; and third, the message, how it makes one feel. Tina believed visceral people are strongly biased towards appearance, behavioural people towards function, and reflective people by brand name, by prestige, and by the value a product gives their self-image.

A product maybe good-looking, even excellently engineered. But a brand starts a conversation; it tells a story, reveals in its history, and connects with the 'now' of the audience.

Tina had realized that the market had shifted. Terms like 'experiential marketing,' 'user experience', and 'engagement' are new age buzz words. The audience is no longer a consumer with a need and interest. They have their own unique story to tell, with their own view of the world. What drives them, their aspirations, how they connect with a product comes from their own narrative of who they are, want to be, and want to be seen as.

Connection is a two-way street; it is empathetic. But how empathetic it is depends on whether the designer is content with the tribe that naturally veers towards them, or if the designer would like to reach out to those on the fringe in a language they understand without sacrificing their own story.

It had been tough for Tina, balancing the topsy-turvy professional life in an ever-demanding industry with an equally unrelenting pressure of domestic life. Though the latter was only a shadow now of what it had been a couple of years ago. Tina and Amit Ray chose to keep themselves busy in their respective professions in an attempt to keep away the memories of little Ayan. But it was not easy. Ayan's smiling face, tiny arms, gurgling laughter came back to haunt them time and again. They cried in solitude, without any solace from the busy and professional world around them.

Magenta was the sole source of sustenance for Tina. This was not only a workplace for her; it was something more than that, almost like a child to her. She had seen it grow; she had made it grow. The organization thrived on innovative thinking, and why not, each and every member of Magenta had an inspired mindset. They had all come together to bring about a revolution in fashion, which they had done quite often, stunning the industry stereotypes into silence. Tina led them from the front, creating apparels so unique, yet so acceptable that people were forced to sit up and take note. But Tina was a woman, competing against unscrupulous wolves and jackals who felt threatened by the ascent of this new wave of change. Change is always resisted by incompetent people who refuse to learn. And time and again, these unhealthy parasites of the industry tried to pose roadblocks in her path.

There were others too who showed false sympathy to woo Tina to their side. Their sole intention being, to get physically intimate with her. After all, Tina was a beautiful, intelligent, and elegant lady. And still there are morons in this country and elsewhere who feel it to be their birthright to lure any decent girl into the confines of their bedroom with promises of a promising future. Time and again the industry had rolled out ethics campaigns to stem these unrelenting misdoings against the female populace. How much more can you educate the society? In a country where a twenty-year-old hangs himself because his favourite superstar's film was not released in his town, how well educated is well educated?

It is the reality that hurts. There were but only a few who rendered out unbiased appreciation for genuine works of art. It was the hard way that Tina had realized that it is better not to trust anyone in this hypocrite, untrue, nefarious industry.

Tina is often reminded of the frightful night a couple of years ago. The phone call shook her out of slumber. It was her sister Daisy. Her voice was full of panic, fear, pain, and confusion. Tina took the first flight to Bangalore in the morning and rang the doorbell as they were having breakfast. There was relief and denial on Daisy's face. 'You didn't need to come! Everything is okay. Don't worry, I'm fine!'

This was not going to be easy.

The day after her wedding, Daisy had recognised the first of a series of lies. She was shocked but didn't want to worry her family. She would figure it out, she was sure that things would be okay. The violent rage, subtle denials, abuse, and manipulations were punctuated with just enough justification; and 'I'm sorry, I love you. It'll never happen again 'to keep her holding on'.

But soon his songs got less pretty. 'There's nothing you can do, you can't go back to your family ; you're stuck with me forever.'

He was a coward. He hung his head in shame and shook his head remorsefully for everything Tina had to say. A brother-in-law turned up to defend his cause, saying that Daisy had provoked him and asked for it. It was all her fault. Tina was quick to file a case of domestic violence just so that the next girl he married didn't hear. 'What can you do? Nothing!' Just for justice and to fix the balance in the world.

This incident had left Tina with anger and indignation at the idea that there are thousands of other homes mirroring this ugly truth. She had realized that no matter how strong, self-aware, and confident a girl is, a situation like this can leave her emotionally paralyzed. Tina wanted to bring out this wrath within her, in her work, leaving a strong message to the society to take note and enhance their consciousness. She wanted to tell women that, as part of their wedding vows, they must also vow to love, respect, and protect themselves, even if the other person doesn't. She wanted them to always remember the power within them. She realized that the best way to pass this message on to women was to whisper it in their ears through the clothes and jewellery they wore.

The typecasting of brides as shy and demure always disturbed Tina, and she wanted to present an alternate image. She visualized confident girls with strong strides. She wanted to see the power and confidence of a career and boardroom presence carried over in the bride.

Tina's first presentation on ethnic wear in Mumbai was a unique one. The theme of the show was empowerment of women. The show opened with a bride in a red *lehenga* and racer-black blouse, with a thin veil covering her face, walking up the head ramp and pulling a *kirpan*, for protection, out of her intricately carved necklace.

Tridents, ceremonial knives, warrior helmets, and spear heads were worked into the apparels and wedding-style jewellery as symbols of empowerment and strength. The message was for the families too: their daughters' trousseaus must contain strength, support, and knowledge and not just gold. It did not take time for these items to become iconic best sellers in Mumbai.

In the subsequent thanksgiving speech, Tina's emotional speech touched the audience to the core. It was a direct explanation of what she wanted to do . . . of who she is.

'Someone once called me a fashion activist, and though I hadn't heard the term before, I think it makes perfect sense. Fashion in conjunction with media can be a powerful way to convey a social message. There are a lot of gender stereotypes, but I believe positive empowering messages will stand out even more in contrast.' She looked around at the silent audience. Many of the eyes were moist, and many had a smile of appreciation. She continued.

'To me, clothes and jewellery are not about ornamentation. It is a liberating expression of one's personality. It speaks of who we are, how we think, our sensibility, and even our ideology. Making designs is not a business for me. It is an extension of me. It is where I place my thoughts and emotions. It is my language.'

The items were quickly put to sale, and they had brides buy these for their weddings, mothers for their daughters, and wonderful husbands for their wives. They say good things come out of difficult situations, and this was a gratifying example.

Tina rarely went to parties and get-togethers but was very fond of guests coming over. But she did not like people sympathizing with her for her plight. She in fact chose to invite people who knew less about her. And most of her invitations were related to business rather than mere recreation.

The cell phone had been ringing incessantly. Kumar had just returned to his quarters after an eventful session of paving, where they had beautifully paved the stretch between Pangorli and Tungarli, two adjoining villages, where the alignment took an elevation. With a sense of satisfaction lingering around, Kumar had made it a point to thank all the team members individually before retiring for the day. His countenance, however, did not betray his feelings, for he knew that there were bigger challenges ahead, and motivation was the key to keep his ever committed team focused on the job. The cell phone rang again.

'Hello, this is Kumar here,' he said picking up the miniscule device.

'Hello, Kumar, this is Tina Ray. Am I disturbing you?' enquired the voice from the other end.

'Absolutely not, madam, in fact it is a pleasure,' replied Kumar in his most pleasant tone.

'Kumar, I need a small help from you. Can you spare sometime?' requested Tina.

'Absolutely, please continue,' Replied Kumar.

'Well, I've heard that you are an expert with Theory of Constraints and other tools pertaining to business excellence. My business, although small, is also showing some growth. I need your advice to inculcate these business tools so that the growth may be sustained without additional pressure being exerted to the existing workforce. Can you help me in this?'

'First of all, madam, I am not an expert,' said Kumar modestly. 'I am just a believer in these sciences and I have also seen the results. And yes, I will do my best to help you with whatever I know. But I need to learn about your business a bit. Your clients, their demands, the present competition, payments, bottlenecks, your offerings, timelines, etc.'

'Well, for that you need to come over to Mumbai for a day. Can you?' asked Tina.

'Well . . . Thursday we have no paving,' Kumar said after studying his timetable. 'Can I come over on Friday?'

'You are most welcome, Kumar. Just let me know when you reach Dadar. I will pick you up,' offered Tina.

'Thank you, ma'am,' replied Kumar before hanging up.

'There can be a lot of process improvisations, madam,' said Kumar as he got himself seated opposite Tina in her overtly decorated and luxurious office, after having taken a round of all the sections of Magenta. 'I will need at least a fortnight to study the files, before making an offering.'

'I would also like to know your charges Kumar,' offered Tina.

'Charges?' Kumar was taken aback. 'I thought that I am only helping a friend.'

'There's no friendship in business, Kumar,' said Tina sternly. 'We are talking in strict business sense here.'

'Madam', Kumar smiled, 'first of all, I am not a businessman. Secondly I am already working for a company and am not entitled to take up any alternative profession. But yes, TOC is my passion, my hobby. My compensation would be the success of my theories in your profession.'

Tina paused to think. She was hesitant here. She was somehow getting restive at the thought of Kumar extending a favour for her business to develop. But Kumar was resolute. His reasoning against accepting a compensation was more than reasonable. Also, she liked this character. His face and total body language exuded confidence and intent. He looked like a powerhouse of positive energy. There was a certain assurance in his thought processes and idiosyncrasies. His opinions were honest and his speech definite. In this world of deceit and duplicity, Kumar was like a gush of fresh air. But the thing that bewildered Tina most is Kumar's grave personality. She wondered how a young person can live a life based on work, work, and only work, without any other form of recreation. At last she agreed to his proposition. Maybe this would give her an opportunity to unravel the enigma called Kumar Sinha.

Tina invited Kumar to have lunch at her place. Kumar had been there before. He somehow liked the place and did not hesitate to accept the invitation. Once they reached home, Kumar quickly brought out a big packet of chocolate from his Laptop bag and presented Tina with the same.

'There aren't any children in this house, Kumar,' snapped Tina almost spontaneously.

'Ma'am, chocolates are for everyone. There is no age demarcation for chocolates. My mother always used to say that when you visit someone, especially for lunch, take something with you. And I could find only chocolate to be appropriate,' replied Kumar.

Tina somehow liked the candid, almost innocent explanation that Kumar provided. Somehow, Tina liked Kumar's straightforwardness. It somehow reflected the honesty of his character. Tina could not refuse the gift though she had refused the same on countless occasions from different suitors.

Tina had prepared Bengali dishes for Kumar. Incidentally, the cook at Tina's place hailed from the outskirts of Kolkata. Kumar was visibly overjoyed. The food and the aroma, somehow, reminded him of home. It had been ages since he had tasted these delicacies. Fried brinjal, steamed rice, sukto (a mix of vegetables with mixes of spices), steamed hilsa in mustard sauce, alu posto (potato with poppy seed), mutton kosha, ending up with sweet curd and rossogollas. Tina took content at the contentment of Kumar. She somehow relished the fact that the food had brought about immense contentment in the countenance of Kumar. She somehow sympathized with him; for he worked hard, physically, and intellectually and, at the end of the day, was served with food that might not be of his liking. But she knew that Kumar had never complained. He had been too busy with assignments. Kumar also did not mix words in complementing Tina for the food.

'How did you find Magenta?' asked Tina as she reclined in the armchair opposite Kumar.

'Fabulous,' replied Kumar appreciatively.

'Just fabulous?' Tina smiled.

'Fabulous as a workplace,' replied Kumar.

After a pause, Kumar opened up a little. 'Ma'am, what I saw in Magenta makes me believe that you are more into ethnic design.'

Tina nodded in affirmation.

'But', continued Kumar, 'have you ever tried anything to do with saris?'

Sari, the traditional Indian wear for women, from time immemorial had undergone tremendous transformations. A lot of contemporary fashion technologists had been working on various aspects of the garment to give it a weave of style, suitable for different occasions.

Tina had also tried several versions of her own with the drapery. But ideas are not easy to come by. The stitched and the non-stitched versions of the sari had been severally been experimented with, but nothing new had come about.

Tina shook her head. 'No, sari is a different composition. It requires a different way of thinking,' she replied.

'Interesting', said Kumar.

'Do you have any idea?' asked Tina curiously.

'Not really, but can be taken up for study.' Kumar smiled.

'You love challenges, don't you?' asked Tina.

'Yes I do. What's life without challenges?' replied Kumar.

'Well then, marriage is also a challenge. Why don't you take it that way?' Tina smiled.

'Ma'am, I believe that marriage should be earned. It should happen and not made to happen.'

'Oh, I see,' exclaimed Tina. 'Are you waiting for love to happen?'

'Never given much thought to it, ma'am. For now, it is the love of machinery that supersedes all.' Kumar smiled.

Kumar departed soon after, promising to stay in touch with Tina over the development of the research work in TOC. Tina knew that they would be meeting again after a fortnight because Kumar looked to be a person who was true to his words, and Tina, somehow, was looking forward to that meeting.

Tina had a soft corner for St. Mary's Convent School at Bandra since she had been educated there. Time and again she took out time to visit the school to relive her childhood albeit for a few hours only. She had redesigned the school classrooms and the school uniform to extend some contribution for the development of the school.

Like other days, Tina had come with loads of gifts, soft toys, and pastries for the children. As she was about to enter the main building, Tina was unaware that she had dropped her purse somewhere while adjusting the load of cartons in her hand. As she proceeded up the stairs towards the faculty complex, she experienced a small pull from behind. As if someone was pulling her softly by the end of her salwar. Turning around, she found a little girl, probably in her fourth or fifth year of existence, standing with her purse in her hand. Tina was enamoured. Taking the purse from her, she handed her with one of the soft toys she had in the carton.

'Thank you, what's your name?' asked Tina smilingly.

Though the little angel did not bother to answer, her twinkling eyes were enough to underline her expression. They stood there for a moment looking at each other. Time had stopped for a moment as if in a picture frame. The small girl and Tina momentarily had lost themselves into an expressionless affection. Love doesn't heed to any reasoning, any appropriation . . . love just happens.

Tina's trance was broken by the voice of Mother Superior. She had seen Tina coming and had come all the way from her office to receive her. She had noticed the rendezvous between Tina and the little girl. So advancing, Mother Superior introduced Tina to her. 'Tina, meet Ria, our new angel,' she said patting the cheek of the little girl. 'She is a darling, isn't she?' Mother smiled.

'Only if she could speak,' lamented Mother Superior.

'Can't she talk?' enquired Tina.

'She is deaf and dumb from birth, Tina.' Mother sighed.

An orphan who is deaf and dumb, having such expressive eyes, Tina couldn't take her eyes off Ria . . . she just couldn't.

Dr Amit was pleasantly surprised to hear Tina address him after almost a year. She called out for him from the doorway. Amit rushed out fearing it to be an emergency.

'What is it, Tina?' asked Amit as he met her at the doorway.

'Nothing, only checking whether you were there,' replied Tina.

After serving Amit a cup of coffee, Tina opened up the conversation.

'Tell me, Amit, can your medical science find a cure for someone who is deaf and dumb?' asked Tina.

'Well, depends. What is the age of the patient?' enquired Dr Amit.

'She is five years old and an orphan. Had met her at St. Mary's,' replied Tina.

'Well, some pre-examination would be necessary to understand the correct form of the disorder. She might also need a surgery,' explained Dr Amit.

'And parents too,' thought Tina as she strolled out of the room.

What you do makes a difference, and you have to decide what kind of difference you want to make.

(Jane Goodall)

CHAPTER 15

The Mandate

BB was courteously welcomed by the coteries of the decorated office of Siddhartha Gowda. At the first glance itself, it could be felt that the gentleman was well read and well travelled. The walls were full of quotations and excerpts from epoch making speeches from enigmatic leaders of the world. BB slowly ran his eyes over the excerpts, which were motivating enough for people in polity. As he waited for Gowda to arrive, he chose to spend his time reading those words of inspiration from leaders who transformed time.

The Gettyburg Speech by Abraham Lincoln:

Four score and seven years ago, our fathers brought forth upon this continent a new nation: conceived in liberty, and dedicated to the proposition that all men are created equal. Now we are engaged in a great civil war, testing whether that nation, or any nation so conceived and so dedicated, can long endure. We are met on a great battlefield of that war. It is rather for us the living, to be dedicated here to the great task remaining before us . . . that from these honoured dead we take increased devotion . . . that we here highly resolve that these dead shall not have died in vain, that this nation shall have a new birth of freedom, and that government, by the people, for the people shall not perish from the earth.

I Have A Dream by **Martin Luther King***:*

I have a dream that one day this nation will rise up and live out the true meaning of its creed : We hold these truths to be self-evident : that all men are created equal. I have a dream that one day on the red hills of Georgia the sons of former slaves and the sons of the former slave owners will be able to sit down together at the table of brotherhood. I have a dream that my four little children will one day live in a nation where they will not be judged by the colour of their skin but by the content of their character.

The Bombay Address by **Mahatma Gandhi**

You may take it from me that I am not going to strike a bargain with the Viceroy for the ministries and the like. I am not going to be satisfied with anything short of complete freedom. Here is a mantra, a short one, that I give you. You may imprint it on your hearts and let every breath of yours give expression to it. The mantra is: 'Do or Die.' We shall either free India or die in the attempt; we shall not live to see the perpetuation of our slavery . . . Freedom is not for the coward or for the faint hearted.

The Midnight Speech by **Jawaharlal Nehru**

Long years ago, we made a tryst with destiny, and now comes the time when we shall redeem our pledge, not wholly or in full measure, but very substantially. At the stroke of midnight hour, when the world sleeps, India will awake to her life and freedom.

The Chicago Address by Swami Vivekananda

I am proud to belong to a religion which has taught the world both tolerance and universal acceptance. We believe not only in universal toleration, but we accept all religions as true. I am proud to belong to a nation which has sheltered the persecuted and refugees of all religions and all nations of the earth. I will quote to you, brethren, a few lines from a hymn which I remember to have repeated from my earliest boyhood: 'As the different streams having their sources in different places all mingle their water in the sea. So, O Lord, the different paths which men take through different tendencies, various though they appear, crooked or straight, all lead to Thee.

The Inauguration Speech by Winston Churchill

You ask, what is our policy? I can say: it is to wage war, by sea, land and air, with all our might and with all the strength that God can give us; to wage war against a monstrous tyranny, never surpassed in the dark, lamentable catalogue of human crime. That is our policy. You ask, what is our aim? I can answer in one word: It is victory, victory at all costs, victory in spite of all terror, victory however, however long and hard the road may be; for without victory there is no survival.

The Audacity of Hope by Barack Obama

I'm talking about something substantial. It's the hope in the face of difficulty, hope in the face of uncertainty, the audacity of hope: In the end, that is God's greatest gift to us, the bedrock of this nation, a belief in things not seen, a belief that there are better days ahead.

'Good morning, Mr Bhushan.' The voice almost startled BB. He was so lost in the inspiring words that he hadn't noticed the quiet entry of Mr Gowda, not only to the room but to his life as well.

Siddharth Gowda, unlike most of the political figures in India, was not clad in the customary white clothing. In fact, he looked more like a professor in his dark blue suit with a light blue tie. His warm smile and the strong handshake somehow personified the confidence he carried with him. As they sat across in discussion, a feeling of admiration started developing in each for the other. Gowda was an accomplished gentleman. Having done his masters in economics, he had for quite some time, worked as a lecturer in various universities. His knack for participation in social activities, for the welfare of the poor and the needy, drew him into politics at a relatively young age.

They were discussing about the industry in general, as a bearer arrived with tea, which he poured out of the tea pot for Gowda and BB.

'Well, Mr Bhushan, it's unfortunate that we have to depend upon branded tea makers for our morning delicacy, yet we don't get the flavour that you are so accustomed to have at Dooars.' Gowda smiled.

'Absolutely, sir. The tea at the plantations is unique. The tea that we drink there is stronger, having an aroma that can fill this room for hours,' replied BB. The talk of tea almost made him nostalgic. He could see some fleeting images from his childhood which had always been lingering in his mind and which, at times, made him long for home—home at the plantations in Vannabari . . . his home.

'Well, Mr Bhushan, what have you thought?' said Gowda in a businesslike tone.

BB was pleasantly surprised at the question. What was there to think about?

'Well, Mr Bhushan, we have spoken about this before, but still I would once again like to repeat it,' said Gowda.

'Our party is not a conservative party. It works more as a social organization rather than a political outfit,' continued Gowda. 'We work towards re-establishing the social equilibrium, which is the only way to usher in progress for the nation.'

There was a short pause. Gowda probably was expecting some response from BB. However, BB was more intent on listening. Perhaps, Gowda was also trying to read through the thoughts of BB since he chose to continue with his explanation.

'Power is necessary to implement your ideas. Mr Bhushan, you don't need to be reminded for there have been times when circumstances might have taught you that a little power in your hand might have shifted the situation in your favour,' he said, almost in a hushed tone. The smile had been replaced by a stiffened jaw. Gowda looked serious to drill his thoughts in.

BB nodded in agreement.

'I know, Mr Bhushan, what you think of politics,' said Gowda unblinkingly. 'Once upon a time, I too had those similar thoughts. I too had those similar feelings of disgust and aversion towards politics and politicians. But just by blaming the politicians and the system, are we doing justice to our patriotic responsibility?'

'If people like us, Mr Bhushan, who do not find the mediums for the expression of our ideas. If we do not find a pedestal on which the foundations of our so-called implemented dreams can be established, then why go about crying foul with everything?'

'Mr Gowda, I understand and appreciate your feelings,' replied BB, still in a state of reluctance. 'But we as professionals are doing our bit for the nation. Then why won't the people whom we have selected to serve us do their bit?'

'They are incapable people, Mr Bhushan,' snapped Gowda. 'We need to replace them with people with scruples, understanding, compassion, and a feeling of responsibility.'

'But, Mr Gowda, politics is not for everybody. Politics requires certain degree of ruthlessness, which might not be a quality easy to acquire,' said BB.

'Look, Mr Bhushan, every trade has its own standards of propagation,' explained Gowda. In politics, in order to have the powers to do something good, you need to, at times, resort to some unscrupulous means as well. The ultimate aim is to have power so that you can realize the dreams that you have always been harbouring.'

'So what is your proposal, sir?' asked BB.

'I propose that you, Mr Bibhuti Bhushan, join our party as a candidate for the constituency of Whitefield,' announced Gowda.

BB could only laugh in dismay. 'Mr Gowda, thank you for your proposal. It is an extreme honour for me that a person of your stature has considered me capable. However, Mr Gowda, I have never thought of politics to be my cup of tea. You see, I am a technocrat. I belong to the domain of technology. What am I to do in politics? I am simply not made for it.'

'Mr Bhushan, I am not asking you to make an instant decision. Take your time but not too much. Remember that your decision concerns a lot more people than you actually think.'

They shook hands again as BB took his leave and headed for his office.

As he approached his car, Gowda's voice rang out, and it seemed almost like a prediction. 'Mr Bhushan, I know this is not our last meeting on this.'

However much he tried, he could not shake off the proposition of Gowda from his mind. There were several thoughts that had clogged up his thinking process. He took the road that led to the centennial park where he liked to spend his time quite often to decongestion his mind. He desperately needed some time alone to come to terms with these emotional upheavals.

✍

The news came to him pretty late. The muffled voice of the receptionist at Oasis informed him that his father had been hospitalized following a very severe cardiac arrest. BB couldn't remember when he had last run so fast to out of office to drive frantically to the airport. As he stood in the long queue at the security check, he wondered why his people back home did not bother to call him in his cell phone. After a quick change of flights at Dum Dum Airport in Calcutta, BB finally reached Bagdogra at 9:30 PM. He drove down to the hospital directly to find his hapless relatives and neighbours stranded in a paralytic animation. No one could clearly tell him what was going on inside the closed door of the Intensive Care Unit.

Finally, a doctor emerged from behind the door of the ICU. Everyone including BB rushed out to meet him at the doorway. The doctor informed them that they had already done angiography and had found three major blocks in the arteries. However, the hospital had little infrastructure and modern medical facility to be able to undertake angioplasty. They were even unsure whether to refer the patient for ballooning or open heart surgery.

BB looked around helplessly. He had the requisite money to have his father treated at the best of hospitals in the country. But it was time that mattered here, and one needed something extra to win this race against time. The doctors too were not adept. They looked to be too junior to be able to provide some viable solution. Only one of them could assure him that the night would pass without worry. But he had to do something desperate the next day; otherwise it would only be a miracle that could save his father. BB had the night to think or expect miracles to happen the next day.

It was exactly midnight when BB got a call from Bangalore. It was Mr Siddharth Gowda.

'Mr Bhushan, I know what kind of a situation you are. But don't worry, my friend and party vice president Ramesh Shetty will book his chartered flight for you for Mumbai in the morning. Fly straight down to Mumbai, don't risk Kolkata, since it is the time of Durga Puja. The ambulance and medical staff of Breach Candy Hospital will pick you up from the airport and come straight to the hospital. By then all preparations will have been made. Trust me, everything will be fine. Mr Shetty will contact you in the morning.' Gowda hung up, leaving BB in a state of daze and utter astonishment. Help had come from a least expected quarter.

After all, miracles do happen.

Mumbai did not disappoint BB. Mumbai has never disappointed people with money, and BB had plenty of them.

With every passing day, Subhash got better and better. Top-notch doctors had been bestowing him with their best of attention, and the excellent facilities in the hospital ensured his steady recovery. BB was relieved that his father could sit up and talk to him. Sometimes he talked about the tea gardens, sometimes about his friends at Vannabari, and at times urged BB to get married and start a family. BB spent most of his times beside his bedside, taking utmost care of even the smallest requirement that his father had.

BB had also befriended a few doctors in the hospital. Most of them were friendly and capable unlike the ones at the Government Hospital at Vannabari. BB was especially fond of the doctor who had been attending his father Dr Amit Ray. His amicable nature and profuse knowledge in his field enamoured BB. He was a great doctor, and on top of it, he was also the most fantastic human being. BB liked spending time with him, of course whenever he was free. Dr Amit had also taken an instant liking for BB. His vast knowledge on a panorama of subjects and open mindedness was indeed a trait for appreciation.

BB was surprised that Dr Amit, being a Bengali himself, chose to work during Durga Puja, a festival that all Bengalis looked forward to. He was amazed at his dedication. Perhaps having read his thoughts, Dr Amit chose to invite BB to his house on the occasion of Navami, the ninth day of Navaratri and the third and penultimate day of Durga Puja. Dr Amit took BB to Shivaji Park before taking him home. The huge gathering at the Pandal there reminded BB of his childhood at Vannabari where they had always celebrated the four days with a lot of pomp and excitement. The puja was different here. It was more of a social gathering than the actual puja celebration. People in bright clothes from all over Mumbai came here to catch up with old friends and relatives and spend some precious time reminiscing the time gone by.

Dr Amit's house was located in a posh locality, where people interact only when in need. The silence of the surroundings demarcated the feel of alienation amongst the bungalows that stood aghast to the ravages of time. There were a few people inside the house whom Dr Amit chose to ignore as he ushered in BB into the seating room. The house had been beautifully decorated, perhaps underlining the fact that Mrs Ray was a fashion designer.

'Namaste, I am Tina Ray,' a lady clad in a beautiful light green sari greeted BB smilingly.

'Namaste,' BB returned the greeting with a broad smile.

The other members inside the room also greeted BB with folded arms. There were six of them and all of more or less the same age group.

'They are all my colleagues at my boutique, Magenta,' introduced Tina as she handed BB with a glass of water and a plate of some baked delicacies.

Tina Ray possessed an air of elegance about her. The pleasant smile that perpetually kept playing on her lips had an added attraction. 'What a couple,' BB thought to himself. These probably are the matches that are made in heaven.

Dr Amit took BB around the house. It was indeed designed and constructed with utmost finesse. Meandering through the various rooms and the big hallway, Dr Amit took him upstairs, right up to the terrace. The terrace too was as beautiful as the interiors of the house. The terrace was beautifully encircled by tubs of flowering plants that were in full blossom. The freshness of the plants suggested that they were well looked after. There were seating arrangements made at the rooftop, and BB could imagine how the couple spent their romantic moments together.

'You are extremely lucky, Mr Bhushan,' said Dr Amit all of a sudden. 'You had arrived at the hospital at the right time.'

BB had heard this for the umpteenth time. But the words did not irritate him anymore. He knew that it was like a dream sequence, which had brought him to Mumbai. He had wondered several times what people without the connections and the money that he had would have done under these circumstances.

'But, Mr Bhushan, my heart goes out for the people who cannot afford such facilities. Why don't the politicians out there build a hospital that is good enough?' asked Dr Amit.

'Well, probably the time will come soon,' BB replied wryly.

Suddenly, the silence was broken by a loud cheer. The reason for the cheer was the entry of a young couple in the house. BB had to follow Dr Amit downstairs to welcome the new entrants. Tina introduced BB to a handsome gentle man and an equally elegant lady.

'I am Ramsingh Rathod, sir. Nice meeting you.' The gentleman in his midthirties smiled.

'I am Bibhuti Bhushan. You can call me BB,' replied BB with a smile.

'And I am Neha Rathod. Namaste,' said the petite lady with a heart-warming smile.

'Where is Kumar, Ram?' called out Tina from behind.

'Kumar is busy with his girlfriend.' Ramsingh laughed.

'Huh?' Tina looked confused.

'And the girlfriend is called Writgen Paver,' Ramsingh elaborated further.

After dinner, Dr Amit dropped BB at his company transit flat. As he entered, he was pleasantly surprised to find Siddharth Gowda at the drawing room. After giving BB a warm brotherly embrace, Gowda took a quick briefing about the health conditions of his father. BB was literally bowled over by this gentleman's humane gesture. He had seen very few powerful people having such humble feelings.

That night BB had trouble sleeping. Several thoughts once again kept coming back to haunt him. Was he not being selfish? Was he not taking advantage of people like Gowda? Was the adventurous instinct that he had garnered from the endeavours of the protagonist of his namesake Bibhuti Bhushan Bandhopadhyaya's, *Chander Pahar*, all irrelevant? What about the dream he had always nurtured about leading India into a golden future? Is his role of a mere employee with a multinational the only dream he was living for? He slowly repeated the words that he had once heard in IIT, 'flow with the times, or be influential enough to change the times.'

Gowda accompanied BB to the hospital, and on the way they had a brief discussion on certain policy matters of Oasis. BB was happy to find his father having a cheerful discussion with Dr Amit Ray. After introducing Gowda to his father and the doctor, BB chose to head for the cafeteria for some coffee and some serious discussion with Gowda.

As they entered the cafeteria, a thoughtful line caught their eye:

> 'If u still want to see hot girls after your death . . . donate your eyes!'

✂

The party manifesto was redone the umpteenth time. BB wanted things to be immaculate and realistic. Already a buzz was around the constituency about a newcomer challenging the might of the great Ajith Seshagiri, who had been the champion of the constituency for the last four elections. BB remained unfazed through appreciation and criticism. His campaigning had been less vociferous but hard-hitting. He had challenged every aspect of life that are run by age-old beliefs. Unequal education, the job market, poor healthcare facilities, the disparity of wealth, inefficient operation of government organizations, unreasonable police force, discrimination against caste and religion, dowry system, child marriage, dubious methods of business processes, uneconomical hoarding of money—every social evil was questioned at every forum. The nation demanded answers, and BB simply added fuel to ignite the intolerance of the countrymen. His speeches started finding more and more space in newspapers and magazines. Some of his speeches even got broadcast within news snippets in the television. BB was slowly and steadily becoming an icon of sorts with the young population of India. The ruling party, however, remained complacent. They had, in the past, seen several upstarts rise and fall by the wayside in countless occasions. The stalwarts remained. Indian politics is teeming with such stalwarts, who have ruled the nation to jeopardy, even at an age when biology had discarded them as incapable. BB had raised questions on the sanity of the electorate over their persistence with people who not only had failed to deliver but also had not made an attempt.

The rich rhetoric, the clarity of assurances, the honest acceptance of the limit of performance, the clear-throated opinions all reached out to the educated and the not so educated equally. People craved for change, and BB seemed to bring in the changes, even before the declaration of results.

Bangalore responded. His inanimate methods and thought processes soon became a subject of debate and arguments at coffee tables, restaurants, college campuses, company buses, canteens, bank porticos. BB had forced people to sit down and think about themselves, about their families, about the nation, and about their own dreams. The slogan 'I am you . . . You win if I do' spread like a conflagration. It was not a hype; it was belief. It was a collective effort to infuse new blood into the ageing, petrifying system.

Needless to say, the writing was on the wall. The invincible ruling party had to unceremoniously bite the dust as BB's party registered a landslide victory with a huge margin. BB was not the only reason for this victory but merely a part of it. Gowda had ensured that many of the unhappy ruling party members join their side for hefty sums, just before the elections. Also, the ruling party had lost its faith from the educated populace due to their inability to govern. The ruling party had also done the cardinal mistake of ignoring two major sections of the electorate: women and the educated. Whereas BB's party had targeted them from the very beginning. The debacle of the ruling party had intensified the political activities in New Delhi. The ruling party at the centre was quick to woo Gowda to join the ruling coalition. Gowda was quick to accept the proposition with a condition to indict at least two of his winning candidates within the cabinet or within the ministry of state. P. Jayaraj was given the portfolio of the minister of state for industry, and BB was given the ministry of state, home affairs.

Siddharth Gowda, the Alex Ferguson of his party, had once again done the trick. His party had slowly reached up to the ranks of the Ministry of State. But Gowda knew that a little more push sometimes later might ensure these two with cabinet berths. And he was going to do just that.

'Cheers to a new life, Mr Bhushan,' Gowda made a toast, raising his glass towards BB.

'Thank you for all your support,' replied BB. 'And cheers to better days ahead.'

Yes, BB thought, he needn't flow with the times anymore; in fact, he should concentrate on how to become influential enough to change the times . . . at the earliest.

The back roads of every Metropolis await. They, the Atlantis of our lands, await, a mutiny of thought . . . a Rodin . . . a revolution in colour, concept, shape, and character.

Cricket is not hard work. Drilling for eight hours a day two kilometres underground in a South African gold mine is hard work. Cricket is stressful. nerve-wracking, and mentally and physically exhausting: but it is always a pleasure.

(The late Bob Woolmer)

CHAPTER 16

Leaders

All young contenders for the national side had congregated in the historical field of Kolkata, Eden Gardens, to showcase their talent in front of the national selectors. It was a big event . . . much bigger than what had been perceived earlier. Keeping in mind the fact that cricket is a religion of India, the National Selectors were determined to select the best possible combination for the forthcoming world cup.

The players had been divided into three teams of almost equal strength: Red, Green, and Blue. The aspirants were of all type. There was the regulars, who had been part of the team for some time now and were almost fixed members of the squad. They had been inducted in these three teams to give the newcomers a taste of international cricket. The experienced, who were part of the team off and on and had good experience of playing first class cricket. The newcomers, who were unknown names in the first class arena . . . and the recommended ones, who had found a place in the side due to recommendations from the various lobbies in the cricketing circles. Thirty probables were to be selected for the conditioning camp at Bangalore. The players would be further screened to the final fourteen who would represent India in the world cup. The stakes were huge for the forty-eight aspirants in fray, and for some of them, it was the first instance when they were sharing the dressing room with some of the big names in Indian cricket.

Armaan was an unknown face here. Though his performance in the Ranji Trophy matches were not remarkable, his performance in the Corporate Cup had been phenomenal. And this year, a lot of reputed players had participated in the tournament where Armaan had lead the PECL team to be the champions. The cricketing community of Mumbai, one of the strongest in the nation, had taken note of it, which resulted in Armaan getting a call for the preliminary selection camp at the City of Joy.

Before coming to Kolkata, he had visited his parents at Jamshedpur. Surprisingly, the city had not changed much. The wide roads, the green avenues, the scenic beauty of Jubilee park with the Great Dalma Hills forming up the background—Jamshedpur still carried the picture-card effect. Armaan had always been in love with the city, especially during this time of the year, just before the winter had set in. It always made him proud to be a part of the city. With its virtues as well as the flaws, Jamshedpur always remained a city of unique portfolio. The city always managed to provide Armaan the motivation to excel in the cricketing field.

Each team was to play two matches against the others before the finals. The teams had been equally distributed with the experienced and the novices so that there would be no clear-cut favourite. This tournament also was a platform for the newcomers to perform, get noticed, and get groomed for the upcoming tournaments and test matches. It was a big opportunity, and Armaan considered himself fortunate to have an outside chance to break into the highest level of the cricket echelons in India.

The climate had become reasonably pleasant in Kolkata. The heat and the humidity had diminished substantially, to give way to a mild chill in the weather. It was fun practicing with the seniors, sometimes in the Eden and sometimes on the Mohammedan Sporting Club ground. BCCI had also provided him with a room in an affiliate hotel where cricketers from other teams were also hosted. Bailey was lucky to have a single room to himself; otherwise his reluctance to converse would have bored to death any room partner who would have opted to share rooms with him. But that was not to be; and that gave Bailey a world of freedom, to think, plan, and prepare.

In the first match, Green India defeated Red India quite comfortably. Though Armaan was in red, he had to warm the benches; there was only one slot for the newcomers and the coach had decided to go for an extra batsman rather than a bowler. Armaan had no option but to wait for his chance for he believed that the chance would surely come.

The Reds were beaten by the Greens quite comprehensively. They were outplayed by the Greens in every department of the game. The factor, however, which was most evident was the uninspired body language of the Greens as if they had accepted defeat even before they had actually been defeated. The communication between players were poor, the bowling changes, ineffective, the batting too was bereft of any definite plan, the field placings were also neither intuitive nor imaginative. The team simply lacked the spirit to perform.

That evening, in the team meeting, the coach Vijay Kanth announced some major changes in the team. A lot of strategy was discussed and the non-performance of the new players severely criticized. Armaan wondered why only the new players were being castigated. The experienced ones should be the ones taking responsibility. Also, the captain, who stood blaming each and every player of weak display, was himself found wanting during crucial stages. He was the one who should have taken most of the blame. Reds played the Blues next. The Blues were being lead by the Prince of Calcutta, Saurav Ganguly and in his armoury were some of the most promising young cricketers of the generation. The beleaguered Reds were no match for the Blues, and as was predicted, they again went down tamely against the stronger opposition. The organizers were peeved with this weak performance by the Reds. Ravi Shastri was visibly annoyed during the post-match press conference. 'Any club team from Kolkata would fare much better than India Reds. It is annoying to see them put up such uninspired performance at such a top level tournament,' he thundered before leaving the room in utter dejection. The players and the officials of the Reds were visibly shaken. They had to do something desperate to redeem their repertoire. And it was not easy. At the moment, the momentum was with the other two teams. Meanwhile Greens and the Blues had played out a tie. It was an edge of the seat thriller, and the spectators were treated with some fantastic cricketing skills from both the sides. It was almost the end of the road for the Reds. They had to win both their matches to be in any kind of contention, but looking at their current form, it was highly unlikely for them to create an upset. However, cricket has always been a game of glamorous uncertainties. But nobody prayed for the Reds, for everyone knew that cricket is also a game of the mind and no less than a miracle was required for the turnaround of a team that looked demotivated and demoralized.

Reds were again slated to play the Greens. Before they went out to practice, Vijay Kanth took the players to the famous Eden clubhouse.

'Do you see this stadium?' he called out as the players looked out into the green outlay that lay in front of them.

'This is the Mecca of Indian cricket. You guys are fortunate enough to play here at this level. Please do not insult this august arena with your ordinary efforts.'

The players themselves had been disturbed by the flak they had been receiving from all around. They too wanted a change of fortune. They too wanted to silence the critics by virtue of their performance. Victory or defeat was not irking them anymore. Their prime aim now was to perform as a team and put up some semblance of fight in the remaining matches.

Captain of the team Vishal Shukla had been receiving most of the criticism for being an insipid, unimaginative, uninspiring captain. His performance as a batsmen had also plummeted due to the additional responsibility. He desperately wanted someone to replace him at the helm, but there were no takers. No one wanted to voluntarily stand in front of the firing squad formed by the selection committee, the spectators, and the media. Some of the cricketers fearing jeopardy to their careers had already stayed away from practice feigning injury. It was truly a desperate situation.

As the officials and the coach of the Reds sat in deep contemplation over the combination of the next match, Armaan approached them with a proposal.

'Sir, can I be the captain for the last two matches?' he asked the gathering.

They were too stunned to reply. What was this guy up to . . . suicide?

But there was no option left. Vishal Shukla had already given in to the ever increasing pressure to step down, and no one was ready to step into his shoes. But how can they bring in a novice, a nobody to lead the team? They would face endless questions. But they had to play the match the next day, and time was not on their side. They had to play within less than twenty-four hours, and they had to play with eleven players and a captain. They could only tender a mute acceptance to the proposal after wasting some precious hours in the process. Things were getting bad to worse, and they could only hope for a miracle. And tell you what . . . miracles do happen.

Greens were bubbling with confidence when they came out to bat. The openers were out there as if with an intention to humiliate the bowlers in the process of building a mammoth score. They started in a whirlwind fashion, plummeting or trying to plummet every delivery out of the boundary. Armaan waited for his opportunity. He had asked his bowlers to bowl wicket to wicket at a slower pace making it difficult for the batsmen to get them away. It was more of a defensive ploy that upset the rhythm of the batsmen, and soon they got frustrated at the nagging line of the bowlers and ended up playing rash shots. Both the openers soon perished in an identical manner. The Reds were slowly getting back their self-belief and their captain. He somehow had infused into them a different kind of confidence, one that makes them believe in their own ability.

Soon, a few more wickets had tumbled without much being added to the total. Even the selectors were amazed at this sudden turn of events. They had come to witness the Greens compete amongst themselves. They had come to see a truncated match, shortened by the low score of the Reds or the quick dismissal of the Reds, trying to chase some unsurpassable score put up by the Greens. But here the story had a different script. All of a sudden the Greens were 34 for the loss of 5 wickets. Armaan was not ready to relent. He now let loose the Diamond Attack System, which he had devised and implemented most successfully in the Corporate Cup. Greens were all at sea against this sudden improvisation. The diamond cut through their thinking mechanisms and defensive techniques to bring an end to their struggle, out in the middle. They could only manage a paltry fifty-nine runs. The players and officials of the India Greens were stunned into silence. They could not fathom what had hit them. They simply had no answer to the schemes of Armaan Bailey. He simply kept astonishing them with each new stratagem that the Greens were totally unprepared for. The Reds came out to chase the target emphatically. The handful of spectators along with the selectors and the others indeed witnessed a truncated match, but they had never even in their wildest imagination had anticipated such a result.

The media was going gaga over the new discovery. Everyone tried to share the honours of the success thus achieved. In one particular press conference, a visibly bloated Vijay Kanth had claimed that Armaan was his finest invention. It was much alike of what Sir Humphrey Davy had called Michael Faraday—'his favourite invention'.

Armaan, however, ducked the media. His job was yet incomplete. He had his job cut out. He knew that he had to defeat the Blues; otherwise this hoopla may end pretty soon. And the Blues were a formidable team led by the iconic Saurav Ganguly. Blues also had a few more stalwarts in their ranks to boast of and one of the most prolific batsmen of yesteryears, Ajit Wadekar, was the coach of the team. It was a tall order to inflict the Blues with the same kind of treatment as meted out to the Greens. But what mattered was the spirit, and it was revelation to kind the India Red players bubbling with energy, raring to have a go at the favourites of the tournament. Armaan stayed away from the spotlight as much as possible, trying hard to concentrate on schemes that might derail the mighty Blues. But the others were too busy bragging about their role in the team's turnaround. This is a prime aspect of cricket that Armaan was yet to come into terms with. Success is fathered by many while failure is a mere bastard.

A lot of hype had been created around the match, and it was evident by the capacity crowd that filled the stadium, though most of them had come with the intention to see Ganguly stroke his way to victory. And Ganguly was in the mood to oblige. He and his opening partner Amay Khurasia were particularly brutal to the opening bowlers of the Reds. Armaan remained unfazed. He was least bothered by the galloping scoreboard and waited for the opportune moment to cash on the mistakes the batsmen committed.

Success came, not once but twice in quick succession. The Blues lost two quick wickets to poor shot selection, and soon Armaan started gaining some control over the game. Armaan and Sourav matched stroke for stroke. It was fun watching Sourav alter his game plan to offset the changes brought in by Armaan while Armaan did the same too, changing the field to make it difficult for Sourav to gather runs at will. However, the experience of the Blues was not to be discounted. They had seen all of this before. They have dealt with bigger pressures at international level. They were equal to the task that lay in front of them. But cricket had always been uncanny, puzzling, and unpredictable. The applecart of the Blues soon got into trouble. Some subtle bowling changes introduction of the Diamond and some clever field placing somewhat created obstacles to their progress. The Blues, however, managed to recover through their experience and skill to post a reasonably respectable total of 235 Runs in 50 overs. Reds were to get 236 runs. Not an improbable proposition, but certainly not easy too. The Reds knew that they have to bat particularly well to get to the total. Eden was already erupting, in anticipation of an exciting finish.

Reds started the chase cautiously. Armaan had given strict instruction to the batters to preserve wickets, and they were doing just that. The Eden pitch had been true to its character, and the outfield was lightning fast. But the batsmen did not fall to the lure of tempting deliveries outside off. Sourav had not removed the lone slip throughout the first hour. He too was playing with the minds of the batsmen, testing their patience, their temperament, and their technique. The tussle was immense, and it was certain that whoever held their nerve would emerge victorious.

And then the Blues struck. The pitch had shown some hints of turn, and Sairaj Bahutule had exploited the same by turning one away from the bat, inducing an edge. Eden erupted. Blues had broken through the resilient opening stand. Surprising everybody, including the opponent players, Armaan walked into bat. They had never thought that he could come out so fast. His record held that he had always batted at number five or six and never at number three. Had the Reds panicked?

Armaan began in the most sedate manner, playing deliveries as per their merit. The asking rate kept climbing, and the bowlers continued to torment the batsmen outside off. The Reds too kept their head and did not allow the Blues to cause further damage.

Against the course of play, suddenly Armaan broke loose, hitting one of the spinners, who also was a debutante, over midwicket boundary thrice for six. The silent phase of cricket was over. The Reds were on a counterattack. The Reds chased everything that was on offer though losing three wickets in the process. The momentum had suddenly shifted. All the bowlers were given the same treatment.

The match had woken up. Wickets, boundaries, wickets, boundaries. The match kept swinging from side to side like a rocking pendulum. Armaan was still there, allowing his other batsmen to play around him.

Ultimately, the match rolled into the last over. Raja Suresh, a successful medium pace bowler, was entrusted to defend the last twelve runs to prevent the Reds from victory. Suresh was a nippy bowler and had never in his career offered freebies to any batsman. But this was a tight match, and he was about to bowl to a batsman who didn't seem to care about the crowd, the situation or the records of the bowler. Armaan drove the first delivery through the covers to collect a couple. The second delivery was short, and he swivelled around in the process of pulling it to the square leg boundary. A diving Sriram could only watch in dismay as the ball rolled over the rope.

Four balls and four runs. A run a ball requirement for not difficult, but the field had closed in, with the sole intention to prevent any single. The third ball was directed at his toe, an in-swinging Yorker. Armaan could just dig it out to the bowler. No run. Buoyed by the success of the previous delivery that had brought out a roar from the crowd, Suresh attempted another. This time, however, Armaan had taken a few steps forward before the delivery, taking it on the full, driving it past the bowler for a straight four. A cumulative gasp went up from the stadium as the Reds humbled the formidable Blues in the last over. Saurav Ganguly was the first to give Armaan a tight embrace. He had done it, as a captain, as a player, as a performer at the highest level.

The stunned capacity crowd could not help giving Armaan Bailey a standing ovation as he made his way to the pavilion. The whole cricketing brethren was spellbound, astounded at this performance.

'This is what real leaders are made of,' said the legendary Sunil Gavaskar as he handed over the man of the match trophy to Armaan.

In the next match, the Blues went on to defeat the Greens, assuring a showdown with the Reds. It was a chance for the favourites to square things up. But the Reds appeared resolute. They were not going to be easy prey to the champions. What a turnaround it had been. The formidable were looking at the minnows with respect. This is cricket . . . the great leveller.

It was a sunny afternoon as Sunny as the presenter himself, who predicted a humdinger. Sunil Gavaskar did not mince words in pronouncing Armaan Bailey as the next big thing in Indian cricket. The excitement around the match had attained a feverish pitch as spectators poured in by thousands to watch their favourites lock horns in a mouth watering encounter.

This time, however, the Reds batted first. The India Blue bowlers had their tails up and welcomed the batsmen with some very fine swing bowling. The batsmen were all at sea against the accuracy and variation of the Blues. The Blues had come out with vengeance, and they surely appeared to have the upper hand from the word go. This time around, the Blues were intent to play to their full potential and the Reds could feel the heat of their intensity. Even Armaan Bailey could not contribute much, and the Reds innings folded up at 205 runs in the forty-fifth over.

Needing 206 runs to win, the Blues went about their task clinically. Though the diamond system did have them in a spot of bother at times, yet they manage to hang around till the last run had not been accomplished. Saurav Ganguly ensured that he stayed till the end to assure victory to his side. It was payback time. The crowd at Eden Gardens heaved a sigh of relief as their hometown hero lifted the challenger trophy. Saurav Ganguly, however, heaped a lot of praise on Armaan Bailey for being a great cricketer and leader. Praise also came from all other cricketing pundits who had witnessed this amazing tournament. They all did not hesitate for once to proclaim Armaan as the new prodigy in Indian cricket. Armaan Bailey had suddenly become a household name.

⁓

There was celebration in the Bailey household, but a muted one. Jonathon's assignment in India had ended and he had been asked to return to Australia. It was not a happy news for them. This was a land that Jonathon had adored for so long. His love for the country had at times made him forget his roots, his place of origin. Yet this was a reality which he had to accept. Though he had offered Alia to stay back with Armaan, he knew she would definitely not leave him alone at such an emotional period, of being detached to the country which had given him an identity. Another case of concern was Jonathon's early stages of Parkinson's. Alia did not want to leave Jonathon alone. She knew that he needed her support for every step that he took.

Her feelings were well supported by her father. Salman Ilahi too believed that they should not hesitate to return to Tasmania, and as far as Armaan was concerned, they should allow him to take his own decision.

Armaan listened patiently to his mother. She took care to explain very minutely the reason for their decision. Surprisingly, Armaan was not shaken. He had understood the fragility of the hour and chose to offer his allegiance to his family.

'You must stay with Dada and concentrate on your career, Armaan,' his mother said.

'Mom, I know I have a career here. I know that Dada needs to be taken care of. I know that whatever I have done here in India may have little or no significance in Australia. But, Mom, I know you all need me. And I cannot leave dad at a time when he needs me most,' said Armaan.

'But, my son, you cannot miss out on this opportunity,' cried Alia. 'It has always been your dream to be a part of the Indian Cricket Team.'

'Mom, had you all not toiled so hard after me, I couldn't have reached at this stage. I can understand how worried you had been, when at the age of eight I was unable to pronounce the alphabets. I know both of you had spent countless sleepless nights, pondering over my future. Mom, both of you are my reality. Dreams can be realized later too,' replied Armaan.

'Oh my god, I cannot believe this.' Alia was almost in tears. 'My son is speaking the language of my father. You have grown up so fast, my son.'

'Yes, Mom. Hazaron Kwahishe aisi hai, ki har kwahish pe dum nikle. Bahut nikla mere Arman, lekin phir bhi kam nikle. Love you, Mom.'

The rest of the conversation was only sobs and sniffles. Alia just could not come to terms with this sense of sacrifice from her son. She had seen him grown up to live a life of cricket, and when he was almost at the doorstep of realization of his dream, he was ready to relinquish it all to be with his parents. This is not what even normal children do. Then why does the world call Arman, an autistic? She was also proud of the big heart her son possessed; otherwise who on earth thinks about parents, when success awaits on the other side of the door? Perhaps . . . perhaps this is what leaders are made up of.

But in vain she did conjure him,
To depart her presence so,
Having a thousand tongues t' allure him
And but one to bid him go.
When lips invite,
And eyes delight,
And cheeks as fresh as rose in June,
Persuade delay,—
What boots to say
Forego me now, come to me soon.

—Sir Walter Raleigh (1), Dulcina,
see Cayley's *Life of Raleigh*, vol. 1, ch. 3

CHAPTER 17

The Return

The phone had been ringing for quite some time. Solomon somehow managed to scramble out of bed to take the call. There had been very little paving for the last two nights because of the lack of front. The PQC team had got a rare opportunity to catch up with some sleep. But the ringing of the phone had created a ruckus. This was the third time Solomon had been attending the phone.

'Who's this?' Solomon mumbled in a state of semi-slumber.

'That's my question too,' snapped the voice at the other end. Solomon could recognise the voice by its terseness, BKT.

'This is Solomon, sir, good evening,' said Solomon, trying to regain his senses.

'Where the hell is Kumar Sinha? I've been trying his mobile for the last one hour.' BKT was almost shouting by now.

'He is in Kushgaon, sir, near the paver,' replied Solomon.

'What the hell is he doing there? We have an emergency here. Contact him fast and ask him to report to the CPO immediately,' ordered BKT before cutting off the phone.

Solomon took his time to figure out what to do. Kushgaon was an area where the reception of mobile phone signals is pretty weak. Solomon worked on the walkie-talkie instead.

'Kumar Sir, come on line. Kumar Sir, come on line,' announced Solomon.

'Kumar online, over,' replied the voice at the other side.

'Solomon calling, sir. You have been urgently called at the CPO by BKT. Over,' informed Solomon.

'Any specifics, over?' asked Kumar.

'An emergency, over,' replied Solomon.

'Thanks, Solomon, over and out,' Kumar ended.

Solomon kept awake, wondering what might be the emergency. The crackled voices kept on blaring on the walkie-talkie.

'Vijay Kumar, come on line.' Someone was seeking the safety chief.

'Solanki Sir, please take your medical team to the Sadar Hospital. Others will join you soon. Over,' another voice poured in.

'Mandal, come on line. Mandal, come on line. Please inform TFL that we have already reached Khandala Police Station, over,' another voice broke in to inform.

'Hospital, police station . . . what the hell is going on?' wondered Solomon. He was wide awake by now. Something was surely wrong somewhere. He could feel a rush of Adrenalin in his system. Hurriedly putting on his shirt, trousers, and shoes, Solomon rushed out to the jeep stationed outside. He drove like he had never driven before reaching CPO within no time.

He could see a crowd in front of the TFL's room. There were safety stewards, officers, and senior officers waiting for the TFL to emerge from his room. 'What's the problem?' Solomon pondered. Right then, he saw Kumar and the TFL emerge from the office and get into the latter's car. Solomon pulled Vinod, who was standing near the TFL room, aside.

'What's the matter, Vinod?' asked Solomon breathlessly.

'Don't you know?' Vinod looked surprised. 'Ramsingh Rathod and his wife have met with an accident while returning from Mumbai this evening. Both have been seriously injured.'

Solomon was rendered speechless. He was the one who had received Ramsingh's phone call that evening and had informed him that paving had been suspended for the next two days. He somehow could not believe what he had just heard. It was unbelievable, unthinkable, unconstruable.

A lot of people had gathered in front of the hospital. Kumar was available at the reception of the Casualty Ward. He informed them that while returning from Mumbai, Ramsingh had lost control of the vehicle while manoeuvring the sharp bend near the Duke's Nose. The vehicle had hit a tree before skidding into a deep gorge. Some of the villagers had spotted the vehicle and managed to pull out Ramsingh and his wife from the badly battered vehicle before informing the PECL office. The condition of both of them was very serious and that the doctors were doing their best under the present circumstances.

Dr P. Chettry, the company doctor, soon emerged from the ICU to announce a grave news. The news hit them like a thunderbolt, rendering them with a feeling of paralytic numbness. While Ramsingh battled on to ward off death, Mrs Rathod had succumbed to her injuries. The doctors, even after trying their very best, could not bring back the fleeting breath. It took time to sink in. Mrs Neha Rathod was no more.

Kumar was called to the conference room. It was way past midnight. BKT and some of his senior team members were already there. BKT gestured Kumar to take a seat. The silence had a murdering effect. Regaining his composure, BKT looked around the team members before speaking out.

'Guys, this has been an unfortunate event,' he said. 'We as a family should stand in support of Ramsingh Rathod in this hour of crisis. He will require a lot of emotional support to be able to live through this tragedy.'

'Sinha.' BKT looked squarely at Kumar. 'You are the team leader for the PQC Unit. You have to handle this very carefully.'

'What do I need to do, sir?' asked Kumar.

'First, we need to inform the families. Ramsingh's and his wife's. You need to do this Kumar. You've known them personally,' said BKT.

'Me . . . sir?' Kumar stammered.

'Yes, Kumar. You're the team leader,' replied BKT in a stern voice.

Kumar was flabbergasted. He had never imagined that leadership would impose so many difficult propositions upon him. Already he had been fighting with tremendous time pressure and work schedule. He had to keep his team and associates motivated. He had to assure the qualitative and quantitative results the project warranted. He also had to ensure proper control over man, machine, material, money, and other form of resources to bring about profit for the organization; but death—this was something that he had never been prepared to deal with before.

No parent or school or college or university ever teach or train anybody to deal with death. They have never even tried. Death is such a taboo that folks at home are not encouraged to discuss. But it is a reality that one comes to face at times of most unpreparedness. Only life teaches us to deal with death and, at times even, most gruesomely.

The news stunned Dr Amit Ray. Though, in a profession, where death is almost a part of everyday occurrence for Dr Amit, the news shocked him out of his senses. He managed to cancel all his schedules for the day so that he can drive down to Lonavala.

It was early morning, and the traffic was sparse on the highway. It took him a little more than two hours to reach the Sadar Hospital. Kumar met him at the parking lot. Dr Amit could see that Kumar had not had any sleep for hours. Dr Amit accompanied Kumar to the casualty. Neha's body had been draped in white and kept at a secluded area. After having discussed a few things in medical verbosity with the doctors present, Dr Amit made his way into the ICU.

Dr Amit was not a man of expression. But Kumar could see streaks of water at the corner of his eye.

'Should we inform Tina madam, Doctor?' asked Kumar.

'Please don't,' Dr Amit said almost in a pleading voice. 'She would be shattered.'

'But at any point of time, we need to tell,' replied Kumar.

'That we will see. But please not now.' Dr Amit was adamant.

'What about Ram, sir?' enquired Kumar.

'Still not out of danger. The next twenty-four hours are extremely crucial,' replied the doctor wiping his perspiration.

'We also need to inform Neha's family, sir. I don't know how to do that,' said Kumar helplessly.

'I don't know too. This is the most difficult news that one can bring home to a family,' said Dr Amit.

'I think it's better that we inform her brother instead,' said Kumar.

'Wait, hang on,' Dr Amit said, bringing out his mobile phone. 'Let me take the help of Salman Chacha.'

Salman Ilahi looked visibly disturbed as he nervously twitched his fingers. A person like him, who had been witness to several tragic events in his lifetime, seemed to have lost words of consolation, words of healing. He looked blankly at Dr Amit and Kumar in an expression of apology. At last he spoke in an almost inaudible voice.

'Let's meet the family,' he said, feebly.

The drive to Bandra was perhaps the most difficult journey, Kumar had ever embarked upon. He prayed, somehow, to let the journey continue forever. This journey should not culminate at the designated destination. This journey brought in a world of grief, woe . . . a parcel of catastrophe. This journey was too painful to bear, too heinous to even think about.

Neha's brother had greeted them at the doorway. Perhaps he was leaving for college. But on the request of Salman Ilahi, he stayed back. They seated themselves in the small but well-decorated living room, unable to find words to start the discussion. Neha's mother was overjoyed on seeing Dr Amit. For the family, Dr Amit was next to God. It was under his intensive care that Neha's mother had found new life. After having discussed general topics, it was time for divulging the heartbreaking news. They waited . . . not knowing how to begin and where to begin from.

'Maa ji, this is Kumar Sinha, Ramsingh's friend and colleague at Lonavala,' Dr Amit managed to say in a faint voice.

'Yes, my son. Ram and Neha had come to visit us this weekend. They were very happy,' The old lady smiled.

'I am sorry maa ji to say this, but they had met with an accident last night. We have come to take you to Lonavala right now?' said Kumar in a choking voice.

'What?' the lady was taken aback and so was her son, seated next to Dr Amit.

'What has happened to them was? How is my Neha?' The woman's voice had transformed into a wailing tone.

'Get ready, maa ji, we'll leave immediately,' said Kumar.

The poor ailing woman, with her son by her side, got into the car, not knowing that darker news awaited them at Lonavala.

Tina was aghast at the news. She could not, for the first time in her life, believe in the words of Salman Ilahi. It seemed untrue. Absolutely untrue. The news had made her uncontrollable, unable to come into terms with the sinister turn of events. The word had spread to Magenta as well, bringing a pall of gloom to the otherwise lively workplace. Time stood still amidst sobs and sniffles and amidst the feeling of an irreplaceable loss of a human life.

Ramsingh was yet to regain consciousness, but on the behest of Dr Amit and Salman Ilahi, Neha Rathod was cremated at Mumbai, in the presence of some of the top officials of PECL.

Ramsingh, unaware of his wife's demise, had been shifted to the Boulevard Hospital, which was a private and thus a more sophisticated place for further treatment. The members of the paving team took turns to spend the night at his cabin, taking care of the medicinal needs as prescribed by the doctors. Dr Amit too visited the hospital every alternative day, keeping track of the process of recovery.

Meanwhile, Salman Ilahi had decided to visit Jaisalmer to break the news with the Rathods. According to him, it was improper to inform them by telephone or post. It was a news, so touchy in nature that it should be personally informed. Kumar Sinha was requested to accompany Ilahi on the behalf of PECL, and Kumar did not hesitate to oblige.

After a week at the Boulevard, Ramsingh began to show signs of recovery. Though, he had regained consciousness, he was too weak to speak or undergo any movement of body parts. Dr Amit announced that the progress would be steady in the next couple of days, and Ramsingh would at least be able to sit or maybe walk by then.

Life was slowly returning to normal. Paving had once again started, from Kushgaon moving towards Pimporli. Ramsingh had been released from the hospital and was taken care by his brother KaranSingh who had accompanied Salman Ilahi and Kumar Sinha. Though Ramsingh was yet to recover completely from his physical injuries, his psyche had been bruised beyond repair. Ramsingh remained mostly silent and secluded, spending most of his time looking aimlessly outside the bedroom window, out into the fields. His conversation with his brother too remained limited and incoherent. He ate less, slept less, talked less. The tragedy had transformed the once lively Ramsingh Rathod into a lifeless lump of jelly.

Kumar, Solomon, Vinod, Goswami, Suraj all paid him regular visits without much success of inducing him into any kind of conversation. His silence was ominous. It was indeed necessary for them to bring about some life into him. They tried, in every way possible, putting up their best effort to bring out some voice from within. But Ramsingh remained quiet, a shadow of the self that he had once been.

The paving continued unabated, surpassing new milestones as it meandered its way past Pimloli to Kamshet. The road with its beautified median verge looked a spectacle in itself. The scenery of the adjoining areas added further colour and flavour to the background. It was an apostle of engineering excellence.

Kumar was astonished at the dull atmosphere at Magenta. The sordid faces, emanating forced smiles in greeting, further added to the gloominess of the otherwise fantastic workplace. Kumar somehow felt uncomfortable in the humourless interims of the office. The otherwise creative workforce was working more like zombies. Had they been reading Pavlov lately?

Tina was expressionless too, like never before. She gave Kumar a dry smile in greeting. Kumar could see a glint of tear in the corner of her eye. Silently, Kumar handed over the file, containing his observations, to Tina. She thanked him in a whisper before keeping the file aside. Kumar wanted to say something consoling to her but didn't know how. They sat in silence for a while before Kumar excused himself from the office to drive down, back to Lonavala.

Ramsingh had returned to work. Though he had been physically present at the site, his thoughts were somewhere else. He didn't bother to discuss programs or take instructions, neither was he too keen to be part of the process of PQC. He generally stood far from the centre of activity, in some desolate corner, lost in his own world of unknown thoughts. There had been times when his group members had tried to get him involved, but his reluctance to join them was way too strong for them to continue with the effort. Ramsingh had also resorted to the comforts of alcohol. His habit of relentless drinking had been upsetting for all the people who knew and loved him. Ramsingh was fast showing a decadence of character, losing himself steadfastly into the realms of self-destruction.

Karansingh had been very worried at his brother's rapid deterioration. Before calling home for help, he decided to talk things over with Kumar and Salman Ilahi. He had given both of them a call and had received the assurance of help from both the quarters.

'Ramsingh needs to go back, Kumar,' said Salman Ilahi after a moment of silence.

'Where, sir?' asked Kumar.

'Home,' said Ilahi, looking Kumar in his eye.

'But he can do wonders here, sir. This is a huge project,' said Kumar almost in protest.

'Kumar, life is not about projects and performance only. Probably one day you too will realize that. Ram has lost the aim of his life. He is just ambling away into the territory of self-decay. He can still be of use to the society. His society. His family in Rajasthan needs him,' the old man sighed the old man.

'But will he agree, sir?' asked Kumar.

'I will make him agree, son, don't worry,' Assured Ilahi. 'You just manage his release from the company.'

Kumar and Solomon had completed all formalities for the release of Ramsingh. All necessary documents had been signed and made ready for posting to the HO, and all his dues were cleared within a very short time, something not very common with PECL. Now, it was time for convincing Ramsingh, who remained unmoved, unperturbed, almost unaware amidst the whole ordeal.

'Ram, there's nothing left here, my son,' said Ilahi, in a voice most soothing. It was only Ilahi and Ramsingh seated across each other in the dimly lit living room.

'You need to return, Ram, to the place you belong. Your people need you,' said Ilahi.

'Chacha, but they are the ones to disown me,' at last Ramsingh muttered.

'It's time to forgive and forget the fallacies of the past, Ram. Let the dead past bury its dead,' said Ilahi.

'Ram', Ilahi continued with his usual soothing tone, 'Arjun needs you, not only to look after his business but also to look after him. Your *kirdaar* is different now. You need to play father to your ailing father, Ram.'

Ramsingh could only silently realize the truth of the statement. Yes, his *kirdaar* indeed has changed. He had to live for someone, live for something. He had to live, for himself, his people, and contribute towards the good of the people who need him.

Almost the whole of PQC team had come to see off Ramsingh and Karansingh. After shaking hands with everyone, Ramsingh locked Kumar in a tight embrace. Kumar was surprised to notice tears rolling down his own cheek—something which was a very rare happening.

As the train increased its jog to a canter and the small crowd started to dissipate into oblivion, Ramsingh caught sight of the once celebrated dream house of his, standing aghast, in a state of desolation in the lap of the green mountains.

He remembered a small quote he had read somewhere, which seemed to be engraved on the blue walls of the Bungalow:

Can storied urn or animated Bust.
Back to its mansion call the fleeting breath?
Can Honour's voice provoke the silent dust.
Or flattery soothe the dry cold ear of DEATH?

And when your fears subside/ And shadows still remain/ I know that you can love me/ When there's no one left to blame . . .

—Axl Rose

CHAPTER 18

A Change of Season

Parents and teachers never teach us certain things because they cannot. They never taught us how to manage our successes and failures deriving a balance between them as we move along. They never taught us how to keep steady at times of crisis, without taking assistance from alcohol, astrology, psychiatry or God. They never taught us how to manage our first salary and also our last, all that we get in the middle off course is dealt by professional manipulators. They never taught us that our first love should be cultivated to be our last, and our best love should be our last. They never taught us how to deal with death . . . of others and even our own.

Ah yes, Rudyard Kipling did put a lot of thought in this regard in his poem 'If,' but again, he should have written more. And besides how many people read such kind of write-ups. Even if they do . . . do they understand?

'Soda or Cola?' asked Manivannan.

'Soda, sir,' replied Kumar.

'You've not changed, Kumar. Still soda with rum? That's not the right combination.' Manivannan smiled, pouring the drink leisurely into the empty glass.

'But this has been the most suitable combination for me,' replied Kumar.

'Then let me try this today as well. Let's have a change of season,' Manivannan said with a broader grin.

'You will enjoy it,' Kumar said raising a toast.

'How can you be so sure?' asked Manivannan.

'I know you, sir. I know your tastes.' Kumar smiled.

The glasses kissed each other before emptying part of its content into the bowels of two of the brightest professionals that PECL could boast of.

'Why don't you try your hand in bidding?' asked Manivannan.

Kumar looked amused. What the hell was he talking about? 'Well, I don't have good exposure to it. But why are you telling this to me?' Kumar asked, surprised.

'Because you need that experience as well. It is a completely different world. And I know that you can do well here.' Manivannan stopped to fill up his glass.

'Had Manivannan gone bonkers?' thought Kumar. Had he got tipsy in the second peg itself? If not, then why was he asking his favourite disciple to change his track, and that too when he was doing quite well.

'You can't be serious.' Kumar smiled.

'I am serious, Kumar. I always am, when I am talking to you,' replied Manivannan, now in a tone of gravity.

'You know, Kumar, I believe, that each one of us should have a feel of other worlds as well. Look at me.' He paused a bit and then continued, 'I will always be known as a jetty man. I will always be given assignments of Jetty. Now, if the world changes and work on Jetty's get diminished, I will be an extinct creature.'

'You mean one should be a jack of all trades?' questioned Kumar.

'Yes, a Jack of all trades and master of some,' Manivannan smiled.

'You see, Kumar,' continued Manivannan with a bit of gusto now. 'You know about panning, execution, manufacturing. You have been trained to think alternately and distinctively in aspects of engineering. But you can never be complete unless you know about marketing, market building, business development, market analysis, and bidding.'

'What you are doing today, even your competitors are. But why are you doing this the way you are is because you have not been part of bidding.' Manivannan paused again to refill before continuing. 'Had you been part of the process, you might have done it differently.'

Kumar looked puzzled. He had never thought in these lines. Probably he should give it a try. He should also try out this aspect of engineering as well. Probably Manivannan is right, one should have all types of weapons in the arsenal . . . And besides, the pressure and stress of execution was growing on him. Probably, he desperately needed a change of season.

Dev Chandra was a comic character. Nicknamed as *Chacha* by his comparatively younger subordinates, he had always been a topic of jest at all company gatherings. His expressions, gesticulations, and thought process were all comic book stuff. Though he was the head of the project proposal group, he was and always had been very insecure about his position. His subordinates too were a non serious bunch. They revelled in the fact that they were comparatively novices in the field of bidding and were given ample freedom to learn as they earn.

'Please welcome Mr Kumar Sinha to our department,' announced Chacha as he stood in the middle of the hall. 'He has come with a rich experience in planning and execution.'

One by one, all the team members came up to shake his hand and introduce themselves.

'Please refrain from unnecessary gossip,' remarked Chacha.

Dev Chandra, alias Chacha, had an atrocious hold over English. The newest addition to his vocabulary was the word 'refrain,' which he tried to use as many times as possible in as many sentences possible throughout the day.

Refrain from shouting, refrain from idling, refrain from being late, etc. And his subordinates too mimicked him by using the same unnecessarily.

Please refrain from using my pen, please refrain from looking into my computer, and please refrain from refraining to talk to me.

It was a department full of comic and caricature. Kumar Sinha sat watching each of them in bewilderment. This was a department of laughter. Time and again, he thought of whether he could ever adjust himself to this atmosphere of tomfoolery.

Magenta was slowly limping back into normalcy. For Tina, it had been a Herculean task to put the tragedy behind and focus on the huge backlog of work that lay in front. Probably, she had taken up more assignments to keep herself busy. The duress of the workload had also started taking its toll. Falling sick now had become a regular recourse amongst the co-workers at Magenta. It was probably the first time that Magenta was handling so many assignments simultaneously. Tina had to take a call; the pressure was not easy to handle.

'Kumar, this is Tina. How are you?'

'Fine, madam,' replied the voice from the other side. 'How are you?'

'I need your help, Kumar. Can you meet me?' said Tina without replying to his question.

'Sure, ma'am. When do you recommend?' asked Kumar.

'This evening, at my place. Can you come over?' asked Tina.

'Sure, ma'am, at around seven,' said Kumar

'Perfect. I'll be waiting.' Tina hung up.

By the time Kumar reached the Ray mansion, it was already 7:30 PM. Kumar was somewhat embarrassed to be late. The house looked unusually quiet as he entered the lawn. He wondered whether he should call on the cell phone before going further. Probably, she would have gone elsewhere after having waited till 7:00 PM. Before he could dial the number, his phone rang. It was Tina's call. Almost taken aback, he looked around. Had she seen him enter?

He picked up the call. 'Yes, ma'am.'

'How far are you?' asked Tina.

'I have actually reached and am in the lawn,' replied Kumar.

'Please come in. What are you doing outside?' exclaimed Tina.

'Sure, ma'am,' said Kumar.

He entered the sitting room and was pleasantly surprised to find it empty. He stood there for a while before reclining in the most comfortable-looking sofa. The interiors of the house had an inherent charm. It somehow made Kumar feel so much at home.

Soon Tina entered with a plateful of delicious looking sweets and pastries. Kumar indeed was hungry but was not quite eager to start eating all at once. Tina looked her usual self, much in contrast to what she had been a couple of weeks earlier. Somehow, Kumar felt relieved. It was a rather agonizing experience to see her so sad and broken down the other day.

'How are you, ma'am?' was all he could ask.

'I am fine, Kumar, thank you. How have you been, and how's your project progressing?' asked Tina.

'My part of the project is over, ma'am. So I've shifted base to Mumbai and have joined a different department altogether. I am in Project Proposals now,' said Kumar.

'Well, that's good to hear. You are now much closer to us.' She smiled.

'Well, ma'am, did you go through my proposal for your processes?' asked Kumar.

'Well, Kumar, had you been always like this? Always talking about work and projects and business? Don't you find time to relax or just have a small discussion or some gossip?' asked Tina.

'I'm sorry, ma'am. I just asked.' Kumar looked embarrassed.

'And secondly, why do you keep calling me madam every time? It sounds as if I am a schoolteacher. Why can't you call me Tina?' There was a hint of irritation in Tina's voice.

'OK, ma'am,' replied Kumar.

This made Tina break into a loud laughter. The laughter had a kind of magic in it. It was so hypnotic that it made Kumar sit up and keep looking at her. She appeared ethereal; he just could not take his eyes of her.

'We'll talk about the project report some other day, in office. I just thought spending some time with you today,' said Tina.

'Yes, yes, that will be fine.' Kumar stammered.

'Tell me about yourself, Kumar. Your parents, your likes, and dislikes. Something you want to share. About the love of your life, if you want to.' Tina smiled.

Nobody had ever asked Kumar such questions before, neither friends nor accomplices. He was unable to begin because he had never known how to.

'My parents are in Jamshedpur, and I grew up there. It's a wonderful city, ma'am. Sorry, Tina.' He looked up to see her smiling pleasantly.

'I was put into a boarding school from an early age. Probably I was only seven then. Life in a hostel, especially when you are too young, is difficult. You cannot sleep till late. You cannot eat whatever you want to. You are not pampered like when you are at home. And you also have to be responsible for yourself. It was rather difficult in the beginning.' Kumar looked up.

Tina was listening silently, intently. She handed him a doughnut, beautifully crafted on the top with chocolate, in a small porcelain plate.

'Slowly I came into terms with the bigger boys. I played hard, fought hard, and worked hard to be amongst the leaders in the race,' said Kumar.

'But wait a minute', he thought, 'why the hell am I telling her all this?'

'You said that you wanted some help from me. May I know what kind of help?' asked Kumar.

'Yes, Kumar,' Tina sighed.

'You know, Amit is very impressed with the way you handled the tragedy that happened with Ram and Neha. You were blunt and honest when required and also soft and supportive. You have a sensitive being within this hard exterior, Kumar. We all have realized this, no matter how much you try to hide.' Tina smiled.

'Thanks, if that's a compliment,' said Kumar.

'It is this nature that makes you very unique. Anyway, coming to the point, I need your help for something very different.' Tina paused, handed Kumar with a glass of cold drinks before continuing. 'Mr Salman Ilahi had been Amit's patient for a long time. We are very fond of him, and he of course considers us a part of his extended family. We are like his own children.'

'Salman uncle's daughter is going back to Australia for good. To make matters worse, Armaan, his grandson, has opted to accompany his parents back to Australia. We know how sad he is. But he seldom shares his grief with us. He needs company, Kumar, of people like you, who are so honest with words and feelings,' said Tina, almost in a tone of request.

'That's all right, but I don't know him that well. I had only spent a few days with him. Why should he open up in front of me? I am still very much a stranger,' said Kumar.

'I know Salman, Uncle. He loves people who are honest. You know, even Jonathon was a stranger to him. But how well they got along. They share a relationship of love and respect,' said Tina.

'And love hurts,' remarked Kumar.

Tina gave a long and meaningful stare to Kumar.

'No, Kumar love does not hurt. Everyone says love hurts, but that isn't true. Loneliness hurts. Rejection hurts. Losing someone hurts. Envy hurts. Everyone gets these things confused with love, but in reality, love is the only thing in this world that covers up all pain and makes someone feel wonderful again. Love is the only thing in this world that does not hurt,' said Tina, her voice getting more and more melancholy.

They sat in silence for quite a while. Kumar felt sorry that his words had somehow hurt Tina in a subtle manner. He did not know whether to apologize or not to. The silence was growing in proportion . . . Kumar raised his head to meet Tina's eyes. Such beautiful, expressive eyes could cause many a heart to skip a beat. Kumar was only a mortal. He tried to look away, but can beauty ever be overlooked? Can beauty ever go unappreciated?

'Ma'am, you are the most beautiful woman I have ever seen.' Kumar could not prevent himself from saying.

Surprisingly, it induced a small laughter from Tina.

'Thank you. That was cute,' she replied laughing.

⚘

Dev Chandra had imposed a lot of regulations in the department. He feared rebellion since he was not the person suited for the position. He always dominated his subordinates in a manner to keep them reminded about the fact that he was the undisputed ruler of this kingdom.

Chacha always kept his subordinates in fear with various ploys and techniques. But now he had a new challenge at hand. The challenge was to tame the newcomer of his department who had come with loads of experience, not in years, but in variety. But Chacha was unaware that he was pitting himself against an enigma called Kumar Sinha, who had faced sterner challenges in his small tenure with the company.

However, Chacha's hilarious nature and atrocious knowledge of English was like an energizer to the department. PECL needed projects. There was increased pressure from the management to bid for more and more projects. It was not easy to win because the cake size had been diminishing. Chacha was in trouble. He looked forward to someone who could help him out from this situation of pressure. And there was only one person who could help him—Kumar.

'Mr Kumar, we need to win some bids,' said Chacha in a commanding voice.

'Sure, sir. I will try,' said Kumar.

'Never tolded me stuff that will make me hurted,' said Chacha in a language of his own.

Kumar looked puzzled but could understand that he had to deliver. That's too fast.

⌘

'Solomon, I need to talk to you,' Kumar said, to a half-sleepy Solomon.

'Yes, sir,' replied Solomon.

'Solomon, have you been ever in love?' asked Kumar.

'Sir, the paver had been wobbling at places of moderate moisture. How to overcome it?' asked Solomon.

'I will tell that tomorrow. You first answer my question,' said Kumar.

'But if the slump is a bit high, can we adjust the augur speed?' asked Solomon.

'Solomon, can we cut off topics on the project and talk about personal things?' asked Kumar.

'Sir, these are personal things only. You only have taught us this,' replied Solomon.

'Solomon, I think I was wrong. Now I have realized this. Probably . . . probably, I am in love,' said Kumar.

'Sir, love is not something as simple as a project. What if you do not get the love back in return?' asked Solomon.

'Love should have a condition . . . that it should be unconditional. Love is a process and not an end result,' replied Kumar.

'But, sir, if the DBI doesn't have a smooth insertion, can we alter the travel speed of the paver?' asked Solomon.

'Solomon, you are incorrigible,' replied Kumar.

❦

The bidding room was taut with tension. This was the first bid for Kumar Sinha. Almost all the heavyweights from the industry were there. Mostly bidders knew each other. They had been fighting each other for years, some for decades and some, even more.

Kumar was new to this world, but that did not perturb him. He could read through the questioning looks of some of the bidders trying various techniques of mind games to make Kumar uncomfortable. But Kumar had seen such things before, though not in the field of bidding. But there are other testing fields as well. Kumar did not smile, did not nod to anyone. He just concentrated in the compilation of summary of prices and taxes to be submitted with the discount letter.

After submission, they waited. These were the testing moments for a bidder. They waited as the client completed their evaluation of the bids. The bid with the least value and the best technical data will stand to be the best bid.

One very young engineer read out the results aloud in the hallway.

EBK Limited: Rs. 4640 Crores.

Sunrise Industries: Rs.4633 Crores

MBF Limited: Rs. 4621 Crores

TBT Private Limited: Rs. 4614 Crores

Emmar Industries Limited: Rs.4611 Crores

PECL: Rs. 4610 Crores.

All eyes turned to Kumar Sinha. The new kid in the block had made a winning start. The rest of the bidders came up to congratulate Kumar and to remind him that this was just the beginning of a long fight against each other.

❦

Salman Ilahi was overjoyed to see Kumar. He had thinned down considerably. Was it ill health or worries . . . or was it the forlorn thought of solitude? Kumar was visibly surprised by the silence of the place. It was a haunting silence. He wondered how a single soul managed to live through this silence for so long.

'Sir, it's pretty lonely out here,' said Kumar.

'Lonely? No, no, there are a lot of memories here. They are enough to keep me busy.' The old man smiled.

'But you manage to keep yourself cheerful and also mange to keep the people around you in good cheer. That's phenomenal,' said Kumar.

Salman smiled sarcastically.

Kya hun main aur,
Kya samajhte hai mujhe zamanewaale,
Sub raaz hote nahi batanewaale . . .
Kabhi tanhaiyon mein aakar dekho,
Kaise rote hain, Duniya ko hasanewaale.

It's the fire in my eyes,
And the flash of my teeth,
The swing in my waist,
And the joy in my feet.

(Maya Angelou, *Phenomenal Woman: Four Poems Celebrating Women*)

CHAPTER 19

The Woman of Substance

Tina Ray had unleashed her latest collection in the Autumn Special of Lakme Fashion Week. The couture had taken special care to draft utility outfits for women on the move. It was a new concept—a new dimension to the even evolving trend of fashion outfits. The appreciation ranged far and wide. Even the galaxy of stars that had graced the occasion had emphatically endorsed the simple and thoughtful line of products launched by Magenta. There were saris, saris, and saris, eulogizing the elegance of the Indian woman. During the felicitation, Tina thanked all the members of Magenta for their outstanding work during testing times. She also dedicated her collection and the subsequent award in the memory of Neha Rathod, who had left the team and the world in a tragic turn of destiny. Amongst the tears and the gasps that ensued during the announcement regarding Neha, Tina had also announced the name of Kumar Sinha for extending unconditional support to her and her team with his conceptual management support that had strengthened Magenta's efficiency to achieve excellence.

The fashion world had been swept off its feet. Tina Ray had been elevated to the pedestal of a celebrity. But still there was an emptiness in this clamour—a silence amongst this din. These accolades, titles, fame, success did not give Tina the happiness she desired. Amongst all the celebration there, somehow, remained a void in her life.

She had taken a great liking for the little girl, Ria. But Dr Amit's indifference towards Tina's growing affinity for this girl. Tina, however, could not prevent herself from going to St. Mary's Convent every day to meet the little angel. She showered the girl with gifts, chocolates, clothing, and shoes every time she visited, and Ria too always waited for Tina. Time and again, she stood at the doorway, looking at the road ahead, anticipating Tina's car pulling up at the driveway. The tie was getting stronger with each passing day. Mother Superior had advised Tina to apply for the adoption of Ria and start the formalities by coming with her husband for a customary interview at the convent.

'I don't have the time for all this, Tina, you know that,' said Dr Amit.

'All this?' asked Tina surprised. 'We are talking of a little girl, who has nobody in the world.'

'I have never stopped you from doing whatever you want,' said Amit.

'But both of us need to meet the authorities, Amit. Not me alone.'

'Tina.' Amit took a pause. 'No one can take the place left vacant by Ayan. No one,' he said, looking away.

Tina was almost in tears. She could not understand why Amit was so very harsh at the idea of adoption. She had to somehow convince Amit to help her out. She knew Amit and probably still loved Amit, even after living like strangers under the same roof. She somehow believed that Amit would relent to her requests, her pleas, her tears. But she did not know when and how. But she also could not for once take her mind off Ria. The innocent little girl was starved of affection, and Tina longed to hold her in her arms . . . forever.

Salman Ilahi sat buried in his thoughts. He could feel the emptiness that had engulfed Tina because he too was an inhabitant of this empty world. Having spent some time in pondering, Salman looked up at Tina as if he had come up with a solution.

'Tina, my child, you don't need to despair,' he said at last. 'Amit might be disillusioned, too grief-stricken to take a decision. But Amit is a bright boy. He will surely understand. Just wait for time to provide the healing touch.'

'But, Uncle, the child needs my care. I know she cannot live without me,' cried Tina.

'Yes, my child,' said Ilahi in the most soothing voice. 'The child is yours. Allah has willed it this way.'

'What must I do, Uncle?' asked Tina.

'Keep giving her the best of your love. She will be nourished by your love,' said Ilahi.

'Tina, this girl required special attention. Give her the best medical treatment. See how she responds. If medication can help her talk or listen, you can save a life.'

'Yes, Uncle, I have already talked to the doctors. We will have her first check up tomorrow,' said Tina.

The doctors intended to have a primary check up of the child. Ria was not a born hearing impaired. Her history depicted that she had been blabbering as an infant and had picked up a few words too as she grew up. But abruptly, she had stopped vocalizing, probably because she had lost her capacity for hearing for some reason. The best of ENT experts had been contacted for this. The advantage of being a family member of a medical expert is that experts of different departments are always ready for help. Amit's position had been advantageous in that aspect.

Ria remained perplexed throughout the medical ordeal. However, she had good company. Sister from the convent had come along with Tina and also Salman Ilahi and a very active Kumar Sinha. The reassuring presence of all the people around her had given a huge respite to Ria. But Ria always kept looking at Tina. She had an immense faith in Tina, somehow, and probably believed deeply that in Tina's presence nothing can go wrong for her. And Tina—she prayed and prayed like never before. She wanted her Ria to talk and be as normal as the other children around. And this wish had almost escalated to be the goal of her life. Other achievements seemed to pale in comparison to the joy that would bring.

As they sat waiting for the results of the tests, Ilahi could feel the tension in Tina's face. He seated himself beside her and patted her hand.

'Good things happen to good people, my child. Though late at times,' he said, smiling.

'Hope so,' said Tina, smiling back.

'And remember for anything worth having, one must pay the price, and the price is always work, patience, love, self-sacrifice, said Ilahi, looking at Tina in the eye.

The doctors informed that Ria would have to undergo a minor operation for the removal of some crusts that had been preventing her from sound comprehension. The doctors also informed that even after the surgery, Ria would have to undergo intensive training in vocalization to regain her power of speech. It required professional intervention and of course a lot of love and care. Tina agreed to spend a lot of time with her so that her recovery became fast. Tina got herself busy, with Ria and the processes proposed by the doctors and other professionals. She knew that with patience, dedication, focus, and a lot of love, she could certainly bring back Ria at par with other children. The tussle had begun . . . and intensified.

❧

BB's father, Subhash, had been staying for some time with BB at his flat in Mumbai. Since he was under the care of Dr Amit, it was advisable to keep him at Mumbai rather than any other city. Though BB had appointed enough people to take care of his father, he made sure that he came down to Mumbai once every week to be with him.

BB liked Mumbai. Though, he now had his official residence in New Delhi, yet the life of Mumbai charmed him. He also liked to spend quiet evenings with some choicest friends, one amongst them being Dr Amit Ray. BB and Dr Amit liked each other. They liked to talk to each other. Liked to listen to each other. While talking to Dr Amit, BB had realized that Dr Amit had always tried to avoid discussion on his family though he urged BB from time to time to get married. But BB could sense that there was something that irked the doctor. But at the same time BB did not want to make Dr Amit uncomfortable. So he decided to wait for the right opportunity . . . and the right time.

Dr Amit had never discussed his personal problems ever with anybody. But with BB, he felt most comfortable. He felt inclined to open up his heart to him. But he did not know how to begin and where to begin from.

'You know, Bibhuti, sometimes I feel very lonely out here,' he said hesitatingly.

'Why so?' asked BB in dismay. 'You are always surrounded by a world of people who look up to you as their god. Even I revere you for what you are.'

'No, Bibhuti, perhaps there is more to life than this,' said Dr Amit.

'Tell me, I am listening,' said BB.

'You see . . . er . . . there is a void. An emptiness here within,' he said pointing to his chest. 'A wound that shall remain green forever.'

'Ayan?' asked BB.

Dr Amit nodded silently.

Before the silence stretched into the realm of soreness, BB placed his hand on the shoulder of the doctor.

'Doctor, heal thyself,' he said slowly, making Dr Amit look up to him.

'Don't let this grief dictate your life Amit. You are still alive. And your being alive is a boon for everybody around you. Ayan is still there in our memories and shall always remain. But life cannot come to a standstill because of his departure, Amit. Give life another chance.'

'Bibhuti, I have always tried. But I still bear the blame in my heart. What kind of a father am I that I could not save my only child?.' Amit's eyes were brimming with tears.

'You had done your bit, Amit. You had played your *kirdaar*. But perhaps God willed it differently. You cannot blame yourself for things that are beyond your *kirdaar*. Look around you, Amit, and mark my words. You will find Ayan in a different form, with different features. Try to discover Ayan in your reality. You will surely find him.'

Dr Amit silently nodded as he looked away.

❧

Tina had been spending most of our time at St. Mary's with little Ria and Jamini Desai, the special instructor. The vocalization program went on in its own pace. Ria had difficulty picking up words, especially those which were alien to her. But Tina was determined. She took the smaller hiccups in her stride and revelled at the fact that Ria was giving her best effort. Sometimes, Tina would take Ria to the Juhu beach, sometimes to the zoo, and sometimes to watch a film with her. Both were inseparable, and both relished each other's company.

Mother Superior, time and again, reminded Tina that she needed to act fast. The rules of adoption may change without notice, and the seemingly easy procedures might become a cumbersome process. Tina was helpless. She could neither force Dr Amit nor counsel him. He was beyond any counselling. Neither could she leave Amit for good. Something needed to be done extraordinary to create a sense of awareness in Amit.

It's not that Tina didn't have support. Kumar Sinha was always within range when required and supported Tina with all the paperwork, applications, and all that was required for the medical formalities. Kumar was very good with papers. All the submittals that he made were near perfect. Only thing that Kumar could not do was submit the application for the process of adoption . . . though he badly wanted to. He somehow felt that Tina deserved all the happiness in the world. And someone needed to assure that.

The evening was unusually silent. Tina had returned early, unaware of the fact that Dr Amit had also returned home early. It was a strange coincidence. There had been rare occasions when they had been at home together in the evening. There was a slight drizzle outside, quite uncommon during this time of the year. Bhuvan, the cook, had prepared some crispy French fries with hot coffee in tune with the inclement weather. The aroma that emanated from the kitchen was too tempting to withstand. Amit peeked into the kitchen to look for a helping. Bhuvan was well aware of the likings of Dr Amit and had been readying a plateful of the mouth-watering delicacy with toppings of mint and coriander leaves. That accompanied by Cappuccino Black was an enviable combination.

'So what have you thought about?' Amit's sudden question surprised Tina.

'About what?' Tina asked in reply.

'About the child,' said Amit as he sipped into the coffee.

'You should tell me, Amit,' said Tina, her voice almost choking.

Amit chose not to reply immediately.

They sat in silence for a while. The rain had intensified outside, and in the fading light, they could see the droplets thicken into a haze.

The patter of the rain against the Cornish reminded them of their days together in during their early days of marriage when they would spend hours together, wrapped in a blanket, gazing out of the window at the rain. After so many years, they were again witnessing rain in November, though seated apart on different levels of mental attenuations. But the rain raged on, bringing more and more memories with it, giving torture to the already ravaged minds of the two.

'Remember the cluster of trees that sheltered us from rain when we returned from Matunga? Those trees got felled some days ago. Wonder where people will take shelter when it rains heavily,' said Amit.

'And also those heart-shaped cookies, which we used to carry to distribute amongst the urchins. They used to literally wait for us.' Tina smiled.

'Also the green umbrella . . . that got battered by the high breeze and yet we could manage to hold on to it.' Amit laughed.

'Yes, we got it repaired several times . . . But never got rid of it until last year,' said Tina.

'And that black dog that always followed us around Shivaji Park. We gave a name to it,' recalled Tina.

'Shadow,' exclaimed Amit. 'It shadowed us everywhere.'

'And we cast the same shadow against the wall,' Tina said in a whisper.

'Was he alive when you saw him?' she asked.

'Yes, he was,' replied Amit softly.

Then there was silence again.

Amit moved closer to Tina and took her shoulders. She was crying. Amit could also not stop tears from forming in his eyes. They held each other tight against each other as tears rolled down in a free-flowing stream. The silence had been rodgered into submission by the sound of sobs and sniffles.

The rain had stopped outside, and the streetlights had taken dominance over the region. But in the darkened room, Tina and Amit perhaps rediscovered their lost relationship, unaware of the time that passed them.

'Can we go there at 9:00 AM?' asked Amit.

'Yes.' It was the only reply that Tina could manage.

❧

The formalities had taken little time to get over. There had been other factors too. Letters from professor and social activist Salman Ilahi and the minister of state, home affairs, Mr Bibhuti Bhushan, had made things much easier. It was a moment of euphoria. Both Tina and Amit were in the seventh heaven. And so were the people who always wished for their happiness. Tina and Amit thanked everyone for their support and good wishes . . . And little Ria, who now had been rechristened as Ria Ray, stood transfixed amongst the celebrations.

Her innocent cute features and expressions were features one couldn't take the eyes off. She had been the cynosure, and perhaps she knew it. But she wanted to be with Tina all the time. As Tina went around distributing sweets and the pastries her father had brought along from King's Circle, Ria feared being left behind.

'Mamman,' a shout rang out from the hall.

Everyone turned around to look at Ria. She had uttered her first meaningful word.

Tina ran ahead and took her on her arms as everyone around broke into a spontaneous round of applause. This was magic. This was history. Tina's hard work had borne results. She stood like a victor on the podium with her prize in her hand.

Tina had proved to the big bad untrusting world that being a woman is indeed a blessing and being a woman of substance is itself nothing less than godliness.

There was but a confusion . . . whether to laugh, or cry . . . whether to die of happiness or live again—the life of fulfilment.

Vasamsi jirnani yatha vihaya
navani grhnati naro 'parani
tatha sarirani vihaya jirnany
anyani samyati navani dehi.

(As a person puts on new garments, giving up old ones, similarly, the soul accepts new material bodies, giving up the old and useless ones.)

—The Bhagavat Gita

CHAPTER 20

Processes of Thought

'Politicians are not the only people who are dark,' thundered BB. 'The common man himself should share the blame. I am not defending anybody, but look, anybody who gets an iota of power, chooses to misuse it. People easily put the blame on politicians, but remember it's not the politicians only who make or mar a nation, its common man too, who contribute.'

The audience was not impressed. They had come to crucify politicians over the increasing corruption in the country. But BB was not one to take things lying down. He had established himself as a clear-throated person. Whether it was the press, the common public, fellow politicians, or any platform, BB had been very honest with his feelings. Diplomacy is for the dead; the truth requires a lot of courage, that's what he had been feeling all the way.

'You see, ladies and gentlemen', continued BB in the same tone of aggression, 'the country runs on revenue, mainly from taxes. Before castigating the government, have you ever thought of the vast population we need to feed? Our population remains our greatest challenge. Everything else is secondary because everything else is a derivative.'

He paused, gulped some water from the bottle of Bislery, kept on the table.

'A country like China uses their population to become their strength.' He continued with renewed vigour. 'For us our populace is a liability. That's because our people are too complacent, languid, uncontrollable. We despise work. We resist change. At the first instance, we try to dodge work. We are too attracted to shortcuts, processes of easy money. In India there are more middlemen in every trade, than any other country. Why? They are also a part of the common man. And politicians, they are surrounded by too many strong middlemen, who keep them in power to earn unscrupulous money. They are the enemies and not the politicians alone.'

'Then what do you propose?' said a young man from the front rows.

'Identify yourself,' said BB pointing towards him.

'Abhay Kher from UTV India,' replied the questioner.

'Well, I have a lot of propositions, but what pains me is the mass indifference that the common man has towards something novel,' said BB.

'And why not, sir? What kind of security have the government provided to the common man?' asked the man from UTV.

'Who are your threats to security?' asked BB in reply.

'You see, when someone has met with an accident and we carry that person to the hospital. Police harasses us, unnecessarily. Then why should we help someone? We should rather save ourselves from these government-aided goons,' replied the young man.

'Look, Mr Kher,' BB's voice had mellowed down a bit. 'Police too has to follow some protocol. I understand that these methods need to be revisited somewhat. We are trying to improve a few things. We would definitely like to have suggestions from you people.'

By now rumblings and murmurs had started from all corners of the auditorium. Suggestions flew in thick and fast—about reforms in law and order, about making police and authorities answerable to the public, about declaration of proper assets of politicians and bureaucrats, about re-organizing the quota system, and about capital punishments to rapists and terrorists and a lot more.

The party workers had to intervene to restore some sort of decorum to the situation. Once the din had subsided, BB once again took the centre stage.

'I've heard a lot many things today. Few of them are new, but most of them are age-old expectations. Our leaders have failed to implement the ideas that had been put across to them years ago. I won't go about promising things like a seasoned politician because I am not a seasoned politician. All I can assure you is that I will try my best to implement certain ideas that has been discussed today, not because I wasn't to create a vote bank but because these are the things that perturb me as well. It disturbs me when I see disturbing pictures of death and gore in the newspapers in the name of religion and caste. It disturbs me when I hear about the misuse of power by the police and the bureaucrats. It disturbs me to see the ugly face of poverty and hunger that still form a large part of our population. It disturbs me when I hear people belittle the girl child and try to disown the baby who is a girl, still in the womb. It disturbs me to see an ever-increasing distance between the villages and cities, between the city-educated masses and the vernacular-educated population. It disturbs me to see the lackadaisical approach to work by the government employees and the lack of facilities in government-run institutions, including colleges and hospitals. It pains me to see people settled in the U.S. or other countries, having earned a comfortable life for themselves in dollars cribbing against the lack of opportunity in India or lack of cleanliness of the cities. I ask them that when you compare, try to see through the surface of the skin—into the bone structure of the skeleton. I tell them that we are feeding or trying to feed one of the biggest population of the world. We might have narrow road, unclean public places, unsystematic ways of administration; but still we survive, every storm, every catastrophe and not succumb the way Lehman Brothers did.'

A huge round of applause went up spontaneously at this declaration.

'Ladies and gentlemen, I admit that there have been times, we have made gross mistakes. I had read somewhere, and to some extent, I believe in it too, that, man is never good or bad. He's always dictated by the circumstances, he is in. There have been circumstances when the polity of our country had gone through dark eras of transition. Probably it was necessary too, to go through such times of turmoil. Those were lessons for us. Lessons for reform because those who forget history are condemned to repeat it. I do not see any reason for India or Pakistan or for that matter Bangladesh to go for partition in another thousand years, also beyond that probably. We have learnt our lesson.

'Well, coming back to the point, there would be several decisions that our core team members will take during our tenure at office. They will be bold ones. We would require your support at every step to achieve, what we aim for. Help me and my team in rebuilding our nation.'

There were more applauses. The audience were slowly swaying in favour of BB.

Jayesh Mathur, an eminent party worker, informed BB that an old man from the audience had been trying to speak to him for quite some time.

'Allow him,' BB relented.

The audience fell silent as the authorities managed to get the microphone across to the old man seated towards the rear of the auditorium.

'Identify yourself first,' yelled a young party worker from the stage.

The spotlight had been focused onto an elderly man, clad in white, with silvery grey hair, and a small shining beard. BB seemed to recognise the figure.

'Wait a minute,' he thought. 'This is Salman Ilhai, the great scholar. It's a privilege, an honour to have a person of his calibre in the audience.'

'I . . . I am your common man, Mr Minister,' said Ilahi in a tone that reverberated in all corners of the auditorium. 'I am he who tries to find his identity in all the forums of society. I am he, who gets harassed by the policies of the government and also at the hands of the auto rickshaw driver while returning home from work. I am he, honourable sir, who is always harassed by rising prices, by the roadblocks, by the unsuppressed hooliganism of the goons of the locality. I am he, sir, who when he goes to work each morning, goes prepared for a war because our buses, trains, public places, restaurants, even places of worship is no longer safe. Our wives and children unnecessarily make phone calls to confirm whether we are alive or not. Sir, the vast majority of the population is frustrated, battered, bruised, afraid. We don't know whom to support and whom not to because our situation never changed and never will. I have no question or any appeal for you, sir. I only have good wishes for you. It is good to have the embers of hope burning within us. Help us transform that into a flame.'

The audience clapped. It was their voice that the gentleman had echoed. Some of the people did recognise

Ilahi, some did not. But it did not matter. People clapped, for they had just heard their very own voice.

BB clapped too as he came forward at the edge of the dais.

'Mr Salman Ilahi, sir,' he said aloud. 'I have always admired you for what you are. I have always read your articles in newspapers and magazines. Let me first use this forum to thank you for the thoughts you have published and hope that you would keep guiding us with your intellectual views on social, economic, political aspects of present-day India. Please give a huge round of applause, for this eminent personality.'

The applauses continued. Amongst the huge clamour, BB invited Ilahi to the dais.

'Sir, one day, a few years back, I had been attending one of your lectures in this same very hall. You had summoned me the stage to speak up my mind. Today, I request you to share the stage with me. I will be honoured,' said BB.

Ilahi gave BB a tight embrace on reaching the pulpit. 'I don't know whether I deserve such accolades. It's an honour to get applauded by people who have never heard me, heard of me, or read my writings. It is an honour to be applauded by people by accepting you at your face value. Thank you, Mr Bibhuti, this has been an overwhelming gesture.'

❧

'What the hell are you talking about, Bailey?' asked Rajat Singh in utter disbelief.

'Yes, sir, it's all true.' Armaan smiled.

'You mean, you are ready to risk your career at this early age? You have a bright future in front of you,' said Rajat who had seen the meteoric accent of Armaan in the world of cricket.

Rajat Singh had been a staunch supporter of Armaan since the time he had first seen him playing. He also had been the influence behind Armaan's selection in the challenger's trophy. After all, Rajat had been in the selection committee for the last three years.

Armaan's decision to withdraw his name from the list of probables had shocked everyone like his performance had. The name of Armaan Bailey had become a source of interest to every follower of cricket in India and abroad after his heroics in the Challenger Trophy. Bailey had also led a team comprising of upcoming cricket stars to victory against the visiting New Zealand team. He had established the fact that his understanding for cricket was immense and that he had an inborn virtue in him to captain any side.

Cricket had been the oxygen for Armaan. It was the only medium perhaps through which he could express his feelings. When on the cricket field, he was oblivious to the world. It was only cricket and him, the finest form of self-expression, the outside world had a little bearing to his life, then. The whole cricketing world was dumbfounded by this decision of his. Already the Indian media had started weaving tantalizing stories around Armaan and his abilities. He was after all an enigma. A person who appeared unperturbed, serious, focused, humble, and quiet. He never seemed to go overboard with success and never appeared overwhelmed while sharing the dressing room with famous cricketing personalities of India.

Armaan had been called to the headquarters of BCCI in Mumbai, to discuss on his decision of withdrawal. Even after hours of discussion wherein the board members did try to persuade him to reverse his decision, by chalking out lucrative plans for him during the upcoming cricketing season. But Armaan had remained unmoved. The firmness with which he had led cricket teams to victory never deserted him throughout the conversation. Armaan Bailey was like a rock of integrity, decisiveness, and determination.

'So what is your plan, next?' asked Saraf, one of the eminent members of BCCI, in dismay.

'I definitely shall be associated with cricket in one form or the other,' said Armaan. 'I have always had a dream of playing for India. But destiny too takes its turn. Maybe, I will have to start afresh, in Tasmania.'

'We all had been unanimous in selecting you for the conditioning camp. We knew you would do well there too,' said Saraf.

Bailey could only smile in reply. He was well aware of the missed opportunity, but the stake was too large, at least for him. For lesser human beings, this would have been an opportunity of a lifetime. It would have been an opportunity that supersedes all other beckoning. Being successful, sadly, is measured by the glitter of money and fame. Success does not count those rare occasions when humans bear the courage to spurn worldly gains in favour of non-tangible attributes. It is true that one who can sacrifice is destined for greater glory, invariably.

ல்ல

There had been very few applicants for the PPP model of schemes of the government. Private Public Partnership was the new approach that the government had adopted to woo investors for the development of infrastructure. However, private entities had their own doubt in the system. They feared the safety of their investments.

Government had opened their doors for investments in schools, universities, roads, airports, hospitals, and other amenities in infrastructure. India needed infrastructure. The economy had slowly shifted gears from being total agrarian to semi-industrial. Foreign investors had been eyeing India as a favourable destination for investment, primarily in steel, power, and mining. However, the dearth of infrastructure had irked them. The FDI was slow small. The government wanted more and so were intent to roll out SOPs in favour of private players who showed courage in matching steps with the Public Sector.

One of the brightest proposals received by the Government of Rajasthan was that of a super speciality hospital in Jaisalmer. Initiated by the Rathod Group of Companies, the proposal had been accepted by the government with a flourish. Government had already allocated the necessary clearances for the project; and land, electricity, and water had been allocated. The process of finalization for the constructor was on for the process of bidding.

Kumar Sinha was somewhat taken aback by the heading of the NIT (Notice Inviting Tender). Design, engineering, procurement, and construction of Neha Rathod Memorial Super Speciality Hospital at Jaisalmer. But after reading through the cover several times, he could not hold back his smile of contentment. He felt proud of his ex-colleague and friend Ramsingh Rathod. He had a strong urge to call up Ramsingh and congratulate him for his momentous effort, but restrained himself; for after all, he was a bidder. And it is against the ethics of bidding to establish contact with the client, leapfrogging over the consultant. Yes, he can wait. Whether PECL won the bid or not, he knew the victory was ultimately of the team. The completion of this project would be an attribute to all the people who had been in close connection to Ramsingh.

Yes, you have done it, Ramsingh. You have done it, Tina and Amit Ray. You have done it, Salman Ilahi. The PQC team of Lonavala, you have done it. The complete fashion team of Magenta, you have done it. And, Neha Rathod, you have been the inspiration . . . you have done it.

The speaker had allotted only twenty minutes for the discussion. The opposition had been stalling the house over useless propaganda against the government over inaction over some stray incidents of crime and lawbreaking. The Home Ministry had been targeted for not being able to assure safety to citizens in the metros and other big cities. BB was given the task of taking on the opposition over the issue. Needless to say, BB was more than ready to deliver.

'The honourable members of opposition are absolutely right in bringing up this issue,' he began amidst the bedlam. 'However, by only shouting slogans and causing hindrances to the procedure of the parliament, what patriotic responsibility are they displaying in front of the nation?'

'Crime is a resultant. Crime is a derivative. It is the source that we need to eliminate. We have always resorted to blame games, which has never got us to focus at the root cause for the growth of violence. Have we ever thought why we are not able to control it? There are several reasons which dictate our inaction. One of them is noncooperation. I admit, I am not a seasoned politician . . . and tell you what, I have been elected because of that.' He paused to wipe off his perspiration. The otherwise hostile opposition members had somewhat settled down to listen. They knew that Bibhuti

Bhushan had become somewhat an icon for the youth of India. Be it the followers of the ruling front or opposition, they all adored him for his honest opinions. He was one who never covered up the misdoings of the government, and neither did he spare the opposition for the nuisance they created.

'An opposition does not mean that we oppose everything that the ruling party proposes. In some of the grave matters, we should work hand in hand. The miscreants who have been spreading violence all around the country are being sponsored by some political party. Without support, these thugs do not have chance to roam free. The goons or so-called dons, who crowd around the culverts near your house, are bloody kith and kin to some idiot who bears some political clout. Let's get rid of these fools before their population increase to uncontrollable limits.' He paused to see the response. There wasn't any. Everyone had been stunned by the spirited counter attack.

'India is not able to use its population to its advantage, unlike China and some other South Eastern neighbours is because of its high count of unproductive population. Look at the unemployment. Do you expect the government to go to your homes with employment letters? Why can't the population find means of productive employment? It's below the dignity of graduates to work in factories. It's below the dignity of high school pass outs to work in poultry farms. But it is quite dignified for them to resort to crime and arson and to be thugs and touts as middlemen and rob honest peasants of their hard-earned money. And also a sizeable part of the population is happy to reside in jails and reformatory centres or amble their life away, begging. Beggars, who are able bodied but not ready to work for their living should be considered as an uneconomic citizen of India.' There was a slight uproar at this from the opposition benches, which was quickly quieted by the upbeat speaker. BB was asked to continue with his high-voltage deliverable. Why were the seasoned politicians quiet? Revolution? Self-realization?

BB waited for people to settle down.

'Please continue,' said the speaker.

'Why don't we put the prisoners who are a burden for the country to work for economy boosting activities? Each big and small prison should be converted into small-scale industries engaged into construction or production jobs for the government. A prisoner who does not perform will not be left to have free lunches. Also, the educated, unemployed youth should be helped to set up their own small-scale units. The idea is engagement of the population.'

'I also would like to request the finance ministry to reform the taxation system. Alcohol, tobacco, and bigger pub and discotheques should attract bigger percentage of taxes. Processions on marriage, celebrations, etc., should also come under the tax regime. Fat Indian marriages should also be taxed. If a business tycoon can spend two hundred crores of rupees in his daughter's marriage, he can also spend another fifteen crores in taxes. This fifteen crore can help the government to set up a good hospital at places like Vannabari, from where I come from or for that matter any other small province which lacks proper facility of healthcare.'

The was a mild round of applause from the backbenches.

'Honourable speaker, sir. People have lost their faith in politicians, and politicians are more than responsible for it. Sir, can we not have a screening system, wherein the candidates filling nomination papers should pass through the process only after furnishing documents pertaining to a minimum level of qualification and experience.' BB looked around. Are they listening?

'At the present moment, we need to win back the confidence of the population that we have lost. We need to look beyond the petty differences that overrule our senses. For once, we should grow out of the limits of the respective parties and work for the nation. Believe me, even if you are in the opposition, your good work will be recognised, and you will stand a greater chance of winning not only elections but several hearts too. Can we not for once stand together, briefly, in an effort to rebuild the nation? Can we not ask ourselves whether our selfish motives as leaders of the ruling party or opposition give us the correct picture to our progeny? Can we not for once be united in the common interest—interest for the nation? I believe we can. And if a technocrat can win elections by beating a seasoned politician, this nation can also wake up to truth and self-realization. *We can*. Jai Hind.'

The Bailey family had migrated to Mumbai to spend some time with Salman Ilahi prior to their departure to Australia. Jonathon had repeatedly requested Ilahi to persuade Armaan to stay back in India to pursue his cricketing career. Jonathon somehow felt guilty that, for him, Armaan was foregoing the great future that lay ahead of him. At the same time, Jonathon knew that Armaan was too simple, too naïve. Rogues would exploit his simplicity for their own benefit, if not guided properly in different walks of life. Armaan was autistic, and autism is not a disease but a disorder. Though Armaan was a great cricket captain, he required help for every other aspect of life. Jonathon knew that Armaan needed him, and he too in turn needed Armaan.

'Dada, why don't you too come with us?' asked Armaan.

'No, Armaan, I have lots of work here,' said Salman.

'But, Dada, this is the time for you to retire. Why don't you just take your mind off work for some time?' asked Armaan, a bit puzzled.

'My work is such that there is no retirement.' Armaan smiled.

'What is your work, Dada?' asked Armaan rather innocently.

'I search for *kirdaars*,' replied Salman, smilingly.

'Can I too become a *kirdaar* for you, someday, Dada?' asked Armaan after a bit of pondering.

'You already are, my son. You are already one of my *kirdaars*,' said Salman Ilahi.

And Ilahi was pleased to see his disciple smile at him in deep contentment.

CHAPTER 21

Confessions

'**B**ibhuti Bhushan weds Bidisha Basu,' Solomon read out aloud.

'They could have put BB weds BB.' Vinod laughed.

'The invitation is for the total team of Mumbai-Pune expressway of PECL,' said Kumar with a proud voice. 'The minister was very happy with the quality of the road when he took the ride on it during the inauguration. He had even personally congratulated our MD for it,' informed Kumar.

'Yes, I was there when the team from NHAI had inspected every inch of PQC and had accorded their appreciation,' said Vinod.

'So this is the reward, invitation to his grand wedding.' Solomon smiled.

'Well, that depends on whether you can manage your leave,' replied Kumar.

'I have never attended a grand Indian wedding. I cannot wait to be a part of it,' said an excited Suraj. 'And besides, PECL can treat this as an honour for the whole PQC team.'

'It's not only the PQC that has brought accolades to this project,' said Kumar in a tone of modesty. 'Look at the tunnels, the elevated corridor, the shotcreting, the viaducts, everything done so immaculately. BKT has lived up to his reputation.'

'That's right,' seconded Solomon. 'But Kumar sir, will your cranky boss allow you to take a leave that long?'

'Boss, who?' asked Kumar spontaneously.

'Chandra, that buffoon,' replied Solomon.

'He's no longer the boss,' replied Kumar straight-faced.

'Your department—' Solomon was interrupted by Kumar instantly.

'If I say, I am the department?'

Suraj almost spilled the tea he was about to sip and looked up.

'Wow, you never told us.' Vinod was as astonished as the others in the room.

Kumar only smiled in reply as he started towards the door, leaving the others in a state of spellbound silence.

The silence was finally broken by an insipid question that only someone like Solomon could ask.

'Is this Bidisha Basu somehow connected to the actress Bipasha Basu?'

The others seemed least interested to even attempt a reply.

'Do you know the uniqueness of this marriage?' asked Gowda to the other party workers inside the office.

Most of these people had been quite discontented by the way BB had been running the party. Though, his strict measures had become very popular with the general public, there had been growing resentment over his strange and stern policies. However, one person had, as always, kept faith with the doings of BB, Siddharth Gowda. He had been a staunch supporter of BB in everything he did. His unconventional methods of operation undoubtedly had made the party stronger and more popular than never before.

Gowda had always been farsighted, and he knew that if BB could resurrect his party from the brink of extermination, he could, with his own methods, take it to the heights of unimaginable glory.

'This is the first marriage that is being taxed.' Gowda smiled. 'Think of the audacious reply that Bibhuti has given to the questions of the opposition leaders.'

The murmurs had subsided. The party members had nothing to say on this. It had swept them as it had the media, the political and bureaucratic circles, off their feet.

❧

'Sir, you will have to come. I don't want to hear anything.' BB was adamant.

'My blessings are always with you, my son. But believe me, at the moment, I do not want to stay away from my daughter and her family for even a minute. They will be going back to Australia next week,' said Ilahi meekly.

'Sir, I have already told you several times. Please come with your family. Your daughter's family. It also will be an outing for them. Sir, please come, it will make us feel good,' pleaded BB.

'Your world is different, Mr Bhushan. Do you think we can fit in . . . in the world of such big people?' asked Ilahi.

The phone receiver echoed the laughter from the other side.

'Sir, you must be joking. You only keep saying all men and women are equal. There is no worldly difference amongst mortals. I repeat, sir, if you do not come, I can even postpone my marriage,' said BB.

'Hum samjhte the hum hi pagal, deewangi kya hoti hai, unhe jana to ye jana [I kept thinking that I am the only one who is mad, but after knowing thou, I have come to know what madness is all about],' said Ilahi in his customary tone.

'Sir, we will wait for you and your family,' said BB before hanging up.

'Who was it?' Alia asked Salman as he hung up.

'Bibhuti Bhushan,' replied Ilahi.

'Allah, that enigmatic politician?' asked Alia, excited.

'Yes. He is more human than a politician,' said Salman.

'A human playing the kirdaar of a politician,' Alia smiled.

'Absolutely. We have to attend his wedding. He is adamant. Please try and convince Jonathon and Armaan to come along,' said Ilahi.

'Don't worry, Dada, we all are coming,' said Armaan, entering the room. 'He is a hero of the nation.'

Ilahi smiled in reply. Then pressing Arman's hands into his, he said, 'Like you, my son. You too are a hero. My hero.'

❧

Gautam Bhadra Jr., executive, Project Marketing Department of PECL, stood hesitatingly in front of the palatial bungalow that happened to be the office of Rathod Constructions Limited. He had been asked by his boss to meet the owner of the firm, Mr Ramsingh Rathod to have a firsthand introduction with him before going ahead with the bidding process of the Super-speciality Hospital project.

Gautam was led to a spacious visitor's room by the security personnel and was asked to wait till Mr Rathod gives him a call. Gautam looked around. The whole surrounding looked very sophisticated, almost surreal, studded with expensive decor, and very tastefully made. He had heard that the owner had once been an employee with PECL. He wondered how he might have ascended to this level of sophistication and wealth from very modest remuneration of PECL. Gautam also wondered what kind of reception he might get from an ex-employee of PECL after getting detached from the company. He had heard that Mr Rathod was a cranky character and had been asked to be very humble and polite with him.

'Mr Bhadra', called out the security from outside, 'the MD wants to meet you.'

Gautam made his way with the help of the security, into another room, more spacious and grand than the room he had been seated in. He was awestruck by the chandelier that hung from the ceiling in the middle of the room. He had never seen a chandelier for real before. It was indeed majestic, probably handed over to the Rathods by their forefathers as legacy.

'Welcome,' said a booming voice from behind the well-spread-out table.

Gautam was amazed by the character. He was quite contrary to the description that had been given to him about Mr Ramsingh Rathod. In front of him was seated a typical Rajasthani Rajput clad in traditional Rajasthani attire, sporting a bushy handlebar-type moustache.

'Sit down,' he said in the most commanding voice.

Gautam could meekly follow.

'Whisky?' offered the man raising a glass of the amber-coloured liquor to his lips.

'No, thank you, sir,' said Gautam shivering awkwardly.

'Cow milk?' offered Rathod again, smilingly, this time.

'Actually, Mr Rathod, I had been asked to—,' started Gautam but was instantly interrupted by the raised arm of Ramsingh.

'Sir. Learn to say sir. I am your senior, and I don't run a grocery shop,' Ramsingh said in a grave tone.

'Sir, I have been sent to—' Gautam was once again interrupted.

'Listen, this is not a brothel that pimps can come and negotiate for clients. Tell your boss, if he wants to bid seriously, to come himself. Now you may leave,' said Ramsingh in a dismissive tone. It was quite evident that Ramsingh was not much interested to converse with Gautam.

He stood up, bowed, and left the room in a hurry.

'What were his exact words, Gautam?' asked Kumar curiously.

'Well, he said that ask your boss to meet me,' said Gautam rather meekly.

'Cannot be,' Kumar laughed. 'Ramsingh never talks so courteously with his dad even. Anyway, we have a date tomorrow evening.'

'With whom, sir?' asked Gautam.

'With an old friend who almost went astray,' said Kumar before leaving the room.

This time, Kumar and Gautam were not asked to wait. They were rather ushered into the MD's chamber immediately on arrival.

'Welcome to the jewel in the crown of PECL,' the booming voice welcomed them graciously.

'Yes, Ram, how are you?' asked Kumar in a tone of concern.

Ram came forward to give a tight embrace to Kumar, then took his hand and got seated side by side on the beautifully crafted sofa.

'Mr Bhadra, what about some whisky today?' asked Ramsingh as if in mockery.

'Thank you, sir, but I don't drink,' replied Gautam almost in a whisper.

'No ice, no soda, only water. Two is to one,' said Kumar, almost out of turn, surprising both Gautam and Ramsingh himself.

'Sabhaash [bravo],' said Ramsingh emphatically.

⁓

Contrary to expectations, the occasion was not as glamorous as it should have been. There were little fanfare, no music, no heavy ornamentation of the venue. Amongst the simplicity of the occasion, what stood out was the thoughtfulness for which BB was known for. There was an arrangement for lunch for the poor. Blankets, saris, and medicines were also distributed amongst the needy. Money had been spent thoughtfully on meaningful activities rather than on decoration and glitterati.

Food was another area which had been taken special care of. Good food always makes a great occasion grand. Though people might forget the date and also the people whom they had met in an occasion, the taste of food stays with them forever. And BB had managed to conjure up the best dishes from around the globe. Guests were presented with the eternal dilemma of what to have and what not to. Food from every part of India prepared with immaculate authenticity filled the giant hall with mouth-watering aroma. It was a foodie's delight, and it could be perceived from the number of helpings that Solomon and Vinod took in short span. Even people who are fussy about food like Dr Amit and Salman Ilahi were seen to enjoy the vegetarian dishes that had been arranged for. BB himself went around taking opinions regarding the preparations, and of course, people did not stop to cast their opinion with a flourishing heart . . . like they did during the elections.

At night, BB had organized a *mushaira*. Of course, the presence of Salman Ilahi had inspired him to do so. It was a fabulous occasion, and Salman Ilahi put a rhythm to the atmosphere through his magical, hypnotic words. Everyone was caught in the spell of words that touch the soul.

Lafzon Ke Fasaane Dhoondte Hain Log
Lamhon Mai Zamaane Dhoondte Hain Log
Tu Zehr Hi De Sharaab Keh Kar Saaqi
Jeene Ke Bahaane Dhoondte Hain Log . . .'

⁓

The succeeding night had a different agenda—a unique one. It was decided, after a lot of coaxing and convincing, though, to have a session of confession. It was a session where each participant should share the most bizarre feeling or incident of his or her life. There would only be a single confidante whom everyone could trust and have faith upon. The person selected to do the duty was, of course, Salman Ilahi. Who else can match the maturity, experience and integrity of someone like him?

Armaan was the first to volunteer. As usual, Armaan never wanted to lose any chance to have heart-to-heart talks with his dada. Though it was a fact that he had never hidden anything from dada, but still there was something left to confess.

'What confession do you have?' Ilahi smiled.

'Dada, I don't know what a confession actually is. All I want to say is what I feel so strongly. Dada, in school, I never had friends. Boys thought that I was different. They made fun of me. They passed rude comments on me. The only friend that I had was you, Dada. You only taught me that there was a life beyond the books. You know, I tried, Dada. And I did what I couldn't have done alone. Now, I know that my dada, my friend, needs me the most, and I find myself guilty to leave him alone. Dada, this is my confession, that I have been inconsiderate towards you. I know you will never come with us to Australia. The lanes, bylanes, bends of Mumbai will never let you go. The *panwallahs*, the newspaper vendor, the milkman will never let you go. The verses that you make and remake from morn to night behind that pillar in the veranda will not let you go. The easy chair where you have your evening cup of tea, relishing the sunset will not let you go . . . because you belong to everybody, Dada. Everyone likes to have a bit of your time, a bit of you. I feel guilty to leave you alone, Dada. But one day, I will surely make you proud.' Armaan's voice was full of emotion. Salman could only give him a tight embrace and say in the gravest tone, 'Ameen.'

And they say Armaan is autistic. If this is autism, thought Salman, then this nation could have been better off being an autistic nation. Perhaps it is better to be autistic than be normal. Look what our normal people have done to the world—division, partition, hatred.

BB was next. He walked up graciously to Ilahi and sat beside him silently for a while.

'Sir, I am aware that today I am very popular. And I am popular because of my unconventional methods of governance. My methods find appeal with both the educated and the uneducated masses. I have reached a level in society, from where I can get things done, whether it be good or bad. But, sir, I too had resorted to dishonest means to reach this level . . . it was necessary. When I was employed with Oasis,

I came to know that hard work alone does not guarantee a successful career. Dedication alone cannot assure progress and growth. Your loyalty for the company does not count when the company faces adversity. There is something more which you need to have to ensure your ascent to the top. Deceit and polity is something that one must attain, not only to grow but also to survive. In Oasis, sir, I went about discovering the weaknesses of my peers and superiors. Sir, I gained considerable ground by making their weaknesses my strengths. This catapulted me to the next level of power, Siddharth Gowda recognised my abilities . . . Yes, sir, I am the one who had ordered for the abduction and assassination of the PA of Seshagiri Rao. It was necessary. But, sir, I want to prove to the world that there are good, honest politicians too. Sir, believe me, I am here to work for the people, for the nation. I am here to create a world which is more comfortable to live in. But for that to happen, I need to resort to activities which by itself is vile. But for the greater good, I will keep doing it.'

'My best wishes are with you, son. Ameen,' said Ilahi.

Ilahi was not amazed by the confession. He was not unknown to political warfare. History of mankind had been witnessing such crossing of swords from time immemorial. Ilahi knew, however, that one who rules by the sword often falls victim to it. In the heart of his hearts, he somehow could feel the emergence of a lurking fear—a fear for the safety of BB.

There was a brief wait before Dr Amit gingerly made his way forward.

'Uncle, you know that I hail from a very humble family. My parents had to struggle to make ends meet. Money was a commodity that I had grown lusting for. My friends were all rich blokes, where as I always used to be the odd one out. I always missed out on important activities in want of money. In numerous occasions, I had seen my parents remain hungry in order to feed me. So as I grew up, my biggest objective became to be rich, affluent. Sir, I never missed a single operation. I even operated in extra shifts to earn fat commissions. Tina and Ayan too had become secondary to my love for wealth. Sir, that fateful day, I could have reached the school much earlier had I not opted for the operation that was not actually slated for me. I took over the case from Dr Kamat because I knew that the operation attracted a fat commission because of its urgency. Sir, had I not operated that day, probably I could have saved Ayan.' Dr Amit had buried his head into his hands.

Salman Ilahi caressed his head softly as he spoke. 'It is a matter of pride that you have been able to speak out the ill that is in your character. It requires courage. Now that you have known about it, I know that you will quickly eliminate this evil from your life. And I know that you have grown out of it now. And besides, Ayan's demise was an accident. And accidents do not recognise any ifs and buts. Do not unnecessarily accuse yourself, Amit. You too have been a father. I know that you will be a good father to Ria. See properly, you will find Ayan within her. Amit, Ayan has gone nowhere. He has only changed form. He is very much in our midst.'

Ilahi had been deeply moved by Amit's words. He always held that Amit was a doctor with a big heart. But he had never witnessed him break down like this before.

'Doctor, heal thyself,' whispered Ilahi to himself. The almighty has assigned you with divine powers to preserve the life he has bestowed upon us. Doctor, when your hands tremble, humanity shakes. When your emotions waver . . .

mankind waits at your mercy in total numbness. Heal thyself, doctor. The world needs you.'

Oblivious of the confession that Amit had made, Tina walked up to Ilahi to confess.

'Uncle, I don't know how to put it,' she said slowly. 'But I had become too ambitious. Magenta had been doing well, and slowly my focus had been shifting from my family to my profession. Uncle, I could feel that I had been giving less attention to Amit and Ayan. I liked the appreciation. I liked to be talked about in the parties and get-togethers. I liked being awed by my contemporaries and also the jealousy part of it too. Within all this, I was losing precious time for my family and probably for myself too. You know, Uncle, had I not been sketching certain apparel designs, I could have reached the school much earlier. I could have saved Ayan, Uncle.' She broke off into a sob.

Ilahi lightly took her head into his hands.

'Tina, my child, don't blame yourself for an accident,' he said softly. 'We all know what a kind heart you have. You have done so much for so many. You, my child, are kindness personified. Don't hurt yourself by even thinking of such things. Look at Ria. She is the transformed form of Ayan. My child, Ayan is very much with us. He has not gone anywhere.'

Ilahi was in fact fascinated. This was something that seemed to emerge from a fairy tale. Both Amit and Tina did not hesitate to shoulder the blame that never was theirs and never will be . . . perhaps this . . . perhaps this is the love that we so wildly search for . . . and it indeed is immortal.

Ilahi could only smile in appreciation. It was heavenly.

Kumar Sinha appeared somewhat reluctant as he walked up to Salman Ilahi. After a moment of silence, Kumar spoke up.

'Sir, all I learnt well in my school, college, and later on at work was to become professional. I had learnt that nothing should come between me and my profession. I should be absolute in whatever I get into and that I should be able to take up greater challenges enhancing my opportunities of growth. I never made girlfriends. Neither did I get into too much camaraderie with my team members. It was work and results. But, sir, after meeting Tina madam, my concepts towards life started changing. Sir, I realized that exhaustion can be relieved by a single smile too. I realized that by simply hearing someone talk or laugh, one can get rid of tons of fatigue and that a single word can energize you into capturing the whole world. Sir, I became a human from a machine, after having met Tina Ray. Yes, sir, I am in love with her. But do not misunderstand me, sir. She is my inspiration, she is my motivation, she is my source of energy. I love her as someone far superior as a human than me. I do not want to know what she feels about me, it is not important. But as long as I keep knowing her, my love and respect for her will keep on increasing.'

'Kumar, I know you are a brave boy,' said Ilahi. 'You also have the purest of feelings. Love is always pure. There is nothing wrong in falling in love with someone. It is the finest feel that Allah has bestowed on us humans. But remember, love should have only one condition—that it should be unconditional. Never expect anything in return, and you will be happy, my boy.'

Solomon was the last to come in. He had been pushed in, rather, by Kumar.

'Sir, I have only one confession to make,' he said rather prudishly.

'Go ahead, son,' said Ilahi in his customary tone.

'Sir, when I was sixteen, I had, you know, had sex with my neighbour's daughter,' he said with a lowered head.

'OK, say it like this, that you had lost your virginity at the hands of your neighbour's daughter,' prompted Ilahi.

'No, sir, I had lost my virginity to her mother,' mumbled Solomon.

'What?' exclaimed Ilahi. 'Then which one is your confession?'

'Both, sir,' said Solomon before leaving Ilahi in a state of utter shock.

I wanted a perfect ending. Now, I've learned, the hard way, that some poems don't rhyme, and some stories don't have a clear beginning, middle, and end. Life is about not knowing, having to change, taking the moment, and making the best of it, without knowing what's going to happen next. Delicious Ambiguity.

(Gilda Radner)

CHAPTER 22

Kirdaars

It was a rainy morning. Not unusual for this time of the year. The date was nineteenth of July, a date that may find its place in historical treatises in the future. The multimillion Super-specialty Hospital stood like a monument in the heart of Jaisalmer, waiting to be inaugurated. The last two days had seen this place buzzing with activity. The police, the media, the bureaucrats, the social activists, and the construction workers had mobbed the place, putting in position their bit of work for the inauguration day. People did not mind the heat, the rain, or the sand breeze to be able to catch a glimpse of something that had been taking shape for the past thirty months. And yes, PECL had achieved the unexpected, completing the project well within the offered time limit and budget. The speed of work had been breathtaking, and no compromise had however been made in the quality of work. The majestic facility spread out over twenty-four acres of virgin land, had been immaculately planned and executed. Thus, people from all walks of life had gathered around braving the rains to take a share of credit for something which was unimaginable till some years ago.

A huge congregation of doctors, who were amongst the invitees, from all over the world had arrived a week ago, to personally inspect the facilities and suggest modifications, if any. Dr Amit Ray had been part of the elite Indian contingent. Though he had received a separate invitation, which was more personal in nature, he chose to stick to the official commitment. Tina and Ria, though, had accompanied him in this trip, a rare occasion when the family had travelled together. It was also an occasion they chose to rekindle the old fire, which time had nearly extinguished. However, the most celebrated guest probably was Bibhuti Bhushan, the would-be Minister of Home in the new cabinet at the centre. The charisma that he carried with him had already given the otherwise dank atmosphere, the necessary pomp and grandeur. Salman Ilahi was another guest of honour. Known for his heavily researched scriptures, Ilahi had already carved his name amongst imminent scholars by his published works on comparisons of thoughts of ancient philosophers with the modern ones, creating a deep-rooted awareness amongst the literate masses regarding the growth of intolerance in the world. He had been especially drafted into the curricula to enlighten the masses with his thoughts on contemporary India.

The lush green landscaping that surrounded the hospital wore a look of a resort. Greenery, with flowers in full blossom has always been a rarity in Rajasthan, and especially in the arid conditions of Jaisalmer, the scenery seemed to leap out of some picture postcard of a foreign and more fertile land. The Rathod clan had always been magnanimous; but the magnanimity that reflected from the gargantuan structure, which would treat, cure, and care for so many people with physical and psychological ailments was beyond any comparison. The organizers too had worked very hard to bring everything to shape within the schedule of time provided to them. They had immaculately arranged for all the requirements that were customary to make the event a grand one. The Government of Rajasthan had done enough to give the event the publicity it required, and of course there were the Rathods who were influential enough to send the word far and wide. There were excitement all around, and a star-studded evening was about to unfurl.

Tina and Amit took some time out to relax in the lounge. The lounge of the hotel was unusually quiet, probably immune to the humdrum outside. Amit and Tina were highly grateful for the privacy, for it provided them with a rare occasion when they could share some moments together without any professional pressure, whatsoever.

'What about your new assignments, Tina?' asked Amit in a rather relaxed tone.

'Why, what about them?' Tina replied, being rather surprised at the question itself.

'It seems that you are not interested in picking up new assignments?' asked Amit.

Tina had been till very recently one of the top choices for fashionistas with lots to spend on every outfit they slip into. Her creative, yet simple manifestations had created a revolution of sorts in the world of fashion in a very small span of time. However, even after having tasted so much success in a highly competitive line of work, she had suddenly slowed things down. Her priority had shifted towards her family, where she had been devoting her maximum time.

'Ria needs my presence, Amit. She needs my attention.' She paused before continuing, 'And I need to take care of you too. Besides, this is not the best of professions.'

Amit looked concerned. Lately, he had been a very frequent visitor to Magenta. He had taken deep interest in the subject and had been inquisitive about the various steps of development of a product.

'Tina,' Amit smiled. 'You just cannot drop the assignments that are coming your way.'

'But, Amit—'

'No, Tina,' interrupted Amit. 'I know I had in the past derided you from getting into this profession. But I was ignorant, Tina. No one ever told me about fashion as a subject. But now I have come to learn that it is one of the most creative and passionate pursuits. Like sculpture or paintings, fashion is also a manifestations of the mind. It originates from imagination and takes a form so tangible that people come to own it, accept it, appreciate it . . . and sometimes cannot live without. Now I know what it takes to be a designer. It is much more difficult than becoming a doctor. We doctors have set rules within the framework of which we work. We do not imagine things. We work with things that are . . . You work with things that aren't.'

Tina was dumbfounded. She had never imagined that Amit would be able to develop such a liking for her profession. She pinched herself. Was she dreaming?

'Tina, have you not forgiven me for being so harsh at times with you?' Amit's voice had almost reduced into a whisper.

Tina had been rendered speechless. She wanted to say something, but her voice choked. No matter however hard she tried, she could not prevent the tears from rolling down her cheeks. Was this actually happening with her?

In the silence that ensued, Amit was reminded of the trip to Shillong that he and Tina had embarked upon after marriage. It was almost like a fairy tale. Amit Ray, the name that he had inherited from the protagonist of 'Shesher Kobita', a marvellous piece of literature by Rabindranath Tagore, had lived up to his repertoire of being unconventional in choosing the time and manner of the trip. And through all hardships and discomforts, Tina had endured all his whims and fancies with a smile. Her love for him had been so deep rooted that time too could not diminish even an iota of the same. Amit knew that he had been lucky, to be with a person who understood him more than he himself did.

'Tina, I know that you need a lot of rest, a lot of love and a lot of care too. I am in the medical profession, and I am pretty good at it. But being with you has transformed me into a much better human being. Give me a chance, Tina, to be at least for once be with you, to savour your success. Give me a chance to bathe in the accolades that people, so selflessly and spontaneously, bestow upon you. Just one more show, Tina, and let all of us be a part of it.'

Tina could only nod in a quiet affirmation before throwing her arms around Amit.

'Thanks, Tina, I am so proud of you. And over the years, I have learnt one thing, Tina, that love is not finding someone you can live with . . . It is finding someone you can't live without . . .'

Tina could notice streaks of grey in the side burns of Amit. No doubt, he had finally attained wisdom. Amit had aged.

✺

It was a huge gathering. Fortunately there was no rain. People had been pouring in since afternoon to grab the most advantageous seating position from where they could not only hear the eminent speakers and performers but also see them in person. The organizers had done a wonderful job with whatever resources they had. The arrangements had been immaculate and very well planned, and why not,

Jaisalmer was poised to once again gain global prominence for reasons other than the heritage palaces, forts, hotels, history, and peacocks. The grandeur of the event even, to some extent, did eclipse the great Desert Festival, which has been an annual affair since time immemorial.

Celebrities were escorted to the dais by a bevy of beautiful girls, where with the lamp lighting ceremony the proceedings for the evening got underway.

First, Mr Anand Kaushal, the chairman of the inauguration committee, was summoned to the dais, where he formerly welcomed the dignitaries and thanked all the people, even remotely associated with the project, for the success of the colossal endeavour. After his short address, Mr Kaushal invited the chief guest, the honourable Home Minister elect, Mr Bibhuti Bhushan, to address the gathering.

BB was dressed, unlike other politicians, in a navy blue Armani suit with a light blue tie. His sharp and fair features reflected the perfect contrast against the colours he had chosen for the occasion. Though, BB was not as tall as he would have liked to be, he had a commanding presence, not only for his formidable personality but also for the way he carried himself. He had about him an air of aristocracy which made him standout in a group. People likened him to Lord Buddha; some compared him to Napoleon and some with Winston Churchill. But truth was that BB was a genre in himself, unique and contrasting.

'Honourable guests, Mr Salman Ilahi Sir, all dignitaries from India and abroad, the honorary chairman of the Rathod Group of companies, engineers, and executives from NHHAI, PECL, and other renowned companies, doctors and dignified medical practitioners, officials from the state government bodies, members of parliament, ladies and gentlemen.

'It's an honour, to be a part of history. When this project was conceived, we all thought that this was just wishful thinking and that it would require a lot of sanctions, permissions and funds to complete it. We thought that it would take a decade for the structure to come to a final shape and that we would have to compromise upon the actual project, trim it short, to make the dream look practical. However, we all were wrong. PECL showed us how a project can be executed in war footing. NHHAI and Rathod Construction Group showed us how effectively resources can be managed and mobilised. The government of Rajasthan showed us how one can effectively mobilize government machinery without red tape and without hindrances.

'Once upon a time, not very long ago, when my father had suffered a cardiac arrest, I experienced the agony of not being able to provide my own father with the proper treatment he deserved. There were no facility available at my home town for proper treatment of even simple ailments. It is then that I realized the need to set up essential facilities first before we indulge into more crafty and sophisticated faculties like IT, Cybernetics, Robotics, Rockets, Satellites, and Nuclear power. We need proper schools more than we require malls. We need proper roads, highways, bridges more than we require bullet trains and underground metro. We require proper drinking water distribution system and electricity transmission system more than we require mobile towers and water parks. We require housing schemes for the poor and modern hospitals more than we require sophisticated restaurants and hotels. Ladies and gentlemen, we always wondered who would bell the cat. And I really am proud to announce that Mr Ramsingh Rathod has done just that. He could have come up with a hotel . . . A five star or seven star resort, which would have been a voracious money making venture at a place like Jaisalmer. He could have come up with several lucrative ventures that would have not been of much benefit directly to Humanity. Humanity—that word should bear a special meaning for us today. As we stand inside this imposing structure, we can only imagine the number of people who will be treated in this hospital at a subsidized price. Probably this will be the only hospital in the world that will treat people as per their economic strength and insurance plans. I can only assure that I would definitely see to it that this unique hospital keeps functioning as it should for many, many years to come. I once again would like to thank Mr Rathod for taking up such a brave and thoughtful step forward in the name of mankind and humanity.

'I won't be using this pedestal for any political propaganda, not only because it will spoil the atmosphere of the evening but also because I know that our party doesn't need it. People of Jaisalmer, we envy you, not only for your culture, valour, literature, food, and music but also because of your support for such a monumental task that has been achieved here today. Will come again and keep coming back . . . and from all of us here . . . Mr Ramsingh Rathod, a big thank you to you. I know you deserve more than that. We, the citizens of India, will remain ever indebted to you. I say this as I find myself fortunate to dedicate this gigantic facility, for the service of the nation and humanity. Jai Hind.'

All heads turned around to have a glimpse of Ramsingh, who could be seen nonchalantly sitting in one of the chairs allocated for the clients in the middle of the auditorium. The loud applause reverberated around every corner of the gigantic architecture and continued undiminished until the next speaker graced the podium.

The master of the ceremony had called upon stage, the task force leader of PECL, under whose careful jurisdiction, the project had come into shape in record time, Mr Kumar Sinha. The solidly built and serious-looking figure quickly took his position behind the microphone. Everyone thought that all they would get to hear from the speaker would be engineering jargon, some marketing talk in praise of the brand PECL, and some statistics that no one would be interested in. However, the tall, dark, and handsome TFL had something else to say, altogether.

'Honourable Minister Sir, dignitaries, my fellow colleagues of PECL, and friends. First of all, a big thank you to the client, the consultant, and the government for helping us to complete this project on time for the people of India. Me and my company stand honoured and blessed to be able to be associated with this flagship project from the very beginning. Not only has this project been a feather in our cap but also it has been a journey of learning through various ups and downs that time presented us with. It has been a challenge for engineering and execution but also a challenge for leadership and perseverance. All of us have come out triumphant together, and that is what gives us the ultimate joy.

'Friends, leadership is not easy. It is something that is synonymous with sacrifice, toil, and selfless dedication. Leadership, I dare say, comes with its own perils, with its own difficulties. It requires a lot of skill, prowess to motivate, passion, control, and humanness. As a leader of this project, I have learnt a lot about leadership, and what I have learnt, I have tried to adopt, yet I feel that there are things that I could have done much better.

'When you work with a group of people, all having separate needs and aspirations, there's bound to be conflict and differences as we move along together. There's bound to be unpredicted problems, unanswerable questions, rough situations to handle. But a good leader finds ways and means to withstand challenging circumstances to keep the show running. In this journey, like never before, I was made to think about my people time and again and not only focus myself on the job alone. A leader is as good as his team, and he should care for his people if he wants his people to care for him. A leader should stand by his team through fair and rough weather, and believe me, that's what I have tried to do . . . and the result is in front of you.

'TOC thought processes are important. It is important because it makes you deal with sensitive problems more reasonably and help you diffuse conflicts more effectively. I have done just that by following the teachings of TOC, laid out by Eliyahu Goldratt, in the most elaborate manner. The result has been profound. The result has been phenomenal. It has evolved me as a person and made me a better human being.

'I must thank all my colleagues of PECL for achieving what we had set out for. We definitely have made mistakes, but we have taken care not to repeat them and learn from them instead. We have made sure that we do not resort to shortcut methods by compromising on quality and intent. We have laid stress on proper practices of engineering and tried to surpass our previous records of excellence, instead.

'My gratitude also gets extended to our consultants for supporting us with their technical guidance throughout this journey and helping us with their knowledge of execution as well.

'My sincere thanks also to the officials of NHHAI (the National Hospital and Healthcare Authority of India) for their relentless supervision and guidance. You have been a source of continuous inspiration.

'I have only admiration of the highest level for Rathod Construction Limited. Perhaps, words will never be able to describe the efforts of Mr Ramsingh Rathod in converting this dream into a reality . . . Ram, if I can still call you that, your dream has become the reality to the nation. You have gifted the nation with the most coveted possession that it can boast of now. I, on behalf of my team, my company, and all the people of India, salute you for this phenomenal effort. You have made the country proud. Thank you.'

As Kumar Sinha descended from the dais to a huge applause, he was met at the passage below by Ramsingh himself, where both held each other in a tight embrace. The audience clapped on as the photographers kept themselves busy capturing the emotional moment from the closest possible quarters. It took time for the applause to subside, but when it did, the master of ceremony called upon stage the dignitary who was not an unknown face to Jaisalmer. Salman Ilahi gingerly walked up to the podium. There was a sway in his gait. A kind of chastity, divinity, and modesty reflected from his whole persona. His simplicity resembled a kind of holiness that was visible to the eye. His white attire appeared to be like a halo of enlightenment that shone about him. The audience had fallen silent and had turned their total attention to the man in white.

'Ladies and gentleman, please accept Salman Ilahi's salaam. Salaam to all the people who have done their bit for this remarkable piece of architecture built with the belief to protect the greatest boon that almighty has given us all—life.

And salaam to my *kirdaars*. You have become immortal, at least for me.

'Every person goes through a number of *kirdaars* during the journey of life. This is the nature of life itself. This is how the almighty has planned our journey. Just take some time off and reflect at what you have been and what you are . . . You can discover those kirdaars from within your lives. The kirdaars that I know of are very much the same. They are like you and me . . . very common people. But circumstances have made them change their role, time and again. We are all victims of circumstances, we all stand at the mercy of time.

'I know Ram since he was a child. He was very comfortable with his life since everything had been made available to him to lead a life of comfort. But a restlessness always drove him, away from the mainstream, away from his zone of comfort into the wilderness of the harsh life of the common man. Ram had taken all challenges head on, winning some and losing a lot in the process. We all lost with him, we all won with him, and in the midst of all these winnings and losing, we saw him turn into a humble disciple of engineering from an arrogant prince of Jaisalmer. Today, Ram is a completely different avatar because he had trained his heart and mind to endlessly pursue his dream. This dream probably was never there in his mind when he had set off his campaign to become a professional. This dream that he had nurtured and finally realized is a reflection of the purity of his mind and heart. He thinks for everybody— you, me, and million others who probably are too feeble or incapable to dream.

'Friends, look at yourselves again. Look at the kirdaar you have adorned today. It is different from what you were or you thought of becoming. Do not let your kirdaar be molded by the ravages of time . . . Try to fashion your kirdaar through the distinctness of your character. Your character defines the character of the nation. Your kirdaar decides the fate of the kirdaar of the nation.

'Kumar Sinha, I was moved by your speech. I love those streaks of emotion from you. I know, your compatriots would find it hard to believe that you too have at times started following your heart. I am a witness to your ascent as a leader not only for the technical acumen that you have but also for your managerial finesse. You have found out means to keep your people motivated, energized, animated, ignited throughout the duration of every project. Kumar, you were always a brave boy, and now you have come of age. Your dedication has been exemplary. We are all proud of you.

'Mr Bibhuti Bhushan, you have been the harbinger to a new India. Though we had been liberated from the British quite some time ago, we had struggled so far to come into terms with our independence. But it is through you that we have started dreaming big. We have started dreaming of a clean and prosperous society. We have started dreaming of a society bereft of the hounds and jackals that run after our flesh. We have rediscovered our rights to live, survive, and be happy. We salute you for giving our youth and our nation a direction. Allah is always supportive to people who try, and Allah surely will provide you the strength to achieve greater heights.

'Remember, one who seeks always blossoms amongst thorns.

'My life has been an embodiment of pain and loneliness. My kirdaar has always been dictated by various degree of torment that time has bestowed upon me. But I have always found solace amongst smiling faces, creative instincts, and the love that people have always smeared me with. This is what has brought me back to Jaisalmer time and again. You people are embodiment of love and care, and you too deserve the best. Ramsingh, you have cleared this debt of mine by presenting such wonderful people with such a world class facility.

'It was a dream . . . which has taken this gigantic shape . . . and folks, it takes courage to dream.'

Ramsingh Rathod was the last speaker before the cultural program was to begin. Ramsingh, as everyone knew, was a man of very little words. But this was an occasion, where people wanted to hear him speak. Ramsingh waited for the applauses to subside, but it continued unabated. Perhaps this was the best way to articulate the gratitude that people bore in their heart. Ramsingh had to gesture to the audience to be silent. He wanted to talk.

'First of all, thank you all to have graced this occasion. The way the previous speakers have heaped accolades upon me, I feel embarrassed. You have all gone overboard in equating me to God. I am not God, I am only human,' Rathod's voice thundered around the otherwise silent auditorium. After a brief silence, Rathod continued with a much subdued voice.

'For me, this is a Taj Mahal of sorts in memory of my bereaved wife. See, there is nothing but a selfish intent behind the planning of this hospital. But yes, this hospital will take care of people who suffer endlessly in want of facility and money. This hospital will also ensure employment to many since there will be a need of a whole lot of people here. We plan to have mobile health centres too that would go around villages administering vaccines and medicine to people located at remote corners. There will also be training centres for women, for developing their skills in nursing.

'There is one person who has always inspired me to set up something like this, though we never spoke about this at any moment of time. Dr Amit Ray, you always have been the guiding force in this endeavour. In memory of little Ayan, sir, we have named the children's ward as Ayan's Cure. I know I did it without your permission, but I know that you and Tina will not mind. And, Tinaji, you have been exceptional. The way you have selflessly helped Neha and me through times of trouble can never be forgotten. I have never seen my mother in person. You have shown me the glimpses of my mother. I am not suggesting though that your age should be equated to the age of a mother for a guy like me, but you certainly have the qualities all mothers should have.'

Seated in the audience, Tina's eyes welled up as she waved her hand to Ramsingh. Rathod too showed some streaks of emotion. The sight of Tina probably reminded him of Neha, who had always accompanied her to all sorts of programs. For a while, he lost himself to his thoughts. Consciousness dawned when the clock above the hospital chimed six, probably announcing to Rathod that he should continue with his speech.

'My team of Lonavala—Solomon, Vinod, Suraj, Ramesh, Goswamy, Srivastav, and Kumar—how can I ever be able to repay you for what you all have done for me? When I am alone and have nothing to do, I get flooded with memories from Lonavala. I must say Lonavala-Khandala had turned us into men from boys, indeed.' He took a pause as the PQC team of Lonavala, huddled together in a group, cheered aloud for the appreciation they received.

'Kumarsa, I have no word to express my deep gratitude I bear for you. You were there, when I had nothing left in me. You were the one who helped me garner the will to live on, fight on, and become . . . You have always been my greatest inspiration and will always remain to be so.

'My brother Karansingh. I know I have troubled you lots, but you have always stood firmly beside me. And yes, thanks for keeping our father's legacy alive, you have taken his business far beyond his imagination. Today dad will be so happy when he looks down from his heavenly abode. Karansingh, I have seen you grow, and today, you have grown into a better human being than your brother here. Proud of you Bhayo, absolutely.'

Ramsingh paused to wipe a few drops that might have escaped his eyes for a moment. The atmosphere had been filled with an emotional silence. Ramsingh, however, was quick to regain his composure, to continue.

'Salman Cha, you have been like the North Star, guiding us all with your wisdom and knowledge. You have always taught me to work for people and share the grief that ails the world. I have tried to do just that, Uncle, just that. You have always said that there are four questions of value in life . . . What is sacred? Of what is the spirit made up of? What is worth living for, and what is worth dying for? The answer to each is the same. Only love. And this is all a manifestation of love.

'People will surely forget me with time. But the name of Neha Rathod will remain immortal with millions whom this hospital shall continue to serve. This is the only gift that I could give her, and I know, she will be proud of it. Neha Rathod cannot die. Neha shall continue to live with us, evermore.

'Once again I thank all the delegates, and especially Mr Bibhuti Bhushan for finding out time for us. NHHAI officials, you have been the best consultants I have ever come across, and of course, Bank of Jaisalmer, without your help, the project wouldn't have progressed this far, so soon.

'Salman cha, allow me to recite a few lines of yours which you had left with me some time back. It resembles my life too:

Raaton ke karvaton se maraasiim puraane hain
Tere khwaabon ke anjuman ki kaynaat nahi hain.'

As Rathod descended from the dais, to a heavy round of applause, the master of ceremony almost forgot to announce the commencement of the cultural program. Emotions had somehow choked every artery of articulation. This was the time for people, perhaps to pause, reflect, and shed some tears . . . of joy.

There will come a time when all of us are dead. All of us. There will come a time when there are no human beings remaining to remember that anyone ever existed or that our species ever did everything. There will be no one left to remember Aristotle or Cleopatra, let alone you. Everything that we did and built and wrote and thought and discovered will be forgotten and all of this will have been for naught.

(JOHN GREEN)

CHAPTER 23

And the Journey Continues . . .

It is when you start examining life. It is when most of what you have been taught so far comes unhinged, gets questioned, is challenged by the insatiable lust to seek, discover, and conquer. When your first regimen of life ends—whenever it is, at twenty or thirty, you start learning, absorbing what you want to, not what they tell you. When you figure nothing is what it seems, you realize history has many retellings, and all great men and women have flaws. It is when you find out that even films can choke you, a painting can move you, music can make tears well up in your eyes, cooking can elate, and travel overwhelm. It is when you feel finally that the only true companions in your life are going to be books or, for some, cricket kits. It is when nothing seems right, you want to rebel against everything: the state, the army, your bosses, your genetic make-up, big companies, your caste, the government departments, the traffic cop, the stupid call centre reminders, acne. It is when you formally start asking, 'Why me'. The age of realization has no tag. It may come at eighteen for some and at thirty for some, even later for a few. But it is when you fall in love every week with new entities. It is when you discover new things about your body and discover new contours in another's. It is when you discover the strength of a caress, when desire burns you, jealousy crushes you, ambition blinds you. It is when you really learn to laugh . . . and cry. It is when you want to try out life, try out people, try out everything. It is when you come to know that this earth is fragile, you know that mankind is solitary, poor, nasty, brutish, selfish, and short. It is when all lies ahead is mysterious. It terrifies you, but you know that you are indestructible. It is when you know that you cannot die . . .

He must walk. Not only for his physical rejuvenation for his cerebral as well. Though age was not very much on his side, yet Ilahi knew that his mind still had the exuberance of youth. He still loved the company of budding new authors and new age politicians like Bibhuti Bhushan, who had revolutionized the thought process of the nation. He walked at a rhythmic and steady pace. The chirpings of the birds or the noise of children playing in the park distracted him. His thoughts circled around the various *kirdaars* life had made him play. Perhaps his thoughts, his words, his kirdaars were the only possessions that he had been left with. Of course, he knew that man will always depart alone as he had arrived. Still loneliness was something he detested, darkness was something that he still could not come to terms with, and silence had always brought along haunting memories from the past. Salman looked around and smiled . . . there was so much to live for in this world.

> Iraada karo to jeene ke sabab dhund sakte ho tum . . .
> Gam ke andhere me hasi ke chiraag jalao . . . to jee sakte ho tum . . .
> Bandisho me rehkar bhi himmat banao . . . to jee sakte ho tum . . .
> Umar ke tarazu me zindagi ko na tolo . . . To jee sakte ho tum . . .

Salman Ilahi smiled as he climbed in to the backseat of the blue Chevrolet. The day may begin.

Australian cricket was slowly coming in terms with the quiet revolution that was taking place in their backyard. The variety of cricket that was on offer from the small state of Tasmania had taken the world by storm. It was cricket that was exquisite, novel, innovative, mesmerizing, and more exciting than before. Cricket had evolved from the slam-bang tendencies of the limited overs and the test of tenacities of five day-encounters into something more exquisite and marvellous. It was the thought process that had evolved and not the game. Tasmania had come up with several new modifications to the way they played their cricket. The diamond format, the crooked stance, the buffer chase, etc., all had semblance to the teachings of Eliyahu Goldratt laid out in Theory of Constraints and CCPM. It was a queer combination of processes of management amalgamated with cricketing skills, bringing out a new variation to the ever exciting game of cricket. Tasmania had stormed every castle. They had even beaten teams from the Caribbean, Indian sub-continent, South Africa, and England. National teams of all cricketing nations were more wary of the Tasmanian team than the Australian national team, not because of any superstar in the team but because of the team itself. It was a *team*, and the slogan was simple: Together Everyone Achieves More (TEAM). And the team got rewarded too. Seven players from their state team had made it to the national side along with their captain. And the captain himself was pitted to replace the present captain for the forthcoming Ashes series. Armaan Bailey, the new pinup boy for the Australian tabloids, had made it to the headlines in a grand way. Forty matches as captain and forty wins. It was not only phenomenal, it was a miracle . . . And yes, miracles do happen.

∽

PECL had emerged from the cocoon of contractual executions, to blossom into a producer of speciality steel and power from alternate sources. Their ingenious approach to technology had made them a global player in the field of low-cost and high-yield products. Especially power, which was being derived from the producer gas based turbines, the input to which is the waste that people keep dumping every day. Indecomposable plastic wastes, which had become a sort of concern for the environment, had finally been dealt with, with the best possible solution the human race could ever think about. This catalytic conversion of the hydrocarbon wastes, without noxious emanations, had ensured the successive generations with a cleaner and greener environ through superlative processes of technology. PECL had become the pioneer for launching such projects at even remotest districts of India and the world, bringing lights to the lives of people who had submitted themselves to darkness. In fact, this pursuit had ensured the world of a baby step towards a sustainable ecosystem. PECL had thus grown exponentially in terms of both the top and the bottom lines, leapfrogging many a global entity to be amongst the top ten companies in the world in terms of fame and net worth. Their foray into diversified fields of operation had been the mastermind of the core group that had put rigorous hours of selfless hard work in strategizing and planning the phenomenal ascent of the company. What changed the company? When faced with this question, there was only one answer that the group members always came out with—thought process. Indeed thoughts do change the world and only if those thoughts are innovative and are implemented in the proper way. PECL had implemented most of their thoughts and had come out triumphant through dedicated and disciplined means of operation. They were now the name that made the country proud. And what made PECL proud? Their dedicated workforce, their steep curve of growth, their enviable credentials, and of course their creative COO, Mr Kumar Sinha.

✐

From the Diary of Tina Ray:

After the show: It's a relief. Some rest was warranted and of course Amit and Ria are exultant about the trip to Mauritius together. But I need to be careful with my health. Amit had been very caring these days. But how to avoid the post show press conference?

During the show: My name is announced for me to take a bow. I feel irritated. Why bother with it at all? But proud to see Dad and Mom in the front row with Amit and Ria.

During the show: The last model walks out into the arc lights. I feel relieved. The show went off without a hitch. Kumar's message and Ilahi uncle's flashes in the phone screen in quick succession.

During the show: Buttoning up garments, tying closures on models. I feel I am on steroids. Adrenaline high, I scream, I hug, I manage to squeeze in a tea break.

Pre-show: I spot Dad, Mom with Ria and Amit seated waiting for the show to begin. I feel happy and blessed.

Morning of the show: I feel nauseous. I need a bucket near me and a bottle of water.

One day to the show: I am filled with trepidation. Preps for the show are done. There really is nothing left for me to do. I still refuse to leave my room, somehow feeling that if I step out even for a second, it'll all go wrong. My members from Magenta are functioning normally. They are so well adjusted. I hate them. Amit and Ria had visited, and somehow Ria seemed pretty excited about the whole affair.

Three days to the show: Model castings and fittings. I feel like the second lead in a Bollywood movie . . . inconsequential. There is nothing really for me to do. I have the shortest fitting schedule always. The entire exercise takes fifteen minutes. There is no point having a sitting with the hair and make-up artist. Even with references provided, they will still do their own thing. Why bother?

Five days to the Show: Prepping guest lists, last-minute dry cleaning, collecting accessories from vendors. I feel like the brain whisperer. I can hear a pop in my head each time I feel like I'm experiencing an aneurism. Apparently, we as a nation do not understand the significance of RSVP. I'm willing to bet any amount that on the morning of my show, I will have people calling and texting me for invites.

Fourteen days to the show: The last batch of printed textiles comes into the workshop. They've turned out great! But wait! Is there enough time to create a minimum of four garments out of these fabrics to have a cohesive sub-story in the collection? Am I crazy?

Twenty days to the show: Ria insists on accompanying me to the workshop. It is a Sunday. I feel guilty of being at work. But Amit has been adamant that I attend the final touches. Loads of Ice cream for Ria.

Twenty-nine days to the show: I feel I need to ameliorate. Actually I don't. This day needed a word that I do not understand.

Thirty-one days to the show: I feel there needs to be a way I can expand time. One month left.

Forty days to the show: I feel, dare I say, happy with the way preps for fashion week are progressing.

Fifty-five days to the show: Pattern cutting and calico toiles are done! I feel like I deserve a pat on the back.

Sixty-one days to the show: I feel a manicure session coming up. Finally, print artworks have been sent across to my printers. Screens will be made, soon, hopefully. Hours on the computer; my right palm can carry out only one function, cradling the mouse. Patterns are being cut; I've got calluses from using old school iron scissors. There is no emoji that can represent my physical state of being. Amit wants to help. I don't know how he could.

Seventy-one days to the show: I feel snails can outrun me at this pace. Colour samples have been finalized. I mean, how difficult is it to decide between two shades of black? Shapes have been frozen. Ilahi uncle had dropped in with some inspiring recitations. I feel revamped.

Seventy-nine days to the show: I feel I am functioning depressive. During ideation, if I am momentarily happy, the ideas I come up with are scrapped within the hour. Creative juices flow well when I brood.

Eighty-three days to the show: Music is sorted. I feel like an entourage is in order. For every showcase, I decide on the music first. I know which tracks are going to be played. These tracks are on 24/7 in my studio, workshop, car, and home. This time I am leading with 'It Must Have Been Love' by Roxette. I imagine myself as being part of the crew, holding gigs in my studio, workshop, car, and home. I'm crooning the number with such familiarity that it seems I am a songwriter too. I am tone deaf.

Ninety days to the show: I feel like I'm exotic. Hotter than the tropics. No, wait. I feel like I need to feel. Three months left. Just the storyline in place. There is, however, no catalyst to get my brain to work. It'll happen on its own accord. I read the report again. Yes, I'm pregnant. Now, I feel exotic.

⚬⁓⚬

Memories, do fade with time, but they rarely stop to torment. It was just memories that remained with Ramsingh Rathod, during the evenings of solitude. These evenings, though, were rare because Ramsingh managed to keep himself busy with the ambitious projects that he went on launching, one after the other. His hospital had been running successfully and so were the school and the academy for sports that he had started. He had also promulgated the technical education scheme for the underprivileged in the rural sectors of Rajasthan, which allowed a lot of talented youngsters to further their education under the patronage of the Rathods who also helped them to get meaningful jobs. Ramsingh's stature had grown in multiples ever since he had taken over the reins of the Rathod clan from his father, who could not fight long against the malicious cancer that had been eroding him. Yet Ramsingh loved to remain unfriendly and humourless. His deep baritone made many a heart to skip a beat or two, for he believed in work, hard work . . . and honest hard work. And people revered him for being so fatherly to everyone in the vicinity, whether Rajput or Gurjar, it didn't matter. Humans were treated as humans . . .

However, Ramsingh remained in the confines of his palatial office and home, taking note of the world as it revolved from behind the silken curtains in company of alcohol and memories of times that were . . . For him life had become 'just froth and bubble'.

⌒⌒

The era was of the youth. A young country had suddenly woken up to stamp its authority across the globe. But things do not change overnight. Revolutions take their own time to yield results, and they take their toll too. The Janata Vikas Party had gone from strength to strength to establish itself strongly in almost all the states of India. The party represented the youth of the country, who were impatient to break free . . . to rule . . . to lead, to grow with growing economy, opportunities of industrialization, and to eliminate the hackneyed policies that only give growth to redtapism and bureaucracy. But there were opposition too. The so-called intelligentsia of the political circles were up in arms against the ascent of this political entity. The opposition parties showed great urgency to prevent JVP from attaining the status of the Indian National Party. There were allegations, accusations, slander hurled at the party to demean its status in front of the media and the general public. JVP too did not hesitate to retaliate. The war of the parties that had broken loose had taken the nation by storm. Too many parties, too much controversy, too many opinions. BB, who had progressed to the ultimate level of national polity, had suddenly become immune to it all quite uncharacteristically. Suddenly, family, property, and fame had taken top priorities in his life. His vision of a cleaner and more vibrant India suddenly appeared a bit hazy in front of him. He found more comfort in holidays at exotic destinations, in high-end models of luxury cars, and in decorated bungalows. His time got spent more in the realms of government circuit house rather than in his constituency. It had been ages since he had visited his roots at Vannabari though, at times, he does pause to remember the times that were . . . Bibhuti Bhushan's 'Chader Pahar' had suddenly been enveloped by the smoke of diplomacy and nonchalance. Patriotism is a short-lived adventure for many. Reality looks different . . . it changes *kirdaars*.

⧼∽⧽

Dr Amit Ray now had only selective patients. Ria, the princess, was the bundle of joy that his world now revolved around. A career in medicine had given him all, and he did not thrive for anything more. He remained busy in the company of the little girl, whose every idiosyncrasy provided moments of joy to Amit. He also found time to discuss in detail about Tina's business ventures with immense interest and enthusiasm. He always insisted Tina to work harder to establish a more vibrant name in the markets of fashion. But Tina appeared reluctant; she appeared more keen to spend more time with her family rather than at her office and workshop. She had also planned to slowly pass over the reins of Magenta to the newly appointed CEO Mrs Savitha Gangadhar, a noted fashion enthusiast, trained and sculpted by Magenta. The Ray household was filled with joy. Come September, September 26 to be exact, there would be a further addition to the family. Amit counted days like a child would for the arrival of another angel to cement the family further.

From the Column of D. Solomon (TFL, PECL), Cross country pipeline Project, Salalah, Oman:

Certain things that I have learnt along the way as I grew from being a college pass out to a TFL:

- A project or a story need not have a twist in the end.
- Mumbai-Pune Expressway is not the greatest road ever made.
- Nationalism is a waste of time. Also, the fact is, contrary to your convictions, ancient Hindus did not discover the heliocentric theory.
- Of course, there is love and unconditional ones.
- Ramesh Guru or Salman Ilahi, if you look more closely, have not answered a single bloody question about life that they put forward at the beginning of a sermon. What you like are their questions.
- Just because there is a question, it does not mean there has to be an answer.
- There are people all around who are in deeper shit.
- Vinod. K., my dearest friend, says that the world is an illusion and that there is a startling truth hiding in plain sight; he says all this not because he is very close to enlightenment but because he is in the early stages of something called schizophrenia.
- She only about likes you, you moron, only about. Move.
- PECL will never ever seriously think about any of your leaves. But the good news is you will indeed have sex one day, surely.
- Roads and hospitals no longer excite.

- Population is no longer the biggest problem, illiteracy is.
- Around this time, right now perhaps, somewhere not very far away, your future girlfriend is naked with someone.
- Leadership is crap. You should know how to wriggle out—that's it.
- You should know how to change your kirdaar as per circumstances. World leaders do just that.
- After a peg or two, nothing looks wrong in the universe.
- Ramsingh Rathod has built seven super-speciality hospitals. But guys, life for him, is still froth and bubble.
- There are good engineers, duds, and good excuse makers; and often it's the good excuse makers who win.
- Money, money, money—nothing else matters much. What's love?
- Ryan Giggs is still playing and scoring. Guys, It is 2014.